Prologue

It was harvest day and the sky had fallen to yellow light to match the stubbled wheat in the hills above Portscatho. The year was 1779 and the land held the summer's heat loosely, releasing it upwards in wavy strands. Men heaved, their backs bent, scythes cutting whispers through the stems, while women bundled sheaths behind them. Soon, the last field would be met. Slowly, the men would circle the outer edges, slicing inwards, to where the final ear – the last wheat to be shorn – would be cut. Crying the Neck was the ceremony's name, though its origins had long since been lost. A spirit lay in the harvest at reaping. She was maid and mother and crone. She was the sugar in the bees and their honey, the strength in the ivy and the gold in the wheat.

'What 'ave 'ee?' came the cries from the men, new tongue and old tongue singing together. 'Pandr'eus genes?'

Then the reply: 'A neck, a neck, a neck!' After its slitting, the severed neck would be kept, to be ploughed into the first furrow next year.

Not far from their parents' activity were the youngest village children. Sticky from the day's warmth and overtired, the little ones crowded around Old Sal, who had been bid to mind the drink and her young charges. Both had loosened her tongue to talking, for, it should be noted, Old Sal was a woman all stories.

'Back when our Cornwall was young, there was a godly man called King Gerent, the last who would ever rule over the land,' she told the children, whose dozing heads were gathered together as close as the wheat itself. 'Handsome, brave and shining, none would stand against him as none would live who tried.' Old Sal leaned forwards, holding up a finger chipped with a fish knife's work. 'Then came along a wise woman, a nasty witch,' for there is always such a woman in these ancient tales, 'who was as ugly as the king was beautiful. She threatened him and all the hills, unless he would marry her upon his return from war.'

A dozen eyes, tired as only babes can be tired, blinked up at Old Sal, who even in middle age was thought long past her prime. Her face was red with sun and lined with years well spent and oft idle.

'Away he went on horseback to fight the Old North, whereupon he came home a victor. Then flew the witch to his castle, skirts high and a lewd command on her lips: take me as a bride and I will spare your life. King Gerent refused. In her fury, the witch seized the seas. An ever-crying storm took bricks from buildings, snatched children from their beds, broke every gull's wing and savaged the land as mean as any raider. King Gerent could not bear to see his people hurt and yet the wise woman was too much a trickster to be killed.'

Old Sal's hands wove through the air. Through a child's

THE SALT BIND

REBECCA FERRIER

THE SALT BIND

First published in Great Britain in 2026 by Renegade Books
An imprint of Quercus
Part of John Murray Group

1

A CIP catalogue record for this book
is available from the British Library.

HB ISBN 978-1-40874-868-8
EBOOK ISBN 978-1-40874-866-4

Typeset in Electra by M Rules
Printed and bound in Great Britain by
Clays Ltd, Elcograf S.p.A.

Papers used by Quercus are from well-managed forests
and other responsible sources.

Quercus
Carmelite House
50 Victoria Embankment
London EC4Y 0DZ

The authorised representative
in the EEA is
Hachette Ireland
8 Castlecourt Centre
Dublin 15, D15 XTP3, Ireland
(email: info@hbgi.ie)

John Murray Group, part of Hodder & Stoughton Limited
An Hachette UK company

To my mother, who gave me the ocean,
and my father, who showed me the stars.

imaginings, the sea was transformed into a terrible beast of talons and claws to steal their lives and Portscatho away. 'King Gerent turned his righteous rage upon the wise woman, yet his sword could leave no mark. Alas, she knew the earth's magic as well as he and for every blow, she blew the wind harder. Still, he would not give himself over to the witch.'

In the fields, the men were almost done their reaping.

'It was here the Pact was formed between the Land and Sea. King Gerent turned from the shore and walked into the waves to place his heart into the ocean, where the witch could never find it. From then on, the storms died and the wise woman – and every one after – had no sway over them. King Gerent was celebrated upon his death and his body rowed across the waves in a golden boat with silver oars.'

'I heard the king was evil and the wise woman banished him,' said Hannah, a small and shrew-faced girl with limp pigtails. 'Not the other way around.'

'Perhaps,' said Old Sal. 'Depends on who's telling the story.' She squinted her eyes at her young charges and noticed one vacant spot at her feet. 'Now where's that Kensa got to?'

Gone was the unruly child, never one to sit still or do as she was told. Indeed, the warning Kensa could have heeded from Old Sal's tale went unheard, for that wild girl had snuck to where the scythes were quickest to watch the wheat neck's cutting.

Part One

Long life to the Pope, death to our best friends, and may our streets run in blood.

A well-known Cornish toast in
the eighteenth century.

Part One

Chapter One

Kensa

At last, the fish had come. Their slim bodies jostled one another against the water's surface, flicking upwards as a coin to a thumb. Portscatho ran on pilchard time, measured in seasons of silver scales. In those weeks, all hands within the village were called upon, even Kensa's. She was twelve and fully capable, as she told those in earshot, with a tone challenging anyone to disagree with her. It was late August in Cornwall, the evening sky thrown to lark and haze, when the cry was heard: 'Avee! Avee!'

In previous months, offerings had been made to the Father of Storms in the hopes he would drive the shoals to their nets – and drive them he did. The boats lay low in the water, heaped with fresh catch. The men in the village waded among them with wooden shovels, filling hand-barrows with pilchard after pilchard after pilchard. Dull red lanterns lit their stern faces, creased in concentration. Next, the barrows were wheeled uphill to the salting house where the women waited, had been waiting all day. Only the miners did not partake in today's work, their riches found in soil, not sea.

A pilchard catch was a large event for Portscatho and the pay was handsome at three-pence an hour. Noise, shouts and curses passed between the villagers, with a laugh or two. This was a practice bred into them. As each person grew in age, their place within the pilchard catch became fixed. Catcher or gutter, salter or packer, each was paid a fair wage.

And tonight Kensa would find her place.

Bread, fat and brandy were offered up and candles lit to shy the dark. There was a feasting air, a mirthful tang, as on Wassail Night or Midsummer's Morning. Only this had a reaper's joy that came from killing. Fish blood ran down the streets. Kensa's skirts were wet with it. Here was a gift to the Father of Storms. Based on its thick flow from land to sea, he would be most pleased and Portscatho would eat well in the coming months, by his grace.

A crystal-cracking sound popped beneath Kensa's boots as she approached the salting house. Here, the women ruled. Nimble hands worked quickly, while tongues slapped lips and spoke ripe talk. Sour tempers met sweet, and lean elbows bashed fuller ones, compelled to band together and complete the work – squabbling or singing, demanding, 'More fish, more salt.' Each woman was intent on her task, fish in one pile, coarse brown salt in the other, to be combined into empty barrels.

Clinging to one woman's apron was a small, fair-haired child. Kensa's mother, Derwa, and half-sister, Elowen. The latter's grip was as tight as a limpet's, which her mother soon suckered onto Kensa's hand.

'You can mind her,' said Derwa.

'But I can help—'

'This is helping,' came the answer, before the grey length of her mother's dress faded into the salting house depths.

Kensa looked down to her charge who looked up in turn, Elowen's wide blue eyes in contrast to her own hazel. Although they were similar in age, with less than four years between them, there was no likeness, bar the shape of cheek and jaw. Even their personalities were at odds. Kensa was first-born and, truly, it was in her nature and name to be first. She was first to wake and beat the other children to the harbour, to swim across the headland and see where the tufted seabirds placed their nests. She was first to call out a lie when she heard it and first to be blamed should trouble arise. Elowen was even-tempered, quiet and sweet: content to wait and be second.

'Kensa?' Always, the fair-haired girl spoke her name as a question.

Those who knew the half-sisters ascribed such variables to the men who'd fathered them. Whenever she glanced into the looking glass, Kensa saw a face once worn by the most feared smuggler ever to roam the coast off their small, crooked finger of a peninsula. Freckles, scarlet hair, a thin mouth better suited to man than woman. Of course, Elowen was as fair and pale as their mother was. Beautiful, even. If ever Kensa stood beside her sibling, she felt rough and bruised in comparison: an apple no good for eating, ready to be pulped for next year's cider.

Kensa was quick to drop Elowen's hand and shunted the younger child into a dull corner where she would not be in the way. 'Stay there,' she said firmly, then began to find her true place within the salting house. It was easy enough, for the busy women called out what was needed. Although she was too small to move the barrels, Kensa could heave their lids off or keep stray cats from the door. Hands shot about, writhing as pilchards when first placed upon the shore. With salt layered, fish atop, salt again and smoothed with a palm, the barrels grew denser, packed and stacked. In coming weeks, oil and salt would drip from the wood, to be collected, for there was no waste in Portscatho. After a month or so, when the pilchards were fully cured, they would be washed and packed into hogsheads, sent to Falmouth and sold across the seas, as far away as Spain and Italy, to feed the papists on their abstinent Fridays. Coin from the pilchard catch could sustain a family for half a year or more, should they be frugally minded.

As the women talked, Kensa listened. Discussions on babes and their mothers, husbands and their wanderings at sea or on the shore of another's bed. Plans were made for the cooler months, for there were pantries to fill and preserves to be made. The words flew as high as fish guts, while Kensa watched, copied, tried her hand until she was ushered away.

For as long as she helped, she was wanted.

It was good, that knowledge: learning where she fit.

Ever since she could remember, Kensa had been unwelcome.

That's what came with being the daughter of Alexander Rowe. Rumour was, after he was hanged and strung up over Percuil River, his body refused to rot. Others say his body disappeared altogether, swallowed by the tides for an unpaid debt. Kensa thought she remembered that day, too – the hanging – and if she didn't, she'd been told of it so often that a memory had formed nonetheless.

And she'd been told what she'd done.

'That chit crawled on to the scaffold and put her hands in his pockets,' said Old Sal. 'Thieved from her own father afore he was cold.'

It was true, but Kensa had not taken money. Instead, she had removed a hagstone from her father's coat. It was as large as her palm with a hole knuckled through it. She could not forget the first time she'd seen it. Her father had come home from sea, rattling with gifts and thick with beard. He'd chased her round their small cob-walled dwelling and placed that hagstone to her eye.

'Here's how I know when a storm's coming,' her father told her. 'Here's how I know to go wrecking.'

Although the hagstone had not protected him from the law and the noose, it was a comfort to Kensa. A weight as natural as her own flesh, carried from one scorn to the next. Her fingers strayed to it now in the salting house, nerves hidden behind that flat, hard mouth.

In the corner, quiet as always, Elowen played with another child. How easily she made friends. Charming everyone with her cow-long lashes and dainty steps. Ones that would always follow Kensa, asking her to slow down, to wait, to stop. And her name a question, always a question, asked over and over: *Kensa? Kensa? Kensa?*

She turned away, stretching to glare inside a half-filled barrel. A dozen pilchard eyes stared back. Her chest grew tight. It always did when she thought on her father. Distracted as she was, she did not see Elowen approach. 'Kensa?' A sudden pull on her sleeve startled her, her fingers slackened, the hagstone tumbled into the dark and bounced beneath Old Sal. And when the heavy-set woman fell, it was with a hard thump. One which brought a pilchard barrel with it, clattering into two others and sending the carefully packed fish and salt across the bloody floor. Four hours' work gone, a hard night ahead, a wage that had to be earned.

Kensa scrabbled for her hagstone and found Old Sal's face pressed into hers.

'I didn't mean to—'

Her excuses fell unheard, replaced by threats to box ears and tan hides. 'You're as twisted as your father was,' said Old Sal. 'He brought badness with him and now you'll do the same. Out, go on! Take the little one with you! I want you gone.'

Kensa's neck burned. Eyes – woman and child and pilchard – turned to her. She opened her mouth to protest and closed it, firmly, teeth clacking together. Head down, she wrenched herself from the salting house, dragging Elowen behind her.

Anger kept Kensa walking. Portscatho's natural incline, a deep slope to the ocean, propelled her towards the harbour. A full moon lit the cobbles, turning what would be red in daylight into a long black stream. By the sea wall, the men had finished unloading the boats and sat together with lit pipes and empty tankards. Only when she felt a tug on her arm did she slow, remembering the shorter legs which struggled to match hers.

'Kensa?'

'No,' she spat, furious.

One word and all the shame inside her reached out to echo against the receding tide.

Elowen gasped, a small huff into Kensa's face, only a hair's breadth away. The men on the wall quietened, their low murmurs fading as they listened. Next came a chance, a beat where Kensa could have sunk down, grasped her sister's arms and apologised. After all, it was not truly Elowen's fault, it was a mistake. Yet she did not, could not admit it. The younger child, eyes spilling over with tears, wrenched herself away and ran. Her buckled shoes slapped shingle and her fair hair trailed behind her. She left Kensa standing there, with curdled sea-foam and fish blood stiff and drying on her skirts.

It served her right. Kensa repeated this to herself as she paced. Near by, the drunken men at the harbour were laughing at lewd jokes, though the few words she overheard made little sense to her. Of course, it was always Kensa in the wrong, never her sister.

'Elowen?'

Where had she gone? Now it was Kensa's turn to ask, call, wait.

Her voice bounced off cob wall and quarried stone. There was no answer. She cuffed her nose with her sleeve and walked.

Uphill was home, a small dwelling elbowed into a long terrace which lined the main road through Portscatho. Elowen had gone the other way, along the path which bordered the coast and dipped precariously close to the sea. Kensa went after her. As she began to move, her anger was replaced with worry, then guilt. She called out again and again. No reply. How far could Elowen's legs have taken her? Kensa pushed on, faster, her path a gloom of ferns and tree roots. She knew the stories, had been raised on them, about the beasts who would snatch a child from its cradle or a maid from her virtue, should the Father of Storms – the Bucka – wish it. Kensa did not like to think on him too close to the sea, lest her thoughts summon him, impossible though it seemed. To her left, the ocean sighed and over the waves came a sound.

It was a low, keening cry. A wail like wind across a rum bottle, clear and high and sweet to hear. Loud, terribly loud: inhuman and unanimal. It tightened a knot in Kensa's chest. Her feet pummelled the earth as she sprinted towards it, that sound, and the creature who made it.

Elowen had got there first.

From a high point on the path, Kensa saw her sister standing on the Towan's shore, dwarfed beside a ship-sized mass. She was a thin stripe against a hulking body. Could it be a whale? It cried again, loud enough to shake the ferns at Kensa's waist and call her towards it, towards Elowen, towards nothing she had ever seen before.

This was no whale. This was a sea monster.

Towan was a beach whose name meant sand dunes, for that was what the coastal stretch held. Uneven heaps, crowned with grass and pebble rings, ran for half a mile. Kensa barely felt her dash across its ridges, hearing shells crunch and pebbles clack.

No sooner did she reach the sea monster than she heard Elowen speak.

'Dydh da,' she said tentatively, in the lost tongue – and one which should have been lost to her.

A chill pulsed from the hulking body, tightening Kensa's lungs. This was not a night for greetings, it was one for good-byes. 'Duw genes,' she corrected, for the sea monster was dying.

Such beasts as these were rumoured to wash up on the shore in colder seasons, when the bracken had rusted and the departing swifts had sailed an absence into being. It had been a long time since such an event had happened, a century, at least. The creature had a dulled spine and twin fins nubbled into ridges, along with a funnelled neck as wide as a cartwheel, which curved inwards like a sleeping swan's. Across one grey flank was an old scar, long healed. Its features were odd, almost human; a woman's face distended across a whale's snout. It was so large, Kensa could hear its heartbeat. A dull *boom, boom, boom*, which rippled the sand beneath it, beneath her.

Elowen's face was small and pinched in thought. 'Eus teylu dhis?' She repeated in English, 'Do you have a family?' Others, perhaps its own kin, who waited in the water.

The question, asked gently, placed an uncomfortable pressure into Kensa's sternum. It was not fear. Had she been surrounded by others, she might have been afraid. Fear is like that, it manifests when there are mouths to feed it. With only her, Elowen and the sea monster, she carried a strange guilt she could not understand. As though she must act, though the actions required escaped her.

It seemed prudent to speak in the voice of the Old Ways. Kensa remembered enough from her father and that of the sailors in the village. Odd, to hear Elowen use it, to know how much she'd listened and picked up without seeming to.

'Who taught you?'

'I've always known it,' said Elowen.

She got like this, her sister, speaking in a strange way when no one else was around. Kensa was used to it, though tonight was different.

Elowen raised a palm to the monster's head and rubbed a soothing circle at a slight dip between its eyes. A shiver rippled the beast's flesh. Its slim nostrils quivered, then stopped, for ever. Throughout its last breath, exhaled for a time as long as time, Elowen wavered. Hand paused, head lolled, knees collapsed. The younger girl fell sideways, as though her bones had gone limp. Kensa tried and failed to catch her. On the sand, under the moon, Elowen's hair lay around her like foam. She did not respond to her name, to a shake, to a pinch.

'Elowen.'

Hard steps pressed shingle, had been pressing shingle for some while, but only now could Kensa hear them. A rhythm that was not the waves crashing, her own pulse thudding or the sea monster's stopped heart.

There, in the shrinking distance, was a cloaked shape.

'Help,' cried Kensa, then halted. Bit her tongue. Shrank her neck into her collar.

No one who roamed a beach at night was good company.

She would know. Her father had lured cargo-laden ships to wreck under a sky such as this. And then there was the sea and its horrors, worse than the one who had washed up this hour. What to do? Kensa could run back to Portscatho. Fetch her mother and get aid. That would mean leaving Elowen. She could not, *would* not, do that. Kensa rose to her feet and reached for the familiar hagstone in her pocket: the only weapon she had.

A laugh rattled the shells.

'You will not need that, child,' said the wise woman, pulling back her hood.

Chapter Two

The Morgawr's Gift

I solde – wise woman, healer, witch and harlot – was said to be more than two hundred years old. Kensa could believe it. What's more, she could believe the *other* rumours about her. That she nursed slow-worms from her bosom, was mistress to the Devil and had birthed each pine tree on the headland's furthest point. And now she had come from her cottage in Bohortha to the Towan, as though drawn to its terrors.

Kensa dug her heels into the sand. 'Don't touch her.'

'She needs seeing to.' Isolde's voice was a hoarse whisper, soft-seeming, belying the hardness beneath it. 'I can only save her if you let me, Kensa.'

It was unsettling to hear her name spoken by a woman

she – by her own recollection – had never met. Save? That word was slower to register. As was the notion that Elowen would need saving and not suddenly come to, pretending to be shy with too many eyes upon her. And yet Elowen did not stir.

After a lengthy pause, the tide hushing in and out to match her breaths, Kensa nodded. 'All right, but if you hurt her—'

'Has she spoken on any ailments?'

Kensa shook her head. How was she to know? It was not as though Elowen ever confided in her. The few words exchanged between the sisters were usually, 'Wait for me,' from the youngest and, 'No,' from the eldest.

Isolde's knees groaned audibly when she crouched over Elowen. Other than that, the wise woman remained silent.

Impatience – at the quiet, at her ignorance – bid Kensa to ask, 'Will she be—'

'Yes.' Isolde pressed her fingers to Elowen's neck, then across her forehead. 'Young girls are prone to sudden turns.'

Kensa frowned. Being a young girl herself, she was certain she would never succumb to a fainting fit; that was typical Elowen behaviour.

'I didn't do it,' said Kensa defensively.

How strange it was to see a woman as aged as this witch, yet sprightly and mirthful, unencumbered by the years gathered across her skin and hair and clothes. Her dress was over-darned wool, the same shade as a hare's pelt. Atop it was a midnight bodice, furred with loose threads where beads had once been sewn. Although its fashion had long since fallen from favour, trends were not followed in the coastal village, where function, warmth and practicality took priority. Layered over Isolde's slim shoulders were shawls, while her skirts were creased with pockets, bags and poultices. At her belt were knives and, bent into one arm, was a willow-woven basket. Long grey hair, longer than it should be, hung in strangled knots about her waist. Feathers, threads, ribbons and vines had been plaited into it. Painted across her lids was kohl in a thick band. And her eyes, milky brown, were the same colour the earth's yolk would run if it were cracked atwain. Unkind talk was that Isolde practised the Old Ways: the forbidden rites which tied land and sea together, spat on the Church and, on occasion, spared a child God had seen fit to take.

The wise woman turned to the sea monster, rising to press her palms to its side. 'Truly, you choose now to die, old friend? You could reconsider.'

For a moment, Kensa thought it would reply.

Perhaps it did, only not in a way the girl could hear.

From the hill came a man's enquiry. Kensa went to shout back, until Isolde silenced her with a hand on her shoulder. 'Soon the village will come. There is little time.' Isolde's dry lips began an untamed song known to those born on Cornish soil – on ship bones and their anchors, seal skins and scallop ears. It was one Kensa had heard her father sing on the nights he went a-wrecking, asking the waves to offer their bounty, however cruel.

> *Mist from the hill, mist from the sea.*
> *Tide in turn has song for thee.*
> *Three to spin a wakening, one to take the crown,*
> *and in there waits a heart-thorn, leading dead-wave down.*

Without being told, Kensa understood that what passed here on the Towan – between herself, Elowen, the witch and the sea beast – could never be told to another. The secret burrowed under her fingernails, gathering an itchy tightness that made her want to put them to her mouth until she could taste it.

Isolde's voice was cracked and brittle as she sang, pausing only to ask, 'Are you the one who found the Morgawr?'

Kensa opened her mouth, closed it again. She had not been the first to meet the creature. That had been her sister. Isolde did not know that. As though summoned, the wind took Kensa's ruddy hair and pulled it from her braid, falling free as easy as her lie.

'Yes.'

The wise woman's eyes turned, at once, to her. 'Humph.'

Next came a knife pressed into Kensa's palm: the witch's knife. Its bone handle was shined from a thousand holdings and inlaid with flint pieces. It bore the same symbols from the ancient stone markers which farmers tilled around, the ones not even the wildest ponies would graze beside.

Isolde squeezed Kensa's shoulder and steered her towards the sea monster. 'You will remove the Morgawr's tongue for me.' Its bulbous lower lip folded forwards, as though in invitation. 'It's a prize seldom found in these parts.'

Kensa's grip slackened on the bone-handled knife.

'Would you rather I find another to do the task?'

'No,' said Kensa quickly.

The witch prised the Morgawr's jaws open with bars of driftwood. A hot smell, seaweed gone to ruin. Kensa placed a knee on the creature's sagging maw and waited for movement. None came. It was really dead, then. Braver now, she hooked a hand around a tooth and pulled herself inside the fleshy cavern. Its fumes were thick as sealing wax, running up the beast's throat and down her own. The carcass began to shake. Kensa would have screamed, until she realised why the monster shuddered: Isolde was hacking pieces from its flesh. Crouching, Kensa leaned across a tongue as coarse as grit and worked by touch alone, for it was too dark to see. She was not shy when it came to cutting and thought herself much like the older women who gutted fish in the salting house – only hers was a much bigger fish. The knife was clumsy in her grip and the tongue was tougher than she expected. Kensa angled her weight behind the knife, took a deep breath. Her first mistake. The sour air was dizzying and the harder she gasped, the worse it got. Her grip loosened on the blade. It tumbled, falling into the nothingness. She lurched after it – bile rising – and bashed her head on the sea monster's gums. Another inhale and spots flashed around her vision. She could not think, could not see. Behind her, the driftwood bars creaked precariously. If they snapped, Kensa would be shut inside the terrible mouth.

Would anyone even miss her?

She did not like that question because she did not like its answer.

Kensa scampered back onto the beach. It was wet, the tide coming in. Already, the sea monster's long tail began to drift in the water. Her own hands were empty. No tongue. No knife. She had failed. Her skin prickled with dread.

There were voices now. Portscatho's women had paused from their salting, despite their hampered progress, while the fishermen had roused from sleep or drunken reverie, eager to see the famed Morgawr. Kensa was surrounded and had yet to be noticed. Prayers were muttered by the more faithful in the village – or, at least, those who wished to appear as such. Others, heathen in nature, touched a hand to the pagan tokens they carried. Knowing looks and uncertain whispers were exchanged. Had the Father of Storms sent it as a warning? If not, then it had escaped his watch. No one knew which was worse. The creatures – once land-based beings – had been cast into the ocean and not troubled them for hundreds of years. Not since the Pact. How could that change in a night?

'This is no good omen to us,' said Branok, the mine overseer, whose authority extended well beyond the tunnels he worked in. He wore a sleep-creased mouth and a long coat thrown over his undershirt.

In his shadow, and with a matching glower, was Jack, who was three years Kensa's senior. Just as his father managed the adults, he managed the children, exerting his will over those who lived in Portscatho. Aside from Kensa, who was far too stubborn to listen to anyone. Even at his young age, Jack had a solidness to him, could withstand anything. Or, at least, Kensa thought so, because he shrugged off any words she threw at him; both criticism and compliment slid from his wide shoulders, and then he'd frown, again. Nothing could impress him, as though he was above it all – above her, what with his father's role in the village – and he'd have her know it. Briefly, his eyes slid to hers, scanned her up and down, then flicked away, purposefully.

It shouldn't have stung, his easy disregard, yet it did.

Hovering nearby was the stuffy clergyman, Mr Aldridge,

wheezing and palming at his bowed legs. Fine dining and a sedate lifestyle had greatly affected his physique. Breathless as he was, he had air enough to chide Kensa. At last, someone had acknowledged her.

'Oh, in Heaven's name! Get yourself away from it, child,' he said, pulling his flopping nightcap from his pasty head and using it to mop his brow. 'Dredged up from Hell itself, I assure you.'

Branok rubbed a hand over his face. He hadn't shaved and there was a thick shadow over his brown chin. It was strange to see a man so trim, tidy and timely be unkempt in these early hours. 'Should we tell Sir Trevanion? It's his land we're on, after all.'

'Goodness, never,' said Mr Aldridge nervously. 'You know the baronet doesn't abide by such talk. We should burn it.'

'It seems a shame to waste it, the fat alone would be worth a fair bit.'

'I would not consider that were I you,' Isolde cautioned the men. 'This is a sacred creature. She will go as she came – with the tide to claim her.'

Kensa did not move. 'Where is—'

'Elowen!' Mr Skewes had a reedy voice. By the time Kensa heard it, her step-father was upon her. Until he saw his daughter, who he sank down beside, bunching and un-bunching his hands. 'What did you do to her?'

Kensa didn't know what to say, so she didn't say anything.

Although he was a stringy man, Mr Skewes held authority in the village. As the Coast Guard, he had the local magistrate's ear. Worse still, he had Derwa's bed. Where was her mother? There standing beside the witch, their mouths tight and quick-moving.

Mr Skewes snatched at Kensa's elbow and shook her roughly. 'I asked you—'

'Pa?' Elowen croaked, sparing her older sister. Her voice was gently lilting. It was a relief to hear it, despite everything.

Kensa longed to touch her. Mr Skewes never gave her the chance.

'Where does it hurt? Show me and we'll make it right, pet,' he said.

A coldness sank through Kensa's boots. Here came the tide, inching the villagers up the shore. Now that Elowen was awake, there was no need to tarry – especially when there were pilchards left to salt. One by one, Portscatho's residents began to leave, having taken their fill and spied the first sea monster to grace the Towan for centuries. If it was an omen, no one knew what for. Elowen was carried to the nearest sand dune by her parents, legs too weak yet to support her. Kensa went to follow, then hesitated.

Derwa and Mr Skewes cradled their daughter and spoke to her in soothing patterns. When was the last time anyone had spoken to Kensa like that?

She could not remember.

The next wave rose high enough to meet her knees.

She welcomed it.

The wise woman began to lift her tools from the sand and slid them into a long cloth strip sewn with endless pockets. Her fingers halted over one particular gap and she grinned, straightened her spine, a bony pillar against the rising gale. She reached for Kensa, who found herself reaching back, if only to touch and be touched.

Isolde held her thumb to the centre of Kensa's empty palm.

'You lost my knife.' It was not a question.

'I did,' Kensa whispered, suddenly afraid.

The witch grunted. She appraised the girl as she had done the monster, as though seeking something of value to cut off and keep. Her hand, tarred with the creature's fluids, came to rest upon Kensa's cheeks, hair, sternum. Its smell: blood and sweetness, gorse-like. There was a question in her eyes and, without speaking, without knowing, Kensa answered it.

'You'll do,' said Isolde.

She took Kensa's wrist and pulled her along the beach, the sea taking their prints as soon as they'd left them. There, she continued her low conversation with Derwa that Kensa could not hear. Mr Skewes ignored her. Elowen did not, the sisters' eyes meeting for a single, wary second.

Derwa shook out her scale-strewn skirts. 'Surely there's another better suited to the task? Kensa does not have the temperament.'

'Your eldest found the Morgawr,' countered the wise woman, showing her stained teeth. 'It is she who has been chosen.'

Isolde glanced out to where the horizon blurred with rain, as though waiting for it to answer her. Kensa understood little and saw even less. Dawn was coming in muted colours, the sun hidden behind a rising cloud bank. Her mother approached, apprehensive.

'When you are ready,' said Isolde to Kensa, 'you'll return the missing blade to me and come with it, to do as I do, learn as I learn, heal as I heal.'

Again, the waves reached higher, a low rumbling. 'I'll be a wise woman?'

Derwa released a strained sound from her throat, nails digging into Kensa's shoulder.

'Many will call you thus.' Quiet, as the wind died. Isolde lost the humoured crease to her lips. 'You will see what is unseen, speak with the sea and draw swords with those who seek to replace the Old Gods.'

A rip in the current began to pull the sea monster back to whence it had come, unlacing their shoes, combing the thin hairs on their legs.

Kensa considered the witch, blood on her hands, mouth melded with spell-work and strangeness tangled in her hair. Kensa had grown up with tales about healers delivering babies, blessing ships and packing charms against the hardest frosts. Figures who held their community together, who were turned to and confided in and necessary. These were not words she could ascribe to herself.

Isolde asked, 'Could you do this?'

Elowen was leaning on her father's arm. Silent, watchful. Kensa met her sister's stare again for the briefest moment. What she took now, she took from another. Kensa had not been the first to find the sea monster. That had been Elowen's discovery. Here was the moment to confess, to hand over a fate which was not her own. And yet, Kensa's tongue remained as still as the Morgawr's, uncut and lost in the sea's rising swell. Better to be a wise woman than a smuggler's daughter. Needed by the village, not scorned and ostracised. Wanted, for once.

A small nod left her. 'Yes.'

'To be as I am is to be lonely,' warned Isolde. 'Unmarried,

childless, relied on, lusted after and yet never truly wanted. Do you understand?'

Kensa spoke as a child spoke, with honesty and an insight she had not yet grown into. 'I am always first,' she explained, 'and to be first is to be alone.'

When at last Elowen had the strength, Mr Skewes and Derwa accompanied her back to village. Kensa followed behind, leaving the wise woman on the beach, her body turned seaward, as though in discussion with it.

At home, as morning began to root itself, Kensa lay on the straw pallet in the kitchen. It was one she shared with Elowen, in their mother's cob-walled cottage halfway down Portscatho. Despite their long night, sleep did not come. Pale, bluish light slid across them. Kensa lay facing the wall. Her sister's warm breath tickled the nape of her neck.

'Will you tell?' Kensa asked her.

A pause and the gentlest exhalation. 'No.'

Kensa did not ask why. It was enough to know she would keep silent. The younger girl wished to be liked, always. Elowen would have given her last crust to make another happy, even as she starved. On the boards above them, their mother and Mr Skewes spoke in low voices and panted questions. No one else would ever know who had really found the Morgawr that morning. This was Kensa's final thought as she fell into slumber, full in the knowledge that her secret was as safe as a stolen crust inside her own belly.

One Elowen would have given her, had she only asked.

Chapter Three

Tide in Turn

Those who lived in Portscatho knew the customs around healers, yet Kensa had never assumed such customs would involve her. Offerings were placed on the front step of the house where Kensa, her mother, half-sister and Mr Skewes lived. Loaves, a shiny buckle, flour as fine as silk, a knitted scarf long enough for the wise woman she would grow to be, who would work and mend and watch over her people. No healer accepted coins in payment. These gifts were exchanges, a contract: the village would keep her and she, in turn, would keep them. Kensa learned much about wise women in the weeks and months and years that followed, though her apprenticeship had not truly begun. Occasionally, she would catch Isolde's eye when the crone visited Portscatho to administer aid or deliver a child, though the answer was always the same: 'You are not ready.' After all, the bone-handled knife had yet to return to her.

From time to time, she was bid to watch a birthing or see how Isolde placed a poultice or set a broken limb. There were some events, however, that she was not privy to. Deaths, usually, when the frail needed seeing to a life beyond this one. Kensa was glad for it. She had no eagerness to see a person breathe their last, though that day would surely come.

Portscatho was built upon a slope that ended with a crescent-shaped harbour. The village inhabitants were primarily fishermen and their wives, miners and their wives, and the occasional crooks with piratical leanings – and their wives – whose blood thickened with the clouds. Kensa's affinity lay with the latter. Perhaps it was her misplaced affection for a long-late father or a need to place herself at odds with the Coast Guard, Mr Skewes.

When it had become widely known that Kensa would work as a wise woman, she was treated differently. Eyes were averted, the nervous ones crossed themselves, and the children began to sneer. It no longer mattered that Kensa was first when there was no one to follow her to the tree, edge or trail she raced to. And should she try to join the others in play, they dispersed as silverfish to candlelight, calling 'haglet' behind them. The unkind name was placed into each new child's mouth as soon as it could talk. Already, Isolde's warning seemed true; Kensa was an outcast, more so than ever before. The only one who did not voice such insults was Elowen, though her silence was condemnation enough.

Since the sea monster's appearance, there was an unsettled quality to the coastal waters. Odd shoals swept up with the drifting seaweed, along with shells as large as fists and jellyfish whose mass and colour were foreign on English shores. More curious than them all was the sea and its barnacled fingers, which curled from the foam in beckoning. Yet only Kensa seemed to notice.

A little after her fourteenth birthday, when the early dawn was an off-colour lilac, a knock startled Kensa awake. It was cold, as February is cold. It had been an easy winter, with fair weather and infrequent storms. Sails were ever-present on the horizon, the majority belonging to the packet ships which transported Post Office communications from Falmouth to the West Indies. Despite the settled seas and plentiful catch, one boat had yet to return to the harbour that morning, as Kensa was soon to learn.

She rose from the pallet she shared with Elowen, bare feet on the rush-strewn floor.

A small voice carried through the shadows. 'Kensa?'

'Go back to bed,' she told Elowen. 'Don't wake Ma.'

The younger of the two girls had a gaunt look, cheeks sunken and bowled. Since that fateful morning on the Towan, Elowen had been prone to sickness. Every head-cold went straight to her chest and too long in the sun would leave her abed for days. A further anxious knock drew Kensa to the door. Men came for Mr Skewes at odd hours, bearing reports of vessels with no flag or an unchecked lantern signalling to a distant schooner. But rather than call for the Coast Guard, the woman at the door had come for her – for Kensa.

'It's my husband,' said Mrs Lowes hurriedly, face slack with sleeplessness. 'He's not come back and it's been over a day.' She was in her nightshift, a man's coat thrown over it. This was what happened at foul times, Kensa noticed. Decent folk on the street in their underthings meant trouble had arisen.

Kensa yawned. 'And what am I meant to do about it?'

'Isolde's away to Bodmin and there's no other who can help,' Mrs Lowes continued desperately. 'You will speak to the Father of Storms for me, won't you?'

'Pardon?'

Mrs Lowes would not accept a rebuff. Predictably, Derwa and Mr Skewes were woken, irate and ill-tempered by the noise from their doorstep. Gradually, the village would muster and Kensa sensed her responsibility pucker around her. She was to be Portscatho's wise woman. She could not refuse to help. Even if she wanted to. What would Old Sal say? Kensa would not dare find out.

'All right,' she said to Mrs Lowes, crossing the threshold with sockless feet stuffed into boots and hair an uncombed tangle. 'I will speak with him.'

Truthfully, she was certain the Bucka did not exist. Yes, there *was* a spirit, a minor sea god who lived in the ocean, though he was only that, the ocean. He was a current beneath the surface or the foam at a wave's tip. If she was bid to speak to the tide, she would, as foolish as it was and for all the good it would do.

There was a place where offerings were left to the sea. A bend in the creek where brine met fresh river. Whenever the tide turned, the two conflicting waters would tussle and roll with a force nothing could stop. It was here the people of

Portscatho left sweet bread or polished glass, coloured ribbon or stones stacked in precarious towers during low tide, only for it to be swept away. Tributes asking for safe passage, firm winds and a bountiful catch. It was an exchange much like that between a wise woman and her charges. Kensa's own father had taken her here and told her to place a token on the ever-moving shoreline. If only she could remember what he had bid her to ask – and what he had asked the Bucka for.

The walk from the village was not a long journey, though the ground was hard and made her ankles ache. With the sun not yet risen, the world was monochrome to her eyes. Bare hawthorn rose along the path. She must have been half-asleep, for it seemed to reach for her cloak as she passed. In the sheltered spaces, which the frost couldn't find, mud tensed around Kensa's boot soles, as though to trap her.

Mrs Lowes stayed close. What good did she think Kensa could do? Were it not for the other's company, she would've waited in a hollow and returned to the village when a suitable time had passed. Then lied about talking to the Bucka and how accommodating he'd been. Now, unable to dissuade the sailor's wife, she had to trudge to the creek and do, well, who knew what?

'You're a treasure, you are,' said Mrs Lowes for the umpteenth time.

She did not reply. What could she say? Her gratitude did not make Kensa's mood less sour or return her to her warm bed, which Elowen now had all to herself.

It was high tide and the creek was a flat, smooth expanse. Thin roots shivered beneath the water, crossed with the reflections of bare branches above. A few bore ribbons in different colours: wishes, prayers, tributes.

Mrs Lowes waited, expectantly. 'Go on, there's a dear.'

Kensa patted her gloved hands together. An echoing *clap, clap, clap* was her answer. Uncertainty brought sweat to the crease behind her knees.

'All right,' she said to herself, throat tight. 'Father o' Storms,' she began, then faltered. She looked over her shoulder to Mrs Lowes, who stared owlishly back. Kensa tried again. 'A fisherman called Mr Lowes is missing and it would do well for you to return him to us.'

'And his boat,' said Mrs Lowes.

'And his boat,' intoned Kensa.

'With a fair catch in it too.'

Kensa released a low grunt.

'If that's no bother, mind.'

After relaying what Mrs Lowes asked, Kensa waited. For a sign, an acknowledgement, a wordless agreement that the Bucka had heard and would do as she wished. *Nothing.* Only the same lapping water, reflecting a waking sky streaked in yellowish light.

Kensa sighed heavily. 'I don't think—'

'That'll do it, I'm certain,' beamed Mrs Lowes. Her features had lost their anxious edge and slackened with relief, as quick as the wind changing. She did not tarry and turned back towards Portscatho with a skip in her step. Kensa could not fathom it. The soon-to-be healer hadn't done anything. Or was this all it took? Perhaps being a wise woman wouldn't be as hard as she first assumed.

Night had folded its blanket from the sky. The emerging sun was as ill-mannered and sulky as Kensa, refusing to leave the clouds around it. She did not return to the village, not straight away. Mrs Lowes was a slow walker and she had no desire for that woman's company. Only, it was quiet, when it had not been quiet a moment ago. The trees were empty frames, leafless and clattering together in near-silent laughter. No birds chattered and no mammals scurried in the underbrush. Even the clouds' scudding progress slowed, everything holding its breath.

Kensa stepped back from the creek.

Her breath thickened to vapour, the moisture catching on her lashes. It was time to go. The damp air had her shiver. And something else. A different chill that did not abate, even when she quickened her pace. A single grouse shrieked its presence and Kensa understood the warning with a second-sense not yet developed: *I am being watched.*

There was movement behind her. Firm steps timed to hers. Too loud to be her own. When she paused, the steps paused too. And when she ran, *he* was right behind her. Yes, she knew, as a woman knows, that it was a man who followed her.

In the half-light, where all that *is* and *seems* and *could* be possible, a thief appeared. This was not a common pickpocket or a chancing wanderer who had spied an easy mark. No, this was a different creature. He had a sickle smile and skin as sallow as chalk. Whatever he planned to steal from her, she had yet to learn and would wait years till she found out.

'Mrs Lowes?' Her voice did not reach far. 'Mrs Lowes!'

No answer came, at least, not from the fisherman's wife.

Hawthorn pricked her spine, her retreat cut off. Water sloshed around her shoes, rising and growing colder. It crept along the path, higher than high tide, hooking her ankles. Kensa could not have fled, even if she wished to.

He stood as shadows stand. He barred the escape ahead.

'You wished to see me, witchling?'

He was tall, which was novel to Kensa, who herself was tall for her age. She had surpassed her mother and several of the hunched octogenarians in the village. Last year she had even forced Jack, the mine overseer's son, to stand beside her, then crowed in triumph when she found herself half an inch higher than he. Jack had avoided her ever since. This man on the path, however, seemed to contain a mass she could not measure. He waited a small distance away, though that distance seemed to shrink and the hawthorn around them grew in size.

Kensa swallowed thickly. 'How tall are you, sir?'

When he spoke, it was with a tongue of silk and samphire. 'As high as the cliffs and as low as the seas.'

'I cannot measure that in inches.'

His coat was long and splendid, spliced together from eel skins and glittering in the not-quite-morning. Across a high forehead ran splintered hair, as silver as sea fog and almost as translucent. His gaze, however, was human. A stark summer-day blue or the teal in a cormorant's eyes. Their mortal tilt made his otherness all the more striking.

'You are the Bucka,' said Kensa at last.

In her eagerness to flee her pursuer, she had run further along the creek's marshy bank. And when she stepped back, it was into its water, skirts billowing around her.

The eel-clad man, if he could be called a man, assessed her. 'Where is Isolde?'

She had been warned about the Bucka. Legend claimed he was a lost sailor, an evil fairy or a cursed prince whose intent was rarely, if ever, good. In fervent prayers he was named the Father of Storms, to be worshipped when summer heat parched the wheat fields or the fishermen's nets ran dry. Kensa had assumed he was a tale used to scare children. Yet, here he was, made flesh or flesh-like, and she a child and frightened.

'Isolde's in Bodmin.'

The Bucka's slim eyebrows rose.

'She's – she's due back within the hour.'

'Do not lie to me.'

Clack. Kensa's teeth snapped together. 'I should go.'

'You had a request, did you not?'

'I—'

It was not the force in which he spoke that had Kensa edge away. Truly, his voice was measured. Soft, even. Yet behind it was a pull that compelled her to set distance between them. And so she did, her foot plunging into the creek and sliding, taking her under. The last thing she saw was the Bucka's smile, as though he'd planned this. Kensa's head fell below the murky waterline. Shock prised her mouth open and brown tidal water poured in. Thick reeds tangled her legs, while her lungs went for air and found none. She clawed outwards and met nothing. Only her blooming skirts, which pressed into her face and caught her hands. At last, her knees hit mud and slipped further down and downwards.

Until the water receded. It fell away to allow her air – heaving, retching. Beneath her was silty ground. It sucked at her limbs as she steadily clambered back on to the dry bank. A hand reached out to steady her: the Bucka's hand. She did not take it. Worse than that, she pushed back. At the hand. At the body it belonged to. At the Bucka.

She may as well have pushed an oak, for all he shifted. She pushed him again, palms flat against his chest. Less in ferocity, more as an experiment. In the near-light, it looked like his feet were rooted to the soil, toes tilted downwards. And he was icy as the sea in winter, enough to freeze the air in her lungs. Kensa's hands were raw from where she touched him. She began to tremble, hair flat against her scalp, clothes sodden and dripping on to the path beside the creek.

'*You* are who the Morgawr chose?' he asked.

Kensa raised her chin. Levelled her eyes to his. She did not speak.

He had told her not to lie.

The Bucka smiled again. 'You called for me?'

'Mrs Lowes's husband—'

'Is drunk at The Wodehouse Arms in Falmouth. He is not lost at sea, though he will tell his wife some grand tale about a windless sky or a great wave and she will swallow it and more, though she knows better.'

Kensa spoke through chattering teeth. 'Then why did she ask me to come here?'

He looked down his long nose at her and she felt her youthful ignorance, heat rising to her cheeks. It did little to dry her clothes.

'When do you begin your work?'

'I don't know.' He was quiet, waiting, and Kensa floundered for a better answer. 'I am to see Isolde when her bone-handled knife returns to me. That will be when I am ready.' Again, silence, hers to fill. 'I lost it to the sea monster, to the sea itself, mayhap you've—'

'I have not seen it.'

He was close enough that she could smell the night on him. Salt and time and cloud-washed starlight. And something else, incense, perhaps. 'You are frightened,' said the Bucka. 'About what will be asked of you, about whether you have the power to do it. You will have power and, in time, it will be others who are frightened of you.'

He referred to the Old Ways, on what the ill-informed called magic. On what she would do, on how she would do it.

Kensa's mouth was stiff and gummy. 'I – I do not want to make people afraid.'

'Then what do you want?'

'I wish to help my—'

'Do *not* lie.' The Bucka's voice was in her mouth, in her throat, in her chest, in her head, as he commanded, 'Tell me.'

And she did.

Spoke on her intentions, frustrations and hopes. Revealed in a babbling stream everything she feared and hated. What she ran from and hoped to run to. Embarrassment flushed her face as she continued to talk, mouth clicking with dryness, tongue harsh against her teeth. She admitted the worries she harboured, about living alone and dying as such, unwanted and ridiculed, exactly as Isolde was. There was a tentative wish in among her words, like a prayer, concerning the experiences – once taken for granted – that now seemed unattainable.

She told him everything.

It was a violation and the Bucka revelled in it.

Kensa gasped when at last her lips ceased their talking. She put her muddy fingers to her jaw, as though to stop its working. Too late, it was done. Her answers satisfied the Bucka, at least, though it left her carved and hollow.

He knew it, too.

Kensa blinked up at him as though to ask or beg or demand he return what he had taken, but it could not be given back.

Without a word, the Father of Storms dismissed her. He slid past her, to the creek's edge, then further. Upon stepping into the water, darkness fanned around him. He sank down until his legs were legs no longer: a cloud with its own writhing intent. Soon enough, his middle was below the water and his eel-skin coat seemed no coat at all, pressed as it was to his angular form, tentacled and coiling. He never once looked back. Even when she willed him to.

Kensa watched his shape, blurred and brackish, until it vanished. Even then, she was not rid of him. Her boots squelched on the way home, as though the Bucka followed her, sitting inside her dampened form, waiting to prise her in two once again. Only when her dress and hair were completely dry did she consider herself truly alone. And later, when she returned to the straw pallet beside her sister, she thought she heard the sea laugh.

Chapter Four

The Convening of Witches

Jack had grown broad enough to fill the doorframe. 'She wants tod's tails.' In fact, he was now taller than Kensa. By four inches at least. 'I'll go with you, though I don't know what to look for.' Worse, he made no effort to hide it. Standing there, back straight and bulky arms folded. 'Are you listening?'

Kensa sucked her teeth. 'Isolde wants me to fetch her plants in this downpour?'

A wet gale pressed through the windows and slid beneath every door.

'She says a storm's good weather for it.'

Jack seemed restless. His brown eyes were unable to meet her hazel, while he shifted his weight from his toes to his heels and scrubbed a hand at his rich dark hair. Well, it was not as though she wanted to spend time with him either.

Kensa sighed. 'I'll get my cloak.'

On the hill overlooking the village, where the oak trees clustered in a wooden spine which ran as far as Fowey, the wind was fiercest. It sought entry into Kensa's mouth and puffed out her cheeks when given the chance. She would have roped Elowen into their task, had she not been helping Miss Latham at the small charity school in Gerrans. Sir Trevanion paid for its costs. Kensa had not been grateful for her own meagre education. Once she'd learned her letters, she'd left. Yet her sister had stayed and now taught the youngest children. At least, when she was able to. Elowen had sickened again. Strange fits, weak episodes, a general malaise which kept her abed for weeks. And her nightmares were worse. Mutterings in the cold and the dark, even when Kensa sacrificed her own blankets (and coat and shawl) to drape atop her. There was nothing to be done. Or that's what Isolde said, when Kensa asked. Claimed it was nought for their divining, and a sea-damp cloth to the forehead was the only help to be given. Yet if ever there was the slightest sign that Elowen might be nearing another episode, Kensa watched her avidly. More than that, she bullied her sister into finishing her dinner, snatched away the books Miss Latham lent her if ever she read overlong, rarely let her go out alone, if at all, and then criticised her clothes when they were unsuitable for the season. And Elowen wasn't even grateful!

The plant which Kensa was bid to find was essential in treating gout. It had thick, long stalks and a mossy quality which fought against her grip. 'Are you going to help or not?'

Jack cleared his throat. 'I've got snares to check.'

Gulls wheeled overhead, waiting out the worst gusts. Not even a seabird would put their trust in the Bucka's generosity today. As such, no sailor did either. Small boats crowded the harbour, straining against their moorings. It had been several months since Kensa's meeting with the Father of Storms. Isolde had been furious when she'd found out. Forbade her from ever speaking with him again.

'If he finds someone desperate enough, he can pluck their worst thoughts from their mind and use them in a bargain,' she'd explained. 'Let's be thankful you're made of stronger stuff, eh?'

Kensa had only swallowed in reply. She was suddenly pleased to have Jack with her. Only because it was a little better than being alone. Besides, he was strong and could lend a hand when it came to carrying the new supplies homeward. Kensa had seen him lift sizeable sacks filled with smoked mackerel when asked. Studied him, intently. In fact, she'd watched him for a whole hour. He didn't seem to strain at the task, his sleeves rolled up to his elbows. Or, on one occasion, with no shirt at all . . .

'Did you hear me?'

Kensa cleared her throat. 'What?'

'There's a rabbit caught on the rise,' said Jack, inclining his head in a request for her to accompany him.

'But the tod's tails are this way,' she replied.

Thus far, he had led her on a roundabout walk that had taken the whole morning. Kensa's legs were already tired and her basket near-empty. He grabbed its twisted willow handle, fixing her in place.

'You're coming with me,' said Jack.

'I've got work to do – and I'm damned well going to do it.'

This was the longest conversation the pair had ever had and now Kensa understood why. Because he was a bully with no manners and even less patience.

'If I have to carry you across the heath, I will,' he warned. 'I will check the snares while the rain's eased and you shall follow.'

'Huh.' Kensa's mouth went dry. Carry? There was rain beaded on his skin. 'I can walk,' she said, and charged ahead lest he see her face, cheeks burning. She would not think on why. Only that it was his fault and she was disposed to hate him for it. No one would make her think thoughts she had not planned on thinking. Besides, it wouldn't hurt to accompany him. Yes, she decided she would go with him. He clearly needed her help.

There was a grim protest from the captured rabbit, prior to a quick click as Jack broke its neck. He worked efficiently, rarely speaking. Even when the rain poured anew, he did not comment. A bright green canopy sheltered them somewhat, though the new leaves struggled against the onslaught.

'Let's wait it out,' said Jack at last.

It wasn't like him to shy away from wet weather. In fact, quite the opposite. Nothing could keep him down or hold him back. And that is when she understood.

'You're keeping me here,' said Kensa accusingly, raising her voice against the weather – and him.

Slowly, Jack rose from his crouch. He glanced to the glassy-eyed rabbit, as though it would offer help. 'Yes,' he admitted after a while.

Kensa's exhale whistled through her teeth. She cuffed her nose with her sleeve and readied herself to begin a tirade, until she thought to ask, 'Why?'

A noise had them both tense: a crack louder than a rabbit's neck.

Elowen burst through the undergrowth, snapping twigs beneath her shoes. 'Kensa! I came to fetch you,' she rasped, her finest clothes soaked through. 'There's wise women in the orchard – there's a whole gathering.'

'What?'

Elowen repeated herself and Kensa cursed loudly.

'It's not my fault no one told you,' said Elowen hurriedly. 'I saw them on my walk home and ran halfway round the village in search of you; Ma didn't know anything about it either.'

'Show me,' demanded Kensa.

'Wait,' said Jack, snatching at Kensa's sleeve.

She pulled her arm free – and failed. When she tried again, he released her, reluctantly. 'You knew about this?' A slow and frustrating truth found her. 'Isolde doesn't need any tod's tails, does she?'

'She wants you to—'

'I don't care what she wants, this is about what *I* want,' said Kensa.

Jack pressed his tongue to the inside of his cheek, as though to stop from speaking – then spoke anyway. 'Isn't everything?'

'That's not fair,' said Elowen firmly, as though she was still in Miss Latham's classroom, chiding a child. Kensa clenched her teeth. She did not need anyone sticking up for her, least of all her little sister.

Jack persisted. 'Don't you think Isolde has a reason for keeping this from you?'

'Everyone thinks I am not ready,' Kensa spat. 'I am ready and I will prove it.'

Elowen led the way through horizontal rain. It grew in strength with every step towards the orchard, forming a nipping barrier. Kensa would not be deterred. The wind smarted any exposed flesh, wrenching at her hair and skirts. Elowen fared worse, with only Jack's palm on her back keeping her upright. She shouldn't be out here. Not in a storm such as this. It wouldn't do her any good and Kensa would be the one stuck looking after her.

Gradually, the three pressed on towards the apple trees above the church, where an old priory had once stood in a forgotten time when early saints were men and no one told stories about them.

Suddenly, the wind died. Past a certain point in the path, the day was calm.

'Listen,' whispered Jack, as he swept the sisters into the bracken using the force of his own mass.

There were ill-tempered shouts. Uproar, even, from eight figures talking over one another, clamouring to be heard. Among the calls was Isolde's. It was her furious words which cut through the din: 'Trust I am fully capable of defending what's mine, Eadain.'

A tall, hawkish woman raised her hand. Silence, anticipation. 'Our concerns are for the Pact.' Her voice had a ringing quality. By her manner and the command she held over the other wise women present, she was clearly the leader. She had long black hair and wore a long black cloak, appearing as a turgid smudge among the blossoming trees. 'You must understand our worry, Isolde, especially with what happened the last time a wise woman waited too long to pass their skills to another.'

'This isn't good,' said Elowen.

Jack huffed. 'We need to go – now.'

'Shush,' said the sisters in unison.

It was rare to see new faces in Portscatho. It was not a place travellers frequented, for it led to nothing and nowhere. Falmouth was the main draw in these parts – well, for the sailors and militia, mostly. And the smugglers, naturally. How far had these people travelled?

Cornwall had its own customs around healers. Although unwelcome in larger towns where men had taken up the practice of medicine, often with brutal results, the poorer folk in smaller communities needed their wise women.

'Only seventy years ago, our kind was hanged by the neck for witchcraft,' continued Eadain. 'If we are to ensure our own survival, we cannot take risks and must be beyond reproach.'

Isolde sneered. 'I am not a risk.'

'You've carried this burden for too long,' said Eadain, her words lacking sincerity. 'It's time to pass it on to another.' She gestured to herself. 'There are warnings carried on the wind, I've heard them; change is coming and we must be strong enough to heed it.'

'I will be,' said Isolde. 'I have chosen an apprentice.'

Murmurs passed through those assembled. Eadain was not convinced. 'Then where is she? If that were true, she'd be here.'

Kensa stayed as still as possible.

'It's a lie,' continued the leader. 'I say we take the Pact by force.'

A toothy wise woman, whose bodice was laced so tightly she near-spilled from it, interrupted the argument: 'We are being watched.' Her chin angled itself towards the underbrush where Kensa, Elowen and Jack hid.

The tall witch in black swept towards them, swift and crow-like. Her face was drawn and hollow, as an old pale stone smoothed by the wind. Kensa stood up, pulling the coven's attention onto herself and away from her sister and her ... well, Jack.

Eadain halted, then pressed on until she was standing over the young woman. 'Do you know what happens to eyes and ears that see and hear what they should not?'

'No,' said Kensa.

'Nothing.' A thin non-smile. 'I leave those in place and remove the tongue instead, so it can never speak of what was witnessed.'

'Enough,' said Isolde sharply. 'This is the girl who is to apprentice with me. Save your scaremongering for the children foolish enough to believe it.'

Kensa could believe it, though she did not think herself foolish for it.

'I recognise a smuggler's daughter, but these two ...' Eadain's long fingers pressed into Kensa's shoulder and forced her to step aside, revealing the others who had spied on the coven alongside her. Reluctantly, they shuffled into the orchard.

'He has tin bones,' said the toothy wise woman as she scanned Jack, who glowered in turn. Next, attention shifted to Elowen.

Kensa stepped in the way. 'They're not important.' Instinct told her not to let them examine her sister closely, and she listened to it. There was a tug on her dress, Elowen's fist at her back, holding on tightly. 'Go on,' she said, ushering Elowen to stand with Isolde. She nodded to Jack to follow – a lengthy stare between the two – a small truce, a mutual agreement: *Keep my sister safe.*

Kensa scanned the wise women present, who were not all women. One man stood with them, with a prominent brow and even more prominent glower. His hands were dirty, much like Kensa's. She had heard of the herbalist Billy Rapson, but had not been told of his smell: darkly botanical, wild mint and mulch. She knew Hawise of the Lizard, for she had stopped at the Jennings' inn once or twice on her travels, keen to tell fortunes about love and lost riches. The others she did not know.

The toothy, buxom woman in her early forties – the one with the tight bodice – asked, 'Is this going to take all day?'

Eadain levelled her stare at Kensa. 'Is it?'

Kensa clamped her lips shut. 'Isolde—'

'You will not talk to her,' said Eadain. 'You will talk to me.' Around the witch, the air was stifling. Not even the insects dared fly by her. A sound, the wind, as it whispered her name to the ear Eadain leaned upwards. 'How lucky you are, *Kensa*, to apprentice here. Do you know how we keep the storm raging? If one wise woman alone were to channel it, to ensure Portscatho's residents stayed away and inside their homes, she would lose consciousness in a minute – or worse. Yet many wise women working together can manage it with only a mild headache. The Old Ways are about balance. When we arrived, the wind was already fast moving. We simply channelled it. When you master this ability, you will understand what it means to obey our laws, to give and take. This is what the Pact does: it keeps everything, us included, in check. Do you understand?'

'I – I think so,' said Kensa.

'We shall see,' said Eadain.

Hawise beamed at Kensa, at odds with the general mood within the orchard. 'That settles it,' she cheered, 'we've no cause to be 'ere if the Pact's secure.'

Tensions existed which had formed long ago. Kensa's own confusion added to it. Strange, to meet others who did not revere Portscatho's wise woman as they should, to have to re-frame in her mind the sway which Isolde had over the village and beyond it.

Quickly, the power which guided the wind disbanded, swamping the orchard with a strong gust. This magic was different to what Kensa had experienced with the Bucka. The Father of Storms had moved through her mind like water, firm and controlled, coaxing secrets from her in a babbling stream. The wise women were an unwieldy force – an uncoordinated weight and haphazard presence. Here was a true taste of the Old Ways, as the witches knew it.

If any other wise woman was uncomfortable with the deci-sion, none voiced it, though two had a sour expression beneath a hood or behind a hand. After a further statement – which Kensa did not hear through her ringing ears – the meeting was disbanded and the wise women began to shuffle from the orchard.

Eadain remained behind. What she said to Isolde no one else heard, before she turned to Kensa. 'I will see you do your duty, Miss Rowe.' As she spoke, her mouth tightened, making her question clipped and sharp. 'Do you know why Portscatho is important?'

'No,' said Kensa quietly.

'Because the Pact was formed in Portscatho, it is here the Old Ways are strongest. Here is an unseen seam from which power flows, resting in the space between Land and Sea. Do you think the Bucka would be half as powerful on any other shore? As such, the Pact requires a keeper with a strong will to hold it, and I think yours shall break.'

With those final words, Eadain swept from the orchard, her strides long and imposing.

Only when her black cloak had gone from sight, did Kensa risk facing Isolde. Portscatho's wise woman had a rounded slump to her shoulders. Jack was close by, purposely avoiding Kensa's gaze, no matter how hard she tried find it.

She wanted to say a thousand things to Isolde. That she was sorry and hadn't realised and was trying to be a good wise woman's apprentice and now she was not sure there was such a thing. Eventually, in a voice as small as she felt, she said, 'I thought it would only ever be us two; I did not think there'd ever be anyone else.'

Isolde raised her head. 'You won't have much to do with the coven.' She frowned heavily. 'I had hoped to keep them from you a while longer.'

'Then you probably should've sent someone other than Jack to mind me,' said Kensa, an ill attempt at humour.

Jack released a long-suffering sigh. Even then, he would not look at her.

One question lingered on Kensa's tongue. 'What happened last time, when someone waited too long to take an apprentice?'

Isolde's answer was pained. She spoke on the Owlman, a legend in these parts, a bird as large as a man. 'I was once his apprentice, in the days when the Roundheads marched on Cornwall.'

That was at least one hundred years ago, as far as Kensa remembered. 'Will you become as he did?'

'If a wise woman does not remember their calling, other forces can claim them.'

'The Morgawr,' said Elowen softly.

'Yes, she was the first, the one who forged the Pact,' said Isolde. 'It was she who stood against man's force and chained herself to an eternal agreement, allowing the Old Ways to slowly corrode her mind and body, changing it for ever.'

Eyes sparking, Elowen asked, 'Do you think she was happier that way, as a creature and not a woman?'

Jack harrumphed at the question, his disapproval ever-present.

Isolde said plainly, 'Yes.'

Kensa sniffed, irritated, as she always was whenever that evening on the Towan was brought to mind. And unsettled to think that any wise woman could change, lose themselves, forget. *She* never would, that was certain.

As though she could read Kensa's thoughts, Isolde asked:

'Do you intend to continue training with me, preparing for your apprenticeship?'

'Yes,' she replied quickly.

As much as today frightened her, it intrigued her more. Truthfully, she had, in part, welcomed the fear. It made her feel as though she was someone – someone worth making afraid. Not overlooked or brushed aside. In the orchard, standing with the coven, she was one of them.

'Get them home, Jack.'

He nodded, leaving Isolde as he escorted the sisters down Portscatho's hill. Finally, the storm had exhausted itself. Tentative sunlight bordered the clouds, promising a better day. Kensa would have shared that sentiment, were it not for Jack's expression. When it came time to separate, he cleared his throat to speak. Kensa did not give him the chance.

'I am to be the wise woman of Portscatho and I will not be lied to.'

Jack was not the young boy she had once known, thick brows drawn together. He had grown, somehow, in more ways than she cared to count. 'You are not the wise woman yet,' he said, 'exactly as I do not run the mine yet, my father does, but I know what it takes.'

Elowen bowed forwards, hiding her face, and ducked inside, leaving the two on the front step with half the village in earshot.

'You are to be a leader, the same as I,' said Jack. 'When are you going to act like it?'

Kensa had never seen him angry. And even in his anger, he was controlled. That did not matter, for she was furious enough for them both. 'Is that how you plan to speak to the healer who'll save your life one day?'

'When she needs to hear it.'

'As soon as I am old enough, I shall be the biggest thorn in your side,' she spat.

Kensa's heart was beating rabbit-fast and Jack's parting words were a snare, delivered as he walked into the fading storm: 'You already are.'

Chapter Five

Mist from the Sea

It was always the whimpering that woke her. Kensa could sleep through the rasps and gasps that came from the space beside her, but not the pain. There was a muffled quality to them, as though Elowen was trying to hide her sickness, even in sleep.

'That's enough,' murmured Kensa, a gentle chiding. 'Come on.'

The sisters lay on the pallet in the kitchen darkness. Despite the dim light, Kensa could see the sweat across Elowen's pillow, an inverse halo. Her fair hair was damp and translucent, while her hands pressed against her ribs, spine curved inwards. She had been getting bad again. It worsened – her condition – each year when the spring tides came. Old Sal claimed it was the stars, their mother blamed the damp once the frosts had passed, while Isolde would not say what it was, only that she had brought a special tonic to ease the symptoms.

Kensa put a hand to her sister's forehead, cold as the ocean. 'Elowen?'

'I'm here,' she replied, spoken in slumber, then repeated upon waking: a reassurance as to where she was and who she was with.

Kensa rolled onto her feet and reached for her shawl. It was always like this, Elowen and her illness. None linked it to the Morgawr's appearance. People became unwell, no one ever wondered, 'Why?' Or if they did, the answer was, 'God.' Whether he be the Holy Father or the Father of Storms. Once or twice, the sisters had tried to discuss it and Kensa had been ashamed and Elowen unwilling to yield her own suspicions. It was their secret – and they would keep it, although Kensa did not know exactly what the secret was or even if Elowen knew it.

'I never know when to wake you – if I should let you sleep through it.'

'Always wake me.' Elowen paused, elbowing herself into a seated position. 'It's dark when I dream – and I think I'm drowning or I'm not drowning and somehow it's worse.'

'Well, you're not now,' said Kensa firmly and with a frown. 'You're here, being a pain, keeping me awake.' If they were not careful, they would disturb Derwa and Mr Skewes.

Kensa slid her thick socks towards the grate. Its fire sat low and underfed. She would stir it to wakefulness in due course, when the house was ready to wake with it. There was little firewood to waste. Mr Skewes's position as Coast Guard did not earn them much. Her mother's sewing brought in a little coin, as did Elowen's role as assistant teacher to Miss Latham. Despite their meagre income, the household did not struggle. That was Kensa's doing. Although she had yet to begin her apprenticeship to the wise woman, she was regularly given eggs, bread, weak beer and even clothes. She could not work, not in the way others worked. Instead, under Isolde's watch, she gave aid to those who needed it. Should an expectant mother be too unwell to milk her cow, Kensa would do it. If there was an elderly chap unable to wrangle the village pump, she would assist him. After all, Kensa was strong enough, able-bodied and did not mind physical labour. The only difficulties she faced were in conversation. *Talking.* People did not want to hear that their problems were their own doing, though Kensa would have them know it.

Begrudgingly, she learned to bite her tongue.

'You learn more,' she explained to Isolde, on the frequent occasions the wise woman came to visit Elowen, tonic in hand. 'Quiet don't stay quiet for long. It gets filled and you'd be surprised by what people fill it with, what they *really* want to say.'

'That there is healing work,' said Isolde.

And it had been a reminder: Kensa was not a healer yet. Almost four years had passed since the witches' convening, yet the bone-handled knife had not returned. No matter how often she begged, Isolde would not relent. Only when the blade came back, would Kensa be permitted to learn her trade. Until then, she was forced to pick up her craft in crumbs, trailing Isolde on house visits and lingering in Portscatho's alcoves and thresholds, offering help where it was needed.

Elowen's tonic was kept in the low cupboard where the sun

could not reach it. The glass vial was cold in Kensa's hand, same as the spring breeze which crept under the door and down the chimney. By the time she returned to their shared bed, Elowen was fully awake. The brief openness in her expression was gone, closed off, chased away.

'I don't want it.'

'Then you'll get sicker,' said Kensa.

Elowen gripped the vial loosely in her slim fingers, threatening to stain her nightdress. 'It tastes awful.' Her fever had finally broken, though it had taken a day. It always did break, eventually, with Kensa to coax her through it. 'I'm not a child who needs minding.'

'Elowen—'

'You will find it today,' she said quietly.

Kensa yawned. 'What?'

Silence. Elowen's speciality. She sank back onto the pallet and set the empty vial on her bedside table. The blankets strained against her outline as she folded onto her side.

'I know you're not asleep,' said Kensa.

She may as well have addressed the moon for all the response her sister gave. Elowen was as sallow as the moon, too. Pale, reedy and often in wane, bar the better days she was full and free and laughing. Equally as distant, too. Now, at eighteen, Kensa bore even less resemblance to her sister. And if she was stockier and broader and stronger, what of it? Her hair had grown brassier with age and thickly tangled, no matter how cruelly she brushed it. Across her face were endless freckles, topped by thick brows, which added a severity to her face. No, there was nothing of the moon about Kensa.

It was a cold morning in March and thick with mist: flat, veil-like, blurring the village edges. Kensa went out to greet it. She could not fall back to sleep. Neither could she lie there beside Elowen and pretend they were – whatever they were pretending. In the fresh air, she was more herself. There were kittens by the salting house. Poorly creatures with crummy eyes and patchy fur. Mr Skewes said they were better off drowned, thereby making it Kensa's mission to save them. Weak mewls greeted her as she leaned between two barrels to find the mother absent, hunting most likely. Portscatho had a tense relationship with its cats, as with most fishing communities. Their presence was a bad omen, for they often stole the thickest herring from the boat's latest haul. However, their rat-catching skills were unmatched and so the half-feral creatures were tolerated. Everything and everyone in the village had a place.

Well, almost everyone. Kensa remained an outsider.

Those children she had grown up with, the ones who had scorned her, were gone. Boys who considered themselves men sought fortunes and rank in the military. At least, those not attached to farmsteads or the mine. Although the war in the Americas was over, trouble stirred abroad in France. Girls who grew to be women were sent to grand houses as lowly servants. That would have been Kensa's fate. It still could be, if she failed in her duties as wise woman, which Mr Skewes took pleasure in reminding her. He had a sister at Trewense Manor, a large house which belonged to their local magistrate. Of course, there were worse options than becoming a maid: one could marry. Become tethered to a man, usually older, with nightly expectations that tightened Kensa's stomach when she thought on it. She tried not to think on it. There was a marked difference between herself and those young women in Portscatho who'd wed as soon as they reached a suitable age. She could not describe what it was. Perhaps how they carried themselves, how they deferred to their husbands, how they looked down on anyone who did not know what they knew. Not that Kensa *wanted* to know. Why would she? She never even thought about it. At least, not often – not that she would tell anyone.

Elowen was too young to wed, though already it was spoken of.

'She'll make a fine wife for your son Jack when she's grown, won't she?' Old Sal had asked Branok one Sunday after church. 'He'll need a woman with a solid head on her shoulders if he's to take over the mine's running, won't he?'

Ever the diplomat – above as well as below ground – the mine overseer had simply nodded.

Kensa had not lingered to hear further. Elowen was too weak to consider a husband. And besides, Jack was – well, he was – it did not matter what he was. No one talked on Kensa's own wedding. A wise woman's only commitment was to her community. It was not deemed acceptable for her to have her own offspring or even partake in the activities which may lead to that result.

Good, thought Kensa, *Good*.

The sea was ever-present at her back. A tidal rise and fall, as familiar as Kensa's own inhalations. Only today, the sea was impossibly loud, bouncing off the harbour wall, eager for attention. As the sun began to appear, its surface shone. A strange winking light. One which stole her focus from the fat-slopped bread she spooned into the kittens' mouths. It was a sharp glimmer, more than daylight's playful sway on the water. As though the sea could talk, it called to her.

Oh, but the sea can talk, Kensa was quick to remember.

Was it a summons? Sometimes she thought she'd dreamed her exchange with the Bucka. Only, she'd no head for wild imaginings and unruly gods. She rose, apprehensively, and moved towards the body of water. There she met the bone-handled knife.

It waited below the harbour's waterline, submerged in sand. Around it were silvery fish, which mistook the blade's shine for their own shimmering bodies. Kensa stared at it for longer than necessary. It did not vanish. This was no trick. Her palms were clammy despite the morning chill. She peeled off one mitten, then the next, and unhooked her shawl. The fog rose around her, as though to shield her. Kensa shucked off her dress, though she kept her undergarments on, body clenched against the air.

With a seal's confidence, and her own gracelessness, she slid from the harbour wall and into the brine. It closed around her. Icy, painful for it. She clamped her mouth tightly against the impulse to open it, to cry out and draw in air. Weightless, the sea's buoyancy slowed her steady drop downwards. At her side was the wall's flaring base, pockmarked with winkles and limpets, ready to skin her knees if she wasn't careful. Kensa's feet hit the sandy bed. It rose to meet her, billowing up, obscuring the—

Knife.

She could not see it. In desperation, Kensa plunged her fist down. Let it cut her. She would risk losing a finger if in her

mangled hands she held her fate. Instinct, or a sea god's inter-
vention, pushed her grip through the water and there she met
the witch's blade. Its handle was bleached white by salt, though
its sharpness had not been dulled. Kensa bent her legs, pushed
up and propelled her head above the water, the bone-handled
knife held high. In the early light, its carvings shone, written
in a script whose secrets had long since been lost, secrets now
Kensa's to learn.

She dressed quickly as the fog began to disperse. Her clothes
stuck to her skin and her teeth clacked together. What did she
care? Elation – no, pride – warmed her. At last, it would begin.
At last, *she* would begin.

At the cottage she no longer considered as home, Kensa
packed her belongings. Three dresses (two simple smocks and
her Sunday best) were curled into a small leather satchel once
owned by her father. Its leather interior smelled of tobacco and
cloves. Next were one or two treasured shells, a handkerchief
embroidered with her initials, and the hagstone.

She left the knife until last. Set it on the window between
the front door and the pallet where her sister lay, yet to leave
the warm covers.

Elowen would not look at it. 'You're going, then?'

Kensa took her time with the buckle on the satchel, drawing
out the action for as long as she could. 'It seems like it.'

'Will you come to visit?'

'Maybe, I don't know.' She rearranged the handkerchief,
unnecessarily. 'I'll be doing a lot. You know, important things
wise women do.' A long pause, then Kensa finally stowed the
knife. 'Unless you'll need me?'

Elowen observed her, pale and wan as their – no *her* – bedsheets. 'Your hair is wet.'

'Should you take a turn, come fetch me,' said Kensa finally, putting an end to their talk. She hesitated at the ladder that led towards her mother, who, along with Mr Skewes, had yet to rise.

'I can tell her you've left,' said Elowen.

There was a lengthy pause between the two siblings. It held much that was unsaid and would continue to be. Kensa ignored it, forcefully. Scraped her boots heavily on the floor, clattered loudly and gave no room for interruption. Even if it came, she would not hear it.

It never came.

She did not turn around as she left. Her life was ahead, not behind. Her chest hammered with a heart too excited to still itself. And wary, too, at leaving. In time with its rhythm, she threw her feet out of the door and her body followed, eager to go, to go and get gone, get away from a self she would never be again.

It was not until Kensa reached the long trail from the village that she remembered the strangeness Elowen had spoken that morning: 'You will find it today.' In some way, perhaps, the bone-handled knife returned to the youngest first. It had chosen her, through her strange and troublesome dreams, at least. This was not the first time her sister had dreamed on a future that had happened. No one else needed to know that and she trusted no one else ever would. Concern twisted in her chest for the younger woman she'd left behind.

Elowen.

Kensa walked harder until her ankles clashed together. Her hair was curled with seawater. Its coldness nipped her skin and she countered it with a brisker walk, head bowed against the wind. She kept the satchel on her right side, furthest from the sea, as though the water might take it back.

And she thought on what she'd miss, her heart aching, until what she'd miss came to find her.

Elowen's hand grazed her sister's wrist, then grabbed firmly. Kensa was pulled to a panting halt, as her sister – exhausted from running – toppled them both up and over into a verge. A hundred grass rivulets, the dull-white moths that slept in meadowsweet, sprang up around them. The young women laughed, knees, elbows, hips damp with dew. Together. The pair lay there a long while, faces turned to one another. Everything and nothing had changed, yet the world seemed different somehow, as though it had decided something on their behalf.

'I'll miss you,' said Kensa begrudgingly, rising to her feet.

'I know,' grinned Elowen, as she accepted a hand up.

Theirs was a brief embrace, stilted and awkward, with Kensa the first to break it. She didn't want to cry and hated that she might and wouldn't have anyone see it. Besides, it was ridiculous to be sad when this was what she wanted.

Beyond them, far from the sloping grass, the waves grew lamps at the tips and doused them on the shore. The weather was turning, clouds churning in warning.

'You should get home,' said Kensa. 'It'll rain soon.'

Elowen nodded, brushed off her wrinkled smock, and turned back. She waved once as her shape receded and Kensa only thought to wave back when it was too late and her sister had turned away.

Although it was only an hour's walk to Isolde's cottage, it could have been another continent. The furthest Kensa had ever travelled was Falmouth. Once with her father and again with Mr Skewes. She barely remembered the first visit. Shouts, fish rot, her father's neck scruff and her own face tucked into his shoulder. Later, when she was grown, Mr Skewes fell into an argument at the draper's shop. Elowen had soothed it, as she soothed everyone, and their mother's embroidery was finally sold for a reasonable price.

The path to Bohortha was steep and slippery, the soil wet enough to slide underfoot. Above, the sky began to darken, as though it had forgotten it meant to rain and was hastily arranging clouds about itself. The bone-handled knife was a weight in her satchel, heavy and growing heavier, the strap biting into her skin. By the time she reached the cottage, her legs were stiff and there was a mark on her shoulder, a bright red slash.

As a child she had found Isolde's home a strange, forbidding place. Now a woman – in her own mind, at least – Kensa saw it for what it was: damp. Squat trees blocked the light, while slime clung to the mould that clung to the crumbling brickwork at the cottage's lower levels. It had a narrow door hemmed with odd symbols and geometric shapes that Kensa could not read. She grimaced, swallowed around a knot at her throat, and pushed the door open.

Knocking was for strangers.

Knocking was for those without a bone-handled knife.

Bohortha had once been home to a manor house, built and

then abandoned around the Restoration era. Rocky clumps stood where walls had been. Ivy claimed its remnants and had brought its beams down years ago. No villagers ever reused the materials, believing the place carried ill luck: once unluckiness gets into stone, you'll never get it out. Bright-beaked choughs nested in the tangled vines, while brambles, thick where floor might have been, kept predators – human, mainly – out. It sat on a cliff's crest with a sea view to the south and rolling fields elsewhere. Only the groundskeeper's abode remained standing, which was now the wise woman's cottage. And Kensa's too, she supposed.

It was cooler here, as though the cottage kept to an older season. Bohortha seemed to cling to an old time, too. At any moment, a man in a ruffled collar and velvet doublet might ride his horse against the thorns to ask if she was for the rebels or the king.

Years ago, Kensa and her peers had invented stories about what could be inside the ramshackle building: a thousand adders knotted together to make a living tapestry, colours no mortal eye had ever seen; a silver chalice that sang whenever a sinner's tongue touched its rim.

Instead, as Kensa eased open the groaning door, she discovered a mess.

Leather-bound books – which cost a year's wage in these parts – were stacked in corners and sloped precariously against benches and lumps which might, centuries ago, have passed for cushions. Tatty furniture sat in leggy tangles, their springs lost and coverings threadbare. Beyond was a staircase reaching upwards, each step cluttered with more books. Then there were the bookcases, the innumerable bookcases, which should have held those endless tomes, yet heaved with jars. Anything that could be pickled, had been pickled. *Anything.* Dried herbs ran from the ceiling in spidery lengths, while the pantry door lay off its hinges. One or two large chests sat at inconvenient angles, promising a bruised knee or shin, should one's concentration waver for even a moment. And that was only the kitchen. At least there was a low fire in the grate, though it desperately needed feeding.

Beyond that chaotic space was a parlour, where live birds sat in cages, docile and slow with sleep. Three high-backed chairs fought one another for space, while flowers rotted in their vases and ash lay among the filthy floor rushes.

'Isolde?' There were no skulls watching from dim ledges, no bloodstains marking the walls, no horned monster with haired thighs perched upon a stool in the furthest corner, guarding a gateway to Hell. Kensa would've happily faced the Devil at this point. Anything other than dusty, filthy chaos. 'Isolde!'

There was a scuffle from a downstairs room, a heaving sound and a loud curse. Slowly, the wise woman emerged from a narrow door off the parlour, licking the dryness from her lips.

'Ah, s'you.'

'I have come to begin my apprenticeship,' said Kensa hurriedly, rummaging in the satchel for the bone-handled knife.

'It can't be time yet, can it?' Isolde scratched herself and sniffed her fingers. 'You're barely twelve.'

'Eighteen.'

'That's old enough, is it?'

Kensa opened her mouth, closed it again. 'I shan't wait no

longer.' She glanced to the bone-handled knife and then back to Isolde.

'All right.' A large yawn. 'Get yourself settled and I'll put the water on to heat.' She thumbed above her head. 'Your room's upstairs.'

Rain finally began to fall, smudging trails down the dirtied windows and pushing Kensa firmly indoors. Was this it? Her shoulders sat tight in their sockets. This couldn't be it. A wild impulse told her to leave, retreat backwards. Where to? She didn't know. Wherever she fled to, shame would follow. No wise woman had ever turned down the role. And if she did, who would take her place? *Elowen*. Who else?

Kensa took a bold step inside.

With her feet reluctantly over the threshold, her fate was set. Today, she was an apprentice. Tomorrow, she reasoned, she would be a cleaner. And not long after that, she would become a wise woman.

One who had work to do.

Chapter Six

Lessons

Her own room. It was small and narrow, furnished with a simple chest of drawers, a nightstand and a bed. She would not share it. She did not need to share it. Here, Kensa would not wake with her sister's elbow in her back or blonde hair in her mouth. It was dusty, although everything was dusty. The crocheted blanket coughed its ire when she slumped on it and a dozen moths scattered when she opened the window. A laugh burst out as the air swept in, right off the sea, from the cliff and the treetops, straight to her lungs.

Kensa's room was the only one upstairs and was held fast by the sloping ceiling. Isolde's room was downstairs. She was not allowed in there. This was a bigger property than the one Kensa had grown up in and looked as though various additions had been crafted onto it over the years. Nothing fit properly, yet it seemed to work. The interior walls were lime-washed, although yellowed with dust and blackened with cooking smoke and fine wax candles, while the exterior structure seemed to be held together with moss, threats and spite, which, having met Isolde, seemed likely.

From below stairs came a question: 'Knife?'

Kensa found the wise woman in the kitchen, palm outstretched. 'Isn't it mine to keep?'

'Not yet.' Isolde took the bone-handled knife back, where it disappeared into the tattered shawl about her shoulders. With that, she busied herself above the fire, mashing dried herbs into grainy submission and tipping in hot water.

Kensa cleared her throat. 'When do we start?'

Isolde sucked on her teeth.

'Learning to do what you do,' said Kensa. 'When do my lessons begin?'

Two steaming mugs were set upon the precariously full kitchen table, whose stained and grained wooden top was hardly visible. Tea was not rare to their ilk, a contraband exchanged for silence. Even the upright Mr Skewes brought a regular supply home. He claimed it was taken from smugglers he intercepted along the coast, yet common talk was he took bribes. This tea at the wise woman's cottage, however, tasted different: earthy and sweet.

Isolde raised her chin. 'How do you treat a boil?'

Kensa took a seat and clasped her tea to her chest. She knew this; well, she had seen Isolde do this in the village. 'You make a poultice with flax – I mean the linseed from flax – and apply it while it's still hot.'

'Tell me a use for blackthorn?'

'It'll loosen your bowels.'

Isolde nodded. 'What else?'

Kensa shook her head.

'Gin.'

'That isn't a healing tonic,' said Kensa.

'It will be when you're my age,' chuckled Isolde, eyes glittering, teeth on show. 'Should a new mother not produce enough milk for her babe, what needs to happen?'

Questions were snapped at with an answer, words bouncing back and forth until Kensa demanded to know, 'Are you testing me?'

'No, I am showing that you've already begun your training; years ago, in fact. You know more than I did at your age.'

By the time the questions had finished, Kensa's tea had grown cold. She had not taken a single mouthful. 'Anyone can bind an unsteady bone.' Her thoughts strayed to the day in the orchard, on the wind and the air bending to a coven's will. 'When can I learn the Old Ways?'

Isolde's steel eyebrows angled higher, almost folding in on themselves.

'The Bucka told me I would learn them,' she added hastily, as though his name would give legitimacy to her request.

It was uncomfortable – his name, spoken here.

As though the cottage recognised it. Bristled back against his presence.

Kensa reached for her tea and chugged it, in an effort to stop herself talking further. Her teeth clicked on the clay edge, her eyes open and wide as she avoided Isolde's unrelenting stare.

Silence, the kitchen did not have room for all the silence that filled its corners.

'I shall hear no more talk of the Bucka,' said Isolde, after a time. 'Nothing good can come from what he tells you. As for the rest, you will know the Old Ways when you are ready for them.'

Kensa slammed down her mug. 'How much longer do I have to wait?'

'Until I say—'

'Why did the bone-handled knife return to me if not for this?'

Another silence followed, though it was not the same silence as before. This one had a presence to it, a tang in the air, a gravity that began to pulsate. Kensa could no longer hear the inhales she took. Even her own thoughts were dimmed. And her tangled hair, newly dried, began to pull at her scalp, as though heavy with water once more.

'You wish to learn the Old Ways, child?'

'Yes, I do.'

Isolde craned a finger past Kensa's shoulder, to a small yew bookcase pressed into the gap beneath the staircase. Every shadow in the room lingered there, as though boiled down and poured sweetly into that alcove.

'That is where the Bad Books live.'

As with all embodiments of ill intent, the tomes had lurked beneath Kensa's vision, sitting as leathery toads on the polished wood, biding their time. Now she noticed their presence, she could not look away. Isolde's next words had the young woman start from her seat.

'Go and pick one up.'

'Fine.'

Her chair legs scraped a warning. Kensa did not heed it. Her steps were muffled by the unswept dirt upon the flagstones, yet they took her to the Bad Books nonetheless. She reached for one. It was heavy in her grasp, its grim contents carrying a weight not measured in ink and paper and leather and twine.

Kensa's instincts told her to put it back, though she would not give Isolde the satisfaction. She was ready to learn, she had been waiting for this. And yet her collarbones grew heavy beneath her flesh, trying to divorce themselves from her body. Her tongue kept sticking to her teeth, no longer its known form, the words sitting on it not her own. Even her face seemed to stretch, yet when she put a hand to it, she found it unchanged. The sensation lingered, a lengthening pull, as though her mouth was trying to fit itself to another skull behind her own, wide as the Morgawr's.

It was then the Bad Book spoke. *You do not belong here.* Its voice needled through her ear. *You will not belong here.* Ancient, long lost and cruel. *Smuggler's daughter, neck to fit a noose.*

Kensa stretched out her arm, intending to place the Bad Book onto its shelf. It would not go. She could not move her hand and her fingers would not loosen.

Do you miss him?

   Do you miss your father?

      Do you think he misses you?

         Do you think anyone would miss you?

            Do you even think at all?

'There were those who knew the Old Ways and succumbed to them,' explained Isolde, distant, quiet, with the same morose tilt to her eyes as when she had spoken on the Owlman. 'Those foolish creatures wrote their madness onto paper to try to rid it from their minds and it did not work, the Old Ways – and a terrible gift of Sight – had already taken hold.'

Kensa's whole body refused to shift its stance and her teeth ached with the effort of it. She could not speak, move her eyes, cry for help. And the Bad Book kept speaking, telling her terrible truths, the coldest thoughts she entertained in the coldest hours.

First to be born.
First to fail.

Worse, there was forbidden knowledge here. About how to corrupt a man's good nature, stop the blood in his heart or the air in his lungs, and how to place his soul in a box for your keeping. In due course, Isolde took pity on her and plucked the Bad Book from her grasp, setting it back among its fellows. 'I do not do this to frighten you, I do this to teach you.'

Tongue unstuck, Kensa blurted, 'What if I am never ready?'

'If you fear that, you never will be.'

And so ended Kensa's first real lesson.

As the day turned on its heel, she was kept busy. She was shown where the herbs were kept and what she could touch in the pantry. There was a brief introduction to the chickens, who quickly lost interest in the apprentice when she refused to feed them, despite persistent – *persistent* – pecking. Later that night, filled with boiled rabbit, woody carrots and dense pastry, Kensa settled in her new bed in her new room in the wise woman's cottage. She lay there on unfamiliar sheets. She listened for another breath beside her own – for Elowen's – which had been present almost her whole life. Instead, there was only Isolde's distant snores, reverberating up the staircase.

Outside, the moon was bright and distant and alone, reflected across the sea.

'Hand me the shears, would you?' Isolde peered over her shoulder, palm extended. 'Always cut a nettle, never pull it or you'll ruin the threads.' New shoots had begun to peer through the soil, bright and green and eager to sting.

Kensa sucked at a reddened thumb. 'You'll be weeding this garden for ever.'

From behind the weeds came several low clucks. The chickens were conspiring again. Kensa shook her skirts to re-cover her bruised ankles.

'It's not a garden, it's a nettle farm,' Isolde snorted.

'O'course, I should've known.'

'Put your wit on the boil with the kettle, will you?'

And with no ceremony, fuss or rite, the women's partnership truly began.

'Are you listening? Go with the leaves, not against, and you won't be stung.'

'I am!'

'If you were, you wouldn't have that sulking face.'

A retort was quick to come. Kensa uncharacteristically swallowed it back down. Each one of their disputes usually ended with laughter, until she forgot the welts upon her fingers or had, perhaps, learned – without realising – how to pull a nettle from its stem. Later, she would find her other lessons from the healer came in such a manner.

'Out, you bloody vixen, out!' Isolde barked, throwing the shears at the back door's frame, where they rang with a heavy *thwung*.

On the kitchen table was a young fox, her snout deep in sweetmeats and her whiskers suspiciously powdered. She leapt off the surface with a graceful pounce and avoided Isolde's temper, enforced with a boot's end.

'This better be the last time I find you in here or so help me, I'll—'

Off went the fox, springing with smugness across the wet grass, sending one hungry glare towards the bushes where the chickens gathered. For once, the weeds were silent. Even a chicken knows to be quiet when a hunter is near.

Kensa's movements were uneasy in her new surroundings. Nothing sat in its logical place. In fact, there was nothing logical about the cottage and its interior. Isolde routinely bid her to fulfil endless menial tasks until she was rushed off her feet. Yet, as the days fell behind her, she learned where the mortar and pestle was, which spices refused to sit beside one another on their shelves and which candles were left for *Best*, should he ever arrive.

Whenever she had the opportunity, Kensa tidied. Isolde bustled about unaware of any changes, and half-unaware of her new housemate. Until she spoke to ask a question, whereupon Isolde became mischievous, cryptic and prone to dry wit, as though thrilled to have a companion to show herself off to. In all Kensa's tidying, there was one chair – the third chair in the parlour – that Isolde warned her must always be kept full. It did not matter what filled it, be it papers or linen or half-finished blankets with their wool unspooling, the third chair could never be empty. She gave this instruction with such gravity that Kensa obeyed. Whoever that chair was for, it was certainly not for either woman and no prodding would draw further explanation from Isolde.

Wednesdays were the busiest mornings of the week and it seemed to Kensa as though the whole village came knocking. First was Mrs Hughes with a question about her ailing husband, second was Pearce, the forge master, who had problems with his feet. Kensa hovered in the background, doing as she was bid – fetch this, bring that – and studied how Isolde worked. Boils were lanced, poultices applied, teeth pulled and conversations had. One or two house visits were arranged by individuals whose relatives were too frail to make the journey to Bohortha, meaning the coming few days would be busy ones. There was talk about a fever in the surrounding villages too, caught by visiting relatives in Truro. Kensa's mind went straight to Elowen, a sense of foreboding reaching into a cavity near her gut. She dismissed it as hunger.

Dinner was a simple affair, as it often was on busy days. Tonight's supper – fish stew – was heated on the stove. Beyond the pot-warmed kitchen, the springtime evening settled in early and the night was sharp company: a cold yellow fading to a colder blue.

In her room, Kensa listened to the house settling now the

day's heat had dwindled, as though releasing one big sigh. She liked her room, had placed her shells about it, while her hagstone was set upon the bedside table. She had got used to her own sole breathing in the night, had got used to solitude in sleep. Kensa's nightdress was cool against her legs, as were the covers she slid into. There was a burden of future upon her, a knowledge that she would spend many a night in this bed, would find the lengths her bones could reach and learn how her features were meant to look, once she'd finished growing into them. Still, doubt came, rising from the yew shelves where the Bad Books waited. Kensa did her best not to listen.

And if she propped a lumpy pillow beside her, as though to mimic her sister's form, the house promised not to tell anyone else.

Chapter Seven

Chicken Shit

It was an eggless day. Not a single chicken would lay, for the fox had come to call. Her predatory teeth and claws marked the coop's exterior and soil around it. Although the chickens remained unmolested, their night-time terrors had altered their behaviour. The birds refused to leave Kensa's side; they either hunched at her ankles or brooded softly beneath the kitchen table if ever a door or window was left open enough to allow their entry. By mid-morning there was no surface, no sleeve, no skin without chicken shit to stain it.

'I won't be long,' said Isolde, 'a day or two at most.'

The wise woman had chosen this particular morning, wet and winkle-grey, to reveal her upcoming trip to Bodmin. From across the South West, the cunning folk – pellars – were gathering, Isolde among them. Her carpet bag stood at her feet, bulging with suspect items, which the chickens thoroughly inspected.

'Is anything wrong? Why is the coven—'

'You can handle everything while I'm gone,' said Isolde, cutting off the questions she had no mind to answer, 'can't you?'

Kensa lifted her chin as though to prevent her own mouth from opening. *No*, she wanted to say. Yet she could not admit weakness. Worse, she knew Isolde had guessed as much. The two women eyed one another across the parlour, their unspoken arguments and counter-arguments straining on too-tight leashes.

Eventually, after several long moments, Kensa ground out a reply. 'Have a nice time.'

'If ever you don't know what to do, simply pretend you do. Our work is about feigning confidence.'

'You mean lying?'

'S'pose.' Isolde hooked her bag into her palm, adjusted her cap and smiled a little too broadly for Kensa's liking. 'And if you get stuck, Jack'll give you a hand.'

Kensa wrinkled her nose at the thought.

Outside, in spitting rain, a stouter figure waited: Hawise, the wise woman from the Lizard. She beamed towards Kensa when she spied her in the doorway. 'Hasn't she grown? Oh, you must be excited to be—'

'Leaving,' interrupted Isolde, hooking her arm into her travelling companion's elbow and dragging her down the lane from Bohortha.

'We should take her with us! Be sure the others will want to see how well—'

'She'll go when I say she'll go.'

Their shapes – one reedy and wooden, the other plump and warm – were taken by the hedgerows and quickly snatched from sight.

Kensa was alone.

Cluck.

Well, almost.

It was not long before a thunderous fist bashed the door. Behind the noise was Farmer Hayle. His cabbages had been ravaged, his turnips had turned-down and his swede had sunk in on themselves. 'A curse as sure as I've ever seen one,' he said, with an expression as gnarled and tubered as the roots he cultivated. 'I need a wise woman to put it right.'

He demanded that Isolde fix it, specifically she and no one else.

'I can do it,' blurted Kensa. 'I will come by at noon tomorrow.'

It did not matter that she did not know how to tackle a curse. She could learn, she thought. Besides, she had deliveries to make in the village, which she could do on the way.

There were three items in her basket. She took them to Portscatho the following day, which was cloudy and wet, though warmer than the last. She made the first delivery to Young Robert: ointment for his sore stump, where it rubbed on the socket to his wooden leg. The second was jam for the joiner's wife: this late in her pregnancy, preserves were the only food she would eat. The last one was a familiar tonic and she knew its recipient without checking the label: Elowen's medicine. Its liquid was clear, as always. Strange, as no other healing potion appeared as such. What's more, this was the only tonic Isolde had not taught Kensa how to make. For the others, she was forced to read instructions and boil down rosehip and mush powders into fats. This concoction was kept from her – and yet Elowen was bid to drink it often enough. Kensa thumbed at the stopper, a waxed leather seal which came free easily. There was hardly a scent, though what there was seemed familiar. She tipped the vial to her lips and instantly spat the contents from her mouth – seawater? This would make even a steel-stomached pig unwell, yet Elowen drank it with no qualms. And it did, invariably, return the colour to her cheeks and bring an ease to her movements, which she often lost.

Kensa rapped on her old front door. An odd gesture for a place she once considered home. She couldn't simply walk inside any more, could she? A fine drizzle rolled in, barely falling, yet coating everything with a misty sheen. Small raindrops beaded on the tonic's glass vial, its stopper returned. What if she threw it away? Or lied about dropping it? It didn't make sense—

'Aye, you're soaked through,' said Derwa, appearing in the doorway and pulling Kensa into a soft embrace. 'Let's dry you off.' It was nice, how her mother smelled, how she knew her mother's smell. And how much smaller she seemed than Kensa remembered, as though the distance between them – only three weeks – had given her a different insight.

'I can't stay.' Kensa leaned around her mother's shoulder, wanting to see the cottage interior. It was the same as it had always been, with her mother's embroidery spread across the kitchen table. She could see the back of Mr Skewes's head on his usual chair by the hearth and frowned. 'I only came to drop off Elowen's tonic. Where is she?'

'Why, she's with you, isn't she?' Derwa quickly unloaded Kensa's basket and placed the medicine – if it could be called that – in its usual place. 'I didn't expect her to go visiting you quite as often as she has. I hope she's not been getting in the way? I told her it was serious work and she wasn't to distract you.'

Kensa's mouth grew slack. 'She hasn't . . . '

'Would you tell her we're eating late tonight? Her father's got a meeting with the magistrate and she'll need somethin' to tide herself over with.'

'Yes,' said Kensa, nothing else.

Because wherever Elowen was and had been, it was certainly not with her. Were it not for Mr Skewes sitting on the chair, within earshot, she might have told her mother. As much as Elowen was his daughter, she was Kensa's sister first. And more than that, a small concern grew in her gut, not that she'd name it as anything other than yesterday's undigested beef.

She gave her mother one last squeeze and carried on, towards Farmer Hayle's property. This was not the first time Elowen had lied about her whereabouts. Occasionally, she had told their mother she'd be teaching with Miss Latham on a morning, then had been elsewhere. Kensa had not questioned it, assumed Elowen had wanted to shirk her duties now and then, the same as everyone else. She'd even been relieved to find her sibling wasn't quite as perfect as everyone assumed. Only, this seemed different.

Her mind rustled up no answers as she strode up the track to the largest farmstead for miles. There she found Farmer Hayle, whose tone was as sour as his soil. 'You'll find the trouble round back.' He accompanied her to the furthest hedgerow, where the earth had turned black and salted, the vegetables wilted around it. Even the nearby field boundary had begun to lean away and there was silence where there should not be silence: no birdsong, no insect buzz, no rustle among the nearby brambles.

Kensa cleared her throat. She looked to Farmer Hayle. He looked back expectantly. She cleared her throat again. Kensa did not know the next step. Her teacher had left and now livelihoods – an entire village and at least four parsnips – depended on her.

'Ain't you going to look at it?'

Kensa nodded. She hesitantly inched forwards. Farmer Hayle stayed back. Root vegetables, already worn through frosts, sponged below her feet. She sidestepped sprouts and ragged leeks, pushing onwards past the winter cabbages to where the land sagged down. There, spiralled within the centre of rot, was a lifeless bird. It had black feathers and a bright orange beak, with talons as bold to match: a simple chough.

'That wasn't there earlier,' said Farmer Hayle defensively.

'Seems to be there now,' said Kensa.

To kill a chough was at best unlucky and at worst, well, it was worse. Silence again, that peculiar silence. Even the nearby sea could scarce be heard, as though the waves held their tumble, straining to see what Kensa decided.

She waited. It was not her place to speak. She waited.

Farmer Hayle drew his chins upwards. 'I mistook it for a crow and knocked it out the sky,' he admitted. He would not look at the dead bird, as though by ignoring it, he could remove it from existence. 'I didn't think much of it until, well—' His confession was bitten off, pride warring with his desire to make amends. Kensa understood that.

'I'll burn herbs and bury it after,' she said, trying to muster as much authority as she could, 'and you best not kill another, else there'll be no saving your farm then.' A pause, then, a barked, 'All right?'

Farmer Hayle agreed without seeming to, turning away to chew on his cheek.

Kensa began to cleanse the farm. At least, she made it seem as though she did. What was she meant to do? How did a person calm soil? And did she have to be calm to do it?

'No one must watch me,' she shouted over her shoulder.

A receding trudge told her Farmer Hayle had left. Her relief came in a long, slow whistle through her teeth. She began to walk. Small circles, then larger ones, counter to the turgid swirl in the earth. After taking a spade from a nearby shed, Kensa dug a little hole beside the hedgerow. In it she laid the chough to rest and spoke a word or two – 'Kosk yn kres' – for its passing. Farmer Hayle observed her from the threshold of his house, despite her instructions not to. Kensa made herself seem busier. Stepped widely and waved her arms and chanted sing-song words. Only when she stopped her work did she find, to her surprise, new sounds: sparrow song and a shrew's skitter.

'By next growing season there'll be no rot to ruin the crop,' called Kensa. And if there was, Isolde could fix it. Regardless, her pretence had worked, exactly as the wise woman had claimed it would. Of course, she could not take payment.

Farmer Hayle would never have offered. Instead, he gave her a gift.

'Now, don't tell no one where you got this,' he said, handing her a bottle filled with untaxed rum. 'It's from a run your father did, years ago.' It was an open secret that many locals helped the smugglers hide their contraband, prior to its distribution in the neighbouring counties and their cities, as far as Bath. No one shared names, as the least known, the safer it was for those who operated beneath the Coast Guard's watch. At her slack features, he continued, 'Yes, I worked with him and hid what he wanted hiding.' He fingered a long, white scar on his cheek. 'And I learned better than to question a Rowe, I did.'

'You questioned me,' said Kensa quietly, clutching the brown bottle, which seemed to grow heavier and heavier the longer she stared at it.

'That was afore I knew how closely you resembled your father – in nature, I mean, as God knows you have his looks.'

Kensa studied the farmer's ugly scar, which ran from eye to lip. It did not sit well in her mind that anyone could do that, let alone a man she was related to. Even the act, dragging a blade deep enough to leave such a lasting mark, tightened her chest. It couldn't be him, he couldn't have done it. Not the same man who called her *poppet* and made coins appear from behind her ears. Who had promised to take her to sea one day, to journey as far as France and dress her in the finest silks.

'Did you like him – my father – did you like him?'

'I feared him,' said Farmer Hayle, as though that was the same.

*

It was late and sunless by the time she returned to the cottage. There was nothing about Elowen's tonic in the usual tomes Isolde consulted. Kensa took each one from their shelf and scanned the pages, seeking answers and finding none. From the mantel above the fire in the parlour, her father's rum watched her. Its brown contents appeared black in the evening light. Around her were the chickens, clucking incessantly. That damned fox was on the prowl again. It slumped through the spring growth, thinner than before, until even Kensa hesitated venturing into the garden.

She had never seen a beast as hungry as the vixen.

In the larder was a pie Isolde had left for her, which Kensa pulled apart, freeing meat from pastry. Afterwards, she placed the scraps in a small dish and left it on the doorstep that led to the garden. By morning, the dish was empty. She did not see the vixen the next day and neither did the chickens. Although the poultry had peace, Kensa did not. Her eyes strayed, continuously to that Bad Book she had opened on her first day at Bohortha. Its presence was a gaping hole in the yew bookcase and if she looked at it, she feared she would fall in. It had gilded edges and script as brown as old strawberries.

Of course, she could only tell the latter by opening it.

Which she did.

Truly, she had not known she'd opened it. Not until it lay restless across her palms. If it had the answer to Elowen's problem, Kensa would risk its hold upon her. She flicked through the pages, looking, seeking, wanting to know. Immediately, Kensa sensed wrongness. Voiceless laughter, mad and maddening. In her head and outside it.

Kenny.
    Kenny.
        Kenny.

The corners of the room split wide in teeth and terror. Cushions unthreaded and gaped into open mouths and laughed then too. From the garden, the fox laughed a throaty, wild lowing and the chickens in their coop laughed and Kensa began to laugh, hideously. Neck bending back and lips spread to cracking, until—

Those wicked sounds were cut from the world with a slam as she closed the book. As though they had never happened. The cottage was quiet and Kensa, trembling, vowed to keep it that way.

Late into the night and worn with travel, Isolde returned. 'You'll find the Bad Books are much the same as bad people,' she said, noticing the disturbance to her tomes. 'There are those who like to be noticed, who'll bully their way to attention, who'll dominate and readily dismiss. It's them who want to be held without being held accountable.' She flexed her fingers into a cradle. 'Do not hold them for long or they shall take a hold on you.'

Kensa squeezed her thumbs in her fists, needing the pressure to calm her shaking. 'Who wrote them?' And *why* create them at all? It was evil, it was insanity.

'I was an apprentice once,' said Isolde, 'to a man I loved.' She did not imbue this confession with any grand intonation or emotion, yet there was importance here. One neither woman could fully confront. 'He was cursed with the Sight more strongly than I've ever known, far worse than— Ah, well, it drove him to madness. It was a cruel madness, driven by righteousness to address wrongs prior to their becoming. To keep the impulses at bay, he poured them onto these pages.' Her aged fingers caressed a spine and it shivered at her familiar touch. 'And when a civil war came, it reached us here, most uncivilly.' In her eyes were flames and kings and sparking flint. 'He had a cell for the Bad Books, a place where his worst qualities were kept, until they were set aflame – released back to him – and he was not the man I knew any more.' Isolde bundled up the last Bad Books, scooping them from the un-swept floor and carrying them as children. 'These were the ones I rescued from the burning, though it was not enough to rescue him.'

'You miss him,' said Kensa.

'Yes,' said the wise woman, 'though I do not miss what he became.' A queer smile reached her and she put her free hand onto Kensa's head. 'He warned me about you.'

'What did he say?'

'Only monstrous things,' she rasped, though no humour was in her voice. 'Only what becomes of us all.'

Kensa carried the strange words to her bed. What sleep she took was fitful and sweaty. And when she dreamed, it was on her sister and on her father and on a cruciform shape against her window, blotting out the glass with outstretched wings and jewel-blue eyes.

Chapter Eight

The Weaver

A knock on the door in the slim hours, when morning has yet to find a foothold, is always – without exception – awful. The Weaver, a sheep farmer who kept to and was kept by the hills, stood in the doorway with his head bare, hat worried between his palms and an expression that was both hopelessness and hopefulness in turns. Isolde already had her work-dress on, pulled over her nightshift, while her feet had been jammed into her walking shoes. Her steel hair was nested with sleep, though her instructions were sharp and capable.

The Weaver's prized ewe had taken ill and he was distraught. Although she had never met the man, Kensa knew the sheep farmer was an odd sort. He did not speak to the other villagers and spent months alone, tending to his livestock. What's more, he wore a wool shirt and threadbare waistcoat, no matter the season, even on the hottest days. He was accepted, mostly, and his need for solitude respected.

Supplies were gathered and Kensa was bid to find wormwood, elm bark, honey and wild garlic. Glass vials, scuffed and scratched, jostled together in her father's old satchel.

'It's only a sheep,' said Kensa groggily, pressing her heels into her shoes.

Isolde's tone was harsh when she replied, 'If it's brought the Weaver to my door at this hour, then it is not *only* a sheep to him.'

That was the end to Kensa's dissent, as she followed the sheep farmer, his lantern aloft, along the drovers' tracks and up the steep hills, to where his small croft lay. It was a neat, well-managed property. Even in wet weather, the flagstones around his stone hut, outbuildings and sheepcote had been swept clean, while the surrounding willow fences were sturdy and expertly latticed. Beyond them, the clear night held more stars than any of them had numbers for.

'I can't face losing her,' said the Weaver.

He led the wise woman and her apprentice into the sheepcote. Its flint-cob walls were topped with a thatch roof, keeping dry the mud-packed earth and straw beneath. Inside, were several fleecy occupants, caught between weariness and wariness at the strangers in their bed.

To Kensa's eye, these animals were housed better than the poorest folk in the village. In one corner, separated from the other sheep, was a sickly ewe. She was no young creature, legs and muzzle marked with age, eyes layered with a thousand grass-fed views. Her breathing was laboured and she did not acknowledge the new bodies in her pen.

Isolde was thorough in her assessment, surveying the sheep, and then the Weaver.

'You need to sleep,' she said to him firmly. 'You're no use to no one if you are too weak to stand.'

'Is there nought to be done for her?'

Isolde shook her head and the Weaver released a sound from his throat, tight and vulnerable. 'What if she passes while I'm sleeping? Going to fetch you was risk enough.'

Isolde chewed on her lips awhile, then turned to her apprentice. 'Kensa will stay, she will wake you.'

Kensa's mouth turned southwards. A refusal crouched behind her teeth, until she caught the Weaver's expression. The pain on his features and the expectation. It was one she had known in earlier days with her sister; an obligation to care, which she could not refuse.

'I will stay,' she said, 'I will wake you.'

If the day came, it did not come for Kensa, whose hours narrowed to a shadowed corner in the sheepcote. The shelter's other occupants were put out into the surrounding fields, their bleats pressing stubborn life into the funereal silence. She sat beside the ewe, heard its troubled breaths. Prayed it would pull through. It slept a while, refused food and water, slept further, and Kensa feared the worst, only for it to stir once or twice. Her fingers stroked, brushed away flies, cleaned what needed cleaning. There is a subtle communication that builds between human and animal when the pair occupy a space for a time. Where sense is shared and talkless knowledge exchanged. It was in this silence that is not quite silence, that Death held back the sheep's breath and began to store it for himself.

'It's time,' said Kensa, upon fetching and finding the Weaver, asleep in a chair at the hearth. His rest had not restored him. He seemed frail and thin, as though he would gladly follow the ewe's descent into those final moments.

'Nineteen years she's been with me,' he said. 'Had her when it was me and my man up here, he hand-reared this girl himself.'

Kensa did not know what to say, although she knew she should.

'That's a good age,' she offered at last.

There had been talk, rumours about the Weaver and his man, Pat. A row with Mr Aldridge, the curate, after he would not marry the pair. Neither was seen at St Gerrans Church again and Pat sadly passed not long after. Kensa had never paid the talk much mind, for she knew what people said about her own mother and her unmarried proclivities with Mr Skewes.

'He loved these sheep, he did, and I've loved them for him.'

The Weaver cried and hummed and sang his grief to the ewe. A warbled offering, yet soothing nonetheless. In his arms, he held a lost love, not a sheep. He did not see the difference now. With a rasping voice, he stumbled through a melody about reunion:

'A guv kolon, deus tre.'

Oh, sweet one, come homeward.

Who was the first person to tend another's ills with song?

That seemed, to Kensa, like witchcraft then, like the Old Ways not yet forgotten. Her own fears gnawed at her, as she pictured him singing to a young woman with blonde hair and Elowen's face. How close Death seemed now, as though its proximity to the sheep could snatch other frail lives purely for the convenience of having them near by.

She left man and sheep to their goodbyes, putting her mind towards food. Her joints were stiff from sitting and she smelled of straw and sickliness. Bread, cooked mutton and fat passed for a simple meal, which she pushed down her gullet. The Weaver could not speak enough to accept a plate and so Kensa left it covered beside the hearth.

'I . . . ' she said, did not say.

When at last she arrived back to Bohortha, the sun had set and its back was turned to her. Upon stepping over the threshold, her legs went. Exhaustion, little food and second-hand loss piled within her, until she collapsed with the weight of it. Isolde was there to catch her. Hands in her armpits, broth fetched from the stove, clothes stripped and blankets heaped upon her. She was guided to the chaise longue and a fire roared: *Welcome! It's safe! Rest! It's safe!*

In her addled state, Kensa could have sworn she heard the flames speak. Perhaps, when one listens hard enough, everything has a voice or a story or a song worth hearing. She only wished she could stop crying enough to hear it.

Chapter Nine

Travelling Moon

Kensa slept the whole day. Now night had come again. Her body said, *Move.* She obeyed. Her limbs were stiff from the long wait in the sheepcote and the long sleep after. There was dung in her nostrils and the seat of the chaise longue was hard beneath her. Isolde's movements in the kitchen summoned her to rise. On the table were low candles below the moon's height, which rounded its fullness through the window and across the two women.

There was a brittle quality to Kensa's walk. She was heavy, all at once, with loss. Her skin smelled of sheep, of urine, of the Weaver's grief. And her own, too. Because she had not done it. Cured the ewe. In those hours, she had convinced herself that if she willed hard enough, the animal would live.

It had not. She was not a real healer. But she had known that since the beginning, hadn't she? Did everyone suspect it – even Jack? Why, even the Bad Books knew it. If she had been a wise woman, she would have known what to do: she could have spared the ewe.

'I need to speak to you.' Kensa's voice was dry with sleep and strangled enough to pause Isolde's preparations, her head tilted as a hound's. 'I shouldn't be here, I don't belong here, I lied—'

'You weren't there to save it, Kensa.'

In the night-time quiet, the sea was loud in her ears. As though it wished to drown her out, to hold her full confession back. 'I don't—'

'We cannot stall death,' said Isolde. 'We can only be present for it and for those whose lives are touched by it.' She put her thumbs to her tongue and, one by one, put out the candles in the kitchen. 'You did all I wished.'

Kensa sniffed. 'Then I am still to be a wise woman, as you are?'

'You will be better than I.' There was a feverish quality to Isolde's movements as she kicked off her shoes, barefoot and wild. 'Tonight we mark spring.' Her gnarled hands reached into the blanket box and withdrew several shawls and throws, which were heaped into Kensa's arms. 'This is April's full moon and it is our duty to greet it.'

Time had moved quickly, with a month having passed since she began her training. Kensa's body confirmed it, with a deftness to her hands and a quickness to her mind. She cuffed her damp nose with a sleeve and wiped her eyes with her palms, pushing hard into the sockets until lights sparked beneath her lids. This was not failure, then; Bohortha would remain her home and she would not need to leave it.

'Stop your crying, girl.' Isolde pushed a crudely carved wooden cup into her grasp. 'There is a witch's work to do tonight.'

At first, Kensa assumed the draught she took would calm her. It did far more than that. Spice, brandy and a looser substance hit her tongue, unwound her thoughts and retied them differently. Her fingertips tingled happily. Oh, this was mischief, this was power, this was magic – this was drink. Isolde began to talk. Oddities, secrets, revelations that made little sense to Kensa or concerned strangers she had never met. She laughed all the same. Outside, a wind stirred the clouds to cover and reveal, cover and reveal, the shining lunar disc in a playful pattern.

'Come,' said the sky to Kensa and through Isolde's lips it spoke.

It's spring, it's spring, it's spring—

Giddy, drunk and high with the starlings, the pair took the trail to Towan Beach. It was a hard path, prone to slippage, oft tread by smugglers who wished to hide their loot, as well as witches when the mood took them to be called thus. Up came the sea to meet them at the shoreline. For a beat, the tide lingered at their toes, then remembered its rhythm once more. Mr Aldridge had once warned the village about powers such as this. Bellowed tales about a dancing maiden who summoned Evil and his entities, drank blood and sipped a man's marrow through his nethers should he succumb to her wiles. This was not that. Here were two women and the skies and Cornwall come a-gathering, in a ritual as old as breath and a womb's first shedding.

It was night and the stars were naked and the moon was naked and the two witches, young and old, followed suit.

Isolde shook her limbs from her clothing. Her hair was silver and her body bare, but for the dirt on the soles of her feet. She was glory as a woman is glory, as age written upon a woman's body is glory. Her skin wore its years in warm shapes, a downwards pull with marks and mottled patches. There was a weight to her breasts, a rounding at her stomach and a large scar, old and puckered, that marked her right calf.

Kensa freed herself from her own garments, hearing the waves and the wind and Isolde's rattling laugh. She had never been naked outside. Bare. Seen fully by another. She was timid and not timid, to be looked at and to look in turn.

Isolde was not thatched as Kensa was and grinned at the younger woman's questioning observation. 'It lessens with age, the thick of it.'

'Do you ever miss it?'

'Being haired and impatient and wanting?' Isolde let out a grand sigh. 'Yes, I do.'

Change. It had taken Isolde's body and one day it would take Kensa's own. She chipped her hand to her own hair, legs, pits, sex.

'Is it wrong to fear it?'

'Only the dead refuse to age,' said the old woman, who wore scars as a diary held its pages. 'A body is a life lived, so live in it.'

Kensa nodded, shared her own small scuffs, a knee with a nick in it, a healed line at her hairline. Flaws earned through needing to be first, through a desire to do what others had not. Of course, now she understood there were no firsts. All the children before her, now grown, had thought themselves first too, as had the children before them and the children before them. Here was a circle as round as the moon: birth, life, death.

Out came the cup once more, the drink within bitter and sweet and blowing Kensa's pupils wide until she could pull the firmament inside them. The older woman fixed their hands together and spun them both, until they stumbled on sand and pebble and shell. Under the Budding Moon they danced, their shapes blurred and the lines between definitions, between age and shape and gender, were chased away. It was a sisterhood of sorts. One which brought to mind Elowen's face, Elowen's hands, Elowen's laughter. Kensa hated it, banished it, drank until she barely felt the sea's patient chill.

Isolde was already in the water.

Waves ran their cold hands up Kensa's arms, across the plane between her breasts and the meeting at her thighs. A sense, kin to lust, bid her to draw away from the shore's reach, curious and yet fearful. Isolde was beside her, years shed as coats. In her place, a younger woman, no less wise, waded further into the sea. Arms spread, head tilted back, mouth wide as she screamed fury at the ocean. Kensa could not look away. The next wave ran to rolling against their bodies and revealed Isolde's former self, with rich brown hair and skin as warm as rose.

Here was a woman of seduction and intrigue, who could conjure terror and did so now, stalling Kensa in her tracks. Here was a witch whose former dealings had been under horse-pelt and princely towers, in a time of black mirrors and sorcery and political alchemy. Oh, she had been terrible, hard and cruel. Memories shone against the sea's churning surface and Kensa saw them as though she herself had lived them. The clearest poison tipped from a lace cuff. A crow-haired lady with blood on her hands. Fire purging wisdom from a wild man with rosemary eyes. Monstrous actions, betrayal and madness, until the moment faded and Isolde was herself again. Old and gently worn, as a shoe thinned with stepping.

'I should not have liked to know you in your youth.' Kensa stumbled, her ankle catching on unseen rocks. Exhausted, tired with knowing, she let the sea pull her in. Its cool embrace was familiar and comforting tonight – almost a friend, filled with reassurances and counter to the sea she'd known all her life.

'I let no one know me,' said Isolde, solemn and prideful and unrepentant.

Here was another lesson: bad women need not seek forgiveness.

Neither recalled wading too far out until their feet no longer knew the sea's bed. Their bodies floated, hands linked with one another, hair lashed with seaweed. And neither recalled swimming into the sky, although their fingers caught on starlight and the ocean, somehow, had a mouth to meet theirs. Kensa's head spun hard enough to break from its moorings, heaving it into limitless space. She remembered drinking more. A sweet syrup brewed with roguery and stormy weather. She looked up to where the blackberry bushes pulsed with unspent foliage, their fruit yet to thicken at the stem.

When at last Kensa returned to shore, she found a fire lit

and Isolde beside it. Flames gummed and gurgled at the stones hemmed around it, warming the water from their bodies. Sand flies nipped at the backs of Kensa's knees and grounded her. She crouched opposite her mentor, the heat placed between them, blankets on their shoulders. Isolde revealed a small basket of savoury pies, which they bit down to crusts.

'Why choose me?' There was no need to summon sentences around the question. Both knew it referred to that first wind-whipped meeting here on the Towan, years earlier. 'There are many other girls in the village who could do the task as well as I.' Flames sparked in sea colours, dyed by the salt in the driftwood Isolde had collected.

'The ones who are obedient and kind and reasonable, those girls?' A laugh, that same rattling laugh. 'How about your sister, Elowen, should I have asked her?'

Kensa's head turned fast enough to pull at a tendon, shooting pain down her back. Her blanket slumped around her and she wore only the firelight, skin cast in molten shades.

'Calm yourself, I meant it in jest.' Isolde's meanness crumbled as old wood beneath a fingernail.

'There were nights I dreamed you'd come to tell me you'd found another to help you,' confessed Kensa, 'and I was not to be a wise woman after all.'

'Ah.'

Crackles, the fire's shift, an eon until Isolde continued.

'There was only one person I would've chosen to be here with me,' said the wise woman eventually. 'When I saw you beside the Morgawr that morning, with no fear or its accompanying follies, I saw the woman you could become.'

'Even though I lost the knife?'

'It was never lost.' A hard *slap* reverberated on the beach as Isolde clapped her bare thigh. 'I found it on the sand after you'd fainted, picked it up and hid it from you. As soon as I considered you old enough, I watched your movements and placed the blade where you would see it sooner or later.' Here came a wide, yellow-toothed grin. 'And I was right, wasn't I? You did find it.'

Kensa surged to her feet, head spinning. 'You—'

'Here's another lesson about becoming a wise woman,' said Isolde, straightening her spine. 'Appearance is what matters, that others believe in you is what matters. You must take each chance to lean into mysticism, to find the connections – the joins in the world – and stitch them together. Most will call it chance, others will name it fate, while the foolish shall dub it devilry.'

'It was a lie?'

If the blade had never come to her of its own will, was she even—

'Remember, there will be many who try to fool you, cloud your vision and write their words across your tongue,' said Isolde, merriment gone, her tone biting once again. 'Do not let them.' As much as the old woman spoke on falsehoods and trickery, her next movements were not that. With a flourish, she reached into nothing – into the blanket at her shoulder – and took out the bone-handled knife as though pulling it free from the folds of eternity.

The Old Ways. *Magic.* Raw power, unyielding and ever-present. The ocean bubbled up the beach, past the tidelines, as though it sought to pull the blade from Isolde's grasp and drink from the well of her power. Kensa could not look away from it, her mind unspooling and rewinding in new patterns and understanding. She eyed the blade with mistrust, exactly as she did her teacher. Both were sharp, their origins unknown.

Kensa's limbs were heavy with self-doubt. The bone-handled knife was no truth-seeking talisman; it had not chosen her, despite her lie. Kensa had been tricked, the same way she had tricked Isolde. It was fitting, somehow, and damning, too.

'Will you fool me again?'

'Yes,' said Isolde.

'And what if I fool you?'

Dawn was edging the sky and the birds were waking in chorus.

'Then we'll be here again on this shore, two mad fools dancing naked in the moon-glow, as I always hoped we'd be.'

Chapter Ten

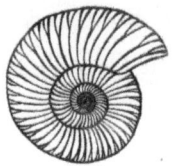

Finger in the Jam

Upon first waking, Kensa feared she was back in the Weaver's sheepcote, nested on straw and waiting for stillness. Instead, she was on the tatty chaise longue in the parlour, clad in blankets and nothing else. Last night's activities made her sluggish and slow, as she scrubbed a hand across her face. Her hair was crunchy and wavy from salt, stuck to her forehead and cheeks.

She had a headache.

There was movement in the kitchen. Low noises – too loud for her fragile temper – which lacked Isolde's usual pitch. After haphazardly arranging blankets over herself, Kensa approached the sound. Pots clanged, cupboards were hefted open and slammed shut, followed by a huff, one heavy enough to demand answer.

'Jack?'

Her pulse quickened. It had been years since Kensa had spoken to the mine overseer's son. He had grown. Although he had been thick-set as a boy, he had only become thicker. His hair was longer, too, and dark as ripe damson fruit. Come the warmer months he would have it cut short, clipped to his scalp. Kensa would have known the seasons by its length.

'Why are you here?'

'It's tidy,' said Jack, incredulous. 'I can't find anything.'

She pointed to the pantry. Previously it had been filled with books, a necklace of mouse skulls and several antlers. Now it stored food. Jack snorted, displeased, and helped himself to smoked herring and hard tack with an ease that came with familiarity.

Kensa raised her eyebrows. 'I asked you a question and I expect an answer.'

Appetite sated, Jack finally took in her blanket-only attire and turned himself, bodily, to the open door. 'Why – ah – where's my aunt?'

'You're *related* to Isolde?'

'Through a fair distance,' said Jack, clearing his throat. 'We don't tell no one.'

'Ashamed?' Kensa leaned into his vicinity to pull a mug off its perch. Her blanket slipped off her shoulders, and, when Jack grumbled his exhale, its warmth found her skin. Strange, how it unsettled her when she'd had every intention of unsettling him. Kensa readjusted her blankets and stepped back, knocking her hip on the kitchen table. She barely knew what to say. Their last conversation was branded onto her mind. It made her hot and angry to think about – and all she did was think about it.

'People talk when there's talk worth having,' said Jack, 'and I don't like to be talked about.' He rammed the remaining hard tack into his mouth, chewing loudly as though to put a stopper on any further conversation.

'You little bugger—'

In the time Jack had taken to eat his foraged meal, a fight had broken out. From the kitchen, the pair heard Isolde swearing at the chickens in the garden who, in turn, clucked their curses back. Jack sighed, though Kensa spied affection in it. How he tilted his mouth at one side, the gesture almost lazy. Unpractised. As though smiling, when he let it, came easy.

Jack's wide steps took him towards the nettles, which were a foot lower than the day prior and relegated to a small corner.

'I've been cutting them back,' said Kensa.

This too displeased Jack. 'Humph.'

Evening was falling and the horizon blurred in the coming rainfall. Another day had gone by with Kensa missing its better half, though the pain she felt at the Weaver's cottage had lessened. Grief, even second-hand, was a weighty burden.

'You know your way around,' she added, in an attempt to make conversation.

At first she thought he had not heard her, until she spoke again and he finally answered.

'I used to stay here as a child, while my father worked the mine,' said Jack. 'I slept in the room upstairs, the one that's yours now.'

Kensa blurted, 'In the same bed?' She pictured his shape in

the mattress where hers had been. It was the same as drinking from the same cup, at the same place, mouths separated by a distance, a moment. By that reasoning, they'd practically, you know – well, she didn't know. Kensa clenched her blankets. 'In the same bed,' repeated Kensa, to herself.

Jack shrugged. 'Ye – yes.'

With one last hiss at the chickens, Isolde emerged, a basket under her arm heaped with nettles and a few soil-covered worms. The healer jostled her way through the garden's overgrown mass and nodded to her nephew, measuring him in the way relatives do, estimating weight lost or gained, complexion cleared or clouded.

'Branok sent you?'

'We're due this season's charms to guard the mine.'

A short discussion followed about cost and what to protect against, as well as Jack's concerns about equipment going missing. He spoke on sea-borne creatures without fear or superstition, only with acceptance and a respectful wariness. Kensa listened to their exchange, telling herself it was her duty to understand the transactions between a miner and his wise woman. She hated how Jack spoke: low and self-assured and so *him*.

'Spring's abating with the season's turn,' said Isolde, 'and I wager you'll meet other forces than the high tide and the creatures it dredges up.'

Jack's hard eyebrows drew together. 'You mean the Bucka?'

'Pah, he wouldn't waste his time with miners,' she grumbled. 'Let's not voice his name in wet weather, lest he come with it.'

Jack would not look at Kensa. Even when she willed him to,

staring two holes into the side of his head. Instead, he treated her as he always had, as a nuisance he had to tolerate. Coin was exchanged, the healer offered advice and the chickens worried Isolde's sock cuffs in placation. It was only when Jack was readying himself to leave that Kensa confronted him. He was neck-deep in the coop, his broad frame comical in such a small space, as he collected eggs.

'You don't like me,' accused Kensa. 'Well, I don't like you either.'

Jack's reply was muffled through straw. 'I don't know you.'

'Exactly, then why not like me?'

Jack took his time to answer, as though he was searching for the shortest way through – and out of – the conversation. 'What do you want?'

Kensa's hands were fists inside her blankets. 'I don't want anything from you.'

'Good.' He stepped back, raking muck from his hair, frowning.

She opened her mouth to scold him and closed it again. When had he grown up? Perhaps, he had done so at the same time she had. Quickly, suddenly, with no warning.

Kensa pulled her blankets even tighter around herself.

'I should be off,' he said.

Jack wrapped the eggs in bunched paper and placed them gently in his coat pockets. For such a large man – for he was a man now – he moved with gentle purpose. There was no doubt, in Kensa's mind, that the shells and yolks would meet their destination uncracked and unscrambled, whole as when he first held them.

'Wait,' said Kensa, stepping into him, careful not to meet his eye.

As quick as she could, she retrieved a small spear of straw caught above his left ear. At least he had not grown any taller, which pleased her for a reason she could not fathom and did not wish to dwell on. Little else had changed, which was good, for she kept them – those changes – in a secret place she'd never admit.

'You should leave your hair long this season,' she said, tongue clumsy in her mouth. 'It looks nice when it's long.'

Jack's stubborn frown grew more pronounced and Kensa was keenly aware of the late-afternoon air against her bare neck, wrists, legs.

Isolde called out from the kitchen with an eavesdropper's knack for timing. 'Do you plan to put clothes on today, Kensa?'

Jack coughed to cover his laugh, dipped his head down and turned his shoulders to the path, tucking through the bushes that bordered the witch's cottage. Kensa listened to his rising absence and waited until his steps had fallen from earshot, imagining she heard them still.

'Round up the chickens and lock the coop, would you?' Isolde sniffed. 'Your legs are younger than mine.'

'Everyone's legs are younger than yours,' snapped Kensa.

Although a yawn leaned her mouth wide and her body was tired from yesterday's excitement, Kensa's thoughts knew no rest. Outside, the sky was overcast and cloudy. Rain began its fall, gentle, soothing. Behind her, the cottage waited. It would always wait and had been waiting for her. For years, perhaps longer. There was a knowledge at the edge of her senses, leftover from whatever she'd drunk last night. It was one she could not name and perhaps it belonged to the Old Ways.

Did those wait for her too?

Or did they wait for another?

'The Bucka promised me,' she told herself.

Beaks pulled at the tassels on Kensa's many blankets, as though to remind her it was bedtime. At the cottage's rear was the small pen where the chickens slept. In that lumped, grassy area was a washing line, dormant cherry trees and raspberry bushes. She could picture Jack's form, his broad back bent inside the small wooden structure. His rough hands, their gentle movements. As soon as Kensa ushered one hen inside, the others followed without much resistance – and then all at once as the trees shivered behind them. A second's movement in the branches. Kensa thought she saw a face set deep within them. Yet there was no one. No man, at least. Instead, a streak of burnt October pressed through the undergrowth and its gaze flashed in the gloom.

'Fox,' said Kensa, letting out a slow breath.

The vixen's pelt was rich with new rain. Her head was bowed and ears pinned back in pleading, as she padded tentatively across the cool grass. Her nose, low and wet, twitched towards the chicken coop. Kensa, never fearing tooth or claw, reached out a hand. There was a pause, a considerable and languid one, before the fox eased back on her hind quarters and inclined her head. Permission. The vixen was silky to the touch, though shivery, her spine ridged as a cockle shell and her cheeks curled in hunger.

Nothing supper would not fix. A rabbit stew thickened on

the stove, seasoned with fern fronds and gorse flowers. Surely no one would miss a few bites? As stealthily as possible when draped in innumerable blankets, Kensa heaped a bowl and took it out into the garden. Its top steamed with warmth and she blew on it several times before she placed it on the ground. The young fox did not hesitate, ravenous as only a wild creature can be.

'There now, is that better?'

Again, a rustle from the trees – hawthorn – at the garden's edge. Kensa squinted into the hedges as the tin bowl clattered on the step and the fox took her fill.

'Jack?'

Inside went the fox, darting past Kensa's feet and into the kitchen. She reached for it. Missed. Its burnished tail tucked low and far from her fingers. No sooner had the creature found its way indoors than it curled up in one corner where an old sack cloth had been left. As though it had lain there many a night. Slipped inside, perhaps, when Isolde's back was turned or her heart had softened to sentiment. Kensa draped one of her spare blankets over its small body.

'One night,' she whispered. 'That's it.'

Later, the women shared a slightly smaller meal than planned and prepared. If Isolde noticed their slimmer portions or the snoring fox, she made no mention. Only after the fire had dimmed, did they separate for the evening. Kensa was tired suddenly. More tired than she had ever been. The new moon's earlier thrill had left and worry had taken its place, though she refused to speak on it.

'You'll learn the movement for a fisherman's charm on the

morrow,' said Isolde at their parting. She seemed distracted, anxious even, as though a mirror to Kensa's own mood. Her hands smelled of onions. She had used their browned bulbs for her divinations. Clearly she had seen nothing good. Strung at the window were their stinking orbs, thick runes carved into each one. Kensa's own skin itched when she looked at their silver casings and she wondered which onion, if any, represented her. The wise woman heaped old parchment, an odd shoe and a dirty cup onto the unused third chair in the parlour. 'Jack should not have spoken his name,' she sighed. 'I'm always put in a foul mood when I think on the damned Bucka.'

Kensa paused, fingers gripping the banister. 'Why?'

'He was a man once,' she said, as though that was enough. 'He's a slave now.'

'I don't understand.'

'A long time ago he tried to force a wise woman to use the Old Ways to grant him immortality – and he did terrible things in his attempts to, ah, persuade her.' Isolde's features seemed worn, tired. 'Eventually, she gave in, yet not in the way he wanted. She chained him to the sea, to live for ever in its swell, and bound the Old Ways into balance, diminishing them, trapping them both, essentially.'

'And she became the Morgawr?'

'Yes, the one you met on the Towan.' Isolde eased towards her bedroom, slippers shuffling across the newly swept floor. 'It is why you cannot ever trust the Bucka. At times I fear he's half-mad, locked in the waves, regretting his eternal life.'

Chapter Eleven

Cider

May Day was thick with pollen and, in the noon-time sun, Portscatho shone gold with it. Spring had turned her face towards the village and with the month's earlier rain – and frenzied hail – the greenery had been sent into abundant growth. Usually the annual fete, which took place upon this day, would have been a cause for celebration in Kensa's mind. Instead, her mood was saturnine. No sooner did she arrive, Isolde clopping beside her, than she saw her sister bedecked with flowers. Of course, Elowen had been crowned the May Queen. Who else? Claps and cheers surrounded her, as she opened the festivities with a ceremonial shower of petals. Everyone, almost everyone, applauded. Kensa fixed her hands to her skirt. Without her realising, Elowen had matured. On her head was a garland of sea thrift, cow parsley and butter-cups woven tightly together with bright ribbon. It was a high honour to be given the title of May Queen. Or so Kensa was told by Old Sal, who was already rosy with libation despite the midday hour.

'See, it's 'cause the May Queen's about cream and loveliness, s'pure and kindly,' slurred the matronly woman. 'You know, I were the May Queen when I were a girl and the boys were struck mute by what a beautiful empress of virginal quality I was. Course, an hour in I wasn't quite a vir—'

Kensa quickly extricated herself. She would have joined her mother, Derwa, who idled in the shade of an ash tree, were it not for Mr Skewes sat beside her.

'Get yourself a little cider, that'll see you right,' said Isolde, dismissive and impatient with Kensa's moods, which, in fairness, were frequent. The wise woman had seemed distracted lately and would not say why. *Onions*, thought Kensa. The bulbs had grown strange in colour, their skin peeling a small fortune of silver on the sill. Despite her inward addled-ness, Isolde had done her best to tame her outward appearance, wearing a brown tunic and cream skirts, which gave her eyes a peaty tilt. Kensa had put on her Sunday best, reserved for sermons she no longer attended. It was a little tighter around the arms and shorter on the legs than she remembered, and it did not quite fit her bust, though it was serviceable. Provided she did not move her limbs too much. As new growth came to the landscape, so it came to Kensa.

'I haven't the coin for drinking,' she said.

'Ah?' Isolde's gaze was fixed on an older chap whose sly wink found her across the field. 'Our kind don't need to pay at events such as these.'

'Then I can have whatever I want?'

'Yes, I— Suit yourself.'

With that last instruction, the wise woman chased her own comforts, which she found in the form of a gnarled sailor with a tufted beard and hands as wide as plates.

As for Kensa, the first ladle of rough scrumpy tipped too easily down her throat. It had been pressed by Farmer Hartie, who owned the cow-cropped field upon which the festival was held. She wasted no time in seeking out further fermented sweetness, until her temper was mollified and her nose happily numbed. Portscatho's villagers took pride in their healer and her apprentice, and Kensa was given whatever she wanted: currant buns, sweetmeats and further cider, which flooded her head with silliness.

Using a gate as a perch, she could see almost every resident in Portscatho was in attendance, bar the Weaver, who had grown more reclusive than ever since his latest loss. Even the landed gentry, the baronet and magistrate Sir George Trevanion, had shown himself. He owned Porthbeor Mine and, as such, owned everyone. His family had funded the May Day festival for generations and it was his purse from which Mr Aldridge, the curate, was paid. The baronet was a mature man in his middling fifties with thin, greying hair and a stern expression. His clothes were finely made and fitted him in a way Kensa had never seen before. She wore hand-me-downs and over-mended attire, too patched to recall its purpose. Nothing as trim and sleek as his waistcoat and jacket, with polished buttons that caught the sun. It was evident from Sir Trevanion's bearing that he was not enjoying the jubilations. A thin mouth, puffed cheeks, eyes scanning the distance as though looking for the gate out. The same one Kensa sat on. She stared at him with unabashed curiosity. Then again, everyone else did the same. It was rare to see a man with such wealth up close and she wondered what he ate, if he felt pain the way she did, if he was built the way that other men were built. At his side was a sleek lady with a placid expression, smooth as a rock pool. She pressed close to Mr Aldridge, who had a blush deep enough to match his Sunday vestments.

At the field's centre was a pole tied with ribbons, which the younger children had been taught to dance around by their teacher, Miss Latham. Within the hour, a small fiddle struck up a country melody. Suddenly, the field was rich with song. Kensa shifted from her seat: she had danced at the fete in her younger days and remembered tripping over her own feet, then someone else's. Besides, she did not wish to see Elowen skipping merrily around the pole, light and graceful and perfect.

Kensa drank more cider.

The festival's hours were long and hot and tiring. She had grown too used to her quiet routine with Isolde, with one or two house visits and Wednesday's controlled and quick-to-pass activity. Give her long coastal walks, a hip bundled with seaweed scraps and her hands deep in nettles. Room for her thoughts to talk to one another, away from noise and people and Old Sal's ever-present chatter. It filled up the whole field, no matter what corner Kensa fled to.

Finally, she spied her mother alone, Mr Skewes having left to converse with the few village men who would speak with him, Sir George among them. Derwa had the May Queen crown atop her head, a gift from Elowen, which made their resemblance all the more striking.

Kensa slumped down, face half-hidden behind her abundant hair.

'I was wondering when I'd find you,' said Derwa. 'I swear you've grown another foot since I've seen you.' Her fingers were sticky with mead and clasped Kensa's hands. 'I ran into Pearce in the road earlier and he was keen to tell me how well you're doing.'

'Oh?' The forge master hardly breathed a word to Kensa when she had rewrapped his chilblained feet. Then again, talk was usually kept to the necessities: where it hurt, bowel movements and a promise, given with reluctance, to rest. It was strange to learn how readily the other villagers accepted her now that she resided with Isolde and had begun her apprenticeship. No longer was she only a smuggler's daughter. Instead, she held a status she had not fully quantified or tested.

'We heard about the Weaver,' said Derwa. 'He's such a poor dear, that man.'

Kensa frowned. 'Who told you that?'

Derwa inclined her head in Elowen's direction. There she was, in animated conversation with the fine lady with the fan. Of course, the prettiest faces at the party would draw close to one another. A remedy against ugliness. Portscatho had plenty of that.

'It's been too long since we've seen you, lamb,' said Derwa.

'I have half a mind to speak to that old crone and tell her she's working you too hard.'

'S'not that,' admitted Kensa, tipsy with drink and hot with fresh ire. 'I didn't want to see Mr Skewes.'

As though prompted, the Coast Guard's laugh rang out across the fields, a high yowl, catlike and reedy.

'Peter has been kind to me.'

'Aye, and we know why.' To her own ears, Kensa sounded like Old Sal, speaking meanness disguised as concern. Or like her father, perhaps, when her parents had argued. She clapped her hand over her mouth. 'Sorry, I didn't mean it.'

Derwa looked to where Mr Skewes stood in a group with Sir George, who still had not managed to extricate himself.

'Do you know who that man is?' It was to the magistrate she pointed. 'He is the one who sent your father to hang.'

It took several long breaths for Kensa to understand. She saw her mother's anger, heard a tone she'd never once used, then registered the words spoken.

Father.

'It was his first act after he gained the appointment and he used *my* husband to secure a reputation for himself. None crossed him after that. There's nights I dreamed on killing him,' continued Derwa, reaching for her mead. 'Yet there he stands.'

Slowly, Kensa's stare returned to Sir George. The shape he cut against the landscape, its sharpness which caught on her lashes. Unwilling to blink, she stared and stared. That man, their region's law-maker, had killed Alexander Rowe. Taken – from her – his warm hands, beard-scratch and oak-round laugh.

'Do you miss him?' Kensa's gums were tight around her teeth, her questions queer and shrill. 'Do you miss my father?'

'I wish I didn't.'

Kensa swore and flung an arm out towards Mr Skewes. 'Then how can you—'

'Because he dotes on Elowen fiercely and I love him for that.' Derwa raised her voice loud enough to summon glances their way. 'What's more, he supported me when no one else would. I had nothing when I was widowed and he gave us all he could spare. More than that, he gave me Elowen.'

Kensa gritted her teeth hard enough to hurt. It was that or cry and she was too close to tears for her liking.

'Your father was never happy,' said Derwa. 'Not a fortnight would go by before Alex grew restless. God, he hated me for needing him, especially when I fell with child. I never knew if he'd return or I'd hear he was shot or hurt or dead. I never knew where he was or the people he dealt with or what he'd done.' Across the field, another song ended and another was begun. 'In truth, I didn't want to know, for the work he did was not Christian. I feared for him every day he was gone and every night he didn't come home.' Down came the flower crown to fall into her lap, dislodged from her head with how fiercely she shook it. 'That's why I wanted Peter. He's a predictable man and I always know where he is, what he's up to and how he thinks.' Derwa eased a slim pink flower, sea thrift, from the crown's arrangement and tucked it behind Kensa's ear. 'Accept it or no, but there will come a time when that's appealing to you, too.'

'A wise woman can't marry,' Kensa reminded her, deflated.

Derwa raised her eyebrows. 'One need not marry to take a man.'

'Ma!'

It was then Kensa realised her mother had imbibed far more than her usual fare. Worse, Mr Skewes was approaching with a swaying gait, as he wound his way back towards Derwa. A hasty retreat was taken: Kensa fled them both, as well as her own embarrassment.

By now, the golden afternoon was ripe and aged, with the entertainment falling into happy disarray, propelled by drink and disorder. Portscatho's community worked hard and toiled long. Whenever there was an excuse to release binds, responsibilities and shackles, it was liberally taken. The miners were the most enthusiastic participants. Their crackling coughs, cultivated in below-ground spaces, were wet with French sherry. Their merriment was contagious to everyone bar Kensa, whose thoughts were claggy in her skull.

In one corner, safely removed from the dancing, were stalls. The neatest one was manned by the church warden, Ephraim, whose thin jacket was as long as his face. He worked for Mr Aldridge and was tasked with selling his honey. It was collected in miscellaneous jars and sealed with tight cloth. Bees were the clergyman's pride. His hives sat within the grounds of St Gerrans Church and the worshippers could hear their hum from the pews. A little sweetness would fix Kensa's sour mood. Or, perhaps not. For as she reached him, Ephraim shook his head.

'Mr Aldridge is precious about his bees and who he sells his honey to.'

Kensa blinked back her surprise. 'Pardon?'

'You heard me.' Ephraim hooked his bony arm around the produce, guarding it from her. 'I shan't be giving you nothin' and the same goes for that old crotch-rubbed dog who suckles you.' He sniffed. 'Especially not when Mr Aldridge is in his moods; no, I know a damn sight better than that.'

A horn-hand gesture was pressed into Kensa's face: a guard against the Devil and a firm dismissal. In her bewilderment, she turned and collided with another. A heavy frame, solid, which reached out to steady her: Sir George.

A single silver coat button, marked with his family crest, caught Kensa's lip as she pulled back. Pain came, as vibrant as the season. His fingers, unyielding against the bone of her forearm, were encased in kid-leather gloves. How soft they were, despite the pressure. And his face, unreadable, when Kensa thought she would see – *something*. He might have been handsome in his youth, yet age had pulled at his jowls and his brown eyes were set small beside heavy lines. Kensa could not speak. Mute, she thought on her father, on his loss, on the hagstone in her pocket, which she had taken from his swinging soul on the scaffold.

'Sorry, I—' came the apology. An unfamiliar utterance. One that tripped treacherously from her own mouth. She thought on the noose, unable to choke out a word around it, as though she bore the rope herself. 'I—'

Sir George, in comparison, was unruffled. Irritated, perhaps. He brushed his free hand down his front, as though to wipe her from it. Shame, like that she'd never known, found her. Although Kensa washed her face daily and scrubbed her nails, her ways were wild and her appearance matched it. Why should she care what he thought of her, after what he had done? And yet she did.

Sir George released her. Took a measured step back. Bowed low. By the time he straightened up, Kensa had fled. Her boot soles were loud against the ground and her feet pulsed. Behind her came a shout. She did not heed it. Only when she was far enough away, a stitch in her side, did she slow. Kensa's hand went to her mouth. There was danger crouched inside it. Her mind spun back to the Bad Books and what she'd read within them. She pictured Sir George on his knees, gasping, dying, begging for his life – begging *her* to spare *him*.

And would she?

No, she thought, *Never*.

Across the field, awash with late moth-light, Kensa saw the wise woman watching her, lips moving. Although the distance was too great to permit talk, Isolde's words came to Kensa as though poured directly into her ear.

We do not take lives, came the warning. *We must not take lives.*

Kensa swore in reply and hoped the old hag heard it. Her hand ached to find a cup. Although she was young, she'd learned early what drink could do and willed it done now. Again, scrumpy was an easy find, though it took her close to the music-makers. Their songs were far too cheerful, which she told anyone who neared her, until no one would. Mean thoughts manifested further as she saw her mother and Mr Skewes get up to dance, especially when his fingers curled onto Derwa's rear.

It was while Kensa nursed her bleak and splintered thoughts

that Elowen chose to speak with her sister. She flopped down on her stomach with an, 'Oof,' and stretched onto the grass which Kensa herself sat upon.

Elowen wore a simple pink dress, hair left loose and flowing. At fifteen, her face was bright and open and happy. She was the perfect May Queen. Girlish, yet leaning towards womanhood; a glass tipped for filling, empty and expectant. Yet, there was a gauntness to her cheeks. As bright as she was today, her face bore signs of sickly shadow.

'Can I have some?'

Kensa drained her cup and belched. 'No.'

The younger of the siblings threaded her fingers through the grass until a dandelion rested on her hand like a giant petalled ring. Silence filled the space between them as the band paused their playing to eat. Eventually, the younger girl asked, 'What's it like being a wise woman?'

'I get a bed to myself and I don't have to share with you.'

Elowen clicked her tongue in a way that mirrored Derwa, in a way that made Kensa's heart sore in every chamber. Again, a quiet threw its weight upon them, wrinkling their sentences until, at last, Kensa lay one flat. 'Where have you been going when you've told our mother you're seeing me?'

Elowen snapped the dandelion stem, the flower tumbling into the grass. Her demeanour changed, shoulders stiffening. 'Why should I tell you?'

'Because I'm your sister.'

'You don't want to be.'

Kensa released a sound from her throat, unbidden. 'I never said that.'

'You don't need to,' said Elowen, her cheeks, ears and neck flushing red. 'I've kept your secrets, haven't I? You'll keep mine.'

A twinned second tied their blood and drummed their earnest hearts, where Kensa could have apologised or explained or made it better. She almost did, opening her mouth to speak, to undo the harm inflicted. She was not quick enough. Elowen rose to her feet. Kensa did not watch to see where she went, for her own eyes prickled hotly.

Not a breath after her sister left, did Jack make his presence known. He was wearing a new shirt – well, his father's shirt, yet new to him. Its cream was bright against his faded blue waistcoat. How smart he looked. Pretty, even, though his chastisement was not.

'Do you have to be so cruel to her?'

'Leave me be,' said Kensa. 'No, wait, fetch me more cider.'

On the horizon, the sun was lowering itself to its end and the light was barley soup.

Jack extended a palm to her. She squinted up at him and hissed.

'You've cut your hair,' she said. 'I hate you.'

'Come on now, up you get.'

His hand hovered between them. Rough digits, calloused with hard labour. She thought on him working in the mines. Feared it, suddenly. Jack was so warm and solid. For him to be buried beneath the ground for hours on end, without the sun to meet him, sent a cold premonition through her.

'I won't have you embarrassing my aunt,' he continued. 'Or yourself, for that matter.'

'Stop telling me what to do.'

'I will when you behave yourself.'

He would not move. She liked that about him. That she could push and push and he would remain, steadfast. Begrudgingly, or seeming to begrudge him, Kensa accepted Jack's hand and got unsteadily to her feet. His palm was a brand and she gasped at the contact, letting its heat settle elsewhere inside her. A squeeze – Jack to Kensa – and her fingers were dropped, his eyes meeting hers a moment too long to be friendly. But when had they ever been friends?

Jack inclined his head to the right. 'I need you to help me fish Mr Aldridge out the stream afore anyone sees him.'

'And you tell me I've had enough!'

'We need to get him home.'

The tense pull to Jack's voice was a grounding force to Kensa. 'Where's Isolde?'

'Last I saw, she was heading down to the harbour with that sailor she passes time with.'

'Uck.'

'You asked.'

The field sloped gently as the pair walked to where the water ran, leaving the celebrations behind. It was nice to be alone – alone with him. She would've told him, were it not for the sounds which found them. Despite the warning Jack had given, Kensa was not prepared for what met her next. Mr Aldridge was sat, fully clothed, in the shallow brook that ran downhill to meet the sea. He was laughing into the water, talking, cooing at it. His whole lower half was submerged, while his palms slapped his damp thighs, cheeks rosy as plum wine.

'I'll take him at the waist, you get his arm over your shoulder,' said Jack.

It was an odd drunkenness that claimed the curate, for it held little resemblance to any inebriation Kensa had known. Rather, it was as though Mr Aldridge occupied a world only he could see. His speech was disjointed, with full sentences dribbling forth or cutting off halfway through.

Kensa hesitated. 'He seems mad.'

'We'll get the wise woman to visit him come the morning, if he'll let her.'

'See, this is what too much praying does to you.'

'Mind yourself,' said Jack, grinning. 'People'll call you a witch.'

Mr Aldridge was a sodden weight. Kensa hooked the curate's arm around her neck and pulled, while he dripped streamwater onto them. *Rip*, went the seams on Kensa's dress, right under her arms. She thought it best not to tell Jack and, if he noticed, he did not comment. Rather, the curate did all the speaking for them.

'Now, I really shouldn't,' said Mr Aldridge. 'Oh, well, go on then, I will! You've twisted my arm, you saucy little—'

'We're taking him to his home, Kensa, not yours,' said Jack, steering them onto the higher path as he corrected their course.

'Oh,' Kensa hiccupped in reply.

Mr Aldridge swayed, blushed and humiliated himself with each step towards his abode. It was a pretty detached cottage with innumerable windows, inlaid with fine Bristol glass (as the villagers had been told at many a sermon). It sat upon Trevanion land, for it was he – the baronet – who funded the curate's hours at the church and ministrations in the village. Unusually, those wide windows, the ones Mr Aldridge bragged about, were closed, their curtains shut tight.

It was there, upon his front step, that Mr Aldridge's sobriety snapped back into place. 'What're you doing here?'

Kensa hastily unravelled herself from the man and Jack eased back, still within arm's reach, waiting for Mr Aldridge to sway again. He did not. His senses had returned from wherever they had been. With them came fury. 'What tomfoolery is this?!' He noticed Kensa, as though for the first time. Mr Aldridge's finger wagged aggressively at her, keeping her at bay. 'I should have known you'd be involved, harlot.'

Kensa reeled back. 'Me?'

Jack stepped forwards. 'You have no right to address her like that.'

'I am a conduit for God's judgements and it is he who decides—'

'Enough,' Jack snarled, with surprising fierceness from a man usually so temperate and restrained. 'Miss Rowe came here to help and this is how you treat her? No, you won't interrupt me when I'm speaking, is that understood?'

The men argued, batting unpleasantries back and forth. Kensa was tired. As if she'd been swimming too long and was too far out to go back. A door slammed and Jack cursed. She had never seen him this angry. It made her feel even worse.

'That damned drunken fool,' said Jack, bouldering up behind her, before coming to an abrupt halt. 'Are you crying?'

'No,' she sobbed. 'Yes.'

Everything tumbled out. Derwa's harsh words, the

encounter with Sir George and Isolde's warning. Until she could barely form a sentence that did not set off another wave of tears. Jack pulled her into his collar where she babbled ridiculous statements about how she missed her mother and had ruined her dress and was sad about the Weaver's ewe and how she never knew what to say to Elowen. And she was going to die one day and for some reason that seemed awfully pressing, even though she knew it would not be for a long time yet. Jack clumsily patted Kensa's back, murmuring softness as one might to a whining pup. It was good to be near him, her face in his linen shirt and its scent: pepper and soap and freshly cut hay.

When at last her tears ceased, Kensa pulled away.

Jack cuffed her nose with his sleeve. 'All right?'

'It'll be my courses,' she sniffed. 'I always get sad whenever they're nearing.'

'Or it'll be the cider.'

'That too,' admitted Kensa. Sunburned, anxious, dizzy, she thought on the cob-walled dwelling she had grown up in, of Elowen going to sleep in her bed, of her mother's late-night voice and how it was to be held by someone who loved you and if – in that holding – he'd smell like a meadow at summer's height. 'I want to go home,' she said at last, then retched and heaved her stomach across Mr Aldridge's front step.

'There we are,' said Jack, staying close. 'Do you feel better?'

'Mmhmm.'

'Good.'

Jack took a measured pause, then thumbed the drool from her chin. Slowly, with patience aplenty, he walked her all the way back to Bohortha.

Chapter Twelve

Come the Storm

Dawn summoned bees. One hundred hive-hewn hums woke Kensa, her window browned with their furred bodies, which were heaped together on the glass exterior. She put a palm against the pane. It was warm with heat and vibration. And there was something else. Beneath what she could sense was another sense. It told her the window was hot with fear. Kensa snatched her palm back and rubbed it down her nightdress. Odd, these moments. When she touched on more than what was there. As though she had opened a box to find another box inside, impossibly bigger than the first. The longer she spent in the cottage, the more it changed her. She called for Isolde and winced, head pulsing in time with her new insect guests. Yesterday's happenings at the fete came back as she clunked down the stairs. If she walked carefully, she could keep from retching. Isolde, in comparison, was shockingly cheerful.

Rosy-cheeked and singing loudly: 'As she swang her buttocks and he raised his leg, a cry fell out from their shared bed. From beneath their mattress was—'

'Bees,' Kensa blurted.

At least that put a stop to the old woman's tawdry humour.

The pair whirled their shawls about their shoulders and padded into the garden to observe the swarm which had consumed Isolde's cottage. The bees poured themselves over the south-facing side and were huddled together in a protective, anxious bundle.

'Those are from Mr Aldridge's hive,' said Isolde slowly. How she could recognise one bee from another, Kensa did not know. There was much she did not know. About her sister, about the magistrate and her father, about her own mother. She was glad Isolde was here. That she could call out in the morning and have her wizened mentor appear and fix it.

'Humph,' said Isolde.

The wise woman turned away and her cracked heels flashed beneath her nightgown. She went to the kitchen window, where her onions bunched: the marked ones Kensa was forbidden to touch. There were at least twenty, if not more, etched and inked with symbols.

'There'll be no good that comes from this.'

Kensa stiffened. 'What do you mean by that?'

At first the onions had been placid and brown. Now, two stood out from the regular yellowed-silver huddle. The one with a shell-shaped 'E' carved upon it was dank and green, while the second, with a crucifix slit into its skin, was dripping, black and pungent.

'Do I have an onion?' And if she did, was it a nice one?

Isolde's mouth clenched into a miserable pucker. Fox shivered and removed herself from beneath the table, padding out into the drizzled morning.

'You look troubled,' said Kensa.

After a time spent in deep contemplation, where she ignored any and all questions, Isolde roused herself. 'Do you have a fine dress?'

'I have the one I wore yesterday.'

'Then you'll borrow one of mine,' said Isolde tersely. 'We are to attend the Sunday service.'

'Are you joking?' Kensa frowned at the old woman and her onions and the rapid exit the vixen had made. Around her was an unsettled quality, a tightening, as though the cottage walls had grown muscle and begun to contract around them. 'I thought the whole point of being a wise woman was that I didn't have to go to church?'

'You'll do as you're damn well told, Miss Rowe.'

'And who's going to make me?'

'I am, because you are my apprentice and it is your duty to do what I tell you.'

'If I only knew why, I would,' Kensa retorted.

Isolde paused for the longest time, then said softly, 'It would not be fair.'

An unsteady quiet followed, nothing solid enough for the younger woman to lean against. It had been like this when

she'd been small: her parents arguing, her father and his secrets, a sense that she'd always be the last to know and maybe,
sometimes, that was better. Isolde ran her hand down her face
and wrenched herself away, to her room. Loud bangs were
heard, fabric rustling. Eventually, Kensa was given a dress with
a faint cupboard scent and told to change. She wanted to argue.
Defend herself. And she would've done, were it not for how
worried Isolde seemed. Gone was her rabid charm, replaced
with an anxiety Kensa had never seen before.

'All right,' said Kensa.

Behind her, a long, black tendril of slime dripped from the
most blackened onion and ran its finger down the wall.

Within the hour, the wise woman and her apprentice were
trudging along the high lane to St Gerrans Church. Outside
was muggy and warm, the sun's heat trapped under a low
bank of cloud to press down on those below it. Neither spoke,
ill-humoured and cross and a tad hungover. The youngest
wore a borrowed garment of brushed brown velvet, which she
quickly sweated through. If she kept her arms at her sides, no
one would know. It was the nicest dress she had ever worn,
complete with gold-threaded leaves at the bust. She pressed
her hands over the embroidery, fingering the pattern: the occasional precious stone glimmered at her touch, betraying the
wealth Isolde must once have owned a long time ago. Although
her chemise was yellowed beneath it, she passed as decent
enough, if you overlooked the musty smell. Isolde wore a grey
smock, the only change in her bearing a bangle which rattled
on her wrist, large and silvered against her bony joint.

St Gerrans Church was a squat, low building with a thin

spire that shot upwards as though caught unawares. Its grey stone was stacked and slated, while arched windows held sallow glass patterns, plain and without adornment. It was attached to the parish of Gerrans, a small group of houses above Portscatho, which had been established long before the harbour's development. For hundreds of years, a clergyman had given a sermon at this place every Sunday. Mr Aldridge was the most recent in a long, long line and was wont to tell his congregation so. At the hill's end, where it ran to the sea, was a new Methodist sect, although none mentioned their ilk, and only one or two worshippers had defected.

Kensa had never paid God much mind and He had given her the same disregard. The Land itself seemed more faith to her and that belief had only increased since working with Isolde. Sometimes she thought she heard more guidance from the Sea than she ever did from a pulpit, the endless waves more real than the Heavens.

The church's Norman interior was beamed and plainly carved, the floor cracked with tiles, and – to the entrance's right – was a large stone font, where Kensa herself had been baptised. Her mother had told everyone how Kensa had cried as soon as the holy water met her forehead, a good omen.

Elowen had not.

'She's still got the Devil in her,' Old Sal had joked once, which brought her a cuss from Mr Skewes and a mean smile from Kensa, which she nursed now at the memory.

As soon as she entered the church, the air grew colder. Its stone could not take the day's Sabbath heat. Inside, the village turn-out was surprisingly high. Sir George Trevanion had taken his pew at the front, while the usual rabble sat in the rows behind. There was Old Sal and her pasty daughter, as well as the forge workers, the wading crew who poached a living on scallops and winkles, Young Robert, the Preventative men such as Mr Skewes and – much to the latter's dislike – the smugglers they tried to apprehend, who sat grinning with tobacco pressed into their gums. Here, too, was Kensa's mother and sister. Yet what drew Kensa's eye was not them. Bright amid the squalor was the pretty woman she had seen at the May Day festival. Rather, the prettiest woman Kensa had ever seen in her life. It was she, then, who had drawn a crowd. Odd, that she sat a distance from Sir George at the church's front.

'I figured the pair of them were together,' said Kensa, as she slid her backside on the wooden seat closest to the door.

'Her with 'im?' Isolde sucked her teeth. 'It could be. Money can make even the ugliest man palatable and it helps that he's not unfortunate looking.'

Elowen's thin face was intent upon the new woman. In fact, she did not once look away, a frown creasing her brow. At last, here was someone to cast shade over Kensa's sister. No longer would the fair-haired girl be the loveliest in the room, for now she had competition.

There were a few grumbles at the healers' entrance. Church was not a place for them, though Kensa had never been welcome. Her father's reputation prevented her acceptance here. It used to make her angry, the same way everything made her angry. Yet with Isolde beside her, she now wielded authority. No longer was she a splinter on a pew. She was integral to the community. As it should always have been. Despite the strong attendance, there was one person missing from today's gathering.

Isolde touched an elbow to her apprentice. 'Who're you looking for?'

'No one,' said Kensa quickly.

Jack was not present, nor his father, their seat behind the gentry empty. A heaviness pulled on her stomach: she'd wanted him to see her dress, to think she might be handsome enough in the soft light, in the right clothes.

Chime went the bell, rung by the warden, to draw in the last stragglers. None had been late today. The congregation had an upright bearing and each face was fixed on the pulpit, where an eagle-headed stand held the Great Book. Never before had there been such enthusiasm around the boorish, droning Mr Aldridge, whose favourite pastime was to point at each villager in turn and divulge their fated punishments should they not ask God's forgiveness. Today, he did not have that same zeal. For when the curate arrived – late – he beamed with the brightness of a pocket-shined pearl. His eyes alighted on the strange woman and widened significantly. She had a dress that buttoned up to her neck, gloves that hid her hands, and sleeves, too, to cover them. A hat obscured much of her features, though what was on display looked fine and sharp, if thickly powdered.

'This ain't right,' said Kensa, too loudly, shushed by those in the pews ahead.

'That be true,' agreed Isolde. 'Over half the people here are self-confessed sinners and yet their backsides are glued to their seats.'

'I ain't confessing nothing,' grunted One-Eyed Si from the row in front.

Everyone quietened down when Mr Aldridge cleared his throat and led the congregation into their first hymn. On went the droning intonations as each voice dutifully churned through the verses. Until the beautiful woman began to sing. Hers was no dreary lull, no tongue skipping over words. Here was a creature with a voice to charm the tide to rising. And she sang to no one but Mr Aldridge. Turned her face on him, unmoving. None could look away. Hush, as all stopped to listen. Elowen was especially transfixed, though her expression seemed odd, mouth thin and disapproving, compared to the adoration carried by the others.

'Merrin,' whispered One-Eyed Si, imbuing this stranger's name with longing, for only Kensa to hear. At its utterance, the singer's pitch slipped into shrillness – as though she knew, as though she heard – then shifted back to gentler tones.

When at last the hymn ended, Mr Aldridge's sermon began. Although the curate usually dressed well, today he gleamed. His double-breasted cassock was brushed, his cap perched neatly atop his head and his golden cross, elevated by a chain around his neck, sat with polished persistence against his chest.

'It must be known that by virtue of being God's dear creatures, we are subject to, ah, certain natural laws that we must, occasionally, succumb to,' said Mr Aldridge. A few amused grunts flitted about the assembled villagers. 'Rather, it would be an unnatural thing should one's affections – coming from self-love as granted by the Heavens – be separate from one's existence. Truly, such love as does grant us goodness in public should then be expressed in private.'

Kensa clicked her tongue. 'What's he talking about?'

'Lust,' said One-Eyed Si.

As he spoke, the curate's features grew rosier and his eyes never left the strange woman.

'Fishiness is afoot here . . .' muttered Isolde.

Her sentence remained unfinished – as did the curate's sermon – for a commotion struck the middle pews where Kensa had seen her mother and half-sister sitting.

'Elowen!' Mr Skewes cried.

Kensa's legs straightened, propelled her to standing. Shouts, then a shocked silence. Worshippers bent over the wooden benches and Kensa craned through the masses to see, to find Elowen slumped in her father's arms, head lolling back. Kensa vaulted over the pews, skirts lifted high and her feet catching laps and hands and prayer books. She landed beside her mother – sweaty, dishevelled – and once there, worked quickly.

Kensa put her hand to Elowen's mouth and sought breath in the way she had seen Isolde do. 'She's warm to the touch.' There were no visible marks on her skin, though she was paler than her usual swan-skinned pallor.

Derwa shook her head, hand clutched at her throat. 'How? There's been no fever, none of her usual signs.'

'What do you think, Isolde?' No answer. Kensa craned her neck and saw the older woman had fled. So, too, had the singing stranger.

Along came the curate, blustering into view, stomach first. 'What is this carrying-on?'

'We need to get her out in the open air,' ordered Kensa, speaking to the masses crowded around them, waving her arms to make space. Villagers fell back in a startled fashion, which might have been humorous, were it not for the circumstances.

'Did you do this?' Mr Skewes asked and Kensa realised he spoke to her. 'Did you do this?' He held the fainting girl to him, clutched like a doll. 'And in God's house, too! In God's house, here among—'

'Peter,' hushed Derwa, although there was no stopping the man.

'If you've cursed her, I'll string you up as high as I did your—'

Elowen gasped into waking. Her fair hair was long enough to fall down her father's arms and sweep the tiles. Even clammy and lips wobbling, she could have been mistaken for a saintly figure in a Bible verse.

'Where did she go?' Elowen trailed off, saw the faces staring at her with gawping mouths, and burst into tears. A dozen voices spoke at once. Mr Aldridge demanded quiet and was not listened to, Old Sal blamed women's troubles and Mr Skewes dragged his daughter – and Derwa – out of the church and into the grassy surroundings, marked with headstones. Kensa was quick to follow.

'Don't you come near her,' warned the Coast Guard. He rounded his wiry body to block Kensa's path and swept a tearful Elowen behind him. At least she was on her feet, if unsteady.

'I'm all right, Pa,' came a rasped reply.

'There's trouble heading to us, we all know it,' said Mr Skewes, his weasel face animated and fierce. 'I saw it when last in Bodmin, that sweating sickness taking hold. We can see the season's slow to come this year, there's naught to catch and foulness in the air.' Although this was not the first time Mr Skewes had fallen into superstition, he had never carried such heat behind it. What's more, he had never directed it fully on Kensa. Theirs had always been an uneasy truce, an agreement to remove oneself from the other's path. It was different now, Kensa was different, and she did not bow her head or avoid his stare. Instead, she stared back. And she did not trust what she saw.

'Let me see my sister.'

Derwa was quick to mediate, seeking a solution. One she pushed, as always, onto Kensa. 'Off you pop now,' she said gently, though not without guilt. 'He'll be calmer once you've gone and I'll see to our girl.'

Our. Belonging to Mr Skewes and Derwa. Even though Kensa's blood was half shared by Elowen, it was as though the two held no possession of each other.

'I've done nothing wrong,' argued Kensa, raising her voice more than she meant to, hating how it cracked at the end.

'Please—' Elowen was cut off, coughing.

Mr Skewes continued his chastisement. It was a droning blur in Kensa's ears. Around the fully fledged adults, the two young women met one another's gaze. Kensa frowned, seeing an odd expression flicker over Elowen's features. One that spoke on need or sorrow or fear. Such wild feelings Kensa never would have put to a girl so seemingly placid. As though she realised her folly, Elowen cast her eyes down and severed their connection.

I don't know you at all, do I?

No, was the reply.

Kensa swore it was her own mind summoning the word, swore it was the Old Ways or her heated conscience, even if it spoke with Elowen's voice.

The tide had turned against Kensa. Heads poked around the church entrance, while Mr Aldridge's sermons on benevolence continued to pound against the pews and beyond, into the churchyard.

There was no such sentiment in Kensa's mind. 'Have it your way.'

She stomped from the churchyard and there, waiting in the lane beyond, was Isolde. The healer turned to her apprentice with a ferocity Kensa had never known.

There was a harried pull to her jowls. 'Where's that harlot got to?'

'She's over there.'

'Not your mother, the singing woman – Merrin!'

'Left, I think, after what happened.'

'O' course she has! I am getting slow and inefficient and fucking old,' said Isolde, nostrils wide and flaring. 'Tell me, where does she live?'

'How should I know?'

'Because it's your responsibility, Kensa! Everything that happens here, to these people, to this place, must be known to you! Have you not been paying attention?'

Kensa's mouth was slack with hurt. She slammed the church gate behind her and clopped out onto the main lane that connected Portscatho to Gerrans.

Bugger each one of them, ungrateful, ignorant bastards.

Her anger took her all the way back to Bohortha and it took her fast. Isolde was not far behind. Their matching tempers rattled around the cottage, batting into one another like the last two spools in a sewing box. Even the chickens adopted their mood and pecked any boots which strayed near them. Afternoon fell to evening and dinner had to be made, no matter their rift. The pair clattered around the space, wordlessly shoving plates or bowls or spoons at the other, while their pheasant supper burned in a pot over the stove.

Isolde used a spoon to lean stew through her lips. 'Humph.'

'You're welcome,' said Kensa.

Fox poked her head through the kitchen door. She sniffed at their distant plates, caught a whiff of their malignant bearing and quickly fled to pester the chickens. Evening was chillier. Fog had begun its unfurling from the sea. Isolde remarked on it. Kensa agreed. A truce was nearing them and the apprentice, despite her frustration, pulled it closer.

'I don't know nought about that woman or the bees, though I recall Mr Aldridge weren't himself at the May Day festival,' Kensa offered, setting her bowl aside. 'He weren't talking to no one, he was sitting by himself in the stream, laughing, speaking oddness, till he suddenly came to his wits again.'

Rather than mend the rift, the new knowledge only made Isolde's temper worse. 'And you didn't see fit to tell me?' Her spoon clattered from her grasp and onto the table. Behind her, the cooking pot's lid rattled, while mounting steam pressed its wetness against the windows. Mr Aldridge's bees, still present in the cottage, found another room to congregate in.

'I didn't think it was important!' Kensa snarled, hacking

bread from a tinned loaf and using the same knife to stab at the butter. 'I am not a child to be ordered around. I am to be a healer and shall be treated as such.'

'Will you now?'

'Yes, I bloody will.'

Isolde lost the tension in her limbs. With a huff, she sank forwards, over the table, and cradled her head in her hands. 'You're a foolish girl, Kensa.' It was not said with malice. She looked old. Quite suddenly, dangerously ancient, the animation gone from her features, until they were slack and runny as egg.

'Are you all right, Isolde?'

'I was old even when the manor house was pulled down. I have seen much and now it seems I cannot see anything else.' She held her palms up. 'Threads I used to hold have fled from my fingers.'

'I can help,' said Kensa earnestly.

'I know – and you do,' said Isolde.

'It's tiredness, only that. After a good night's sleep you'll be fine again.' A strange expression gathered on the older woman's face, bidding Kensa to ask, 'Did I say the wrong thing?'

'You're to stay in your room tonight, you hear me?'

'What for? I didn't do—'

'You're not in trouble.' Isolde spoke quietly, as gently as she would to the chickens when she came to put them to bed. She cast a meaningful look to the third chair in the parlour. Only then did Kensa see it was empty and cleared of rubbish. 'It's nothing you've done wrong; it's only my own oversight and a conversation I must have.'

It was unsettling to hear Isolde talk on making mistakes. Surely, she knew everything, could do anything? She was a witch and witches did not make errors. Did they?

'I don't understand.'

'When I ask you to remain upstairs, Kensa, it is because I am expecting . . . ' Isolde reached around her teeth for the word and chose, ' . . . company.'

No one had ever visited the cottage outside the Wednesday hours. Even young Jack came on that midweek day, in between the sun's rising and setting.

'Am I to know who?'

The wise woman closed her eyes and shook her head. 'Let me hold this knowledge for us both, while I still can.' Isolde ladled further pheasant stew into their bowls and reached for a third: the latter intended for a visitor she would not name.

Midnight was as thick as cream when Kensa awoke to voices downstairs. The late air was different. Heavy and heaped with musk, akin to storm-weather, though the skies were silent. Here was a scent Kensa had met before, yet the memory was slow to reach her. It ran as minnows through her fingers, flashing silver to mock her folly. Isolde's crackling laugh was easy to discern. It leapt from the parlour and into Kensa's room. The secondary voice, belonging to whomever had gifted the woman her amusement, was also familiar. It carried a depth, a weight, as stone pulled over stone: a man's voice.

She could not sleep through it.

Kensa had the notion, a thought as purposeful as a seed planted – unfurling – that she was not meant to.

Fox had made herself a nest on the bed's far end, head resting on her tail. A slight yawn revealed her needle-bone teeth. At least the vixen could settle back to sleep. Kensa, in comparison, was alert.

Possibilities bounced through her mind. If the old woman had a suitor, then who was Kensa to listen and spy and judge? Besides, she had no desire to listen to *that* particular activity. She blanched upon remembering the innumerable sordid items she had found upon first tidying Isolde's cottage.

'You needn't be so prudish, they're fertility charms,' had been the old woman's explanation. Kensa only half-believed her.

As for this man who had come to call, he sounded far younger than Isolde. And his voice, well, it was easy to listen to. The small dark hairs on her arms began to rise and her body moved with them. With a mouse's caution, Kensa set her feet upon the floorboards and tested them. The house did not betray her. Slowly, she ventured into the hallway and sank onto the stair's highest step, the better to listen.

'I have seen the markers, the rising mists and the dead-waves coming,' claimed the visitor. Next, the sound of a cork's whine as it's released from its neck. What followed was a glugging noise, spirits poured from a bottle. 'You should have done this sooner.'

'I did it when she was ready.'

'I am too ancient to be lied to,' he said. 'You called her when *you* were ready, Isolde.' A gap in speech, glass drained, a tap as it is put upon a table. Kensa could guess which: the one with a shell top, beside the high-backed chair neither she nor Isolde ever sat on. 'You should test her, to make sure she's what you require.'

'Perhaps.'

Then the third chair was the Bucka's chair, Kensa realised with a strained gasp. That was how she knew his voice, it was his – *the Bucka's* – voice.

'If you don't, I fear there won't be enough time to train her for what's ahead.'

'Fear? We both know you fear nothing, old friend,' was Isolde's reply. 'She's a resourceful one and many healers have scraped out their path alone, exactly as I did.'

'And look at the good it did you.'

He shouldn't be here. He was hard and cruel and so abominably *wrong*. If she was braver, if she was better, she would march downstairs and command him to leave. Yet she did not feel brave in that moment; she felt small and pebbled, buffeted by the waves of him.

'I can feel the earth pushing back,' said Isolde, 'telling me what needs to happen, warning me that I have a choice to make and I cannot be selfish with it. As it stands, the Pact is fragile and she needs to be strong to carry it – and be carried by others.'

'You fear she's too weak to be its keeper?' The Bucka released a long exhale. 'From what I have seen, she is a surprising one. I do not think your fears unfounded, yet if the Morgawr chose her, then it did so for a reason and you cannot go against her wishes.'

No laughter followed this time, only a waiting silence. Kensa's whole body tensed. What the Bucka said was a lie. He knew the Morgawr had not chosen her. On the morning they'd met he'd isolated her untruths and fished inside her mind for others. Now he told Isolde differently, reassuring her – why? Her confusion mixed with a strange, unwelcome gratitude. She never wished to owe the Bucka anything, let alone that. Yet he had kept her secret. He had done that for her. Kensa leaned forwards, longing to see his face, as though it could tell her more, and the cottage forgot its promise to hide her movements.

Creak, it whispered.

'Should anything befall you, I could instruct her in all she's ignorant of,' said the Bucka slyly. 'I'd drape her in pearls and crown her in coral and be master to a most obedient servant.'

Kensa held her breath. He knew she listened. Goaded her, mocked her, his *witchling*.

'Never.' Furniture scraped on the parlour's floor, almost burying Isolde's next words. 'Do not come here again,' she said. 'Swear to me, now, you will never set a foot in this house while she lives here?'

An unsettling pull had the cottage constrict. It caught the breath in Kensa's throat and rattled the Bad Books in their cabinet. What followed was danger, akin to a misstep on a high cliff, a fall to which there would be no end. Kensa was afraid. Here was power she did not yet understand – and it raged.

'Do not bind me to your tricks,' said the Bucka. 'I will not be chained again by one such as you.' He sounded as calm as ice underfoot, in that long, slow moment before it splits.

When the old woman spoke in reply, she did so with an authority Kensa had never heard her use, as though she spoke with many voices, not one. 'You will do as I command, Gerent.'

'Hah, invoke a dead name, will you?' Here was his laugh, all mockery now. 'You're lucky I remember it.'

'I am the wise woman on this shore,' said Isolde, 'I am the Land to which the tide bows – and you will bow to me.'

'For the moment.' Tension fled, as quickly as it had come. 'Fine, I shall not step over this threshold, not unless she bids me to, and that day will come.'

'Not while I live.'

A hum, an agreement or the impression of one.

Deliberate, hard footsteps sang through the kitchen. A long shadow paused at the staircase's end, cast by a shape Kensa could not fully see. Even when she dipped her head downstairs to view the man, the creature, the sea god who had cast it, who had exchanged such hard words with the witch – sensing he watched her, sensing he waited – she saw nothing. And she did not even hear the door click shut to mark his exit.

Trailing behind him, an unwanted gift, was the scent of salt and time and cloud-washed starlight. And something else, incense, perhaps. Kensa wondered how he lived when he was not on land, where he went and what he did when not salt-bound and sea-tied. When sleep finally came, her dreams were his threats – a coral crown and pearls enough to drown in.

Chapter Thirteen

Chime for a Change

Bohortha's tangled cottage remained unsettled the following morning, as though it had absorbed the foul words from the evening prior. One consolation was the weather's improvement. Blazing sunshine had eradicated the mist and set spring firmly on her course to summer. Blackbirds, robins and wrens cheered the joy of it. However, on the horizon were lumped clouds. Whatever fine day had come, it would not last. Kensa could tell as much from her bedroom window.

Upon waking, she stepped clumsily downstairs. She checked the third chair in the parlour and found it piled high once again with odds and ends. The Bucka was long gone, yet he had left a peculiar atmosphere behind. A sense of being watched. As though he had forgotten his jacket on their coat stand and its pockets now gently lipped at their movements, collecting and heaving with all it overheard. Kensa wrapped her shawl tighter around herself.

On the kitchen table were feathers. The bird cage was empty. Isolde's nails had red beneath them. She bid her apprentice to tie twig bundles, combining magpie, dove and jay with birch, ash and holly. Each item had a meaning, yet to be memorised. It was hard for Kensa to hold a lesson in her thoughts when her thoughts were already full. Isolde ran rosemary oil over her fingers, lips twitching with words Kensa could not quite catch. Around them, the chickens were content to warm themselves on windowsills while Fox slept at their feet, her body curled around the younger woman's ankles.

Kensa puffed out her cheeks. 'Why was the Bucka here last night?'

Isolde hit a twig across her palms. 'Pay attention to your work.'

'How can I do that when you're keeping things from me?'

'Whoever I entertain in the small hours and however I do it is a private matter. Now, bind your damn feathers and do it with a more cheerful disposition. I won't have you tarnishing the shipping charms or else I'll have enough capsizes to fill the spare soil at St Gerrans.' Isolde's words had a falsity to them. A studied, practised air, as performative as a dog rose, sweet to spite its name. 'That reminds me,' continued the wise woman, 'I'll need you to visit Mr Aldridge this afternoon, to ask if he'd be wanting his bees returned and how he proposes to do it.'

'What's that smell?'

Onions, the ones strung together for divining purposes, were weeping. One was blackened and shrivelled, the other oozing clear fluid.

Isolde kept her eyes on the table, feathers and twine in her fingers. 'Don't you mind that, it's nought to worry over.'

Another lie, then. Or at least an inability to tell the truth.

'Suit yourself,' said Kensa bitterly.

She was too proud to pry. Even if she tried to, Isolde would never relent. As ever, there was work to be done. Kensa had no desire to see Mr Aldridge, but it seemed the only way to calm the bees who had begun to pester both the wise woman and her apprentice. Thankfully, any concerns about being stung were eased when she saw the insects wrapped around Isolde's neck like a living scarf.

From the kitchen door, Kensa called, 'I won't be long.' Isolde opened her lips, downturned, as though to speak. Her getting-ready rustle paused when the apprentice dropped her boot laces. 'What is it?'

After a long wait, Isolde said, 'You mind yourself, now.'

'Don't I always?'

Kensa retraced her steps from yesterday and walked up the hill to Gerrans and then along, beside the church, to the curate's cottage. The drizzle had finally sulked to shore and brought with it rain showers, quick to arrive and slow to leave. By the time Kensa was at the clergyman's gate she was soaked through. Sadly, there would be no warm or dry reception here. In fact, after their last meeting, Kensa was apprehensive.

What would be the worst of it? Cruel words, an insult, perhaps the same as spoken at the May Day festival. A sense that she had diminished in the eyes of the village's most influential resident. Her fear was smallness and she wore it then, in the damp and the cold.

She did feel small, lately.

As though every single word cut her too deeply, too keenly.

Mr Aldridge's windows were dark and the curtains closed, as they had been before. This time, however, his door was ajar. It revealed a dim hallway. Beyond that came singing. It was not Mr Aldridge's wavering baritone. No, this was a high, haunting melody which tipped over into cascading, flooding, bubbling laughter.

It *was* and *was not* a woman's voice.

And it was not unknown to Kensa, either. She had heard it only yesterday in church, radiating from that front pew. Her steps were loud in the hallway. 'Sir?' At her call, the singing ceased. *Drip*, her skirts ran puddles. Behind her, the rain continued.

Kensa went to speak again, until she came level with the curate's front room.

On this grey morning, the beautiful singer she had seen yesterday, the lady called Merrin, was no longer wearing her prim Sunday clothes. In fact, she wore no clothes at all. She lounged on a small settee and only the day's dim shadows preserved her modesty. The wider Kensa pushed the door open, the smaller those shadows became.

A fishy scent rolled through her senses.

'I was looking for ...' trailed Kensa, as her eyes adjusted to the gloom in the room and what the gloom held, '... Mr Aldridge?' There the curate was, propped beside the now-quiet singer on the settee. He did not resemble himself. There was a shrunken pull to him, skin tight and shiny like a cured ham. His smile, if it could be called that, was the worst part. Lips peeled back in a grin, neck bent, nostrils wide and gaping.

'He's dead,' said Kensa, disbelieving.

'Yes,' replied Merrin.

'What will I tell the bees?'

Kensa did not exactly giggle. She was not sure what she did. A sound left her, unbidden. She could not have moved had she tried. Dread was a pebble. One dropped from a great height and into a well, stirring the silt at the bottom where instinct lay. The ones that told her to run. She tried to, she wanted to.

The cushions at Merrin's back squelched as she adjusted herself, shiny-wet with matter. 'You are the wise woman's apprentice.' She spoke oddly, stilted, as though her mouth were filled with sand. It was then Kensa looked at her, *truly* looked at her.

Merrin's feet were webbed and green as sandwort, darkening to sea holly across her body, stomach, breasts and throat. Gone was the white complexion she had sported prior – the powder to hide her tint. Here was a monster, almost human in appearance, yet decidedly *off*. She was high-cheeked with wide-set eyes, a too-small nose and stringy black hair. Her dress, chemise and gloves lay torn and discarded on the ornate rug. Lying beside them was another immobile, lifeless shape: Wenna. She was the servant who tended to Mr Aldridge's fires and prepared his meals. At her neck were bright marks – strangle marks – latticed and leathery, which matched the casing on the creature Kensa now stood before.

'You – you did this?' Kensa's stomach lurched. 'How could— You did this?'

The single breath where Kensa might have screamed came and went. Her dress continued to *drip* onto the rug, already sopping and darkly stained.

Merrin tilted her head to the side, watchful.

Those who lived by the shore had names for what this creature was. Whether from the West Country or the Scottish Isles, local folk knew such beasts existed. Called them selkie or mermaid or siren or – in Cornwall – asrai. Kensa had never met one. No one had. Indeed, what lay in the sea was bid to stay in the sea, as far as the Pact told. Wasn't that what the Bucka did? Kept them there, within the waves, imprisoned.

Kensa threw up. Upended her stomach loudly across the floor, exactly as she had done the last time she was at Mr Aldridge's door. With a thin yowl, the asrai pulled her long, webbed feet clear.

'You killed him,' said Kensa.

'He wanted me to,' said Merrin. 'Asked for it.' Her voice was one of coral walls and sandy beds. 'You saw how he dress-ss-ed for me, buttoned to chin, wrapped as a gift. I enjoy a clergyman's plumpness – they are fed *so* well – taste of hypocrisy.'

'And you killed him,' repeated Kensa.

She put a hand to the doorframe and steadied herself. The room began to tilt and fly into curves around her. She could not rip her gaze from Mr Aldridge's stretched, dried face, from the speckled pepper-red marks on the wall behind him, from his ever-staring eyes and the last sight he'd taken.

'You will be calm.'

It was a simple instruction delivered by the asrai. It soothed the waves in Kensa's blood and cooled her heart's beating:

a spell, wild magic, the Old Ways. Merrin moved from the settee. Came close to bare her teeth against Kensa's cheek. Beneath her words was a shrill melody. 'You will pour me tea.'

Unable to resist, Kensa did exactly that.

She could not remember the action of putting the tea kettle over the range in the kitchen, though her hands must have done it. Nor did she recall stepping from room to room. Occasionally, she would blink and realise she had walked or moved or opened a cupboard. If ever she cast her eyes around her, the bodies no longer evoked emotion. Mr Aldridge's dried husk was the norm, as was Wenna's strangled form. Besides, there was tea to make, wasn't there?

'We are fine ladies,' said Merrin. 'This is what fine ladies do.'

Kensa nodded.

Her host was pleased: 'Yes-ss-ss.'

A pot and tea leaves were already laid out, as was the milk. What's more, when Kensa searched the larder, she found Wenna had made scones prior to being throttled and lumped onto the carpet. *Oh*, mused Kensa. *How thoughtful*. She could think nothing else. Her mind was one big *Oh*-shaped chasm. Her hands began to shake as she carried the tray, heaped with what Merrin had asked for. As for the asrai, she had placed herself once again on the settee, wearing only blood and churlish glee. Outside, the rain hardened to bruising taps on the window panes. Icy pellets shot down the chimney and melted, spotting Mr Aldridge's trouser legs.

'Do – do you take sugar?'

Merrin bared her teeth to mimic a smile. 'I will take it.'

There were bits in her canines. Kensa wondered where the

bits had come from and grew determined not to roll Wenna onto her back, lest there be pieces missing from her front.

Merrin waited with a child's impatience. 'What are you named?'

A hard swallow, mouth dry. 'Kensa.'

The ivy-painted cups rattled on the tray and Kensa's own teeth rattled in their gums. She carefully negotiated around Wenna's remains and placed the tray upon a low table. Merrin, with spidery movements, assigned cups to each person sitting, including Mr Aldridge. His parched skin was mask-like, his molars on show in a never, never, never-ending grin. Kensa matched it.

'Yes,' the asrai encouraged, rocking in her seat. 'Pour.'

Kensa did not refuse. She tried to. As soon as she did, there was a pull in her consciousness, body reacting and mind dampening. Was this how sirens sang sailors to rocks? Even now there was a humming noise emanating from a pit in the creature's throat, the same note reverberating over and over.

Did either of them scream? Or did they lie there, contentedly, while she killed them?

'Say when,' muttered Kensa. She heaped sugar into Mr Aldridge's cup. Spoonful upon spoonful upon spoonful. Only after there was a small heap did her movements jar and she was able to stop serving the dead man.

Merrin grinned as a toddler might who has roped an adult into her game. Only, she was a toddler with fangs and a monster's appetite. Her uncrossed legs were impossibly long, back straight, as she dipped her fingers between the sugar bowl and her mouth.

She offered the bowl to Kensa. 'Eat?'

'No, thank you.'

Kensa's spine tingled. Her movements were blunt. She clumsily poured her own tea and kept pouring, hot liquid blooming over the cup, saucer, table and onto the rug. A hot trickle, fibres soaked, tea and blood.

'We are fine ladies,' repeated Merrin.

Kensa squelched her shoe against the carpet, watched it bubble brown over the worn leather that encased her feet.

I ain't cleaning that up.

Anger came at the prospect. It was raging fury, one that overrode her fear. *Snap*, and her mind cleared. *Crack*, and she dropped her cup. *Whack*, and the asrai struck.

Merrin launched herself across the table, sent the teapot spinning and showered their laps with sugar. A blunt force, the creature's hard palms, smacked into Kensa's chest and sent her body careening backwards. She did not land on a hard surface. Wenna, or what remained of the housemaid, cushioned her fall.

A weight landed on top of her: Merrin, knees on Kensa's stomach, a hand around her throat. With the pressure on her windpipe came a harsh burning. It was not hot, like the tea that scalded her legs as it splashed across them. No, this was cold. As raw as the polar sea under snow. It brought a lung-shredding pain. Kensa scrabbled at the asrai, whose long arms easily kept her back. Panic had her buckle and arch, splayed over the housemaid's body, yet Merrin did not budge. She brought her face close to Kensa's and watched, carefully. Stroked her free hand down warm flesh. Merrin's breath was rotten. It stank of fish guts, far stronger than the salting cellars when the catch came in.

'Sink, yes, with me, a fine lady.'

It was hard to see, to feel, to move.

Kensa's vision began to melt at the seams, popping with light. The asrai's sharp teeth neared her, pressed onto her cheek, almost a kiss. Kensa's arms dropped to her sides. Her hand grazed an edge. On the rug, tassels wet and cold against her palm, was a shard: a split saucer and hope in its sharp edge. Kensa grabbed it. With a final effort, she swung upwards. The cracked porcelain caught Merrin's cheek, sheering her from Kensa's body.

Coughing, heaving with drool, blood running down her chin, Kensa pedalled back to the room's corner. On the floor, the asrai cradled her face.

'I was not going to *kill*,' snarled Merrin.

Kensa made a sound that almost could have been a curse, had her bruised throat allowed it. She dragged herself to standing, using the curate's fireplace to do so.

'Bucka won't allow it,' came the hiss. 'Soft, he is, as chalk.'

'Why did you do this?' Kensa would not release the split porcelain saucer. It was her only weapon. Her fingers were tired from holding it and her legs tired from holding her up. 'Mr Aldridge did nothing to you.'

'Do you not need to eat? I do.'

'You do not eat *here*, not from *my* people.'

'If they are yours, then why hate them?' Merrin's face was open and heart-shaped. 'I can smell it on you.'

It was a simple question from one who lived simply, with rules and knowledge far beyond Kensa's understanding.

'I – I don't,' she answered.

'Lies.'

Kensa raised her chin. To her left was the door, leading into the hall. Beyond that, outside. Rain-soaked grass, a breeze that swept in and chilled her wet woollen socks. It called to her: *Run*.

Merrin smiled, too wide, disconcerting. Sank her shoulders down and shifted to a crouch, boxed and ready to pounce. Kensa had always assumed she would be courageous in a moment such as this. As brave as her father, who laughed even on the scaffold. The door was there and Kensa could not move. She was barely eighteen and two people she had known since childhood were slumped, dead, in the room with her.

Was this what being a wise woman was?

Kensa could not do it. Had already failed.

Mr Aldridge began to slowly lean forwards, dislodged by the asrai's sudden flex as she primed herself to leap. His doll-mask face did not change. Was this what Merrin would do to her? The floor groaned. Kensa held up her porcelain shard, ready to fight, ready to die.

Let her be buried by the Weaver's ewe, let her be sung to, as she lay in the soil, let her—

'I think that's enough,' came Isolde's thundering voice.

Nought but the rain dared answer.

The wise woman was tall and furious, filling the doorway as though she had lengthened her bones since last Kensa saw her. Merrin's feral nature thinned. She bowed, trying to look penitent, her long, seaweed hair falling demurely across her face. Kensa, meanwhile, did not dare move.

'You should leave here, Merrin.' There was no heat behind Isolde's order, only sadness. For the second time since Kensa had known her, the wise woman looked her age. 'What led you from the sea – why now, tell me?'

'Mr Aldridge has been keeping me,' said the green-hued creature. 'He taught me to act well, wear a dress, talk on weather,' she stuck out her tongue, 'pray at night.'

Isolde withdrew the bone-handled knife. Its hammered metal glinted dully. 'The Bucka will kill you when he learns what you've done.'

A hiss, attention on the blade, and the reply, 'I know no father in the Father of Storms.'

'You will leave,' Isolde repeated, firmer now, as the wind rose.

Merrin seemed to consider the wise woman's words. 'No,' she said, as the fishy smell in the room grew fishier. 'Stay.' Slim gills on Merrin's neck opened. She took a breath, filled her lungs and pursed her lips to sing.

Kensa clapped her hands over her ears, forgetting she still held the saucer. *Drink tea.* It dug into her eyebrow. She felt the same sway over her body once again, a tug at her conscious-ness. *Fine ladies.* One that overrode her sense of who was friend and who was foe. *Fine ladies drink tea.* Isolde was the one with the knife. Was she not the danger here? *Fine, fine, fine.* And poor, innocent Merrin, who only wanted to wear pretty dresses and drink tea and – *eat people* – that last point stuck, had Kensa hesitate.

Isolde, on the other hand, wasted no time. She rolled up one sleeve and brought the bone-handled knife down onto her flesh. As soon as the asrai's first sour note filled the room, blood poured. Isolde's own, rich and dark. It streamed from her arm to lather on the rug, joining the puddle-water. Her mouth moved quickly against Merrin's wordless song.

One that had already begun to warp Kensa's thinking.

Eat, was the asrai's next instruction. *Lift porcelain shards from the sugar heap. Swallow them down. A sharp piece after a sharp piece. Then the silver spoons and the shattered glass. Take it, there's a girl, fine lady. Rip a smile in your belly. Tear a hole in your chest. A puncture is slower than poison.*

Kensa put the split saucer to her mouth. It was cool against her lips. She could taste sugar, blood, cold tea and a thread of carpet.

'I call on the Pact between Land and Sea, made when the last horse ran through the Mounts Bay forest and Lyonness lay above the waves,' intoned Isolde, as she bled freely.

Die, the asrai's last instruction.

Rain heaved even harder and the front door swung on its hinges. The wispy hairs on Mr Aldridge's head began to rise up, though he remained as dead as ever.

Instantly, the song faltered. Kensa dropped the cup shard and collapsed inward, elbows braced on her knees. The room smelled like burnt skin. And something else, perhaps, that was distinctly Isolde. Her act was no herbal remedy, no vervain to tonic a wound, no hawkweed to still soreness. This, here, was the Old Ways against the Old Ways.

'Ankevi dha davas ha ty a wra ankevi an pyth a'th kelm,' spat the wise woman, curling a hand over her arm and the wound she had made.

'Forget your tongue,' Kensa echoed, 'and you'll forget what ties you.'

Merrin grasped her neck with her green hands. Her throat was soundless and scratching. She swallowed with a dry click. Her face looked as gaunt as the curate's.

'Should ever I see you on this shoreline again, I will touch my blood to the sand and you will be banished,' said Isolde. 'Here be your only warning.'

With that curse on her heels, the asrai streamed into the rain with not a single look back. If anyone in Portscatho saw her seal-skin rush into the waves, none spoke on it. The Cornish had long ago learned not to look too long at sea-folk and their kin, lest they look back harder.

Chapter Fourteen

A Fair Hand

As soon as the wise woman and her apprentice recovered themselves, Isolde began her work. There was no time for Kensa's sobs, which were quickly stifled with a hard look. Porcelain crunched underfoot, the rug squelched and blood trailed from the wise woman's arm. She ripped a line from the dead curate's cassock and used it to bind her wound.

'Get yourself as clean as you can,' said Isolde. 'Borrow a coat from Mr Aldridge and hide the blood on your clothes, lest anyone see it.' Her thin cheeks puffed outwards as she exhaled. 'We have work to do, you and I.'

Kensa lifted her head slowly.

'Haven't you learned yet?' Isolde was grim-faced and serious. 'Healing is cleaning, more often than not.' It took a while and

Kensa was largely kept to the kitchen and garden, drawing water from the well nearby and heating it over the range. It was a kindness, she realised. A forced distance between herself and the two bodies her thoughts dwelled on. As she brought another bucket to the front room, the previous one soiled and to be chucked outside, Isolde began to speak. Fractured words, apologetic, then hesitant. 'If I had known she was as strong as this, I never would have sent you.'

Kensa's hair was wet and hung heavily across her features. 'You knew?'

'Aye, I knew what Merrin was and I wanted to teach you, to show you what it takes to be a wise woman,' continued Isolde, a dirty rag palmed from one hand to the other. 'I did not think she could do what she did; it does not bode well for the Pact.'

'I could have been—'

'I think it time you learned the Old Ways.'

Kensa's face bore the same blank shock as Mr Aldridge's. She turned from his deathly mask to meet her mentor's grim expression. 'Am I ready?'

'You will have to be.' Isolde's tunic was heavily stained with blood and sweat and spilled tea. She wrung its end into the dirty bucket. Spoke to it, rather than Kensa. 'Are you well enough to run to the mine? I need Branok and his son if we are to hide what has happened.'

Kensa's brows rose into her hair.

'Would you have the villagers know their curate's been murdered? No, we'd be strung up at Percuil River.' Kensa flinched at the thought and Isolde continued, 'It is our role to balance the work of Land and Sea. Should we falter, we'll lose far more than our livelihoods. Tell the men to bring their picks and shovels, for I wager we shall need to shift soil if we are to sleep in our own beds tonight.'

Kensa's hands trembled. She hid them in her pockets. Well, these were not *her* pockets specifically, because they belonged to Mr Aldridge's coat. Was it still his now he was dead? The wool smelled like him: plum wine and sweetmeats. Although she had not liked him much, Kensa's face crumpled at the thought. Her mind reeled. Her throat burned. When the wind reached where the asrai had touched her, her skin stung anew.

It took a whole hour to get to the mine. Kensa passed through that space and time as though flying. Shock, she supposed. Her mother told her it could kill little birds, but she was a young woman, not a bird, and so all she did was shake.

Porthbeor Mine was a gash in the cliff face, accessible only at low tide. Its tunnels were held up by stulls – wooden pillars – that seemed too thin ever to support the rock above it. Kensa lingered at the entrance, the sea behind her, licking at her boot soles. By now the rain had exhausted itself and fell in persistent, though light, spatters. It mattered little to her, as she was already soaked through and shivering. Miners were as superstitious as sailors and Kensa's presence was not a welcome one. It was not due to her sex, for many a woman worked below the ground. It was her craft which singled her out. Although wise women were often needed by the men and women at Porthbeor, to see one at the mine's mouth was a foreboding sight: it usually signalled the imminent death of a worker within.

'Branok?' Her voice was hoarse. Were it not for the shapes who moved near by, Kensa would have assumed she went unheard. 'Branok!'

A miner's uniform comprised thin layers, draped over one another. Feet bore hard shoes, including clogs. From outside, Kensa could hear regular wooden taps against rock, joined by songs that appeased whatever strangeness might be levered up with the copper. Branok wore the same as his workmen, though he had a higher status among them, as their overseer. Mining was a hard occupation and it hardened those who did it. He emerged squinting into the weak daylight and Kensa saw how much his son took after him. She could guess, then, which features Jack must have inherited from his long-late mother.

'You should not be here, Miss Rowe,' said Branok. 'Taking a charm into the mines is one thing, taking in the charmer is another.'

He had a low voice, as though enriched by the mineral veins he hunted for. Kensa had never spoken to him. She'd had no need. Besides, he cut an intimidating figure, taken seriously – and respected – by landowners and labourers alike. He talked sense, he spoke carefully and he never took part in gossip. It was hard to know what he thought or who he liked and it made Kensa unsure and uncertain around him.

'Isolde needs you,' she mumbled. 'She asked for Jack too, if he's here.' Kensa's lip caught on his name.

'Where else would he be?'

Jack was not happy to be summoned. He took his time, wading from the shadows – which seemed reluctant to leave him – and out into the day. For a man who reminded Kensa of summer's height, it was strange to think he was so frequently underground. After setting his lantern down, Jack clapped stone-dust off his shoulders and asked, 'Is it important?'

Father and son both raised their brows in a gesture so alike in its condescension, Kensa could have screamed. Instead, she took a measured breath.

'I wouldn't be here if—'

Jack reached forwards. 'What's this?' He pulled at her collar to reveal her bruised neck. With no looking glass, Kensa had not seen the mark the asrai had given her. Judging by Jack's expression, it did not look good. 'How did you get this?' His thumb was gentle on her chin, though his face hardened. 'Tell me, please.'

Kensa leaned into his hand. It would be easy, wouldn't it? To cry, rupture, let him hold her and find comfort. In the past she might have done, if only to be close to him. Not that she needed it. She didn't need anything. After this morning, her impulses seemed foolish and she a fool to have them.

'I will tell you when we leave,' she said, 'and we must leave now – your picks and shovels with us.'

Shielded from the dotting rain by Branok's hat, Kensa trudged back to the curate's abode with the overseer and his son behind her. She revealed little about what had taken place, her tongue stumbling whenever she touched on a memory that was too raw. She did not know how much the wise woman wished to reveal and kept her details vague, with mutters about an 'accident' and little else.

It's not my fault, she longed to tell them. *Isolde could have warned me! If she had, I would have known what to look for, I could have saved Mr Aldridge.*

Kensa clutched the hagstone tight in her fist. It calmed her. When at last they reached the cottage beside St Gerrans Church, it was grimly evident that Isolde had kept busy. The bodies of Mr Aldridge and Wenna lay side by side on the bare boards in the front room, shrouded in white sheets. There was a third, thin length beside them: the stained rug, too saturated to lie neatly. The crockery had been cleared away and its remains sat in a reed basket usually allocated for kindling. A large stain wounded the room's centre: blood. No scrubbing had erased it, though Isolde's reddened knuckles betrayed her attempts. It was those Jack reached for, scanning his aunt for injury and finally closing a hand around her forearm.

Branok rubbed at his chin. 'I see.'

Kensa would have expected disbelief or shock from the men, as – with not a word wasted – Isolde relayed what had taken place. Instead, the two seemed thoughtful and their questions thoughtful too. Although this was not a regular occurrence, it seemed incidents such as these were not entirely unknown.

'I take this to be the Bucka's doing?' Branok spoke with such ferocity that it betrayed an eerie familiarity with the Father of Storms. 'If he has—'

'No, his acts are far subtler,' said Isolde plainly. 'Few can easily cross the sea's threshold without his permission and he would not grant it to her.'

'And you?' Branok asked. 'It is the Bucka who controls the Sea, whereas your place is the Land. Are you capable of defending it, Isolde?'

The wise woman raised herself to her full height and angled her bony shoulders back. 'Don't forget who raised you, boy.'

'That was fifty years ago and you were haggard *then*,' said Branok. 'I am ignorant to the Old Ways and their uses, and I don't know how they change a person, but you have to admit you've slowed?'

Isolde chewed on her tongue and would not meet his eye or anyone else's. 'Yes, the Pact is weakening, because I am weakening. I can feel its tethers loosening from me, leaving gaps for creatures like the asrai to exploit.'

Loosening? The apprentice wished to ask, to pry and learn, and yet, this was not the time. Besides, she was loath to seem foolish, especially in front of—

'Will this creature return?' Jack interrupted. 'That's all I want to know.'

'Not for a long while and not like this,' said Isolde, groaning as she sank down onto the settee in exactly the spot where Mr Aldridge had sat. 'Despite her reckless behaviour, she fears the Bucka and I believe she fears me.'

Branok nodded. 'Well, the curate will need to be buried in the church grounds, as is Godly, the same for Wenna.'

'It's too big a risk and we'll be seen,' said Jack. 'Plus, the warden digs each grave, he would spot a new one.'

The soil would be sodden, too, and heavier for it.

Kensa wrapped her arms around herself as she stared at the two bodies. 'Then what do we do with them?' She had no urge to sing. A violent death did not require melody, it needed action or vengeance or justice. 'Are we going to kill Merrin?'

'We're still in the church grounds here,' said Isolde, not deeming her question worth a reply. 'Why not hide them in the garden, below the hives? No one will disturb the bees.' What's more, the hives were vacant, their occupants taking up space at the cottage in Bohortha. Kensa had never thought bees to be clever, yet they'd known enough to flee Merrin's unnatural presence – or, at least, sought the closest help where it could be found.

It was done at nightfall. Both the mine overseer and his son were used to working in darkness and were left to churn the earth to the right depth for a grave. Meanwhile, the wise woman and her apprentice devised a plan to cover the curate's absence. Wenna had no family and had been a widow since her late husband's loss. Mr Aldridge had never married and his only relation was a brother, mentioned in his sermons and never in a good light. There had always been rumours about him and his housemaid, which was what Isolde preyed on.

When the men returned inside, treading filth onto the newly cleaned floor, she explained their plan. 'We'll leave a letter for Sir George Trevanion and he'll inform the main church in Falmouth that the pair have absconded. Now, my scrawl is too recognisable, for it marks every tonic and salve from here to Portloe. We shall need another to write it. What's your handwriting like, Kensa?'

'I can't do the joined-up letters, but—'

'That won't do.'

'Who could we trust to help us?' Branok's clothes were stiff with mud and his fingers were clasped around the last unbroken teacup, though it held only water. 'A scholar with fair penmanship? That will mean a trip to St Mawes and Mr Aldridge's absence will be discovered by morning.'

Jack cleared his throat and swung his head slowly in Kensa's direction. 'There is one who comes to mind, one who could help us.'

'No,' barked Kensa.

'Elowen is the best student Miss Latham has ever had,' continued Jack. 'She's good at her letters and young enough to not have her hand recognised, not by the magistrate or his serving folk, either.'

'Who says we can trust her?' A long pause greeted Kensa's question. 'What if she tells people?' It was a weak defence. 'There has to be someone else – anyone else.' Again, no reply came, only a lengthy silence exchanged between the three who stared her down. 'You don't know her, she's not – I mean, she is, only— Ah, fine!'

The hour was late in Portscatho. Kensa brought no lantern with her to her mother's front door. It was safest to go without light, to avoid stares or enquiry. And she knew the way. Everyone in the village slept, bar the occasional cat who flashed its watchfulness in Kensa's direction. Her clothes stank, sour with lime and bodily fluids not her own. Worse, she was nervous. Truthfully, Elowen was a good choice. And yet to go to her now sat ill in Kensa's chest. As though, by asking for her sister's help, she was losing her own place in the community, handing it over to the younger girl who – by rights – should have it anyway. What's more, pulling Elowen from her warm bed and into this dangerous situation knotted her stomach, even if the worst threat was gone. She was fragile, after all. Would learning about such a creature as Merrin affect her health? Perhaps it would spark further nightmares . . .

Kensa's rap on the door was a quiet one. She half-hoped no

one would answer it. Elowen did. Her nightdress was short on her frame and a ribbon held her long plait in place. When she spoke, her voice was rumpled from sleep. 'Are you here for the Coast Guard?'

'I need your help.'

Elowen froze, momentarily, then stepped out onto the street and gingerly closed the door behind her. There was a shrewd fit to her face. 'Pardon?'

'You heard me.' Kensa wanted to turn around. Throw a snappish retort over her shoulder. Thunder all the way back to the curate's house. Only, that would mean returning to Isolde's frustration and Branok's impatience and Jack's disappointment. It was the last one which stuck, which bid her to say, 'Grab your coat and I'll explain on the way.'

Elowen did not budge from the front step. 'Why should I trust you?'

'Because I'm your sister,' Kensa said, the same excuse as at the May Day festival. It hadn't worked then, why would it work now?

'You are when it's convenient.'

A grumbled call came from within their mother's cottage.

'It's nothing, Pa,' replied Elowen, though she took a long second to do so. 'Only the baker's dog out again, I'll fetch it home.'

Mr Skewes's reply was a low snore.

Elowen dipped inside briefly, then returned wearing her boots, a warm shawl and a guarded expression. 'Should I bring anything with me?'

'We only need your hands,' replied Kensa.

Elowen's step faltered.

'Don't worry, you'll get 'em back after we're done.'

As the pair climbed through Portscatho, the first stirrings began. One or two hull-scrapes over stone. Slaps of rope and basket. Tallow candles or rush lights flaring in the harbour-side houses. Soon, the fishermen would row to meet the dawn and the shoals it brought. Even high on the hill, the pair could hear the sea's heavy rolling.

Kensa expected her sister to ask questions and demand to know what was happening. Elowen said nothing. Grew smaller. Stepped carefully. Spoke only when they reached the curate's cottage and stopped outside its door.

'This is about Mr Aldridge,' Elowen said hurriedly. 'Am I in trouble?'

'No,' said Kensa, confused.

Elowen's fingers toyed with a loose thread on her shawl as she was taken inside, to the day room, where Isolde and the miners waited. As soon as she entered the space, Elowen's eyes landed on the empty boards at her feet where the rug had been. There she saw the bloodstain.

Her head whipped round to meet Kensa's. 'What's going on?'

Jack was gentle in his words and wording. 'It seems Mr Aldridge has decided to—'

'He's dead,' interrupted Isolde.

Before any other explanation could be offered, Elowen asked, 'Was it Merrin?'

Kensa began to cough, spit catching in her injured windpipe. Both miners had matching frowns on their faces. Isolde, however, remained impassive. 'Yes.'

'What! No,' blurted Kensa. 'How'd you know? Are you—'

'Mr Aldridge asked me to teach his new *companion* manners and trusted me to keep it secret from everyone,' said Elowen. 'I showed Merrin how to conduct herself, what to talk about in polite society and how to dress herself and powder her face.' A glance down to the bloodied floor. 'When we were alone, Merrin told me what she was, though I do not think she told Mr Aldridge. Or, if she did, he was too besotted to care.'

There was no shift in Isolde's tone. 'Did you keep this affair secret?'

'Yes, until now,' said Elowen.

Kensa pulled on her sister's arm. 'You should have told me.'

'Would you have listened?'

'Yes!'

Elowen's forehead wrinkled as she studied her sibling's face. 'Who says it's your business to know what I do? Merrin understands me; we're more alike than you or I—'

'I think that's enough,' said Isolde hastily.

Elowen drew away, pulling her arm from Kensa's hold, careful not to stand on the stained wood. 'May I go now?'

'Not quite yet,' said Branok.

Quickly, the overseer explained what must be done and how, gesturing to the writing desk in one corner, where ink, paper and quill sat beside a stubby candle. Of course, it would be necessary to remove Mr Aldridge's treasured possessions to make it seem as though he had taken flight. Jack offered to hide them in a forgotten shaft at Porthbeor Mine.

'If you want my help, I will give it,' said Elowen, 'for whatever part I played in Mr Aldridge's passing, even if he was a fool.'

Kensa shook her head. 'I thought you liked Mr Aldridge?'

Elowen shrugged with one shoulder, a mannerism Kensa recognised in herself. 'Everyone assumes I like everyone.'

The fair-haired girl worked quickly, taking a pen in hand and practising her script on a blank parchment page. 'Mr Aldridge had me transcribe letters for him on occasion and he wrote exactly as he preached.'

'You mean boring and self-important?'

'Kensa,' chided Jack.

'No, she's right,' said Elowen.

It took several attempts, as the sun began to show herself – spearing onto the desk where the younger woman worked and turning her hair sun-white, almost Bucka-ish – until the five settled on a letter that suited their proposed lies. It was likely that the warden, Ephraim, would be the one to find it, set on a low table in the hall. A new rug was brought down from an upstairs room in order to hide the floorboards, then Branok fed Mr Aldridge's sermons to the fire, those ones he had yet to preach and now, sadly, never would.

Elowen pressed her wrist to her mouth and released a sob. Kensa wondered if her grief was for the deceased curate or the waste of fine-quality paper. As the sky brightened enough to see by, Kensa noticed how thin she was. Here, for the first time, her sister had made a mistake. The guilt Kensa had felt over Mr Aldridge's demise was suddenly heaped on Elowen's shoulders. She thought she'd feel better about it.

'We have done what we can,' said Isolde.

Once the group departed, the door was shut on Mr Aldridge's cottage. Their goodbyes were stilted, with Jack lingering only a second longer than his father, keen to sleep for an hour or two prior to his next shift starting.

Jack's hands smelled like earth.

Jack's hands had buried Mr Aldridge.

Yet this knowledge did not seem to be a burden to him. In fact, he seemed to take it all in his stride. Kensa found herself staring at his sleeves and the grit collected there.

At his cleared throat, she lifted her eyes, yet Kensa was the one to speak. 'This isn't the first time you've helped Isolde clear up a mess, is it?'

'It's never usually as bad as this, though it isn't unusual.' He looked as though he wanted to say more and eventually settled on, 'You remember the Morgawr.'

'Yes,' she said, frowning.

Jack held the tail to her coat, to Mr Aldridge's coat, fixing his stare on that and not on her, rubbing at the felt. 'I couldn't stop looking at you on that beach, I kept wanting to pull you away from it, it was so big and you were so small.'

'You were small then, too.'

'I suppose,' he admitted.

It seemed a sad comfort to know he'd seen her, that when she'd thought herself invisible to all, ill-placed and unwanted, he'd seen her and cared.

'Kensa . . .' he began, trailed off.

She did not know what to say either. They had always been good at starting things, fights, mainly. It was the *continuing* and the *what came after* that stumped them both. Because that seemed riskier, like something they couldn't come back from.

His grip tightened and it pulled her a fraction closer.

'Kensa ...' he said again, and she liked her name in his mouth, how it sounded, with a rasp and wanting he'd never state.

'Jack,' she replied, quiet and soft, both like and unlike herself.

'Be careful,' he said at last, releasing her, making their exchange sound like a chastisement, the way he made everything sound.

'I am,' sniffed Kensa, though he was already gone. And sometimes she wondered if she was too careful when it came to him, and she wondered why he was too careful with her, too.

Lingering in the cottage doorway was Elowen. There was a strange set to her expression: resolved and hardened. Her shawl sat lopsidedly on her shoulders. By now, it was half unravelled with how often she pulled on that loose thread. Kensa's satisfaction was a smug toad in her gullet. Finally, Elowen was in trouble for a change. And yet, she noticed a sallowness to her sister's skin enough to rival the dawn sky.

Kensa's question was quiet enough, one she had often uttered: 'Are you well?'

Elowen raised her eyes and did not reply, though she had most certainly heard.

'Go, I will see you at the cottage,' called Isolde to her apprentice. 'I must speak with your sister privately.'

For once, Kensa did not argue. She affixed the dead curate's coat tightly around her soiled clothes, turned her back on Elowen and returned to Bohortha alone.

Chapter Fifteen

The Old Ways

Percuil River was a place Kensa usually avoided. Her father had been hanged over its waters, where the rocky ledges and outcrops leaned against the nearby village of St Mawes. She could not see the scaffold from here, the river's bends too numerous, but she held it in her mind's eye – or it held her. Kensa heaved a coracle onto the bank next to the wise woman's own vessel. Despite its resemblance to an upturned walnut shell, the one-person boat had been sturdy enough to transport her along the tidal channel and to the narrow tributary of Polingey Creek. Apprehension, or the past hour on water, had weakened her legs.

A long two weeks had followed Mr Aldridge's absence. As always, Old Sal was at the forefront of local gossip, claiming she had suspected such an elopement would happen between the curate and his housemaid. No one spoke on murder. As local magistrate, Sir George Trevanion had called the village to a meeting and promised a new curate had been sent for, to replace the missing Mr Aldridge. This was news Kensa heard second-hand, delivered by the visitors to the cottage on Wednesdays, their ailments brought along with them.

The wet bank where Kensa found herself was thick with dry seaweed, empty shells and tangled roots. Ahead were tangled vines and waist-high ferns. No path to recommend itself. She squinted into the thick undergrowth with a sense that something, somewhere, squinted back.

'Come this way, child.' Isolde's grey head dipped into the greenery. 'Remember, crush no shoot and bend no branch.'

'Why don't I fly while I'm at it?'

Kensa was not as light-footed as her teacher. As she crunched forwards, a heron started, its breakfast – a half-eaten frog – dangling from its beak. The bird left in an offence of wings and the apprentice pressed on, freckled arms raised to shield her face. Insects bounced in her ears while salted mud pulled on her boots; a remnant of the spring high tides.

At first, the trees were small and stunted, changing as she walked. Moss replaced the cloying soil underfoot and squelched her progress back to her. Ahead came a brown flash as a rabbit's ears cupped her tracks, then folded below ground. Kensa contorted her body to pass through the tightly packed copse, branches raking her hair and marking her wrists, until at last she came to a small clearing, alive with silver birch.

Dizzy, she sat and blinked through the light which seemed

to taste different to what she had passed through. Tangy, akin to wood sorrel or apple skin. Not unlike the Bucka's scent. It unsettled her to realise she knew what he smelled like.

Kensa pressed her palm to the point between her brows. 'What is this place?'

'A bridge to the Old Ways,' said Isolde, appearing beside her, manic and be-twigged. Her bony hand clutched Kensa's plumper palm. 'There are few wild places left in Kernow,' she said, using the old name for Cornwall, 'those not touched by a man's plough or spade or round.' Her lips peeled back to show uneven, murky teeth. 'That is where we are, that is this place, Kensa Rowe.'

'It's a bog.'

'An *untouched* bog.' Isolde flung her skinny arms out. 'This was the last stronghold of the Folk and it is here the Old Ways can be found.'

Kensa squared her shoulders and took a mossy seat. No one in the West Country was ignorant of the tales of fairies, pisk-ies and sidhe: cruel beings whose rules were unknowable and beauty unfathomable.

'Once, power ran unchecked and its people ran with it,' con-tinued Isolde. 'Over time, the Folk emerged alongside man, the Old Ways deep-set in their blood. Conflict was commonplace, islands were made and unmade on a whim, miracles ascribed to strange new gods or half-forgotten ones. It was chaos, until the first wise woman of Portscatho bound herself to the Land and trapped another in the Sea, with the Old Ways anchored between them in a Pact. Finally, the wild power which surged through the earth was brought into balance, as were the Folk.'

'What happened to them?'

'As man ravaged the earth further, the Old Ways dwindled from it and most fled to the sea or died.'

Kensa thought on the creatures she had encountered or heard about. Sickly, salt-shaped and sly. 'What happens if the Pact breaks?'

'There is worse than Merrin under the Bucka's heel; a whole sea and its vengeance could well make claim to what we have made ours, and I would not blame them. Before the Pact, anyone with enough power could do terrible things. Now, one cannot use the Old Ways without giving something of themselves in return.'

'If I wanted to mend a cut?'

'You'd tear your own skin in the process.'

Kensa closed her fists, uncomfortable at the thought. 'Then what are the Old Ways good for?'

'Not much,' admitted Isolde, leaning back on a tree trunk, 'but a coven together can manage more than a single witch alone. Besides, it does extend our lifespan somewhat, which has its own challenges. I've lived longer than a century and a half and I have learned that everything must remain in check. For that reason, no wise woman who holds the Pact can take a life, for she has given one, forever, to the Bucka. To do so would be to rupture that bind.' The wise woman leaned forwards, cupping her hands around Kensa's ears, heightening the noises around her. 'What can you hear?'

'I don't know.'

'You will.'

Kensa shook her mentor's grip from her head. She could

not deny there was a nice quality to their surroundings. A peacefulness without livestock's lowing or a cart horse's hasty clop over road. No net-slap against the harbour wall or gasping scythe through stalk. Quiet, without civilisation, only bird chatter and bug scatter. The way the world was meant to be: manless and emerald.

Her foot was going numb. One sleeve was damp from where it had trailed in the river. Her own hair tickled her mouth when it escaped the leather tie she had bound it with. There was no hidden force seeking entry into her mind. Only her own blood in her ears. She tried harder, although she did not know what she was meant to try.

Beneath her, the soil moved and wriggled. A hundred insect lives carried themselves around her. It was there she began, considering the land and her imagination supplied –

Her father, rotting in an unmarked grave. His corpse, its eaten decay, carried in invertebrate stomachs, crawling around her. The last words he spoke to her: *You will always be my little girl, Kenny.* She heard him, from the millipede and the worm and the woodlouse, she heard him. *No one can take my place, do you understand?*

'I think I get it,' she lied, swallowing around a tightness in her throat.

Isolde's fingers came to rest on Kensa's chest, in the space above her heart. 'Each of us has a wildness inside us, one unbent by man's will,' she said. 'It is that spirit I saw on the Towan, it is why I sought you out.'

Kensa's hope caught against her teeth. 'Then the Morgawr had nothing to do with it?'

'She brought you to the beach, did she not?'

'Not only me.'

'Elowen has her own concerns,' scoffed Isolde. 'Don't you mind that. Listen, hear it? Isn't it—'

'I already told you,' came Kensa's waspish reply, 'I can hear it.'

She braced her hands on her knees and pushed onto her feet, a ridiculous prickle at her eyelids. A thousand explanations jumped into her skull, telling her she was wrong and the Old Ways knew it, that she was bad and everyone suspected as much. She was her father's daughter, she was his and nothing else – would never be anything else.

There was no impatience in Isolde's demeanour. She took Kensa's mood in her stride, limbs spread easily under a bracket mushroom as wide as a shelf. 'Why do you want to be a wise woman?'

'I was chosen to be,' said Kensa automatically.

'That's not what I asked. Do you know why I wanted to be a wise woman? I wanted to be listened to and admired. I desired status and control – and to control others. Of course, I soon learned you end up responsible for them, fond of them, even.' Isolde sighed. 'You don't need to be the best wise woman Portscatho has ever had, you don't even need to be that good, you only have to try.'

'I am trying,' said Kensa defensively.

'That's all I would ask. Once you have tapped into the Old Ways, you may call them to help with small favours, provided they are known to nature.' It was here that Isolde paused, waiting until Kensa's face tilted towards her own. 'The greater the ask, the larger the sacrifice needed.' She held up her arm to show the long, deep cut she had etched into her flesh to stop the asrai's voice. Its scar was pink and puckered, marking her for ever. 'That moment in Mr Aldridge's front room, I cut myself and bound Merrin's throat, briefly, for long enough to give us the upper hand.' A smile, then. 'Consider our friend Young Robert,' said Isolde. 'If I wished to help him regrow his leg, I'd have to hack off my own and bind it using the Old Ways. Even then, it would not be enough and I would not survive the process. I'd be dead and no use to anyone in Portscatho.'

'I s'pose if anyone knew it was possible, a few might try to convince you to trade your health with theirs?'

Isolde's expression shifted and became darker. 'Yes, may the Pact protect us.'

For the next hour, Kensa was bid to listen for the Old Ways. Her father's voice returned, with gruelling visions: his wide-knuckled hands, their clawing progress. Each time, she convinced herself it did not mean anything – it was her own thoughts troubling themselves – until bile rose up her throat and she emptied her stomach onto her shoes.

'I think that's enough for today,' said Isolde slowly.

And yet, the wise woman took Kensa back to the clearing the next day and the next, had her sit and strain her ears and listen with her centre, whatever that meant. Perhaps this place, too, had been tampered with? Or, alternatively, Kensa was unable to hear what she was not permitted to hear. Nothing reached over Alexander Rowe's entreaties, demands and promises.

She remembered the night he was taken. He'd come in late, roaring about betrayal and how the woods around Trewense were crawling with militia. The hand not carrying a blade had come to rip Kensa from her cot-bed in the kitchen. Derwa got there first. She'd been faster, as though she'd been waiting, as though she'd known.

'Get yourself here, woman; we have to leave,' snarled Alex.

Derwa recoiled from him. 'I knew this would happen, I warned you—'

In the following argument, the patrol came: a newly appointed Coast Guard with utmost authority on the shore. Kensa blamed her mother. If she'd done what she'd been told, the three would be together now. And yet, had that been the case, she wouldn't have a sister.

If she had to choose, well, there was no one like a father to a little girl.

A pistol fired outside, a window shattered.

Alex shouted behind him, 'I have a wife and child in here.' His eyes – the same eyes Kensa bore – sparked with a thought. He went towards Kensa, extending a hand to her.

Derwa snatched her back, keeping them apart. 'Oh, don't you dare.'

There were boots on the lane, heavy and numerous. Mr Skewes was heard pleading with someone well above his rank. 'Please, hold your fire, hold!'

It was hard to remember what happened next. Her mother accidentally knocked the kitchen table over, blocking the back way out. Then she'd grabbed a chopping knife for protection, though she'd kept it levelled on her husband and not on the men who came for him, barging down the front door to the cob-walled cottage and wrestling Alex to the floor.

Kensa had cried and struggled against her mother's arms. 'Da!'

'I'll come back for you, Kenny,' he'd promised. He'd always been filled with promises.

Cruel memories hounded her. Whenever she reached for the Old Ways, she found her past instead, shown to her for a reason she could not fathom.

On the morning he died, in the moments afterwards, she could have sworn his hand had moved. When she had reached for the hagstone, his fingers twitched ever so slightly. As though he would have given it to her, if he could. And when she turned around, it was into Sir George Trevanion's face she looked. The baronet – younger then – had stared at her with a hard expression, his eyes a flat, cool brown. Being young, she had not considered that others knew what she did not. That secrets could be strung from one mouth to the next, and many were strung between him and her father.

Kenny, her father called her. She would've done anything, given anything, to hear his voice again. When he was there, she'd been wanted. Her hagstone was a reminder of that: once, she had been precious to someone.

Eventually, she convinced Isolde to let her visit the clearing at Polingey Creek by herself. Of course, she did not. When she set off in the coracle, she diverted. It was easy to lie, it was in her nature. One that took Kensa to the bend in the river, where she beached her craft and curled up on a dry rock, to stare out at the place her father died. It was a sea-swept curve in the lane to St Mawes, a meeting place for traders and travellers where a scaffold could be set: a warning to those who'd flout the King's law, which Alexander Rowe certainly had.

What did he want? Did the dead want anything? Was it even him or was it her own doubts gnawing at her or the Old Ways acting up? Besides, she had nothing to give.

By this time, Mr Aldridge's replacement had been found. None knew his face and no one had seen him, though the curate's cottage showed lamplight in the evenings and once, when Kensa caught sight of it, she felt anxiety claw at her stomach. Feared this stranger would know, somehow, what she had done.

It was on such a morning, with thoughts as anxious as these, that she returned to the wise woman's cottage and found a lanky man making his own fast pace to Bohortha. He was an individual – familiar and unwelcome – who had never once set foot in Isolde's nettled domain.

Kensa's mouth grew slack and dry. 'Mr Skewes?'

Chapter Sixteen

Oh, Sweet One, Come Homeward

'It came on quick,' the Coast Guard blathered, 'I do not know the cause.' As he paced before the porch, the ends of his long brown coat, once smart and now fraying, twisted on the wind. 'You will come now,' he said with a jabbed finger. 'You will heal my daughter.' It was an order, yet his red-rimmed eyes were desperate and his tone pleading.

Kensa stood, numb. Elowen sick? Her heart tightened. It was not as though her sister's illness was a new occurrence. Mr Skewes was here. He never would have stepped a single foot in their direction if he could help it, not unless it was urgent.

From behind her came Isolde's voice. 'I shall fetch my cloak.' Hers was a heavy presence at the cottage doorway, offset by the hens at her ankles. An urge to hide with them, to chick under their wings, almost moved Kensa's feet backwards.

Mr Skewes looked directly at her. Since she was a little girl and he had first begun to court her mother, the Coast Guard had never met Kensa's eye. He avoided it, glancing over her shoulder or to a mid-point, if ever he need address her. Now, his irises were fixed to hers and she knew she could say anything, demand anything, and he would obey if it helped his dear Elowen. It was power, of a kind. There was temptation in it.

Leave my mother and I will heal your daughter, was Kensa's first thought.

She dared not speak it. Instead, she fetched her satchel.

Kensa turned her collar against the cold morning. Her boots flayed mud from the path, growing heavy with it. Isolde was unreadable, as she often was in such situations. Occasionally, she checked an onion in her pocket, though each time it looked no different. Always was it dark and rooted and weeping.

Kensa cleared her throat. 'What does it say?'

Isolde's mouth tightened in reply.

Elowen. Elowen. Elowen.

Mr Skewes half-walked, half-ran ahead, halting often (and impatiently) as though his cricket-hop steps and shaking fists could propel them to move faster.

Isolde would not be rushed. 'I am no use to no one if I am too fatigued to offer assistance upon reaching them.'

Portscatho came into view soon enough, first with a church spire and second with the cob-walled houses squashed together along the lanes. Kensa was reluctant to enter her mother's house, fearing what she would find. The front door was ajar and Derwa soon appeared at its frame. She looked tired.

'Oh,' she said, the softest 'oh', and pulled Kensa to her chest. It was serious, then.

Elowen lay on her pallet. Her pale hair was matted with sweat and bunched at her ears. As for her eyes, they were sunken in their sockets, above a red rash that marked her cheeks. She barely stirred when Derwa sank beside her, to place a hand on her forehead.

'It's the same fever that's been running through Truro,' said Derwa. 'I thought she was doing well and through it, back on her feet again, until she wasn't.'

Kensa thought on that night in Mr Aldridge's cottage, to the perspiration on Elowen's face and her trembling which came and went. Had she been sick even then?

'Let's have a look,' said Isolde, stretching her mouth into a non-smile. This was her kindly face, the no-nonsense and reassuring one she always started with, which would either soften to sadness or brighten in gladness.

Please be the last one . . .

Kensa stood awkwardly to the side. Mr Skewes paced. In fact, he only ever stopped pacing to look to his daughter, though he never seemed to like what he saw. Not for the first time, Kensa viewed herself as an intruder in this home. Her breath came hard, as though her lungs had fused to her other organs and, when she inhaled, the expansion pressed and pulled on places it should not press and pull against.

Kensa did not feel like a healer here. Usually, she was at Isolde's elbow. There, she watched and made her own guesses based on what she had learned. Now, she hovered, unable to clear her mind, and stared unrelentingly at Elowen's face.

Kensa cleared her throat when the silence had gone on too long to be bearable. 'Is she all right, then, Isolde?'

The old woman's fingers tarried at Elowen's wrist. 'Has she been sleeping long?'

Derwa shook her head. 'She had a chill and shivered as I've never seen, then caught a fever I could not cool. After, she complained her chest was sore and then could hardly stay awake till she grew faint.'

'Why did you not call on my services sooner?'

Derwa looked to Mr Skewes, her silence accusation enough. The Coast Guard only swore under his breath and uttered nothing else.

'We shall know in the next day how she fares,' said Isolde. 'If she can get through tonight, she will mend well enough.'

'Get through tonight?' Mr Skewes said it once, slow, then again, quick. 'No, you'll help her now! You'll do your potions or your chanting, everything you bitches do, you'll do it.'

Isolde brushed off her skirts, nails finding a mark only she could see. 'The illness must run its course; there is nought anyone can do bar keep her comfortable.'

Mr Skewes stared at Isolde blankly.

Dust motes were the only motion in the room, alongside Elowen's fitful, uneven rasps.

No one spoke, until Kensa did. 'I don't catch your meaning.' Over by the small hearth, Derwa's back heaved with sobs, though she made no sound. 'Do you mean she might die?'

Isolde rose slowly to her feet.

Kensa blinked. 'Wait, I don't— What should I do?'

'You will set up a cot beside her.'

'Until she's on her feet again, yes?'

A long sigh followed, yet no reassurances came.

'I shall be back shortly.' Isolde readied herself. There was a forced and controlled tone to her voice. 'If we are to stay here tonight, I must see to those now who I'd planned to see later.'

Kensa barely heard a word. The door shut behind the old woman and the cob walls closed in on the apprentice, as her mother and Mr Skewes both looked to her. For answers, for action, for hope. What could she offer? Nothing, only a hand to help. Kensa began by boiling hot water, fetching spare linen from her mother's blanket box and keeping her sister clean. All that could be done, Kensa did. Made broth, ignored grumbles from Mr Skewes, reassured her mother, swept the house and kept busy in body to quiet her mind.

'You must eat, Kensa,' said Derwa, herself weak with the care she had given. Occasionally, her mother slept, although it was a fitful sleep and yielded no strength.

'I will eat,' said Kensa, 'I am eating,' though not a spoonful passed her lips.

The day ran its length and ran it long. Evening fell outside and pushed its slim lights through the kitchen's small window. It was then that Isolde returned. She had a basket tucked under her arm laden with loaves, preserves and a wrapped and roasted pheasant.

'Portscatho sends what help it can,' she explained.

Mr Skewes curled his lip in disapproval at the last bundle.

Game birds were Sir George Trevanion's property and meant for his table, guarded by poacher's traps which could take a man's leg clean off, though none in the cottage refused a bite. Well, none aside from Elowen.

'Has she stirred while I've been gone?'

Kensa shook her head, almost to the ground with how heavy it was.

Isolde thinned her mouth even further. 'Sleep now,' she said to Kensa. 'I will need you rested for what's to come.'

Kensa would normally have objected, although these were not normal times. Mr Skewes jerked his chin upwards, to where the main bed lay in the rafters. Her steps were heavy on the ladder and she almost missed the last one. The straw-tick mattress smelled of the Coast Guard and her mother. Kensa's nose twitched. Yet, no sooner did she lie flat than sleep took her and took her soundly. She heard nothing and dreamed on nothing. Only eternity and its unpricked stars, blank in a blank sky. Kensa woke hours later to a liver-spotted hand on her shoulder.

'Your mother should rest herself,' said Isolde. 'Watch over your sister, would you?'

It was dark, the heavy dark of early hours.

Kensa nodded and blearily knuckled herself awake. Beside Elowen's pallet, Derwa was already asleep. Her upper body lay against the bed's end and her hand – outstretched – was limp and curled, having once held Elowen's. Isolde kept to a chair by the low hearth, while Mr Skewes had bunched himself at the window, his slumber a growling, contorted one that stank of brandy.

After changing Elowen's soiled sheets and gently cleaning her slim form, Kensa's eyes found no fixed place. She gazed out to nothing while the fire worried the grate at her feet. In her daze, she almost missed her name, whispered and small.

'Kensa?' Elowen's speech was near inaudible.

'M'here,' said Kensa, pushing a small cup to Elowen and bidding her to drink from it.

She did, slowly and a little, though not enough.

There was a translucency to Elowen's features, where blue veins had pushed up against her skin, making patterns like cold faces on a glass window. 'I meant to – I meant to tell you.'

'You rest now,' ordered Kensa. 'Guard your strength.' She busied herself. Checked the blankets and pulled them straight, convinced herself nothing bad could happen if she smoothed out each wrinkle, as there would be nowhere for the bad to hide.

'I'm sorry I lied to you – about what I'd been doing, where I'd been doing it.'

Kensa stilled her movements.

Whenever Elowen inhaled, it was with a rattle. A distinctive sound, like a body filled with broken pottery for wet air to whistle through. Kensa had spent enough time around death lately to recognise it here, in this room.

'Don't,' said Kensa. She was dizzy with the notion, with the realisation that Elowen was failing. She brushed her sister's pale hair back from her paler face, ran a warm cloth over her skin, kissed her, quickly, on the temple.

'I should have told you,' said Elowen, lids heavy.

'Hush,' said Kensa, mouth clumsy.

The sheets were wet. It wasn't Elowen's doing. Kensa did not know when she had started crying. Her cheeks were sore, indifferent to the salt tracks running down them.

'It was my fault, not yours,' said Kensa. 'If I'd have been better, you'd have been able to talk to me about this, about everything.' No, it would be fine. She had decided. 'You'll get well and come visit me,' continued Kensa. 'You can meet the chickens and there's a fox and on Sundays we make currant buns.' She told Elowen she loved her. There was no reply. She said it again. Kensa held the girl's hand harder. It did not hold hers back. Slowly, the fire lost what heat it had given. Kensa's whole body slumped, as though a weight had pushed her spine down and she could not push against it.

'Elowen,' said Kensa, hiccupping. 'Elowen.'

Had her breathing stopped? No, it was faint, growing fainter. Kensa must have spoken or shouted or shrieked in those moments, for her ears rang afterwards. She could not recall it now and would not later. Whatever was said, it woke the other occupants within the house and Kensa was bid to drop her sister's hand. She rose on stiff legs and stepped back. Mr Skewes collapsed on his knees beside his daughter and mumbled inaudible words. Derwa was quiet, stoic, smiling for ever at her little girl, stroking her forehead and humming, singing under her breath. Isolde kept to her chair and turned away, as though to escape the room's tragedy.

Then this was what it was like? Those days administering to others, easing them into grief as a babe into a washbasin. Here was Kensa's turn. She did not want it. In those fractured moments – no time at all and endless time, when mourning begins to gather itself as a cloak upon its wearers – Elowen's eyes stayed fixed on Kensa's, until they closed.

'No.' Kensa repeated the word until it was shapeless in her mouth. She meant it. 'No.' This would not happen. 'No.' Because she knew a way to stop it. The apprentice spun her body round to where the wise woman sat on a narrow chair. Anger, such as she had never known, had her snatch at her mentor's clothes. Behind her, Derwa and Mr Skewes continued their gentle talk, soothing Elowen though she was too far gone to hear it.

Kensa spoke low enough to avoid their ears. 'You can save her.'

Isolde's jaw was set and firm.

'There has to be a way.' Kensa was hoarse, as though her voice had been pulled from its box, boiled and burned, then tipped back into her throat.

'I can do nought.'

'That's a lie, it has to be a lie.'

'This is a mortal sickness and Elowen, being what she is, is affected differently.'

Kensa squeezed her fingers around the older woman's hood. 'What does that mean?'

'You need not rush back to Bohortha.' Isolde eased onto her legs and readied herself to go. 'Take what time is needed—'

'No!' She quietened her voice at Mr Skewes's hiss and repeated, 'No, please, help me, fix her. There has to be . . . ' Kensa trailed off, swiping a hand at her face. It came away hot and wet. 'I will do anything, I cannot lose her or I will lose myself.'

Isolde's hand was in her pocket, clenched around that

blackened onion. Was it Elowen's future foretold in its shrunken skins? It couldn't be. Kensa's mind reeled. She thought back to the Bad Books on the yew shelf and the dire warnings held within them. At the pages which had eased open, wanting to be seen, as if they had known she would one day need them.

'I've read about it, I've read about ways to cheat death,' said Kensa. 'It can be done, don't you dare tell me it can't be done.'

'There will be a cost.'

'Then I will pay it!'

'And what about balance? One cannot give a life without taking—'

A sharp knock rattled the door. Their heads turned, aghast at the pervasive sound. Kensa was already on her feet. She lurched round, strode to the small entrance and yanked the door open. Morning had already come and gone without her notice and it had brought a man. He stood on the threshold, dressed in black. Tall, he was, taller than Kensa. Wiry, too, with a wide-brimmed hat and the King James Bible in his hands.

Set between his high cheekbones was an expression of re-hearsed sympathy. 'I—'

'You're the new curate,' said Kensa dully. 'Why are *you* here?'

He took in a long breath. Spoke carefully and with a churchly intonation. 'I came to offer my services at this truly sad and—'

BANG.

Kensa slammed the door and turned back to the room. It was that or strangle him, this stranger, the replacement clergyman who had seen fit to believe local talk and take Elowen into the next life.

'It's all right,' said Derwa, though it was not and could never be. 'It's all right.' Only then did Kensa understand that within those unassuming words was a request:

Come say goodbye. Oh, sweet one, come homeward.

The cob walls pressed in around Kensa until she could taste their mottled structure: hay, clay, piss and earth. No, she could not say goodbye. No, she could not let this happen. No, she would not lose Elowen. She wanted to curse and scream and cry. Perhaps she was and that was why Isolde placed a hand to her arm.

Kensa shrugged it off, violently, movements wild and exaggerated. She would rage and snarl and fight. Someone had to, if Elowen was too sick to do it herself.

'I won't allow it.'

Could she make it back to Bohortha in time? She had to try. There would be answers there, help in a beastly form, advice on inked pages.

'Did you hear what I said?' Isolde's question checked her. 'Get your parents out of the room,' said the wise woman. Her lips formed such a grave shape, it was as though she could speak to the soil. 'Get them outside.'

'What? I don't understand.' Kensa's speech was slurred. 'You'll heal Elowen?'

'I will try.'

A strangled noise cracked Kensa's mouth open. She flung her arms around Isolde and went to kiss her cheek, until the wise woman stopped her.

'I have not succeeded yet and may easily fail.' Her wrinkled palm turned upwards. 'Finally, I know what the Old Ways have been telling me. Give me what is precious to you, no tawdry bauble, only a token that has meaning – now, do it now.'

Kensa's hagstone, the one given to her by her father, was exchanged. She gave it without question. There was an odd distance in Isolde's voice, which Kensa had never heard before. Still, she did as she was told and, with some reluctance, Derwa and Mr Skewes obeyed instructions to wait outside. Of course, there would be consequences. Those could be dealt with later. For now, what mattered was Elowen.

'What'll she do?' Mr Skewes was unusually pliant in his exhaustion.

'I don't know and I don't care,' said Kensa, 'as long as she bloody does it.'

Her head was ringing, all bells, all ache.

Derwa was the one to hesitate. She looked to her eldest daughter and to Isolde, a shrewd expression in place. 'Is this Christian?'

'If you have to ask that then you already know the answer,' replied Isolde.

Derwa nodded and let Kensa pull her outside, onto the sloping street. Another day was over, the sun was setting. Time had stopped flowing the way Kensa expected it to.

It was a fine evening, with clouds brushed to frills and dyed a merry pink.

Her sister would be saved tonight and she would help to do it. Only, when Kensa went back to enter her mother's home, did she find the door locked against her, as it had been for the unwanted curate.

'Isolde?' Kensa rammed her shoulder against the wood.

Neighbours gathered as cats to the harbour when the catch has come, pulling Mr Skewes and Derwa aside, mumbling their sympathies. Kensa could hear the platitudes slapping against her ears like wet fins and fishtails. It was only when Kensa beat her fists on the wood and yelled, that Isolde finally inched it open.

'I cannot do what must be done in this noise, Kensa.'

'Let me in.'

'I may be your teacher,' said Isolde, a resigned fix to her features, 'but I will not teach you all things.'

Kensa tried to ram her elbow inside. 'You don't trust me?'

'Do as I say and look after your parents.'

'Mr Skewes is not—'

'If you want your sister to live, then get out!'

Kensa halted. Nodded, once. Stepped back and waited. Confusing thoughts found her. She was meant to help Elowen, to give what needed to be given. That wasn't happening. What *was* happening? She did not want to consider it and could not, mind unable to click into place. Kensa knew what she'd asked for, yet did not let herself think on it fully.

It took an hour. Mr Skewes and Derwa stayed close. The Jennings family soon came out to offer hot wine and supportive words. Kensa ignored them. Ate nothing, drank nothing and sat on the front step, alone. She would not leave the doorway. Her bottom was cold from the porch's flagstones and her knees held tight to her chest.

Gone was the sun and the shadows grew around her. Craning above was a pilchard sky, the stars collected as shoals.

Kensa swore that if the night had a tide, it was high tonight. She prayed to it, bowed her head and gave her loyalty to whatever force – God or Devil or even the Bucka himself – if it would save her sister. In the end, it was Isolde who came through. Just as Kensa was beginning to fall asleep, the cottage door eased open. The gnarled wise woman stood behind it, spent and sodden with sweat.

'It is done. She will live.'

A slackened quality poured down Isolde's face as she teetered forwards. Kensa reached out to catch her, arms thrust around the older woman's torso. Behind her, on her pallet, was Elowen. Asleep, though with colour to her cheeks. Mr Skewes almost knocked the healer and her apprentice aside in his effort to see his daughter, loud and not a little drunk. His caterwauls were silenced by a forceful hush from Derwa.

'There she is,' Derwa said, her fingers to Elowen's forehead. 'There's my little girl.'

Elowen stirred. 'Ma?'

Relief. Kensa's whole body sagged with it. Or would have, were it not for Isolde who leaned heavily against her. 'Let's get you settled,' she said to the wise woman, attempting to angle them both inside. 'You'll have the chair and I'll take the sill.'

Yes, she would stay the night. Curl up beside Elowen and plait daft things into her hair, tell her she smelled bad and make her laugh, somehow, as she had on occasion. At last, they could be true sisters after years spent in sourness. And she would forgive Kensa, she had to.

'We must go, child.'

An urgent note marked Isolde's request, despite the

weariness beneath it. If Kensa was to be truthful with herself, the wise woman looked terrible. Eyes puffed and bloodshot. Hands clutched to claws. Even her hair seemed whiter too, skin lacking colour, as though her blood had fled with the daylight. That could be fixed. Couldn't it? Yes, there would be potions and poultices to mend her in the cottage, Kensa knew that and trusted herself to administer them.

'All right, I will get you home,' said Kensa.

As was always the case with wise women, there was work still to do. But her sister was alive and all would be well from now on. She willed it, believed it.

Over their heads, the pilchard sky watched and knew better.

Chapter Seventeen

The Balance Between Us

One foot after the other. Shuffle, step, shuffle. Due to the wise woman's ragged pace, the journey back to Bohortha was a slow one. An owl's call bucked shrilly against the night, then was silent. Even the waves paused to listen to Isolde's fitful heaving, bile trickling up her throat, as they went on their way. When the pair were halfway there, Kensa sensed another presence and saw, in the dull half-moon's light, that Fox had come to corral them home.

Kensa's stomach complained its emptiness. She was bitterly hungry. Not only for food, but for sleep and reassurance. Isolde barely spoke. Her feet were stones, dragging lines into the ground with each step. Kensa was the only support keeping her upright. When at last the pair reached the cottage, the younger woman's arms had seized in the effort to support the elder's weight. Despite her exhaustion, from both Elowen's care and the trudge home, Kensa was elated. Her sister would recover. She could not think on anything else. Fox darted inside and, with great difficulty, Isolde was manoeuvred through the parlour and onto her bed. Kensa managed to ease the wise woman's boots off, though the rest she left. Even in the dim cottage, with no illuminance, her feet seemed a strange shade beneath her wool stockings and were frigid to the touch.

Kensa hesitated. 'What – what can I do?'

Isolde rolled her head on her pillow, left, then right, leaving a film of grease.

'I'll get hot water,' added Kensa hurriedly. 'I'll put a stew on, you need to—'

A horrid, strained laugh. Isolde inhaled heavily, and seemed in great pains to do so. Strange, that sound, how familiar it seemed. A low, rattling wet rasp. Elowen had been the same during their first hour in Portscatho.

'Get us light, child,' was the witch's request. 'I would have light for what happens next.' Kensa's brain was loose in her skull, as though it had lost its stem and now sloshed in its crucible. With unsure movements, she woke the fire and reminded it as to its purpose. Poker to grumbling coals, she kindled it anew, before finding stubby candles and lighting them one by one. At last, Isolde said, 'Enough.'

The bedroom was a hushed glow. In its warmth, Kensa was able to study Isolde's face. It was almost beyond recognition. Her eyes were sunk in their burrows, while her cheeks dripped into jowls and her lips dragged at the mouth. Her skin's hue had lost its pallor, falling into a grey no living creature could sustain.

'I'd been alone for a long, long time, frightened to be known and know another in turn,' said Isolde, reaching out to touch the younger woman's hair. 'Now I wish I'd done it sooner.'

'You need rest,' said Kensa.

'For an eternity I have put off dying and now it comes for me.' A spread of brown sludge began to mark the sheets beneath the wise woman as her bowels shut down. 'Ah, to think we could have made such mischief.' One candle sputtered, sending shadow-ribbons up the walls and down again. 'Hold my hand, would you?'

Isolde's voice was so fragile that Kensa dared not cup it in her ears. 'You're frightening me.' Her fingers, too, were thin and liable to crumble, as delicate as last year's leaf litter. 'What have you done?'

'I did what you asked.' Another breath, a wave receding over shingle. 'I did what would be done.' An owl cried in the distance once more, as though to call its lover home. Fox dipped her head round the door, then bent her back into an arch and left. 'The Old Ways are about sacrifice, remember? If one wishes to make a change in the world, for good or ill,' continued Isolde, 'one must give the world something in exchange – I would give this to you.'

Kensa extricated her palm, too-warm against her teacher's too-cold. Her own feet prickled with pins and needles when she put her weight upon them. 'I can't do this alone.'

'You'll have to.'

'How?'

Isolde croaked, 'The same way everyone faces loss – they keep going, until eventually they find where they're going to.'

This was not real. Kensa had come in, deposited the old woman on the settee and drifted off herself. Her body told her different. There was a new burn mark on her knuckle and wax drying on her wrist, both aching. She had been too hasty in lighting candle after candle after candle. These were not the markers of a dream. There was no pain in a dream.

'I don't—'

'You *do* understand.' Isolde was dying. 'You are as ready as you'll ever be, as we ever are when it comes to this.' Her grasp went for the bone-handled knife and Kensa tried to quiet her, soothe her, only to be gripped tightly. 'You must take it,' she ordered, putting the sharp edge to Kensa's hand and pressing down until blood ran. Kensa tried to pull her hand away, yet Isolde's grip was strong, possessed by another force. 'You will take the Pact from me. You will take a wise woman's curse and chain yourself to its rules, to the Land, to the shore that speaks to the Sea?'

Next came the hilt, stained red from the fresh wound. The puckered edges around Kensa's cut quivered, as though to mouth at the bone handle. She paused, stared into Isolde's blackened eyes. She did not know what she was taking. She did not know what it meant to agree.

'Yes,' she answered.

Isolde's hold slackened. There was no final word, no last confession, nothing bar a long, long, long exhale. Isolde was dead.

Kensa stood, unmoving, bent over the bedside, while blood seeped from the hand which held the knife.

One by one by one, the candles went out, or her consciousness faded, or both, it seemed. Kensa's mind split open to a
memory, to a dream, to her childhood—

There was a tall and fair lady at the last field's centre, the reaping men around her. She was not alone, for beside her was a
little girl with brazen hair. The lady knelt down and asked,
gently, 'Will you help me?'

Kensa remembered this day – it was harvest time. A few final
wheat stems remained standing, their fat heads nodding in the
low breeze. 'Won't it hurt her?'

It had been Old Sal who had told Kensa about the spirit
who lay in the harvest at reaping. She was maid and mother
and crone. She was the sugar in the bees and their honey, the
strength in the ivy and the gold in the fields. As she looked
down, she saw her father's body, wheat growing through his
eyes, nose, mouth. Isolde was in the far distance with a scythe,
flanked by wise women from times before.

'Crying the Neck is a tradition,' said the lady patiently. She
was no stranger, though Kensa could not recall her name. How
fair she was, how pale. 'You see, the Land's spirit waits in the
last field for reaping and must be bundled into one fistful – a
neck – to be slit.'

Slowly, she bent Kensa's fingers around the standing wheat
and closed her own fist around them. Through the stems –
now suddenly taller than her, as thick as the curtain which
separated her childhood bed from the kitchen – she saw her
parents arguing.

'You traded our family's next child for a pebble?' Derwa

threw the hagstone on the ground, where it bounced across the flagstones, skidding to a halt within Kensa's reach. She took it, warm in her hand. 'No, this can't be true, I won't believe it, Alex.'

'Calm yourself, love,' said her father, sneering. 'It's not like you've let me rut between your thighs in months: I can't give the Bucka what doesn't exist. Unless . . .' He trailed off, breaching the space between them, running his thumb along Derwa's jaw.

Kensa hid her face behind the curtain, heard a *slap* and her father's jaded laugh. 'Easy now, I know where I'm not wanted.' His footfalls grew closer as he found Kensa in her bed, sat upright, holding the hagstone to her chest. He took it, gently, and placed a kiss to her forehead.

'You're my best girl, Kenny.'

In his eyes was a promise, that however many times he went away, he would always come home. And that little girl was still waiting, even now, for Alexander Rowe to return – for her father to come back to her.

Part Two

The hour is come, but not the man.

An old warning from Cornish folklore.

Part Two

Chapter Eighteen

Decision

There was a knock on the door. Kensa opened it, blearily. She did not understand how time had passed or what she had done with it, though an overcast morning had arrived to Bohortha. Her dreams on wheat fields and the coarsest beard-scratch sang through her head till she was sick with it. Several faces peered at her from the cottage threshold. There was a small queue, comprising villagers belonging to Portscatho and their surrounds, who had come to call.

Kensa cleared her throat. 'Yes?'

'It's Wednesday,' was the befuddled reply from Muggersly. He was a fisherman who frequently came to fetch ointment from the healer, in order to ease his shaking hands.

'Huh,' said Kensa.

Her palm hurt. She must have spoken, for Muggersly whick-
ered like a horse.

'Died, you say?' He slid his cap from his head and nodded.
'A real shame, that is. I shall give my respects now. You'd be
wanting us to leave, then?'

Kensa nodded or did an approximation of a nod, sliding her
chin up and down.

Beyond the front step, the day was intermittently cloudy
and unseasonably warm. Its heat stuck Kensa's tongue to itself.
As word spread, the paths around Bohortha began to clear.
Finally, dazed, the apprentice – was she still an apprentice? –
closed the door. Her feet took her to a chair in the parlour. It
was warm from the last time she had sat on it and she supposed
she must have sat on it all night, in fitful sleep. This had once
been Isolde's seat. The other one had been hers. Then there
was the third chair, the Bucka's chair, heaped with rubbish as
it always was. Well, almost always.

Kensa sat for a long time. Despite her weariness, she could
not sleep. Occasionally, she checked on Isolde. Yes, very dead.
Kensa laughed, caught herself. Sat back down again and knew
she should eat. Outside, the chickens pecked and clucked at
the kitchen door and were not permitted entry. Fox hid herself
away. Mr Aldridge's bees buried their hum in one corner, quiet
and moving infrequently.

Kensa wished to hide too. What was she going to do? She had
only been learning the wise woman's craft for a few months.
That wasn't long enough to see a village right. Mr Skewes's
warning – about sending her to serve at the magistrate's house,
wear a starched collar and mind her manners – rang in her

ears. If she could not heal, would that be her fate? With her mentor gone, there was no one to help her, no one who cared enough to help her. If she turned to Jack, he'd turn her away upon learning what she'd done, wouldn't he? Of course, she'd always fail. Because it was not she who should be here, in this house, in this role.

It was another.

There was a pressing ache behind her eyes. Was it grief or the Pact? She did not feel herself. Kensa stared into the downstairs bedroom again, hoping this time that Isolde would be alive. No, as dead as ever, deader even, the deadest. Kensa stood there for the longest time, as though she could fix everything with a look. Eventually, she crawled back to the parlour chair. If she slept, well, she must have slept, for she woke again. At a certain hour came a tentative knock at the door. Kensa did not answer. It went away, to wherever tentative knocks go when they are not welcome. And if she saw Jack's broad shape pace the garden for an hour, then leave, she did not care to remember or share her grief with his.

Night gathered and did so suddenly. The room was bunched with grey when Kensa next opened her eyes. A noise had woken her. From a low shelf fell a Bad Book. It thumped as it hit the floor: *thud*. Another fell, *thud*, and another, *thud*. Each tome collapsed as a bad weight on a bad floor in a bad hour. Kensa approached the yew cabinet in the kitchen to find it had flung itself open. Spines creaked and pages turned, each one holding a new and uncertain horror. She reached for them. Flipped a cover open, scanned the contents, went to another, then swayed, trying to think and read and understand. There had to be a guide or instructions somewhere, written for a new wise woman. Surely, there would be an answer: a way forwards, as Isolde had told her. Kensa searched everywhere, through every book, hurling the pantry apart, pulling jars off shelves, tipping everything off the third chair, searching Isolde's cold pockets, raiding the chests and wardrobes. Something, somewhere, would help her – wouldn't it?

Until a scent trapped itself between the smoke from the grate and the heaviness of the evening and her own sweat, dried and flaked and heavy on her skin. The sea's swell sounded near, though the wind was in the wrong direction.

Mordros, her father called it, when one can hear the ocean without seeing it.

Outside, rising above the waves, came footsteps. Kensa had heard them before. Her eyes snapped to the third chair, now empty and waiting to be filled. The Bucka's chair. There was a knock on the door. This time, she answered it.

Chapter Nineteen

Spin a Wakening

She could smell the night on him. Salt and time and cloud-washed starlight. And something else, incense, perhaps. The Bucka wore his eel-skin coat and looked, Kensa could admit, quite regal. He was not old, although he was not particularly young either. A man who stood between seasons, but he was not a man, nothing close to a man.

Kensa's speech was clumsy. 'What do you want?'

'You called for me.'

She glanced back to the empty third chair. 'I didn't mean to.'

Kensa did not ask how he knew; he knew everything. If her senses had been dulled before, they were not now. She was frozen in the doorway. Her hands were shaking, hidden in the folds of her skirts. His face was hard as quartz, as though his bones pressed too firmly against his skin; against whatever could be called skin, for it bore little resemblance to the wrapping Kensa wore around her own skeleton. His eyes were the worst part, unbearably bright in a way eyes should not be.

'I wish to offer my condolences.'

'Yes, I – I thank you,' said Kensa.

The Bucka did not once break her stare. 'Should I come in?'

'No,' she said quickly.

Because she remembered what he had promised her predecessor: *I will not step over this threshold, not unless she bids me to and that day will come.* When he clenched his jaw, a slow and subtle change in his expression, she knew he remembered it too.

Kensa lifted her chin. 'You should go.'

How motionless he was. If ever he took breath, it seemed to be an afterthought. As though his towering form remembered it should at least try to mimic mortality: a wolf that can pass for a dog in low lighting, so long as he hides his teeth.

'We are to be partners,' said the Bucka, at last. 'We must work together, as equals.' He twisted his long fingers in the air, as though to gather it. 'How strange to be tied to yet another.' He drew his hand back and Kensa felt a tug in her chest, forcing her a step towards him, as though a physical rope was strung between them. 'Each time the Pact is passed along, I can sense its change, as weak or as strong as she who carries it.'

The cut in her palm stung anew, as though salt was packed against it. Being near him worsened it. She could taste it – him – the sea, the brine. The Bucka was not harmless, the same way her father had not been harmless.

'I have a lot to do,' said Kensa.

'Can you feel it?'

Yes: the Pact was an adder in her chest, hiding in the long grass of her ribs.

'You need not do this alone,' he assured her. 'Many a woman has asked for my help, be they wise or no.'

Alone. Everyone would leave her, eventually, wouldn't they? Her fists tightened. But not the Bucka, she realised. He couldn't leave. They were bound together now. Theirs was a marriage of sorts.

He inclined his head in a respectful gesture. 'I shall leave you to mourn—'

'I don't know what to do,' she confessed.

'Who could, in your position?' Only then did the Father of Storms smile. 'Remember, witchling, no one will trust you if you do not trust yourself.'

He was right. Portscatho had respected Isolde, even if they had not always liked her. Now she was gone and it was Kensa's fault. A loud sob split her mouth and she turned away, into the kitchen's gloom.

'You have been very brave,' said the Bucka, when her crying finally ceased. 'Anyone else would snatch her from Death and return her to us, and who could blame them?' At her confused look, he repeated himself, emphasising each word.

Her lips parted. 'Can it be done?'

Now it was his turn to look bemused, as though she had asked a foolish question. 'Did no one ever tell you?'

'Isolde said that—'

'You know as well as I that a wise woman does not always tell the truth.'

A pulse fluttered behind Kensa's collarbone. This was madness or sin or folly. There were stories. Sailors lost at sea, saved by his grace. Fishwives with empty hands, soon filled with his catch. Barren nobility who bore children with teal-tone eyes, exactly the same as his own. What's more, while he was here, the cottage wasn't as horribly quiet.

'Come in,' she said.

And he did.

The Father of Storms drifted inside with the ease of smoke. The cottage knew him. From the grate came a fire which burped in greeting. The bees, usually content to lump on the ceiling, spun a dizzy circle at his forehead like a burnt-gold halo. Fox, who had finally decided to emerge from her hideaway, bounced up to the Bucka as though he was an old friend.

'Lowarn,' he called her.

Fox chirped back, paws bouncing and tapping. The name he gave her was the Cornish word for a fox. It irked Kensa to learn the two were familiar; how the land and its creatures seemed to want him more than her, even though he was a tide-trapped being and she the soil-bound thing.

If Kensa had been numb and tired prior to the Bucka's appearance, she was awake now. 'Go on, away,' she said to the fox, who dipped her head and skulked behind Kensa's legs.

When the Bucka sat down, he did so smoothly. His clothes folded neatly and battishly around him. The room's temperature dropped, to match his. He sat up straight, aligned with the high-backed chair. Those eyes – oddly, oddly blue – were fixed on the fire, which grew and warped and danced with salt-licked shades, as though driftwood sparked upon it. Kensa, in comparison, could not settle. She gripped the side of the seat usually taken by Isolde. The bees settled against the back of the Bucka's chair, while Fox watched him from beneath Kensa's feet, ears pricked. Slowly, the Bucka shifted to meet the young woman's gaze once more, brutal and piercing.

He made her wait. Observed her, as though to take her measure. 'This is a noble feat you consider, truly, yet it is not easy.'

'I can try,' said Kensa earnestly.

Once again, a *thump, thump, thump* sounded from the bookcase. Fox bellied herself away, while the bees tipped to the kitchen window, as though to turn its latch themselves and escape. Even the fire quietened. When the Bad Books skittered into the room, they did so in a jerky motion. Pages clapping – open, closed, open – on the floor one moment and in the Bucka's hand the next, on Kensa's lap, then the floor, hand, lap. She blinked, one stopped, fell open on her thighs and revealed itself.

'If you are to do this, it must be done soon,' said the Bucka. 'The door between life and death is a narrow one. Once she fully passes through, no will – however strong – shall force her back.'

Inside the Bad Books were drawings, interlocking circles, skulls, wild words in languages Kensa could not speak. If this was an old tongue, it was too old for her knowing. Hopelessness engulfed her. 'I cannot translate this,' she sighed.

'I can do it for you,' said the Bucka.

It was reassuring: how he spoke, gently, as though to a cherished one.

The hairs on Kensa's arms stood up. Somewhere, she knew this was wrong. Yet, now the thought was lodged in her mind, she could think on nothing else. And if time was running short, as the Bucka described, she had not a moment to lose. Curiously, she didn't want to lose him, either, to disappoint him or turn him away. Though the Bucka was ancient and terrible, he was here and hers and he understood her, or claimed to.

Her dry voice clicked on her tongue as she said to the Father of Storms, 'Please, help me, show me what to do.'

The Bucka was firm and detailed in his instruction. Kensa stripped the dead woman's body and bathed her, before cladding her in a white nightdress, wrestled over cold limbs. She then put Isolde's clothes on herself. The material dragged at the young healer's body, shushing on the floor and gathering muck about the skirts. Next, herbs and bread and milk were sent to bubble and blacken over the fire. Their foul smell filled the cottage and the walls began to sweat. Kensa was glad she had not eaten, despite the hole in her stomach. When the tincture was complete and ground together in a big cauldron, Kensa used it to draw a circle on the floor in Isolde's room, big enough to fit herself inside. A spoonful was kept behind, for her to eat. It stank. Kensa took a deep breath and rammed it into her mouth. Her gut roiled against it. She heaved, kept it down, before she rubbed soil into her wrists and temples.

'Consider those qualities Isolde had and carry them tight within your chest,' said the Bucka. 'Remember who she was, how she spoke, what she liked or disliked.'

Kensa recalled the woman's bossy, mean and secretive qualities. Her penchant for a pipe after dinner and how she gossiped
about her old lovers after too much sherry. Then, without
meaning to, Kensa considered her own troubles: anxiety and
fear and desperate, maddening want. No matter what, she did
not want to be alone. And now she needn't be.

The Bucka did not interfere, for it was not his place to. Kensa
did not mind. The more difficult the work became, the better
she felt. Exhaustion numbed her, distanced her from her own
actions.

'Blood,' said the Bucka.

'Whose?'

'Any, we only need a cupful.' He gestured idly with one
hand. 'Take it from the chickens.'

'No,' said Kensa, appalled. 'I'll use my own.'

The Bucka raised his fair eyebrows. Beside him, the fire
burned with odd shapes and rumbled, as though it spoke.
Kensa was too busy to listen, for it did not speak to her.
Although the cottage was alive with strangeness, she felt like
the strangest thing in it. That she did not know herself in all
she did, for she did as the Bucka bade her.

Kensa lit the candles once again. She wanted their light to
banish the growing unease within her belly. Then wine, mixed
with hemlock, nightshade and poppy tears in a silver goblet.
Kensa found the ingredients in the pantry and ran a nail along
their labels, each handwritten by Isolde. Many vials were down
to their last dried remnants. She would have to forage for re-
placements when she'd brought the wise woman back. They
could do it together. Yes, why not? Summer was coming and

the harvest would follow: their larder would be stocked with ripeness and goodness. Wouldn't that make Isolde happy?

Kensa did not recall moving from the kitchen to the down-stairs bedroom. It was hard to process each action from one to the next. Using the bone-handled knife, she ran a line along her forearm and, as the Bad Books told her, beaded drops around Isolde's immovable body. A rotten smell emanated from the bedsheets. It made Kensa work quicker. The last task was the worst. Kensa filled a pot with earth and placed it unsteadily on the pillow next to Isolde's body. Kensa hesitated. She did not want to touch it. A few hours prior would have been no matter. Now, decay had set in. She wanted it gone: the body, the smell, the rattle the Bad Books made whenever she passed them, pages whispering their venomous encouragement. However, she wanted to be rid of loss more. Haltingly, she opened Isolde's mouth to find a lolling and yellow tongue. Suddenly, she was a child again, a little girl climbing into the Morgawr's maw. With the trowel, Kensa packed Isolde's mouth with mud. Grit spilled over the sides and caught on the dead woman's chin hairs. Isolde would be cross when she woke up. But she *would* wake up. That was the point. Several insects crawled between the body's muddy teeth. Kensa swallowed bile and wiped her hands on her skirts, until she remembered whose skirts she was wearing; her hands came away fouler than before.

Never mind, it was done. She had done it. 'Is that it?'

The Bucka unfurled from his seat and stepped into the room with one movement, when it should have taken him ten. He looked bigger, somehow, coat fanned as though caught in water. Outside, no creatures cried the late hour and no scurries stirred the undergrowth. Inside, there was a charge. Energy, like the ocean's pull, tugged at Kensa's knees. She took her place in the crudely drawn circle and held the spiced wine mixture in her hands.

'Wait,' said Kensa, remembering. 'Balance.'

The Bucka did not move. Had she spoken? Or did he pretend not to hear her?

'There has to be a balance, doesn't there? What's asked of the Old Ways demands payment,' she said, recalling her lessons. 'What is it?'

'This is Death Magic,' said the Bucka offhandedly. 'Unlike the craft you've known before, the payment is not given prior to the spell's working, it is taken after and not for your choosing.' As usual, his tone was level and calm. It soothed her. Because he was in control and there was nought to worry about. And so she didn't, too tired to care.

'Drink,' commanded the Bucka.

He was closer now, though he never stepped inside the circle. Kensa was not sure he could, even if he wanted to. She put the cup to her lips. Her teeth chattered against it. The warm mixture flooded her mouth. It tasted earthen and sweet and terrible, as though she had bitten through the blackened sky and found a worse darkness beneath it.

Every candle in the room began to shout. Flames growled high into the air, marking the walls and ceiling. Their heat pressed against Kensa's back. She could smell burning cloth and hair and skin: her own. The wax melted quickly. It ran from the shelves and tables around her, rooting across the floorboards, almost touching the circle she stood inside. It was too bright.

Kensa dropped the cup and shielded her eyes. 'Bucka?'

He was gone.

And the whole room was on fire.

And the whole room was not there.

And the whole room was a beach.

Chapter Twenty

Eyes of Wool

Towan Beach was the same as it had been on April's full moon and the marking of spring. That night whereupon two women, young and old, had shed their skins and swum from land to sea to sky. Trapped within the workings of a spell, not everything was as Kensa remembered. The pair faced one another across a sandy expanse. It was dark and the wind howled and the seas churned and Isolde's mouth was wide and open. She wore her nightdress, then she wore nothing, then she wore the Bucka's eel-skin coat, her visage changing with every blink.

Kensa's feet were bare on the sand. Isolde's dress, the one she had put on to complete the ritual, hung against her frame and bowled outwards through her legs when the storm caught it.

To her left, the sea was no more a sea, the sea was the colour of Elowen's hair, the sea *was* Elowen's hair, and a song came from it – a high crystalline lament for home.

Rain, as hard as the bone-handled knife, slashed against Kensa's cheeks. She ran forwards, reaching for the wise woman. Their bodies connected and she buried her head in Isolde's shoulder. She was here and solid and alive, wherever here was. It seemed real, it felt real, though its edges were shiny and blurred. Kensa wept, apologised over and over, until the wise woman pushed her back, thumbs to her clavicles. It hurt and was a good hurt, because Isolde gave it to her.

'Do not do this,' said the wise woman, her voice frayed and distant. 'End it now.'

'I can't.'

Even if she wanted to, it was too late. She could sense it. Whatever had woven itself around them was tied too tightly for her to unravel. Horribly, Kensa did not want it to. She was with Isolde. It was working, she would make it work and never need be on her own.

Ever since her father died, ever since her mother had birthed another daughter – a better one – ever since she could put a name to the tightness in her chest, she had been alone. A smuggler's dregs with a noose waiting, a belligerent child who courted trouble, a little girl who carried a man's indignant rage. Until she had stolen her sister's fate and became a wise woman's apprentice. This was not her life to live, but she would take it, steal it for herself.

Tangled thoughts poured forwards, unspooling from her mouth, nostrils and ears, as black as fog. They surged from

Kensa's body and flew at Isolde's, forcing entry. A choking, binding mass, which wrapped itself around the old woman with smoke and sulphurous hands.

Kensa shouted, 'No!' Her heart cried, *Stay*. No one else would leave her. She would not let them. Ever.

Isolde's head rocked back as though to scream. No sound came. Only the sea's heaving as its hairs rose along the beach, while the sky fell in scales around them.

In a single blink, the downstairs room and the cottage returned.

'Stay in the circle,' warned the Bucka.

Kensa was on the ground. Her palms flat on the boards, knees grating against the wood grain. She began to heave. She vomited seawater. She vomited earth. Aimed it down her dress and skirts, rather than smudge the barrier she knelt inside. The candles lowered themselves to their smallest glow. Another *thing* was here. Its name was Death. It pressed against the light and held its warmth at bay. Kensa fought the white spots eating at her vision and raised her head.

There she saw the Weaver's ewe.

In the room's pitch was the dead sheep, reanimated. Its glassy eyes reflected the body on the bed and the Bucka's towering shape, kept there and removed from the indistinct darkness Kensa now occupied. There was nothing else around her. Only the sheep and the circle she stood in. If she left it, she would die. She knew this without asking.

'Hello,' said Kensa.

Because it seemed polite to greet Death.

The sheep's mouth opened, as though it would speak. From

the creases where the sheep's jaw hinged came a tearing sound. The sheep's mouth began to widen further, separate, its body peeling apart to reveal another mouth, the Morgawr's mouth. Its sea-monster shape filled the space as its mouth began to open, as though it would speak. From the creases where the Morgawr's jaw hinged came a tearing sound—

A dozen mouths inside mouths inside mouths ripped themselves into the world: beaks and jowls and tearing flesh. Throughout it, Kensa screamed. Until she felt her own mouth begin to split at the corners.

'Come now, witchling,' came the Bucka's voice. 'Do not get distracted.'

It would be easy to leave the circle. She could not be alone if she was dead. How tempting it was. And cold, though not a bad cold. The endless mouthing creature split again into the sheep. Kensa could smell the ewe's wool, see its eyes – whole and rotten and pitted at the same time, multiple realities which stared and stared and stared at her. There was a strange power in it: to choose your time of dying. Why not make it now? Everything she worried about or had done wrong would no longer exist, because she would not exist. That would be nice, wouldn't it?

'Kensa,' said the Bucka, stern and with urgency.

She was in the room again. Where had the sheep gone? The Father of Storms sank to his knees outside the circle and levelled his face to meet Kensa's. It was a strange sight to see the Bucka, a sea god, the most dangerous creature she'd ever met, crouched earnestly beside a dirty village girl in a dank cottage room.

'You seem worried,' said Kensa sleepily.

If she closed her eyes, the current would take her: woollen and bleatless.

'You cannot stop,' said the Bucka, and he looked concerned, afraid for her.

She smiled sadly, reassuringly, and he smiled back. He seemed almost human, then. Boyish. How old had he been when this was done to him? When was he made the Father of Storms? She'd never thought to ask. Yet his was a fleeting expression, quickly concealed, as the Bucka rose to full height.

'Death will take your soul if you allow it,' he said, to himself, to her. 'What's left behind will be a husk and the woman you are now shall never see the morrow.'

Kensa nodded, though she barely understood. 'I want to go home.' She did not know which home she meant.

The Bucka swallowed, lips twisting, then pulled straight.

From the other room, the Bad Books came. They pounded against the boards, the windows – shining day, swallowing night, shining day – as the end came. Those vengeful tomes toppled into one another, swirling about the pair, passing straight through the Bucka and clipping Kensa's elbows. A tunnel formed around her, the Bad Books as swift bats. From their pages came shouts and cries and weeping sounds: voices lost to time yet no less angry for it.

'Speak as I speak,' said the Bucka insistently, calling over them. 'I will guide you.'

A cold sweat threatened to break the circle she had drawn as Kensa forced herself to stand. It hurt, everything hurt. When she repeated the Bucka's chants, it was with a croaky shout. She did not understand it. One or two words caught in her mind as hooks, as though she should have known and feared them, yet nothing stayed. Through him, she was plunged into the Old Ways. The ground trembled, as though to shake her from it. This was power. No sooner did she acknowledge it than it was ripped from under her. A rushing in her ears, like a snapping of fine threads, and a jolt to her sternum, which plucked at her final shreds of consciousness.

Fleetingly, she thought she heard the Bucka speak down their Pact – *I will not ask your forgiveness* – yet there was nothing to forgive, she tried to tell him, only gratitude that he would help her. Her mind strayed to Elowen, prayed she would be well if Isolde returned, that the exchange made in her mother's home would stand against this dark magic.

When at last the spell was done, Kensa did not leave the circle. Exhaustion pinned her down, curled her tight into a helix. When had she fallen? Every candle was low in its cradle and sputtered its end. The Bucka was gone. Quiet, bar her own laboured breathing. And no other's to match hers; hers the only lungs working. The Bad Books lay where they had fallen, spent and twitching silently.

'Isolde?' Kensa's mouth was rank and soil scratched at her teeth. 'Isolde?'

It took the apprentice two attempts to rise to her feet and tumble forwards, hands reaching for the bedpost. She could barely stay upright. Even the weight of her own hair on her scalp was too much. Before her lay the wise woman, as she had been prior to the ritual beginning. Nothing had changed. There were the same cold sheets, run brown with stains, and a body that had not moved an inch.

She had failed. Kensa's eyelids dragged shut. She felt nothing.

Tomorrow. She would know what to do tomorrow. Now, she could only sleep and wait for the sadness to come. With no strength to carry her elsewhere, she collapsed onto the dirtied bed and lay beside the only friend she'd ever had and had no more.

Kensa woke to an empty space beside her. Isolde was gone. The cottage rustled with movement. It told her she was not alone and it warned her that someone had taken the body. Was this the Bucka's work? Ankles wobbling stiltishly, she rose to where sound lengthened like twine. There was a mid-morning still-ness to the hour, as though the day had not yet decided what to do with itself. Hesitant sunshine pounded a headache into Kensa's skull, which throbbed in time with her steps into the kitchen. That strange noise increased: an orange peeled too close to the ear, a knuckle clicking inside a glove, a tail bending inwards to slap itself.

One copper-coloured feather fell from nowhere and onto her sleeve. A second, third, fourth feather, paved her way forwards. The kitchen was heaped with them and, at first, Kensa could not understand why. Among them were gem-stone colours, like garnets, only these pooled into runny puddles and the smell—

It was blood.

A hunched figure sat, legs splayed, on the floor. It wore a familiar nightdress, wet and red. Around it were chickens, dead, necks snapped and open, as though their mouths had been widened and moved further down their bodies: Death in another form. Through a matted lump of hair, Kensa saw stained teeth, as Isolde – for it was her – pressed raw poultry to her cracked and scaling lips.

'You're back,' said Kensa.

A high chord rang between Kensa's ears. Where there should have been relief and happiness was confusion. Because the chickens were dead, somehow. Behind it was that lip-smacking and bone-sucking and blood-drinking *slurp*, with feathers between teeth and a wish-bone promise, broken and chewed and swallowed down.

'You ate them,' said Kensa, with a catch in her throat.

She should make breakfast. They could talk. It would be fine. Of course, Isolde would be hungry upon waking up. How remiss of her not to plan ahead. This was a small price to pay for having her back. Wasn't it? Only, Kensa's clucking companions were now in pieces and her own hands were shaking and she was going to be sick and, and, and . . .

'You're here now, as it should be,' continued Kensa. 'Don't be angry with me, I had to do it, I couldn't manage without you.' A hundred excuses, offered quickly, to intercept the chastisement that never came. 'Isolde?'

Quiet, the eating stopped. Two cloudy orbs lifted to meet Kensa's. These were not Isolde's eyes. Kensa jolted backwards and banged her side against the table. Her fingers twitched. She wanted to snatch the carcass, as though she could save it. Perform another ritual, summon everything back to life, to her.

God, all the chickens were dead.

Hesitantly, from the kitchen's far corner, came a faint and questioning, *Cluck?*

Kensa twisted to her right. Isolde saw it first.

The wise woman bolted from her seat upon the stone floor and sprang towards the last surviving hen. She was impossibly fast, her speed nothing she had ever previously possessed. Like an animal, like a predator. Kensa shrieked and the bird sprang up, into her arms. Its thumb-sized heart beat against the young woman's chest as she held it tight. Isolde's head swung wildly towards them and, without a second thought, Kensa ran.

Her dress, Isolde's dress, was too long for her frame and dragged at her toes. Behind her, Isolde's bare soles slapped the floor as a chase began. Kensa bolted to the stairs. Each step sang her footfalls – and there was another pair behind her. When she reached the landing, cracked nails swiped at her ankles. Even with Isolde's quick pace, Kensa was younger and she had something she loved in her arms. She made it to her bedroom and slammed the door behind her. A *bang* signalled Isolde's weight upon the other side. Bizarrely, she did not turn the handle, though Kensa grasped it in anticipation. Instead, the enraged wise woman hammered and scratched at the wood, as a rabid beast might.

It was all right, it would be all right.

Soon, the other woman would remember herself. Wouldn't she?

Kensa dropped the chicken and dragged her bed, lengthways, as a barrier. When at last the door's mechanism gave out, it only opened an inch. It was that slim crack which Isolde attempted to stuff herself through. A rolling eye and dirty fingers, clawing outwards. A blackened tongue, licking the paint along the doorframe.

Cluck, said the chicken, once more.

'Yes,' agreed Kensa grimly.

This was not – could not be – Isolde. It had her body, yes, though not much else. Tentatively, the chicken approached Kensa. She buried her face in its quivering feathers. The safest place was below the window, where she slumped, as far from the door as she could get. Her mind spun with a thousand questions. Had she made a mistake? Perhaps it would take time for the wise woman to settle. Yes, that was it. Kensa need only be patient. After all, what a shock it would be to find oneself alive again, like being born, only the wrong way round. These comforting thoughts carried her through the next hour.

'I've got you,' whispered Kensa, over and over, to the soft body nestled against her own.

Eventually, Isolde sought out a new distraction. With an inhuman gait, she shuffled away, leaving Kensa and the chicken in peace.

Occasional crashes came from downstairs. It was strangely reassuring. If she could hear Isolde, then she knew where the woman was. Could she get out? Unlikely, if she could not remember how to open a door. Exhaustion made Kensa's limbs clumsy. She stripped off the grimy clothes she had worn for the ritual and put on her own: a tatty sage smock which had once been her mother's. It was serviceable enough and left her feet clear of bulky skirts. On a belt at her waist she secured the bone-handled knife and its sheath. Next, she scrubbed her face, armpits and groin with a damp cloth from her washbasin. It would have to do.

'You need to go,' she said to the chicken regretfully.

Her selfish desires told her to keep it, to shut the bird in her room and seek comfort in it later. But she doubted Isolde would be kept out by a lock for long and couldn't face another dead chicken on her hands. Kensa pushed her palms to her eyes, then quietly as she could, unlatched her window and opened it wide. It was a reasonable drop to the ground. She pressed a kiss to the chicken's neck, leaned out the window and let go. Thankfully, the hen softened its fall with ample flaps and landed gracelessly into the garden below. To cover the bird's escape, Kensa pulled her bed away from the door and thumped her feet on the landing. Hopefully, the bird would be sensible enough to hide itself. If it had evaded Fox for long enough, surely it could stay clear of Isolde? At least, until she recovered herself. As for wherever the vixen was, Kensa hoped she had fled to her own safety and hadn't succumbed to the chickens' fate.

Nothing stirred. In fact, the cottage was eerily silent. Cautiously, Kensa crept downstairs. There she found Isolde, hunched and rocking in her usual chair. From her ragged mouth came a hum, then a yell, followed by a chuckle, then nothing. Silence, unmoving, as though she were dead again. For the longest time, she did not twitch. Until her eyes began to roll and settled, at last, on Kensa. The fire had long since gone out and the room was cold. Isolde did not seem to feel it. Her bare soles tapped the floor, almost playfully.

'You're filthy,' said Kensa, risking a step forwards. 'Why don't we get you a bath?'

She was given no reply, bar the *tap, tap, tap* Isolde's toenails made on the flagstones.

It was a long process to clear the fireplace and light it once again. The heaped ashes beneath the grate carried the Bucka's peculiar scent. Kensa was quick to sweep them up and chuck them beyond the front step. As tired as she was, it was good to work; it stopped her thinking. She unhooked the tub from the back wall and set it beside the hearth. Fetched water from the garden well – quickly and with the door closed lest Isolde venture out – and then heated it. After a long and laborious effort, there was a reasonable depth within the tub and she began the process of negotiating Isolde into it. One foot in, knee bent, the next following. At first, the wise woman resisted, drenching them both. Eventually, as Kensa's disgust grew, she began to settle and allowed her nightdress to be removed. It clung to the filth on her body. Odd patches discoloured her skin, which no scrubbing could remove. This wasn't dirt. It was decay. And the smell. Kensa held her breath whenever she drew too close to it.

You bury those smells, she realised. *You can't bathe them.*

Lifting a jug, she rinsed Isolde's hair and lathered it with soap. 'See now, that's better?' It came out. Large clumps, matted grey and silver, stuck to Kensa's wrists and formed circling islands on the bath's surface. The water began to turn a strange colour: brownish-red with clotted lumps and hair and shit. A warbling sound rose in Isolde's throat, akin to a song, only flat and monotone.

Kensa leaned in, across that foul water, to listen:

'. . . *you'll fail, tit-sucking whore, can't do it, housemaid for you, what will your mother say, Jack'll hate you, first means nothing, first means alone, you'll always be alone, Mr Skewes*

*was right, you've ruined it, never should have taken it, father's
daughter, useless cunt—'*

Kensa whipped her head back and met Isolde's eyes, those
limpid-white eyes, and saw a wild grin beneath them.

'Let's – let's get you dry, shall we?'

It was another difficult process to coax Isolde from the tub
and rub her down. The wet-cloth came away filthy. How could
she be dirtier now than she'd been prior to washing? Kensa was
brittle and dry as tinder. This was not what she had envisioned. It
took several tries to push a loose smock over Isolde's head. Shoes
were unacceptable, communicated not through words, no, for
she much preferred using her teeth. Kensa narrowly avoided
losing a finger. And, when left alone for two minutes to allow
Kensa to strip the soiled bedding, Isolde began to eat live bees
from the windowsill, popping them in her mouth like cherries.

'You should rest,' said Kensa forcefully.

Isolde continued to mumble, repeating what Kensa had said
to herself in low moments. She had never told anyone about
the doubts she fed, about her growing insecurities. How could
Isolde have known? It scared her more than the balding and
the shitting and the inane giggling.

'You should have run away, little bitch—'

'Isolde,' said Kensa quietly.

Slowly, the wise woman eased back onto the clean sheets,
squirming. She did not respond to her name. Whatever inhab-
ited Isolde's body was not the wise woman, it was something
other. Kensa was sure of it. Although she had no knack for the
Old Ways, she heard them, that ancient power spearing the
land and telling her that her mentor was truly gone.

For once, she listened.

Kensa fled to the kitchen and kept a closed door between herself and the rotten, broken creature she and the Bucka had brought into being. What had she done? She could not think, would not think. For now, there was chicken blood to clean off the floor and the walls and her dress, again, filthy with horror she could not wash out.

Chapter Twenty-one

The Maiden and her Monster

Midday arrived with a knock at the door and the cold sound of spadework. Kensa dropped her scrubbing brush and craned her ear, as a mother would to its babe, anticipating a cry. Instead, there was only silence behind Isolde's door. Perhaps that was worse. With careful steps, the floor wet from her efforts to clean it, Kensa heaved open the front door. Sunlight forced her eyes shut. When was the last time she'd been outside, truly outside, aside from when she had gone to fetch water? Her skin itched. When her sight adjusted, she saw a burly man on the front step.

'We should be done by the afternoon,' said the blacksmith, Ern. 'A drink wouldn't go amiss, mind you, this is thirsty work.' He thumbed to the garden at his back, overgrown as always, yet with a new person-sized square cut into the earth. 'For the funeral,' he explained, at Kensa's baffled look. 'Don't say you've gone and buried her already?'

Kensa shook her head.

'The village'll be here tomorrow morning to give her a send-off.' He looked her up and down disapprovingly. 'Enough time for us to put our best faces on, aye?'

Kensa was not sure what her 'best face' was, but she certainly wasn't going to give it to him. 'Mm.' Reluctantly, she thanked the blacksmith and pointed at the small garden well. She was a wise woman, not a scullery maid. For years, she'd considered herself separate from the village, an outcast with a bad man's blood in her veins. That was nothing compared to now, isolated by a secret far bigger than anything she'd known before. And the one person she would have turned to was gone, replaced by a creature she did not recognise. Fat tears rolled down her face as she sank into her usual chair in the parlour, hands over her cheeks, as though she could press her weakness back into herself. It didn't work, she couldn't make it work. No one would understand. Everyone would blame her. Why wouldn't they? Here, finally, was the evidence Portscatho needed to condemn her as worthless, no good for anyone, as callous as her long-dead father.

Gradually, the spade-on-soil faded to quiet again. An hour or a minute could have passed. It was intangible to her. Fatigue pulled on her limbs; she hadn't eaten in a day, hadn't had the will to feed herself. Did she even deserve to eat, deserve any-thing, after what she'd done? Maybe if she let herself starve to near-death, everyone would forgive her.

Yet another fist rapped at the door. Kensa scrubbed at her face, then halted. It was normal to cry when grieving a lost one, she need not hide it and no one would know the real reason for her upset. She checked on Isolde first and found her gnawing at a pillowcase, feathers about the room, as though she could find chicken skin beneath. Grimacing, Kensa dragged herself to the door and answered it, ready to survey the blacksmith's work.

'If you'll be wanting more to drink ...' she began, then trailed off.

Gone were the men and their shovels. There, on the door-step, was Elowen. She was thinner than usual, though sturdy enough despite her recent illness. She wore black. In her hand was a small carpet bag, as well as a bundle which she would later reveal as packed with bread, cheese and sausage.

'Ma was worried you'd have no proper clothes for the fu-neral,' she said, fidgeting her feet nervously. 'I offered to bring them.' Elowen's cheeks grew rosy. 'I didn't like to think of you here alone and even if—'

Kensa flung her arms around her sister. Buried her face in Elowen's bright hair. Pulled her close until she gasped. It took a moment. There was a gentle *plod* as the carpet bag dropped on the floor. Gradually, the other girl brought her own arms up and held on tight.

'Oh,' said Elowen.

Kensa did not let go first. Only when the snot drooped from her nose in roping lengths did she finally pull back and mutter, 'Sorry.'

Elowen shook her head. 'There's no need to apologise, we all need a good cry when we've lost a friend.'

Kensa rubbed at her own nose. 'It's not that.'

'Oh,' said Elowen again.

Although the pair stood close, toe to toe, there was the same divide between them which no apology could permeate. It struck Kensa how little she knew about Elowen. Did she have friends? Was there one she had ever lost? How was she feeling after her sickness? Questions with answers she had never cared to learn.

Kensa struggled with her words. 'I've done somethin' terrible.'

'You were fairly awful.'

'No, this isn't about you and me.'

'Then I am sure Jack will understand,' said Elowen, easing back on her heels. 'You know how he is around you.'

'What? No, it's Isolde,' said Kensa, wincing. 'Wait, what do you mean—'

A loud *clank* interrupted their talk, followed by a high wailing sound. It grew louder, the wails shifting to yowls, then glass breaking and a long, slow ripping sound. Kensa's shoulders sagged low enough to reach her knees. She looked to her sister, desperately, though an explanation was hard to come by.

Elowen's features hardened and her eyes narrowed. Quickly, they flicked up Kensa's form, noting the marks on her dress and the bruised quality to her appearance. She looked sharp, intelligence burning with light blue clarity in her irises.

'I think I'd better come in.'

It took a while for Kensa to explain what had happened. When she reached the turn in the tale involving the Bucka, Elowen paled right down to her bones. 'Merrin told me about him,' she said. 'How terrible he can be, how cruel and unyielding.'

Kensa chewed on her lower lip, teeth worrying at a scabbed corner. 'It's not his fault, he was helping me. I must've done it wrong.'

'What did he want in return?'

'He asked for nought,' said Kensa.

Elowen's expression stayed forcibly neutral. She took charge over tea brewing and bid Kensa to sit, thrusting food into her lap. Neither one sat on the Bucka's chair, which remained ominously empty. In that silent, tricky moment – of which there had been many in the sisters' relationship – the only interruption came from Isolde's room, which had been filled with more cushions to occupy the captive within.

'Come on, out with it,' barked Kensa. 'Tell me everything I've done wrong! This is what I hate about you, Elowen. You have these thoughts in your head and never speak them!'

It was good to shout. Even if guilt came after. Kensa needed the rage. It was better than sadness, than confronting, well, anything. Especially herself. From the yew shelves, the Bad Books rattled against one another – and one let out a small burp – as though in encouragement.

'You want me to tell you what I think?' Elowen did not raise her voice. She never did. Instead, she leaned back on her chair, slim shoulders bunching up to her ears. 'I think you're a fool,' she said simply. 'No Devil makes a deal without asking for payment, Kensa. It's what Old Sal talks about when the Falmouth sailors come to call at the Jennings' inn, hoping to sway a simple girl with fancy talk. It's what Mr Aldridge told us every Sunday about sin and temptation, and what Mr Delavaud will tell us too, when he preaches his first sermon this Sabbath.'

'Who?'

'Besides, if Isolde is not dead, then we have to tell people,' continued Elowen. 'Her funeral takes place tomorrow and if she suddenly appears, there'll be questions.'

'You don't understand,' said Kensa, exasperated. 'She's come back different.' Then, quietly, she added, 'I don't know what she is.'

She grabbed her sister's hand – an unfamiliar gesture, even if it came naturally to her – and pulled Elowen into the bedroom where she had imprisoned the wise woman. It resembled a bedroom no longer. The straw mattress had been de-strawed and its contents strewn about the place. No feathers were left in their pillows, for they too had been spread wide as a poor simile for snow. It was dark, the daylight obscured by brown smudges on the window panes. Kensa did not want to speculate as to what that was; the stench told her enough. Then there was Isolde herself, whose gown had begun to unravel at the side.

The crone squatted in the corner, wet again somehow, and stinking. Her hair, what remained, was matted. She was almost the same as she had been earlier, aside from one key difference: Isolde's eyes were sharper now, no longer cloudy. That strange grey had shifted to a charcoal hue, bird-like and menacing. Kensa stepped back from the doorway and her boot struck a small white stone. No, not a stone. A tooth, gum caught on one side and bleeding.

Elowen, ever controlled, betrayed nothing. She ventured forwards. 'Isolde?'

Kensa didn't understand it. Her sister spoke as though to a stray cat, gentle despite the vileness around them. There was nothing in Kensa as disciplined, as quiet, as kind.

Isolde did not move.

'Do you know who I am?' Elowen stretched her fingers out, palm upturned.

With a jerky, inhuman quality, Isolde twisted her head to face the newcomer. Slowly, she opened her mouth. Not to smile, no, her lips stretched beyond such an expression, jaw clicking and straining as its twin sockets popped and her chin dropped. A humming came deep within the wise woman's gangrenous throat, growing louder and louder as a single bee rose up. It was heavy, flying in a zigzag, to fall at Elowen's feet. A further two flew out, stronger, then five, then eight, buzzing forth in quick succession. Isolde spread her arms and laughed through the hive, tendons in her neck vibrating with force. Elowen started backwards, stumbling into Kensa. The wise woman's ripped gown fell to the side, revealing one filthy breast and a tattered hole in the flesh. Where her ribs should be was honeycomb, as dull in colour as Isolde's eyes, dripping with a tar-like substance, down her hip, leg, knee, foot. From her mouth spewed a growing swarm, encircling the ceiling, bashing against plasterwork, angry and violent. Until one single bee arrowed towards the two sisters. The rest of the hive, with a sudden precision, began to follow. Kensa yanked Elowen out of the room by her collar. A pretty pearl button *pinged* to the floor, the door was *slammed* and then *drummed* a dozen times as the bees pummelled it from the other side. Safe, the sisters collapsed into one another, panting hard.

'I, ah, think you're right,' said Elowen tactfully. 'She isn't quite herself, is she?' The smashing and ripping and pounding began anew from the creature. 'Whoever that is in there, it isn't Isolde. I'm not even sure it's alive, Kensa.'

For all her youth, the fair-haired girl had a level head. Kensa was glad for it. Despite her talk about needing no one, she needed Elowen now. Both knew it, yet the younger girl never remarked upon it.

'You must speak to the Bucka again,' she said, as the pair righted themselves. 'If he was involved in its doing, he can undo it.'

'Yes.' Kensa nodded, trusting their bind – the Pact – would align their cause.

Elowen paused, troubled. 'Did this happen because of me? After what Isolde did for me when I was dying?'

Here was an opportunity, sword-like and glinting. Kensa could say, 'Yes,' or even, 'No,' haltingly enough, and Elowen would blame herself. If she let Elowen take the fall, no one would doubt her. It would be easy. And then she looked to Elowen, truly looked at her, and the choice was no choice she'd ever make.

'It's nothing to do with you,' said Kensa resolutely. 'At least, nothing you did.'

Because it had been Kensa who wished for Elowen's life back and it had been Kensa who refused to let Isolde go when asked. Whatever mistakes had been made were Kensa's own and she'd claim them, finally. It was freeing, in a surprising way.

Elowen asked quietly, 'Why did Isolde help me? She didn't have to.'

Kensa clicked her tongue. 'I – I asked her to.'

'Oh.'

'That's the Bucka's chair,' said Kensa, pointing to the vacant high-backed seat beside the fireplace, quick to change the subject. 'When it is empty, he fills it. Only, it's been empty all this time and he's not come.' She pushed her untamed hair from her forehead and began to collect odd ends and discarded objects. One by one, she placed them on the chair, then took them off once more. Kensa even balanced a Bad Book on top, its cover fizzing when she touched it. Elowen refused to go near, her expression one of distaste at the tome and its brethren.

'It might take a while,' Kensa explained, as though she knew what she was doing.

A nagging wrongness told her it would not work, confirmed by a crowing laugh from the bee-infested bedroom. No imposing presence arrived at the cottage entrance, no shape against the window outside, no Bucka-Boo to frighten them, though the pair waited long enough, hoping – and fearing – to see the Father of Storms himself.

'We'll ask Merrin how to find him,' said Elowen. 'Do you have anything we could give her? She will want a present.'

Kensa did not understand right away. 'You want to consult the asrai?'

'Why not?'

'She's *killed* people, she tried to kill *me*.'

'Do you have a better idea?'

Kensa shook her head.

Elowen straightened. 'Get your boots on and let's go.' She brushed two firm hands down her front. 'Do I look all right?'

'You're coming with me?'

'You don't have to do everything alone, Kensa,' came the exasperated reply. 'Besides, you've no clue where she lives and I do and, well, she likes me.'

'That's all right then, isn't it? So long as she won't kill *you*.'

As for what could be given: Kensa took her father's rum off the mantel, the one Farmer Hayle had given her. Its weight was heavier than anticipated, as were all things tied to old memories.

The sisters piled furniture against Isolde's door as a make-shift barricade and headed down the old farmers' paths to the shoreline. The sandy tracks they followed were used by labourers who fetched seaweed as fertiliser for the crop fields. Loose strands of dried sea-oak and dulse crunched underfoot, sounding their strides back to them in delicate *pops*. A strong wind brought frequent clouds overhead, blotting out the blue and the sun's steady warmth, tugging at their clothes and hair.

It was not an easy path, yet Elowen walked it with confidence. She explained that the asrai lived in a crevice in the cliff face on a slope where a mill had once been, prior to the tide taking it. Portscatho was far behind them, over the hill, while St Mawes and Falmouth lay ahead, jutting forward on slips of land like fingers into the ocean. Kensa could make out St Mawes's castle over the water, a low-squatting heap built by a long-dead king, now used by naval men who rarely ventured over the tidal river to pester their small community. The coastal route curved round to clasp a cove, where the fresh-water Fal River pushed back against the sea's salt. Next was a steep drop, which Kensa struggled with and Elowen managed deftly enough. The latter slid her blonde hair into a braid as she went, tying it with a ribbon she kept in her pocket.

'You've been coming here a while,' said Kensa.

A non-committal hum came in reply.

'Why have you been coming here a while?'

'Watch your step,' said Elowen lightly, at the same moment Kensa slipped. The younger girl looked back, once, with an *I-know-something-you-don't-know* grin. And, despite herself, Kensa laughed. It was good to have a sister.

'I'm glad you're not dead,' said Kensa.

'Me too,' said Elowen drily.

'No, really.'

The weather was breezy, with cloud over sun like a fist over stone. It whipped Kensa's hair around her face, in contrast to Elowen's neatness.

'Thanks,' said the youngest, after a beat.

Against the pair's heels came persistent, low waves, cold and strong. Silverfish skittered away at their progress, while anemones, lying in the watery gaps between boulders, watched each movement the pair made, their tentacles waving in greeting or warning. Overhead, gorse crowded the hills, stacked where landslides had left them. Their yellow flowers were bright and sweetly scented, shielding them from any who could have seen them. It left Kensa uneasy. No one knew where the young women were and Isolde had been left, as securely as possible, alone in the cottage. Kensa could only hope that the books she'd shoved under the door would keep the old woman occupied, whether she read them or ate them.

'Not far now,' said Elowen, leaping over the pointed terrain.

Kensa's neck burned where Merrin had pressed against it during the fight in Mr Aldridge's day room. 'If she attacks us—'

'She won't, I promise.'

Carefully, the two negotiated each slippery spike, arms out for balance and skirts tucked into their undergarments. They neared a small worn-away section in the rock, smoothed into a narrow tunnel. Here, the shadows grew denser. By turning sideways and breathing in, Kensa and Elowen could nudge their bodies through the slim crack. Sand sucked at their boots, while limpet shells dragged painfully at their chests and backs. The wet stone reflected the dull, infrequent sunlight back to them, growing duller still, until the sisters found themselves crouched below a small wooden roof, bowled the wrong way. There was another next to it, and another. Kensa's brows pinched together in confusion.

'Boats,' said Elowen.

A dozen fishing vessels were wedged into the stonework above them, creating small platforms: floating wooden islands. Ahead was a ladder which Elowen ascended, simultaneously fixing her skirts and gesturing for Kensa to follow. They climbed until Kensa's thighs screamed in protest and a larger platform was revealed, marked with tidelines and decorated with a thousand shiny objects. Heaped coins, spiralled shells, broken chests glittering with jewels and, alarmingly, bones. Femurs, skulls, picked-dry ribs placed with precision on shelves carved into rock or positioned on driftwood planks secured with rope. Their size varied: rat, cow, horse and many which were undeniably human.

Elowen cleared her throat and trilled, 'Merrin?'

Kensa's nose wrinkled and she yelled, as though in correction, 'Merrin!'

The asrai took her time. Scuffles could be heard from above, until, when called again, she appeared, peeling herself onto the deck behind Kensa and Elowen. Merrin wore nothing, as was her habit, and moved with a sloping gracelessness.

Her green eyes fixed on the youngest of the sisters. With one long nail, she picked at the loose thread where Elowen had lost a button. 'What is for me?'

Elowen blushed fiercely and produced the rum. 'I got you this, in exchange for helping us to find the Bucka?'

Merrin accepted it with a chirp and sank onto a low bench, intricately carved though bitten with rot. It must have been belonged in a ship's captain's quarters once and now had a home with her. As for the captain, he had likely found his final rest here too.

Kensa tried not to look at the skulls. Her neck throbbed. When she put a hand to it, Merrin smiled, her fangs on show. She rubbed her greenish legs together and shivered sand across the wood they stood upon.

'Why should I?'

Elowen paused, considered. There was no sternness to her voice, only a calm challenge. 'Remember when I helped you?'

'No,' said Merrin sulkily, setting the bottle aside.

'When that fishing hook caught your shoulder, I took it out and treated the wound. Each day I came to visit and changed your dressing, too.'

'No,' repeated Merrin. 'No.'

'And I let you play with Mr Aldridge.'

'No.'

'And we'd swim together and you'd show me your treasures?'

'You'll tell us where the Bucka is,' said Kensa, unsheathing the bone-handled knife. 'Or I'll finish what Isolde started.' She began to roll up her sleeve with her free hand. 'Do you want that?'

It was an empty threat. Kensa didn't know how to banish anything. Not that it mattered, for her warning had the desired effect. Merrin hissed and lurched towards Kensa, teeth bared and hands clawed.

Elowen darted between them. 'She doesn't mean it, I swear!' A meaningful glance to Kensa. 'If you do help us, I'll bring another treat soon, the next time I visit. How about cake or a sticky bun? You like those.'

'You could bring the new curate,' said Merrin slyly, retreating to her bench. 'Or I fetch him myself soon enough.' She spread her fingers across her lap and breathed deep, her gills flexing. 'Ken-*sa*.' She pulled the name apart with her tongue and giggled in her wet-fish voice. 'What business have you with the Father of Storms? He's as bad as your father was; I've met them both, I have, I have.'

Kensa bit down on her tongue and lifted her knife, higher, its point angled towards Merrin. 'Why should I tell you?'

'A resurrection gone wrong,' said Elowen, as though it happened every other Tuesday.

Kensa barked, 'Don't tell her that!'

'She's my friend.'

'Hah,' snorted Kensa, only to realise she meant it. Indeed, there was a familiarity between the two, a shared knowledge, a secret joke only they were in on. A sickening disgust curled in Kensa's stomach when she understood that her sister – a woman she'd once thought innocent and pure and not a little dull – would choose this murderous harpy for company.

Merrin eased herself to standing, taking the bottle with her, and took two long steps towards Kensa and her blade, as though it were a young boy's wooden sword. It might well have been, for the notice she gave it. 'Here is a wise woman ordered to keep balance and instead she tips scales.' Below them were other creatures. Numerous faces lurked below the waves, ever watchful, flat and fish-like in appearance. Their bodies were crab-backed and spined as an urchin shell's. Fey-kind remnants lingered in their long fingers and tipped ears, bearing tortoise-shell markings. How long had they been there? And did this asrai lie when she'd claimed to know her father? Creatures such as her only spoke what people wanted to hear . . .

'You should be respectful,' said Merrin. 'Before, we took a fisherman's catch right from his stomach or pulled the pretty girls down to the deeps with us, until the Pact drove us to near-extinction.' She reached for Elowen, played with that loose thread on her dress. 'I was as you, once,' she said, lulling, 'would you like to be as I, my little-fish-from-water, fine ladies together? You've never belonged with them, you know?'

Elowen remained silent. Unreadable, as ever.

Kensa slashed forwards, separating them. 'Tell me where to find the Bucka.'

Merrin smiled her horrible smile. She tipped the rum to her mouth – Kensa's father's rum, dry and sweet and potent – and did not say, 'No,' again.

*

The seabirds nested on Killigerran Head, not far from Towan Beach. Their home was a small island where the Bucka was also thought to reside. No one truly knew where the Father of Storms lived, Merrin had claimed, for he was no more than fog and the riddles it keeps. The outcrop was known as Last Leap, for legend stated it compelled the heartsick to run along the edge and dash themselves on the rocks below. Kensa swallowed thickly. If she intended to scramble down without being swept away, she would need to do it soon; the tide was low and would not be for long.

'If I don't come back, get Jack to help,' she said, removing her boots, stuffing her socks inside them and tying the laces around her neck. 'He'll know what to do.' Or, she hoped so. A desperate pang – a longing to be near him, touch him, hear him say her name – reverberated in her chest.

Elowen's bare feet joined her sister's in the grass. 'You're not doing this by yourself.'

Kensa shook her head. 'It's too dangerous.'

'For as long as I can remember, you've run ahead into every situation, without me,' Elowen continued, 'and I won't be left behind again.' Although it had only been a few days since her recovery, Elowen insisted she was strong enough. 'I owe this to Isolde.' She hitched her skirts even higher and descended to the waiting ocean. 'Are you coming?'

Cormorants watched their wading progress, wings out-stretched: a dozen crosses to mark their passage, teal eyes flashing ill luck, the same hue as the Bucka's. Noise from the nearby mines ran on the wind and bounced on the water's surface. Sonorous calls, a pick on stone, loud and pummelling machinery. When the land ran out, the sisters were forced to swim. It was not a kind sea around them, the current strong as though to guard its master. With a final surge onwards, the outcrop grazed their palms.

'We'll count the waves and pull ourselves up on the highest one,' shouted Kensa, above the rushing sound in her ears, above her mounting doubt. There was no real proof the Bucka would be here. Wouldn't they have seen him from shore, if he was?

One, two, three – foam crashed on their chins and burned their eyes – then *four*. A last effort, knees bent, fingers reaching. Kensa was almost there. And then she wasn't. Underwater, there was no up or down, only pain as a hard ledge punched her chest. Elowen's hand fumbled through the brine, seeking hers. It guided her to the surface. The waves came higher and Kensa slipped again. Elowen would not let go. Every movement took strength neither sister possessed, as Kensa finally hooked her knee onto a firm surface and heaved herself out of the water.

Kensa lay flat, coughing and heaving. Elowen slumped beside her, a cut streaming from her eye. Their boots were lost, though the bone-handled knife held fast to the belt at Kensa's hip. Soon, she would give it back to Isolde – the real Isolde, not the ghoul she was now. As she rolled onto her side, she took in her surroundings. It was a small plateau with little to recommend itself. Cormorants watched them, unperturbed, their feathered bodies within touching distance. An ever-present breeze whipped the clouds overhead and curdled the seaweed. There was a large circular rock pool, framed by a bed of mussels, who clenched their lips tightly. In less than an hour, the jagged mound would be lost beneath the waves and the young women with it.

'There's nothing here,' said Kensa, cursing loudly. 'Merrin tricked us.'

'Not everything with the Folk is at it seems.' Elowen rolled onto her elbows and leaned towards the rock pool. 'Here?' She dipped her hand into the water and pointed to a channel running through the smooth stone. A *splash* had the pair scream and roll backwards, as a cormorant dived into the rock pool. The bird vanished into the tunnel and barely a ripple marked its progress.

'The tide's rising,' said Kensa. 'If we're going, we're going now.'

Elowen grinned and her braid – a slick, dull tail – bounced on her back as she sank forwards, taking the path the cormorant had shown them. As the eldest, Kensa was disgruntled to realise she had not gone first. For once, she could only follow.

Compared to the sea's temperature, the rock pool was warmer, having captured the sun's heat. She sank into the sloping channel, which plummeted downwards and levelled out, to reveal strangely coloured sand: cobalt and white, pearlescent in turns. It was bright enough to light her progress. Kensa's foot grazed it as she kicked her legs. Movement. It was not sand. She flinched away. *Eels.* Hundreds coiled together in thick shapes, writhing around themselves and flashing with an eerie luminescence. A queer light, the kind Kensa only ever saw if she pressed too hard against her closed eyelids. Among them was the cormorant, who caught one, wings beating, and retreated the way it had come. Doubt grew in Kensa's mind. What if there was no way out? She was not worried for herself; Elowen's lungs were smaller, ravaged by illness, and yet the younger woman swam onwards with a peculiar ease. The tunnel narrowed. Enclosed by stone, the water's stillness bottled Kensa's pulse and repeated it back to her, a shell to her ear, a shell to her entire body.

When she thought she might burst or faint or drown, the tunnel expanded and the rock above them opened. The light was low. Kensa didn't realise she'd broken the water's surface until the weight of her wet hair pulled at its follicles. Elowen was beside her, alert to their surroundings. It was a rounded cave whose eel-light trickled along a narrow walkway. Thick blue streaks veined the rock face, which Kensa identified as copper left too long in stone, and hung as stalactites like a dead man's fingers.

The only sound came from Kensa and Elowen's own movements, the gentle lapping water and their breathing. Occasionally, the eels would thicken or collide against one another, slapping and splashing, prior to settling once again. Kensa shuddered when one slithered against her thigh. The sisters' clothes were saturated and heavy as they crawled out onto the pathway that stretched ominously into the blue. Kensa cleared her throat to speak and the cave echoed her nervousness back to her.

'I know,' said Elowen.

It had been a brave notion back in the cottage to confront the Bucka and ask him to fix their ill work. Now, it seemed unwise. One could not forget who he was, nor the stories told about him, but what other choice did Kensa have?

She went first along the tunnel, which tilted lower and lower. Above her, Kensa could sense the weight of the ocean, a pressure which made her head thicken. It was quiet enough to magnify their breathing, steps, the *drip, drip, drip* of their clothes. The tide would be well above the entrance to this place by now; it would be a long wait until they could leave – *if* they could leave. Gradually, the tunnel flattened into a chamber, shaped like a giant bulb, with another pool in the centre, wide as a house. There was a ringed platform around it, raised above the water. Inside were further eels, their bodies circling the water's edge in an undulating cyclone. There was another body moving in the pool, this one tentacled, with an eye as large as a dinner plate and a beak that opened menacingly.

'Is he here?' Elowen leaned her head over the water, saw the creatures within it, and leaned hastily back again.

Kensa put a hand to her belt for reassurance, seeking the bone-handled knife. Her fingers met an empty sheath, the blade missing.

'He is,' said a low voice behind them, 'but why are you?'

Kensa whipped around, hopeful and afraid, to meet the cormorant eyes of the Bucka.

Chapter Twenty-two

The Bucka

The Father of Storms was as he always was. Unreadable. Whatever his mood, it was as hidden as a riptide. He placed himself at the copper-blue tunnel entrance – and their exit. In the Bucka's long fingers was the bone-handled knife. He angled and rolled it across his knuckles, as though it were liquid, not steel. When he spoke, it was with an ocean and its fathoms behind him. 'Witchling.'

'It didn't work,' blathered Kensa. 'Isolde's not herself; she's wrong, somehow.'

The Bucka's mouth twitched and his eyebrows rose a fraction. Not enough to be called a frown, though near to it. He seemed less human than ever. 'For a wise woman, you do lack wisdom.'

A pounding throbbed in Kensa's head. She wanted to lie down. Not be here, discerning conundrums posed by a minor sea god. Anger, ever-present and easy to summon, pressed against her teeth. That didn't mean she wasn't afraid. On and on, that blade swam in his grasp. Kensa could not draw her eyes from it. 'Tell me how to fix her.'

'She isn't broken,' said the Bucka plainly. 'Give her time, she'll recover.'

Elowen secured herself at Kensa's side, suckered like a limpet, as though they were kids again. 'He's lying.'

'He can't lie, we have the Pact.'

'A man can always lie,' said Elowen.

And the bind between wise woman and sea god was never about truth, Kensa realised.

The Bucka inclined his head, a queer lean. 'If I hand a child an apple larger than his fist and he chokes, am I to blame?'

Kensa slid her eyes to her bare feet, thoughts a brambled mess, until the realisation came to her. 'You tricked me,' she said slowly. 'You knew it wouldn't work.'

'It will not be long until she kills, for death needs death to sustain itself.' A solemn shape took his lips, while that knife continued spinning. 'Once that happens, I will have what I want.'

'Why?' Elowen asked. Her voice was far steadier than Kensa's and she did not flinch at his direct stare, which remained on her a beat too long. Surprisingly, the Bucka turned away first.

Kensa's fury was lost, replaced by shame. How ridiculous she'd been to forsake the warnings she'd known since birth. He was a cat in a dovecot and she a thing with feathers. What else would he do but bite?

'I know what it is to be ignorant, to ask why and gain no answer,' he said. 'I will give you this, at least.'

He slid past them with steps that were not steps and appeared at the pool's edge. It began to shiver, flat, then churning, pouring itself into shapes: a dozen horses in white. The mirages weren't alive, Kensa realised, they were no more conscious than the shadow-puppets her late father once cast against the walls. Yet these were far more detailed. Sweat shone on the horses' flanks, while riders appeared on their backs, bearing spurs on their heels and spears in their hands. Hooves pounded the pool's surface and yet the beasts galloped on the spot, sending water surging outwards, as opponents rose up in challenge – and were swiftly cut down. Translucent spray fanned out: seawater now, blood back then.

Men such as these had not been seen in centuries.

Men such as these should be run from.

Among their number and cast in salt was a warrior in armour, longsword clasped within his powerful fist. When his mount reared between his thighs, he held on to its back as though nothing – no wind, no rain, no blow – could take him down. A fierce battle rang through the cave. Elowen pressed her back to the wall, while Kensa heeled forwards, though she too was afraid, and reached out to touch one running beast. It pulled away, eyed her, then leaned its watery muzzle to her palm.

Here, the Bucka explained, 'In the forgotten age, when our land knew another name, there was a man who would be the last king to rule it.'

'Gerent,' said Elowen quietly.

A name which Kensa already knew. For once, she was not annoyed at her sister's vast knowledge and quickness. Now, she needed it. *King Gerent.* Could it be? She roamed the Bucka's sharp features, his stance, that eel-skin coat as weighty as a royal cape.

'King Gerent was arrogant – *I* was arrogant – and the first wise woman of Portscatho punished him for it.' As he spoke, the pool's visions shifted. Arrows were loosed and with them a spear, which shot straight into Gerent's thigh. 'She was a clever bitch, this wise woman,' continued the Bucka, as the water-king staggered off his horse and fell to his knees, hands lifting to plead with a graceful figure. 'She thought to punish him for his cruelties, for she had witnessed what he had done to her village. Her hands salved the lash marks on his servants' backs, her hands delivered the babes he put upon the local women, her hands set the bones of the men who survived the wars he courted. Upon receiving a mortal blow, it was his turn to demand her help. He wished to be immortal, undying, to rule the Land for ever and have it bend to his will for eternity.' The shapes in the pool were seen to argue, a watery hand reaching to wind, harshly, into the wise woman's hair. 'She refused.' Kensa flinched, the pain splintering through her, as the Bucka's own fist tightened. 'He persuaded her.'

From his tone, he had not done it kindly.

'Even then, she tricked him,' said the Bucka. 'Promised him unending life if he would forsake the Land for the Sea. King Gerent was greedy and knew the waves to be a powerful force, so he agreed to the Pact.'

In the wise woman's hand appeared a blade. Although it was

translucent, Kensa recognised its shape. Her watery double slashed at the king's throat, which ripped open to become the pooling saltwater.

'Now he would live for ever, yet not as he envisioned. She had bound magic along with the sea and King Gerent was trapped within both, never knowing peace from the tide. Finally, he was forced to serve the people he'd abused; send the day's catch to them, cradle their ships or pluck a sailor's wind from his lungs when he was too far from shore to live.' Even this the Bucka showed them. 'At first, he brought storms to lash the coast, surging as high as the wise woman's home though not one met their mark, for the Pact offered protection.'

In the pool, the wise woman was depicted on a clifftop, hands raised to quell a tempest. Years spun around her, features twisting, changing throughout time, shifting sex and height and skin, until one became Isolde and, after her, Kensa, standing there to keep back the waves. Curious, the real Kensa approached her brine counterpart – evading her sister's hand – and met its cold stare with her own.

'For as long as a wise woman preserved the Land and protected its peoples, the King would be tied to the Sea and its monsters.' The Bucka grimaced. 'I do not sleep, I cannot eat, I cannot recall joy or pain or living. I am unending and bittered with time. Through you, witchling, I can end it.'

The counter-Kensa in the water reached out to her fleshy double. Behind her, shifting up through the water, mouth agape and screaming, came a monstrous form – a sea-hag – who tore the pool apart. It was an unstable foam and liquid-boned mass, surging and bubbling and wrenching the pool apart. Quickly, the water – and the sea-hag with it – fell back to a flat surface with not so much as a ripple to stir it.

'If a wise woman causes deadly harm to the village she is bound to protect, the Pact will fail,' said the Bucka, holding the bone-handled knife close to his face. Kensa willed him to slice his own pointed nose open with it. 'As soon as your creature kills, which she surely will, everything shall end, and it will be your doing.'

Elowen hissed through her teeth, though kept her back flush to the copper-stained wall.

'If you want to die, I'll fix it,' spat Kensa.

The Bucka took her at her word. He vanished, fading to vapour, then materialised a mere foot away from her. The weight of water in the air soaked Kensa's hair anew. He grasped her hand, pulled it to his and pressed the knife – that bone handle – into her palm. She gripped it, hard. The Bucka was impossibly strong as he wrenched her fingers up, clawing coat and faded layers aside, to press the blade's point at his chest. Kensa needed no further encouragement.

She was tired and cold and scared. He was monstrous and cruel and frightening.

'There,' he said, thumb pressed to her knuckle. 'Come tear through breast and bone, see what good a heart of barnacle gets you.'

He was too close. Breath rigid and icy, like the sea at night upon her.

Kensa could not do it. For as much as she wished him ill, she could do no harm. It was not in her nature and he knew it. She pulled back, fighting to loosen his hold.

He let her go.

'I cannot die, as the ocean cannot die,' said the Bucka finally.

No sooner did he disappear from her sight than he appeared behind her again. Chain-linked droplets encircled his wrists and tethered him to the water, as slim as a spider's craft and stronger. 'As soon as I met you, child, I knew it would be you who'd undo what was done centuries ago and free me from the Pact,' he said. 'You are arrogant, as I was arrogant. It is your undoing as it was mine.'

'I didn't mean to,' said Kensa desperately.

He looked at her with pity, and for a moment she wished she had stabbed him.

Elowen had not budged an inch, though pursed lips showed her shrewd mind turning. 'What will happen without the Father of Storms?'

'War, I suppose,' said the Bucka indifferently. 'Those surviving Folk who fell with the ebbing sea will reclaim the shore that was theirs. Soon, there will be nothing to keep the deep's predators from making prey of men.'

'How can you do this?' Elowen's anger was startling. 'You've had a thousand years to become less selfish and you've only become worse.'

'If I could do this without spilling blood, I would,' said the Bucka regretfully. Only then did he change his focus, shifting to stare at the youngest in the chamber as though she had arrived at that very moment. 'Does your family know what you are? Born with too much salt, fey-blooded, siren-bound.'

'Leave her alone,' Kensa growled. Her attention shifted briefly to her sister, to find her lips parted and brow furrowed in worry. Because here was a secret, one neither had touched or fully understood. Although there was shock in hearing it bandied about so openly, Kensa schooled her face into neutrality, into acceptance, into whatever she thought Elowen needed.

'It is getting late and the sun is setting,' said the Bucka, though how he knew, none could tell. 'Your hag does not tolerate sun. When the horizon dims, she will find her way out and sate her appetite and the Pact will break.'

Kensa shook her head. 'Isolde would never hurt anyone.'

'She wouldn't, yet this creature would; a corruption of existence, a living grief come to enact its woes.'

The sisters exchanged looks.

'How long do we have?'

The Bucka's cheek twitched. Tension drew on his shoulders. In that minuscule gesture was apprehension, which stripped his severity to nothing. He became a lost young man, his soul blunted by a crown's merciless weight. That did not mean Kensa could forgive him.

'It could be hours, no more than a day,' he surmised, closing his eyes. 'Do you think I will feel it, when it happens, or will it simply end?'

Kensa edged closer to Elowen, who leaned her head towards the tunnel, towards their freedom. Would they reach the cottage before nightfall? Kensa could not hazard a guess. There was no measure of time here. Only darkness, the water, the eel-light and the Bucka.

As though waking from a dream, the Father of Storms heard their careful, cautious feet on the stone, saw Elowen's hand reaching for Kensa's.

'You cannot leave how you entered, not without drowning,' he said. 'It is high tide and we must let the hag do her work.' His frown deepened. 'I would – I think I would see the sun set upon the waves one last time.'

Kensa reached for him. 'Wait!'

That was all the farewell he offered as he stepped into the pool and was gone.

The sisters dared not move, lest he return. He did not. After several long moments had passed, Kensa said, 'Stay here until low tide, then get help.'

Elowen snatched for her sleeve. 'You heard him! You'll drown!'

'I can't stay here and wait, can I?'

'There's another way out,' said Elowen, blinking quickly. 'In the pool is a long tunnel leading to Porthbeor Mine.' Her hand fidgeted with her braid. 'You'll ask how I know and I've nothing to tell you, only that I do and always seem to know what no one else does.' She fixed her eyes on Kensa's, nostrils flaring. 'I never blamed you for hating me. I thought, somehow, you knew what I was, that Isolde had told you.'

'I don't understand.' Kensa shook her head. 'I never hated you.'

'Please, trust me,' said Elowen.

There was no chance to stop her. No sooner had she spoken than Elowen ran, straight into the pool, blonde head diving down towards the eels who parted at her approach. In their sallow sheen was another tunnel, exactly as she'd described, which the younger woman swiftly swam into. Cursing under her breath, Kensa sheathed her knife and went in after her sister. Below, a rumble began. The kraken sensed their movement. Despite her weariness, muscles clenching, Kensa propelled herself faster, into the tunnel, behind her sister.

The eel-light faded. Around them was nothing. A dead end and it would be their dead end. Worse, no one would ever find their bodies. A cold brush met her ankles: the kraken. The Pact kept it at bay, yet how long for? Its slim tentacle began to curl towards her legs as she groped forwards, grazing Elowen's calf, then her hand, which met hers and began to pull, lifting her out – *out* into fresh, cold air.

She only realised they had company, and that more than Elowen's hands gripped her, when the first lantern bloomed against the dark.

Hard feet slapped on stone, a shout, a heave, 'Drehevel!' A bulky fist pulled her up by her armpits. She was dropped, unceremoniously, beside her sister and beneath the austere disapproval of the mine's overseer.

Chapter Twenty-three

The Hag

'What in God's name are you doing here?' Branok directed the question and his simmering fury to Kensa, the eldest. 'There's none allowed in the mine's lower recesses. You're lucky we heard you.' His glower was so like Jack's. 'How did you get in?'

'I . . .' Kensa trailed off. What could she say to the miners crowded around them? She met her sister's eyes in the gloom, bloodshot and wide. If she was to be their wise woman, she wouldn't show weakness here. Murmurs ran along the copper-rich walls, melding into the mineral veins and damp hollows.

Branok, ever astute, sent an order over his shoulder. 'Get to work!'

Swiftly, though with dissenting talk, his men did as they were told.

'Where's Jack?' Kensa's wits restored themselves enough to notice his absence. Seeing him would help, somehow, she was sure of it. Even if he was cross with her.

'Is he not with you?' Branok's nostrils flared. 'I sent him to the cottage not an hour ago after you did not answer his earlier call. I thought it better he be among others who cared for his aunt, rather than pushing himself to exhaustion here.'

In her selfish actions, Kensa had forgotten she was not the only one who'd loved Isolde. What's more, Jack had a far greater claim to her loss. Slowly, her mind distant within her own self, she pieced together what Branok's words meant. Her stomach leapt to her mouth.

Elowen, as always, was faster to understand. 'We have to go!'

Kensa pushed past Branok, drawing her sister behind her. Lanterns threatened to catch her scalp and picks swung to avoid her, as she fled through the tunnel and dodged miners' bodies. It was high tide and the lower entrance was no longer accessible, forcing them higher, through the rat's maze in the cliff side. Eventually, a ladder led them up and into what remained of the day's light. A booming voice carried to her, over the brittle grassland, which she knew to be Branok's. Kensa had no time to tell him and he gave them no chase.

Bohortha was close, a short way along the hills. In the distance was Portscatho, hidden behind the coast's bend. It didn't matter if the Bucka had tricked her; she'd let him. And now Jack was in danger. In her frenzied run, Kensa barely noticed the sunset, which looked as though the sky's forge had poured molten metal from cloud to sea.

The cut on Elowen's forehead bled anew, painting a stripe down to her collar. Her weakness slowed her, legs seizing. It was no more than a mile, though it may as well have been several to the youngest sibling. In the sea she'd soared, on land she struggled.

'I'll go ahead,' called Kensa.

She did not wait for a reply.

Her body arrowed forward, bootless feet barely sensible to the stones that jabbed her. A stitch buried into her side, though she did not relent. She had to save Jack. If the Pact was going to break, it would not be through his loss. She wouldn't allow it.

The nettles did not sting her – or if they did, she did not know it – as Kensa crashed through the front garden and into the cottage. *Jack.* He was pinned to the parlour floor. His arms locked as he pushed back the rotten body craning over him – the hag – a keening, drooling creature, whose maw bent towards Jack's neck. Blood soaked him, but he was alive, thank God, alive. Around him was chaos: the shell table cracked, glassware in pieces, a single Bad Book twitching against its broken spine and lying in a puddle of its pages. In his struggle, Jack did not notice her. Did not see Kensa. Until she barrelled into them both. She knocked Isolde to the side and fell down with her, against her.

'Rope,' wheezed Elowen from the garden path. 'Tie it up.'

A broken canine scraped Kensa's temple, while a gargling liquid dripped into her ear as Isolde – or the woman who had been Isolde – snapped at her. The hag's features were sunken as Farmer Hayle's rotten turnips, breath putrid and gums shrivelled with fly and maggot. Kensa shielded her face with a forearm. Her free hand went to her belt. She pulled the bone-handled blade loose. As soon as it left the sheath, the hag shrank back, knees bending crablike, freeing Kensa.

'Don't hurt her,' said Jack, a desperate shout.

Kensa waved the steel closer to the hag and received a clawing swipe for her efforts. Beetled eyes watched her from behind a stringy lump which once was hair. 'Isolde,' she tried. 'Speak to me.' Nothing, not a flicker of awareness. Kensa inched forwards, brandishing the weapon, using it to corral the hag backwards. Did she recognise it? Whatever the reason, whether its memory was painful or it tapped into the Old Ways and their terrible might, it brought discomfort to the creature. At least, enough to ward her off. As soon as the hag's bare, broken feet crossed the threshold to her room, Jack slammed the door on her. He swiftly put a chair under the handle, jamming it and securing the hag inside. Jack's heavy panting betrayed his pain, his shock.

Kensa reached for him.

His snarl was her answer. 'What have you done?' She flinched at his tone.

'We should have left a note,' said Elowen, breathless as she entered the cottage. 'One telling you not to open the door under any circumstance.' The overseer's son levelled her with a hard look usually reserved for the eldest sister.

Kensa's voice was unusually small as it left her. 'Jack—'

'No,' he replied, swinging his attention back to her.

'I hoped I could fix it myself,' she confessed, 'and you'd never have found out.' She raised her chin and truly looked at him, to see the gash on his shoulder. Its slim-sickle shape was the fit of Isolde's gaping mouth and ran fast with blood. A healer's instincts kicked in and her hands moved automatically to his injury.

He pulled back, yet the movement brought a pained gasp from him. Only then did he relent, allowing her to assess him, though he made it clear he was not happy about it.

'Good, it's not too deep.'

'It doesn't hurt much,' said Jack.

Kensa's mouth thinned. 'Don't lie to a wise woman.'

'It hurts a lot.'

'I'll need to clean and bind it or else it won't heal.'

It was a simple act to wash his neck and put a sling together using an old skirt, as gentle as she could be. Kensa's mind shifted back to what she had been taught, a healer's actions, careful and precise, even though it was Jack beneath her fingers. If she thought about it too much, she knew she'd never stop thinking about it. Him, neck laid bare to her, shirt falling open to show the warm brown skin beneath.

A more complicated task lay ahead. It was Elowen, practical as ever, who broached it first. 'What do we do with Isolde?'

Kensa's stomach dropped into her shoes. 'I can't think.'

'We fix her,' said Jack, pallor faded from the blood he'd lost.

'Is there even a "her" any more? Although that may be Isolde's body, she's not in it,' said Elowen. 'Or if she is, she won't listen to us.' She relayed what the Bucka had told them. Jack's expression was stone, if stone had anger.

Shame had Kensa's bearings falter, the room growing small

for a moment as she looked at him. 'You hate me,' she said
dully. 'Don't you?' When had she taken a seat? There was
suddenly a cushioned chair at her back – one she did not remember slumping into – and Jack's hand on her arm, which
he hastily removed.

'You need to rest,' he said, unreadable. 'We'll take turns
watching her.'

She had to explain. He couldn't hate her if she explained.
And if he did, she could explain again. Reason and argue and
pester until he relented. 'Jack—'

'No,' a pause, then repeated, firmly, 'No.'

There was no retort. Nothing she could say, even if she had
all the words known to every scribe who'd ever lived. Nothing
that would make him forgive her.

'I think I will sleep,' she said eventually. It was better than
staying with him and his unwillingness to meet her eye. And
confronting the realisation that she'd lost him – it – them.

No sooner had Kensa spoken than she found herself in her
bed, the movements which brought her there lost in a dizzy
haze. In the quiet that precedes hard slumber, she heard
Elowen speak from the parlour.

'You handled her well,' she said to Jack. 'There's few who can
get her to see sense when she's off on her nonsense.'

'I know,' he replied, slow and strained. 'She must be tired.'

Were it not for the truth in their words and her own exhaustion, Kensa would have flung off the covers and marched
downstairs to spite them, herself included. Make it right, somehow. Or worse, no doubt. Instead, she slept.

*

Kensa carried her dreams into waking: cormorants and wheat fields and a Jack with blue eyes who hated and loved her in turns. It was night still. Fox had finally deemed it safe enough to return and slept at her feet, curled nose to tail. A full bladder and a dry mouth told her she had taken enough hours' rest. Grogginess dipped her head below her shoulders, chin to sternum. When the bleariness subsided enough to let her move, she filled her chamber pot and then thought on filling her belly. There had to be enough ingredients in the pantry to rustle a small meal together.

Elowen was alert, on guard outside the hag's door, her back propped against the parlour wall and legs tucked inwards. Blankets cocooned her, pale features owlish amid the heavy wool. Jack snored rhythmically on the rag-rug beside the hearth, his face aglow with roaming embers. He looked young when he slept. He *was* young. It was easy to forget. To see him now was to see his maturity gone, along with his persistent frown and brow forever knitted in an *I-told-you-so* or *you-need-to-listen* or *for-goodness'-sake-Kensa* or the other phrases (ones she would never admit) that Kensa spied upon his forehead and read too much into.

After scraping what she could from the pantry – hard bread, old cheese and a winter-softened apple – Kensa sat beside her sister, knees splayed out.

'It's your turn to sleep.' She chewed as she talked. 'I'll keep watch.'

Elowen nodded and leaned sideways, until her head was on her older sibling's shoulder. It was as natural as breathing. A strange knot loosened in Kensa's chest, one she had held fast to ever since her sister had been born. Strange, how quickly she could relinquish it.

A question had been rolling around Kensa's mind for too long and she voiced it now, quietly. 'How long have you had the Sight?' Few could see into the future. It was a rare gift and an unwanted curse, claimed Isolde, who mentioned it on occasion, as though arming Kensa for this moment. At her questions, the Bad Books shifted slightly on their shelves. 'That's how you knew about the tunnel to the mine, isn't it?' Onions, bone charms and seaweed on a line could predict large events, in a vague way, yet nothing as accurate and troubling as the Sight.

Elowen tensed. Her lips parted with a small, wet sound. 'Since that morning on the beach.' There was only one morning and it was with the Morgawr. 'As I saw her die, I heard a voice and there was a change in me. As though I'd eaten enchanted fruit or split my finger on a spindle.'

'You read too much,' said Kensa.

Elowen hummed a non-committal response. 'After that, I began to sicken.' Long nights with a heaving chest, weakness and peculiar rashes, there one day, gone the next. Kensa had seen her sister fail and suffer and fret against her illness, though she had never thought any reason behind it bar poor luck or attention-seeking. 'Unwanted visions found me, memories passed down from another. I came to know what I should not and, try as I might, could not forget it. When I tried to tell our mother, she wouldn't hear it. You've noticed it, haven't you? How she only ever wants to hear the good and not the bad.'

Elowen unfurled one arm and Kensa was permitted entry

into blanketed warmth. With some adjustment, the pair tucked their feet together and sat shoulder to shoulder, encased in wool and each other.

'Ma wasn't always like that,' said Kensa. 'Only after my father died did she get distant. She never wanted to see trouble, would rather be ignorant and unquerying. If she pretended it was enough, then it would be.' Quiet, but for Jack's snores and the fire's reply to them. 'Are you angry with her?'

'No, I'm not.' A pause. 'Yes, I am.' Elowen rolled her head sideways and Kensa sensed a hardening around her, an internal wall she kept high and would let few climb. 'I understand it, though, which makes it easier. Besides, if she hadn't been that way, you wouldn't be your way.'

'And what way's that?'

'Stubborn, naming the truth when you see it, eager to face everything first and beat the others to it.' Elowen took a deep breath. 'I could never keep up with you.'

In the silence that followed, Kensa offered, rather charitably, she thought, 'Well, I'm not as clever as you.'

Elowen laughed softly. 'There's nought else to do when you're ill but read.' There were always books around her, ones Miss Latham loaned her, which only increased Kensa's resentment. Their teacher adored her, and who wouldn't? It made sense now. Why she chose dusty tomes over people, why she was so guarded and did not speak her mind, lest another's slip through and reveal a destiny.

Kensa puffed out her cheeks. 'Do you know what will happen to us?'

'No and I do not think I would want to,' said Elowen. 'Only

in a particular moment do I learn how it will unfold, as though another hand is guiding mine and telling me what to do.' Her lips were pursed in thought. 'I think if the Sight did not attack my body, it would attack my mind,' she confessed, glancing to the Bad Books. 'I think I can accept that.'

Another question dogged Kensa and she threw it clumsily onto their tangled legs, if only to be rid of it. 'Why don't you hate me? After what I've done, I thought ...'

'I did, at times.' Elowen sniffled and wiped her nose on Kensa's shoulder. 'You were determined to do everything alone and I saw how lonely it made you. I don't think you realised that it made me lonely too.'

'We're together now,' said Kensa, though it was weak-sounding to her own ears. There was a pause as the eldest opened her mouth to speak and thought better of it.

Elowen asked, 'What is it?'

Kensa cleared her throat. 'Are we going to talk about you lying to our mother and visiting Merrin in secret for months and not telling anyone?'

'No.'

'All right.'

'I wanted to have a person who was solely mine, who I did not have to share with anyone,' admitted Elowen finally, 'the same way you and Jack are.'

Kensa's teeth clacked together. 'We're not—'

A *thump* shook the door on its hinges, the one which Kensa and Elowen sat beside. The pair jumped, Elowen squeaked. Through a small knot in the wood, Kensa heard ragged breaths and an exhale that passed – stinking – through a minuscule gap. Kensa *thumped* back, as hard as she could, and the hag cackled in response.

'Go on upstairs, I'll take over,' said Kensa.

Elowen was sent to the vacant bed and Kensa took her place at Isolde's door. Her ears listened for the hag's movements, while her eyes fixed on Jack's shoulders. Traced his chest as it rose and fell, followed his back and the gradual slope downwards to— Well, she looked at him a lot. Until she feared he might guess, somehow, the thoughts she nursed in her unseen spaces.

A wise woman could not marry, she had been told. No midwife could deliver babies when she was having her own. The village – Portscatho – was to be her family. Its residents would be bonded to her, as she was to them, partner and child and brother and father combined. Unbidden, heathen notions danced through her mind. Had not Isolde entertained herself with a man come May Day? She had not been a wife, yet she'd done what wives do and no one spoke against her. A thousand scenarios danced through Kensa's head, as many ribbons as on a maypole. Perhaps her mother's advice was right when it came to lovers and dalliances.

Jack. What would it be like? What would *he* be like? Strong, she guessed. Firm, yet gentle. Focused, the way he was with every task he set himself. Surely it would be the same if he set himself to her? Kensa held the blankets tight against her lap. She remained seated. Poised at the door, thighs clamped together. Kept her thoughts as thoughts alone, barred from intention and action, though sweet enough for now.

*

Elowen did not sleep long and when she woke, it was with a noisy impetus that pulled everyone awake with her. 'They'll want a *body*, Kensa,' she said loudly. 'For the funeral, they'll want to *bury* a *body*.' Jack made a low, sleepy grunt that had Kensa's mouth go dry, while Elowen continued, 'I was winner two years running for the village scarecrow competition.'

'Of course you were,' said Kensa, talking over her. 'Why does that—'

'I can make a scarecrow and we'll wrap it with cloth! No one will know there's nothing in it and then we can figure out what to do about Isolde after the service.'

'Or bury me,' grumbled Jack, 'then I could get some sleep.'

Kensa's throat tightened. 'Please don't say that.'

He had grace enough to nod and mumble an apology. Despite his careless words, a small thrill found her: Jack wasn't a morning person, she'd never have known if not for this. Now the information was hers to keep, to revisit whenever she wanted.

Under Elowen's direction, Jack and Kensa collected whatever items they could find. Stones from the garden – brushed pink in the morning light – and swaddled with cloth. A heavy pot, its bottom burned to uselessness – Kensa's own mistake, which she was now grateful for – and other miscellaneous items from Isolde's fertility box were roped together and slowly bound into a human form. Even with their frenzied activity, no one left the hag's door unattended, lest foul activity be heard.

'It's too heavy,' said Jack.

'Bodies get heavier after death,' said Kensa, who had learned as much these months past. 'Or they feel heavier, anyway.'

'It's the limpness that concerns me.' Elowen clicked her tongue as she surveyed their work. 'Jack, you'll need to carry her out. No one will know the body's not real if you're the one holding it. Are you strong enough?'

Jack gave her a long look. 'Yes.'

'Try it now and—'

'I'll be strong enough,' said Jack.

Kensa's laugh startled them, though it was short-lived. When her chest deflated she had a jagged piece within it, a strange dread she breathed around. It had gone unnoticed until now and appeared only when she remembered what it was to be lighter, to find humour in odd places.

'I'll put on breakfast,' said Kensa, eager to be clear of Jack's disapproval. Her feet took her to the kitchen door, until she recalled there would be no eggs for morning as there were no chickens left to lay them. *Oh.* A soured mood brought her to nod at Isolde's door. 'Does she – it – need food, d'you think?'

Jack frowned. He was a man who frowned often. This frown, however, was more pronounced than usual. 'She's been quiet.'

'Um,' said Elowen meaningfully.

After several long seconds, the other two caught up with her thinking.

Kensa swore loudly. She charged across the room and yanked the chair away from its place under the handle. When she opened the door, she found Isolde's room without Isolde in it. The mess was there, pillows, filth and dead bees lying on the floor with their small bodies curled into themselves.

'Kensa,' said Jack, in warning.

She checked in the wardrobe. Nothing, only Isolde's old

clothes. Next she pulled the covers away and looked under the bed. There were bits there, too: old toenails, faeces and a small finger which the hag had left behind. Feathers. Black ones, silken and sheening, as a water bird's are wont to do. And through the shadows on the bed's other side were boots, familiar ones at that.

'Kensa,' said Jack again, with gruff urgency.

Only then did she straighten up. As she did so, her back tightened, vertebrae fusing together. How long had it been river-cold? Since when had the air been this tight in her lungs? She knew then, with certainty, who stood in the room with her.

'Witchling,' said the Bucka.

Kensa wrenched the bone-handled knife from her belt. 'Where is she?' There was a freshness to the space, an airy quality which brought her focus to the window. It was ajar, the rusted latch gone. Water lay around it and she had no doubt it would taste of salt.

'You did this,' she accused.

He did not need to confirm it. His expression told her enough. There was an even stranger quality to him now, distant, here and not here. The Bucka had taken something from her she'd never get back. Worse than that, he was part of her. When she searched inside herself, the Pact was there, a subtle thread binding them. Yet when she thought she'd feel satisfaction radiating from it, there was nothing, only a pitiable aching hollowness. She hated him even more.

Jack and Elowen stood in the doorway, their expressions matching thunder and not a little terror. Both looked to Kensa. She did not look back. How could she, while the Bucka was here? Under his wrath she was ridiculous and small and fool-ish – a fool made fool again.

Her voice stuck in her throat. 'How long has she been gone?'

The Bucka gave her no answer and spoke instead on Kensa. 'You would have been a fearsome woman to behold had you lived in my time.'

'I am fearsome now,' she whispered, though her knees pressed together under her skirts and their caps knocked in time.

'Make your peace, for there will be none once the hag fin-ishes her work,' said the Bucka. 'Let it be done, do not interfere.'

Kensa inched closer to the Father of Storms, around the bulky furniture that stood between them. 'How could you do this to her? She invited you into her home, she—'

'Isolde was as much a friend to me as she was to you.'

'Is this how you treat your friends?' Another step and Kensa rounded the bedpost, while the Bucka stood and watched and waited. How could he be this calm? Stand there and meet her eye. 'Is this what you'd do to me, given the chance?'

'If I had to,' he said simply. He stood as tall as the baronet and held the same authority, as though built for it. If men like him were born to lead, she did not consider herself a woman who'd follow.

Kensa's fury reached new heights. 'Oh, so you *had* to?' It did not matter that he was the Bucka, one who commanded tempests and dragged ships to the depths. Now he was simply another man who'd disappointed her.

Before she could act, Jack saw an opening. He pushed out from the doorway and struck, curving a fist into the Bucka's side. Kensa's mouth went slack with terror. Yet his hand went straight through, leaving an odd missing section behind. Icy water ran across them, as though the miner's son had merely punched a puddle's surface. Jack's balance went, stolen by his own momentum. His knees hit the floor, arm sling forgotten and his wound splitting anew. Despite it, he barely cried out, mouth clamping shut.

'I knew your grandfather,' said the Bucka to the miner's son. Slowly, his shape rippled and reformed to patch the gap Jack had made. 'It was I who saved him when he stowed away on a ship which sank near Falmouth Bay. In his last moments, when he thought himself lost, he asked me to deliver him, and did I not deliver him?'

'For a price,' spat Jack.

'He paid it gladly,' said the Bucka. 'Tell me, what price would you pay if I gave you what you crave most?'

Jack raised himself and swung again. 'Bastard.'

Kensa let her instincts guide her. The bone-handled knife was heavy in her hand, as though it knew its purpose. Her only wish was to get the Bucka far away from Jack. Neither saw her approach. She closed her eyes and slashed forwards, wildly. She hit her mark. Of course, she doubted she'd do any real damage to the immortal man, yet flesh gave beneath her blade and she gasped in triumph. Only, it was not the Bucka whose skin tore beneath her. Her lids split open to find the Bucka had moved, drifted from one space to another as easy as vapour. Kensa had not hit the Father of Storms. Instead, she had sent her knife straight into Jack.

She stared, numbly. Blood pooled anew from his shirt,

already stained from the night prior. There was a small fresh gash on his arm, bubbling crimson. It was on her hands, she could not put it back in, she tried, there was—

'It appears I do not need a hag to break the Pact when you can do it for me,' said the Bucka cruelly. 'Your duty is to protect these people, is it not? And look at you, look what you've done, witchling.'

'I didn't mean to!'

'You never do and yet it happens nonetheless, doesn't it?'

'Yes,' said Kensa breathlessly. How could she deny it? Her eyes were wide, growing wider, as she stared at the wound she had made. 'Jack.' She reached for him and yet hated to touch him, to make it worse, to hurt the one person she—

'I'm all right,' said Jack, clasping his palm over the cut and pushing Kensa's hands aside, 'I'm all right, look, see, I'm all right, it's nothing.'

Her shock came and went, quickly replaced with rage. 'You!'

Lurking behind Jack's shoulder was the Bucka, his entertainment flashing with his bleached-coral teeth. Kensa sidestepped her friend and stood right against the Bucka's chest. This time she kept her eyes open and her bone-handled knife found its mark. It was as though the Land beneath them came to guide her strike. And unlike Jack's failed punch, the Bucka could not escape it. His eel-skin coat tore, as did the skin of his chest, sundered from stomach to clavicle. Kensa's wrist shook with the effort, heels anchored to the flagstones, tendons flexing as she pulled free.

Confusion took the Bucka's lips. He put a hand to his middle. There was no blood. Instead, his wound lay open and pale, as though the blood within him had already gone to tide. Slowly, he began to leak seawater.

'I wish it were that easy,' encouraging, desperate, mad, he said, 'Come try again.'

'Kensa,' warned Elowen, poised in the doorway, her fear palpable.

The Bucka asked her, invited her, and she knew it would make no difference. One cannot kill the sea as one cannot love the sea. As she struck once more and met his cold flesh, the small leak released a torrent. The Bucka split apart. From his heart came a wave, as tall as Kensa, which flooded her lungs and slammed her back against the wall. It was relentless, fixing her to the hard stonework. She would drown here, in him, a mile from the ocean. When her body weakened and her ears lost their last sounds in rushing water, it receded. She hit the floor, chest flattening against the ground and chin meeting a hard edge. Kensa palmed up and onto her rear, to find the room's furniture washed to one side, every surface dripping with salt.

Jack coughed his ire and Elowen shouted her distress. It did not seem to register in her mind, for the Bucka was gone and Isolde had escaped and there was nothing Kensa could do to fix it.

Chapter Twenty-four

The Funeral

Elowen twisted her braid over a bucket to free the saltwater from it. She looked furious in a way Kensa had never seen. 'It's like he's *in* my hair,' she hissed. 'Why did he stay? He could have freed Isolde and left.'

'Gloating, probably,' said Kensa, elbows on the kitchen table, head in her hands. 'It's what I would do.' There was a single white chicken feather sitting on the floor beneath her shoe; another hook in her conscience that would not let go.

Elowen huffed and tugged her hair harder. 'He's trying to shake your resolve, Kensa.'

'It's working.'

'No, it isn't.' Jack's sling was back in place. He was even worse for wear, another bandage around his injured arm as he proposed, 'Elowen and I will look for Isolde together.' Kensa surged upright and he quelled her protest with a single raised palm. 'You need to stay here for the funeral; the village will need its wise woman to show strength. Or, well, at least show herself.'

'No one can know I've done this.' Kensa's plea was coarse as it left her. 'You can't tell anyone, please?'

Jack's nostrils flared. 'We can right it.'

It was a thin reassurance, as he did not promise to keep her secret. Kensa was ashamed she had even asked him to. He did not complain about the knife wound on his arm, yet it must have hurt him. *She* must have hurt him. Everything was her fault and she could sense him pulling away from her, distancing himself from everything she'd wrought upon them.

'You can't carry the body now,' said Kensa. 'Not after what I did.' She referred to the hastily made scarecrow propped up in the Bucka's old chair. 'It'll pull on those wounds and they'll bleed anew.' Jack's shirt soaked in the same bucket Elowen dripped her hair into. His body was wrapped with bandages and Kensa could barely look at it. 'If what the Bucka told us about the hag is true, she'll avoid sunlight and hide in a dark place.'

Elowen glanced out of the window, muddy with a morning haze. 'Everything will be dark again once the sun sets.'

'Then we have only a day to recover her,' said Kensa. 'If we can tempt her here, we can shut her away – properly, this time – and find a cure.'

There was no expression on Elowen's features, ever guarded, yet she was somehow pessimistic. 'How do you propose to lure her?'

Kensa raised herself to standing and leaned into the cupboard where the poultry feed was kept. 'We have one chicken left alive.' She sighed heavily. 'At least, for the moment.'

Almost everyone who lived in Portscatho and its surrounds was present at Isolde's funeral. There were residents from Gerrans, as well as the few who resided in the Customs House opposite St Mawes and even one or two Falmouth dwellers (as Kensa's mother told her afterwards). They arrived in twos, threes and fours – families, neighbours and friends – to pay their respects to Isolde. Mr Skewes had not shown his face and neither had the other God-fearing types, who put their faith in prayers rather than wise women. With how warm the day fared, none wore a heavy coat and cloaks were quickly plucked from shoulders.

Kensa wore the dress her mother had sent. It fit her arms and bust, though she could not shake the notion that the last time Derwa had worn it had been during the funeral for Kensa's own father. A nervous energy itched her elbows and she repeatedly stuffed her hands up her sleeves, to dig at the skin beneath. Jack and Elowen had fled out back to go hag-hunting and she was left to mourn a scarecrow.

Could she lie to everyone? Yes. She'd lied before.

Of these familiar – and unfamiliar – faces present at Bohortha, there was one who did not seem to fit. He was young, though older than Kensa, and wore black: a clergyman. Remembrance came and it was bitter. She *had* met him. Here was the figure she'd slammed a door on, the night he came to read Elowen her last rites. Kensa's hands balled into fists, like small fleshy boulders at her side.

How dare he?

She would have ordered this new Christian man to leave, and cruelly at that, were it not for her audience. His presence was as irksome as a tick beneath a hound's pelt. Worse, he seemed to know it and sought her out, breezing through those assembled in the garden. The curate was tall, much to her annoyance, with chestnut hair and a certain disposition which said he spoke crisply and not in the Cornish way. Yes, she could tell that afore he opened his mouth. And then he did and she was certain he did not belong here.

'Mr Delavaud,' said the curate, introducing himself.

'I can see that,' said Kensa, with no mind to give her name nor manners.

Not even Sir George Trevanion took such airs about himself, though many claimed he was born from common stock, a dalliance of his father's. Perhaps this was what made the new curate so ill-placed among the coastal people. He did not have the sea in his blood, only water: weak and saltless.

'I thought I'd say a few words,' continued Mr Delavaud.

'Did you now?'

He spoke in a pinched, deferential way. It made Kensa feel powerful. Here was a man who sought her approval. He wouldn't get it.

'Do not bother yourself,' she said, 'few are church-goers here.'

There was a bully, squatting as a toad, in Kensa's gut. She wanted him to be small and would enjoy the process of small-ing him. She opened her mouth to speak, to be cruel and feel better in the process, only he interrupted her.

'I do enjoy a challenge,' he said jovially, 'and perhaps one day I might win you over and see you in St Gerrans?'

Kensa's reply took several long moments to manifest. She wished she were clever, as he was clever. 'It weren't so long ago that your stock burned witches, killed the wise women and drowned the cunning folk.' She spoke to him down the length of her nose, chin raised. 'It's lucky there's any of us left.'

Mr Delavaud nodded, listening intently, fingers steepled together. His hands were soft, more used to books and quills than hard labour. Nothing like Jack's hands. 'If I keep the fires to a minimum, will I see you in a pew?'

'No.'

'I'll ask again,' he promised, 'each time I see you.'

'You'll be wasting your breath.'

A laugh, he had the *gall* to laugh at a *funeral*. 'I doubt any conversation with you would be wasted breath, Miss Rowe.'

Kensa bet she could fling shit in his face and he would remain quietly smug, as though he possessed all knowledge about everything, shit included, if only she would ask him. He knew her name, too, even without her telling him. She did not know what to do with that. Her arms grew uncomfortable. As though she remembered, suddenly, that she *had* arms and had forgotten their purpose. An expectant hush fell over the villagers. Kensa would have to speak, address those gathered, lie about Isolde's passing and conceal the truth.

Mr Delavaud remained beside her, as though he knew her thoughts.

'All right,' she huffed. 'Do it.' She waved her fingers and

even that gesture was awkward, as she accidentally brushed his elbow. 'Pray and sing and do your God bits.'

He smiled again. 'Conduct a service, you mean?'

Kensa turned about with a loud, 'Ugh,' and headed back inside the cottage, the door flung open. There was a mess within, though she needn't worry as none would enter it. She had no means to organise a wake and trusted most funeral attendants would head to the Jennings' inn to drink, as was the custom in Portscatho.

Thankfully, the men who carried Isolde (or rather, the scarecrow) out and into the earth never questioned her weight gain. Kensa had scarcely moved while the fake body was laid to rest, lest a saucepan clamour out from its wrappings or a teapot spill forth. Derwa cried silently, in contrast to Old Sal's loud honks into her handkerchief. Around them was the low wood and the hawthorn-swept paths. She listened for a chicken's final cries and a hag's crushing bite. Instead, there was only the curate's lulling speech and the occasional breeze, new leaves rustling its presence. Above their heads, in a gnarled oak which overhung the garden, was a cormorant. Its teal eyes flashed at Kensa and she did not doubt it was no bird at all. Had the Bucka come to pay his respects or did he watch her? She assumed the latter. If he was here, Kensa guessed that neither Jack nor Elowen, nor the chicken, had found Isolde. That meant wherever she was, she had yet to take a life.

'We lay to rest a soul whose hands touched every brow and tended every wound in Portscatho and its surroundings . . .'

Mr Delavaud had a nice voice. Kensa was reluctant to admit it. Mr Aldridge had spoken grandly, wanting attention and believing himself a true extension of God's will. In stark comparison, this new clergyman preached in a conversational manner. Worse, he had a sense of humour. Perhaps, thought Kensa darkly, it was not too late to let Merrin eat him.

'Are you all right?' Derwa spoke quietly over yet another prayer. 'Where's Elowen?'

'She – she was too upset to come.'

'Heavens, that girl is a sensitive soul,' said Old Sal loudly. 'A shame she's a sickly sort. Why, I wager it shan't be long till we're gathered together for her own passing. Now, I don't mean to offend, Derwa, it's only that she was never going to last to marrying age, not like my Bertha. A sturdy one, with a firm—'

To do him credit, Mr Delavaud barely wavered in his speech. Kensa gritted her teeth. After the last 'Amen' was uttered, she clapped her hands together.

'I appreciate you coming,' she said, 'now I would ask you to leave.'

Grumbles were passed from one person to another.

'There be healing work to do and I would have the peace in which to do it.'

Nods came, widened mouths in 'O' shapes, as shoes raised themselves quickly off the ground and turned towards Portscatho. Naturally, there would be innumerable tasks to complete with Isolde gone. Wasn't this young girl their healer now? It was best to leave her to it, let her settle into the role. Many folk smiled kindly at Kensa as they left, while others mentioned drinks to one another, beer being the general consensus. Isolde would likely have approved. Soil was heaped high on the scarecrow and thirst declared. Old Sal's tactlessness faded away and Mr Delavaud went with it, though not without a small nod to Kensa, who did not return his farewell. Slowly, the garden cleared and Kensa could see the nettles again.

Her mother was the last to leave.

'I never got to thank Isolde for what she did for Elowen,' she said. 'I never truly understood what that was, either.'

Kensa tried not to look at Derwa, lower lip trembling. An infant wish compelled her to press her face into her mother's skirts, to be picked up and held, though she was far too old and fat and grown. Instead, she admitted, 'I don't want to do this on my own, Ma.'

'Hush,' said Derwa.

Quickly, without needing to ask, Kensa was pulled into her mother's arms. It was hard to be a person and not a child, to have to fix her own problems and not rely on another. Now she was a wise woman and could not run home whenever life's burdens grew too heavy: it was her role to carry the heaviness of others. She was tired, knew she would always be tired, and knew there was no one else to shoulder it.

'Let's get you down to the inn,' said Derwa. 'We'll put a drink in you.'

How tempting to leave this mess and be soothed with ample scrumpy. In the treeline, the cormorant had yet to depart. Its shape was a blot against the blue, blue sky. One which watched her, unendingly. She would not let him see the pain he caused her. Pride, always her pride, brought her back to herself.

'I have work to do,' said Kensa, speaking more to the Bucka than to her mother, 'and I shall get it done.'

*

Kensa's relief was audible when Jack and Elowen appeared not an hour later, the chicken still alive and clucking. 'I wager she's hiding in the mines,' her sister said. 'No one's shared any sightings with us, though many a worker sees weird goings-on and won't speak on it.'

'And no one's been hurt?' Kensa's arms ached from scrubbing the floors again. Everything which made life or marked its end had been trodden into the flagstones she once used to diligently brush. Strange, she thought, how obsessed she'd been with keeping the place tidy. Now, it didn't seem to matter. She missed her mentor's clutter about the place. No longer would Isolde leave her dirty socks or, alarmingly, her frayed undergarments, hanging from a chair or heaped over a candlestick.

Jack shook his head. 'Not that we've heard.'

Elowen was quiet and withdrawn. Her fingers stroked the chicken's neck. 'We need to warn the village,' she said. 'That'll give them time to shut their homes and bar their doors and find weapons.'

Kensa dropped her brush in its cleaning bucket with a loud clang. 'No.'

Elowen continued, 'Surely the wisest course—'

'I am the wise woman and I will say what is wise.'

The chicken squirmed from Elowen's grasp and squawked nervously. 'This is about more than you, Kensa.'

Jack made a gruff noise in his throat. 'She's right.'

'Is she really?' Kensa laughed without humour. 'What a surprise! Elowen's right, as always.' Her voice was thin and reedy to her own ears. 'I can mend this.'

'How?' Jack sounded tired, his wounds reopened from the day's activities and his sling red with it. 'Cleaning the kitchen floor isn't going to do it.'

'I don't know!' Kensa had searched the Bad Books again. There was nothing there, no hope and no solace. She'd found no writings on the ritual performed with the Bucka and it was clear his memory and manipulations pre-dated the tomes within the small cottage library. Worse, Kensa had lost hours in them, stroking the fox on her lap, her head buried in the Bad Books' pages, forgetting what problems she had that needed fixing, only letting herself be lulled by their voices:

Beware the undrowned man.
A dawning throat is best for cutting.
A boy's pride is death to lovers.

It was too late for the first warning. As for the rest, there was little meaning to be made. She did not share them with the others, sensing she was not supposed to.

'I can't do this,' she admitted.

'You're not the only one who's lost someone.' For the first time, Jack wavered. 'I can't even grieve the woman who raised me after my mother died, and now you want to endanger everyone else I care about? I won't allow it.'

Kensa bared her teeth. He was close, exhaling against her mouth. When she pulled in a breath, it was the same he pushed out. She loathed how wobbly it made her. In her anger, she almost didn't hear the hard steps on the lane above the cottage. A heavy pulse, a hollow sound upon the earth: a visitor.

Whoever it was would get an earful and Kensa was determined to be the one to give it.

'You've missed the funeral,' she shouted over the threshold, pushing past Jack in her haste. He grunted in pain and she regretted her thoughtlessness in an instant. It was too late to apologise now – for that, for everything.

Rather than meet late guests, she found two large men and their long, long strides reaching into the cottage.

'Can I help you?'

Kensa's recognition was slow to come. These were rough types drawn to rough work beyond Portscatho's rural boundaries. One was a groundskeeper who set traps for poachers along Trethem Creek – the magistrate's land – while the other managed the magistrate's hounds for hunting.

'We have come for the wise woman,' said the groundskeeper, mouth obscured behind a bushy pepper-black beard. Had word spread, somehow, as to the crimes she had committed? The magistrate was the law in these lands and she had betrayed it. At least, as far as known customs went.

'I am she,' said Kensa quietly.

The men exchanged quick looks and the hound master, a sour-cheeked man with two missing fingers, said, 'It's the older one we need.'

'She's dead.'

They did not know, then, what she had done. Kensa sensed Jack behind her. His hand came to rest on her shoulder. She had the petulant urge to shrug it off, this singular mark of possession. Even though she wanted him, to be possessed by him, if only a little. Because that small action, that claim, meant he did not hate her, despite what she had done and may still do.

With inarticulate grunts, the magistrate's men conferred and the groundskeeper's beard flapped towards her again: 'There was an accident.'

'Come off it, lad,' said the hound master.

'While out patrolling the perimeter, we thought we saw— Ah, I won't name it.' He cut himself off. 'It were the magistrate, though, Sir George. He got scared, see, and walked right into his own poacher's trap.'

Kensa turned back, quickly, into the cottage. 'I shall gather my things.'

As it was not a direct attack by the hag, only a mishap, she did not know if the magistrate's death would lead to the Pact faltering. Her duty was to heal whoever had been harmed. She could not refuse. At the same time, a hot coal had been set inside her at Sir George's mention. It burned and it burned with one truth: the magistrate had killed her father.

Jack's steps caught hers as she took her satchel off its hook. 'If it's Isolde who's caused this, she'll be close by in the wood and we can grab her.'

'And then what?' Kensa placed a stained apron over her funeral clothes, for there was no time to change. 'Do we lock her up for ever? How long will you live, Jack? Will you introduce her to the woman you'll marry? Pass her on to your children who can watch her day and night while she tries to rip their throats out?' She retied the laces on her best shoes and mourned her lost boots. On her belt was the bone-handled knife, always worn. She'd even slept with it around her waist, lest the Father of Storms emerge in her dreams.

Jack's hand found her forearm and held her there, beside him. He was always so warm. She watched his eyes and how they didn't meet hers. She watched his eyes and how they dipped to her mouth.

'Yes,' she said, despite herself and her fury, ever-present.

He paused and Kensa took the moment for them both. She leaned in to broach the distance between them. He did not let her. Pulled back, sharply, the grip on her arm slackening as he angled his jaw away.

'As I said,' he grumbled, shingle in his throat, 'Elowen and I shall take the low path and search the wood by the manor.'

'Fine, have it your way,' said Kensa waspishly, striding briskly out of the cottage without a goodbye to him or her sister.

The road was hard and hollow-sounding. Above, a late-sun sky was drawing long shadows. Sir George's men flanked her and she had the overwhelming realisation that her presence had not been requested, it had been ordered.

Chapter Twenty-five

Passed like a Spirit

Trewense Manor was a vast and unhappy estate. It had latticed windows, Tudor beams and a history of ill-luck and ill-fated wives. It officially lay within the Gerrans boundaries and a thick wood pressed about it, as though to keep the coastal views of Portscatho at bay. Kensa had been to the manor once, when Mr Skewes had gone to see his sister, though she had not gone inside. It was smaller than she remembered, draughty too, which she confirmed when she was escorted through the servants' entrance and into a dull kitchen, one she could have worked in had Mr Skewes had his way. A single scullery maid ignored her, a snivelling face pressed close to the dishes she washed.

'Wait 'ere and you'll be seen to,' said the groundskeeper,

ducking his head out of the door where his accomplice had already fled.

Kensa called after him. 'Where are you going?'

'Where everyone else has gone,' he said, beard shaking. 'Far away from here.'

Kensa would have recognised Mr Skewes's sister anywhere. It was common knowledge that she considered her brother's dalliance with Derwa to be one below his station. For that reason, neither Kensa nor Elowen had ever met the woman. Mrs Howard did not introduce herself, though Kensa knew her name. Beneath the woman's greying hair was a chestnut warmth, though one would not have known it with how tightly it was bunned behind her skull.

'You are not who I sent for.'

Kensa's tone was measured and flat. 'I am all there is.'

'Humph.' Mrs Howard turned as a reed in wind and down a narrow hall. After a small, belligerent moment, Kensa followed. She had never seen as many paintings as held in Trewense Manor. Their gilt frames portrayed people who appeared as grim as the dark-panelled wood at their elbows. Men stared down with austere expressions as though to pin her to the polished boards. Women smiled wanly, draped over settees or dressed as Grecian visions, each arranged in beguiling poses, as though waiting for a lover standing outside the frame. One wall held a large tapestry, an old battle in faded colours, where horses raged and spears flew. It was horribly familiar to Kensa. Below it was a gold plaque and the inscription:

THE LAST KING OF CORNWALL

Kensa recognised his blue, blue eyes, despite their muted thread. Across these walls were Sir George's family and here was the Bucka, a man once: a relation, it seemed. Did the Father of Storms know? He must. At her belt, the bone-handled knife called to her grasp and she longed to run it through the weaving, slice him from his horse and crow her victory. Instead, she kept walking – through the house owned by the man who'd taken her father.

'You are not to address the baronet unless asked.' Despite her quick and precise pace, Mrs Howard was never breathless and seemed far more competent than her brother, as though to compensate for his many losses. 'If you are spoken to, you shall keep your eyes downcast. Give only the information required, nothing more, and refer to him as Sir, is that understood?' Kensa remained silent and Mrs Howard continued. 'We summoned the family doctor from St Mawes first, only he's come down with the sweating sickness. That left either a wise woman or a naval surgeon and, quite frankly, Sir George chose the former.'

'Why?'

'I suppose he wishes to keep his leg, not have it cut off.' Mrs Howard put her fingers to her mouth. It was only then her steps wavered, masked quickly with a cleared throat.

The floor fell from chequered tiles to polished wood and a grand staircase led them upwards. Yet, despite the manor's size, it was strangely empty.

'Where is everyone?' Kensa had not seen another soul aside from the housekeeper and the scullery maid. 'Doesn't a house this big need people to run it?'

Mrs Howard lingered on the top stair. 'When the staff heard

what happened to Sir George, nothing could keep them here.' Her judgement was so pointed that Kensa could have hung her coat upon it. 'Only my daughter and I remain and we are no fools as to believe a ghost story.'

Kensa's conscience flared. 'What if I told you the others were right?' She was rooted to the mid-stair point. 'There is a monster here, though it is no ghost, it is flesh and bone and will hurt you if it gets the chance.'

Mrs Howard sniffed. 'Far worse has been claimed of the baronet.'

Along the final corridor on the manor's east side was an open door. There was an odour – musk and over-boiled sweetness – blood. It met Kensa as soon as she stepped into the room and it met her as a regular acquaintance. She halted. She'd never been in a man's bedchamber before.

Sir George's room was large, as one would expect it to be. In the expansive bed was a shape. Kensa did her best not to look at it. She was abruptly aware that she was a young woman and, when Mrs Howard left, she would be alone with an older man. The magistrate lay flat and unmoving below a thin white coverlet. A purple hue stained his lips and red blotches fanned across his pale sheets.

Kensa cleared her throat. 'Sir?'

There was no answer. Perhaps she was too late to save him. Had she wanted to be? Uneasy, Kensa dropped her satchel and began her ministrations. Mrs Howard lingered at the room's edge, hands bunching the keys on her waist.

'I gave him ample laudanum,' said Mrs Howard. 'It's what he asked for, I could not refuse him.'

This is the man who killed my father, this is the man who killed my father, this is—

Kensa peeled the sheets away and found the magistrate stripped from the waist down. It saved her a job to cut away his clothes. Although his leg was bound, it had been done poorly and in haste. Throughout her examination, Sir George did not speak or groan. Did he know she was here? Kensa had never heard his voice. Even at the May Day festival, when she had collided with him, he had not uttered a word.

'If he dies, it'll be on your head,' warned Mrs Howard.

Kensa allowed the encouraging threat to drift over her head. Regardless, death would come and it would wear Isolde's night-dress and she did not know what to do when it did.

In her determination to ignore Mrs Howard's vulturous hovering, Kensa did not see the spare individual in the room with her. He had been still enough and it was dim enough that he blended into their surroundings. Worse, he wore black, cut close to his form, like another man she knew. Caught unawares, Kensa's peripheral sight translated his slim clothes into an eel-skin coat.

'You.' She leapt back from Sir George. Her palm flew to the knife she carried, then froze. It was not the Bucka. It was the curate in his clergyman's garb and his eyes were mercifully blueless. 'You,' she said again, with less heat in it, her heart beating a protest against its confines.

Mrs Howard called from her perch in the doorway, 'Is there anything I can fetch you, Mr Delavaud?'

'Tea would be most kind,' said the curate and his voice leapt into Kensa's ear like a flea. 'For myself and, well, it's Miss Rowe, isn't it?'

Kensa shook her head, aghast.

'Oh, I beg your pardon, Mrs—'

'No, it is Miss Rowe.' Kensa returned to Sir George's injury. 'Why're you here?'

'Tea, I think,' he confirmed, and Mrs Howard bustled along the hall.

Kensa would rather have dealt with the Father of Storms himself than with a holy man. He walked to the bed's other side with a candle's upright and unyielding shape. And, like a candle, she supposed he would melt easily enough. There was road dust on his travelling cloak, which he had untied and draped on his chair. In his hand was the King James Bible and Kensa realised he had appeared for the same reason he had visited Elowen on the night she almost passed.

'I will not let the magistrate die,' said Kensa fiercely, trying to convince herself.

Mr Delavaud's brow creased, a thin line drawn at the middle.

Rationally, it was normal to send for a curate in such times, as none knew how quickly the end could come. It was no insult, it was practical. And yet it made her uneasy; the thought that she could fail, might want to fail.

'Are you well, Miss Rowe?'

'Aye.' Kensa pushed her palms to her eyes, cursed and turned back to the bed.

Sir George was hairy in the way men are hairy. What's more, there was a lot to him. Kensa tried to cover it – *him* – with the bedsheets. She could sense Mr Delavaud watching her and tried in vain to keep her hands from quivering. Frustratingly, the whole coverlet was heavily soiled. Her attempts to protect her patient's modesty only spread mess further along her arms and the bed and there were *still* man-parts in her sight-line that she was not keen to see or touch. Eventually, with some manoeuvring, she managed to hide enough fleshy bits to observe Sir George's injury. Along his upper thigh were gory marks where a poacher's trap had pressed its metal teeth through flesh. As soon as Kensa removed the bandages, blood pulsed anew. She was quick to act, going through the motions and remembering what she had been trained in during her short time as Isolde's apprentice. Sir George was hot with fever. Occasionally, he groaned: a good sign. 'Twas better than silence.

Mr Delavaud leaned closer. 'Can I help?'

'No,' said Kensa.

Mrs Howard returned with a tea tray, which she placed at the curate's side. The housekeeper's lips grew thinner each time she entered the bedchamber and, as such, she did not remain long, speaking on a meal to be readied if the magistrate could eat it.

'I won't get in the way,' said Mr Delavaud.

Kensa's words came thick from her throat: 'I want hot water, wood for the fire, any spare linen as can be found and the window to be opened for air.' She wiped her forehead with her dirty sleeve. Her mother's dress was ruined. 'After that, you'll watch him while I rest.'

Mr Delavaud's frown became more pronounced. 'I think that's a job for the housekeeper ...' He petered off at Kensa's glare. 'Yes, right away.'

It was Mrs Howard who returned with the necessary items, while the curate trailed behind her and spoke loudly about gathering wood when there was an ample pile by the grate. He occupied himself in the way men do, pretending to appear busy while being quite the opposite. Kensa changed the bedsheets as carefully as she could and spoke while she did it, explaining any movements she was making to Sir George. He did not reply.

In her work, she never once thought to harm him or conduct herself poorly or allow his wound to fester. As soon as she had entered the bedchamber, her vengeful impulses left and she had seen only a man who needed help. It confused her, to not know herself or what she wanted until it was right before her.

Outside, the day was ending, fading into a soft-baked indigo only seen in the warmer months. What had the Bucka said about the hag and her aversion to sunlight? A trickling dread began to pool in Kensa's kneecaps and she wanted to settle them somewhere. Kneel down and tuck herself into a ball and not move until it was over.

Kensa asked the curate gently, 'Have you ever done this before?'

Mr Delavaud managed to nod and shake his head simultaneously. 'Been at a sickbed? I've had siblings who were—'

'No, administered last rites to someone who's dying,' said Kensa. 'That's what you're here to do, isn't it? Should he start to fade, you're going to read him verses?'

'There's a lot more to it than that.' Mr Delavaud swept a hand down his torso, in the way she had once seen Sir George do. 'He has to be conscious, for a start.'

'Then you *have* done it?'

'Um, well . . . ' He took in a large breath, then deflated as it left him. 'No, I haven't.' He cleared his throat anxiously. 'Is he dying then? Should I—'

'I think he'll pull through,' said Kensa, and she found she believed it. 'He's exhausted as he's bled a load and I doubt the laudanum did him any favours. Plus, his breath smells like alcohol and I wager he was drinking prior to standing on a poacher's trap.'

'That isn't a surprise,' said the curate, the tension leaving his body. 'Then I suppose I best be on my way?'

'No!' Kensa almost shouted, though Sir George did not stir. It would be dark soon and the hag might be wandering the woods outside. 'No, better to be safe, surely?'

'I thought you said he wouldn't die?'

'I mean, who can say?' Kensa flapped her ensanguined hands. A sudden gust shook the trees as though to agree with her, and when the night came, it came suddenly.

Mr Delavaud studied her, reading her as he might his psalms. A distant clock in the hallway marked the hour and he said softly, 'I will stay.'

Mr Delavaud was poor company. She wished she'd sent him away, even with the looming threat. He fell asleep immediately and sprawled on a plump throne at the fireside. It was hard not to compare him to Jack, the only other man she knew around her age. Their builds were starkly different, and their manners at odds. And there was a smugness about the curate's mouth, even in slumber, as though he was amused by a joke only he was privy to.

Mrs Howard placed supper in the bedchamber's doorway, prior to giving a stern, 'Goodnight.' There were three bowls and Kensa assumed her helping was the smallest. Sir George showed no wakeful signs and, considering the curate was also indisposed to slumber, Kensa ate all three portions.

There was one candle by the sick bed, which spread buttery gold out from one corner. Kensa had never seen a candle as fine and clear as this one. It did not smell, either, unlike the other lights she was familiar with. Aside from that, the only other luminescence came from the fire, quiet now without the curate's persistent prodding.

'Mm,' came a rasp, filtering over the bedsheets.

Sir George was awake.

Kensa's hatred rose anew, summoned by his open eyes – brown, thankfully – which met her own. She moved to his beside and stood as a statue to observe him, to wait until he registered her.

'Where am . . . ?' He trailed off, confused.

He trembled as he reached to his bedside, to the water she had placed there. He could not manage alone and Kensa, teeth gritted, raised the glass to his lips. The magistrate drank large gulps, the water flowing over his mouth and down his chest, dotting the sheets. It was a good sign; he was alert and thirsty. If the wound was kept clean, he would recover well enough, though he would always know pain when he walked.

Good.

Kensa withdrew the empty glass and set it down loudly. 'Do you know who I am?'

Sir George's fingers moved awkwardly, one coming to his

face, to the stubble grown there, while the other felt at his leg. He did not rise and Kensa doubted he could.

'I need more water,' he said.

'Are you listening?'

'Do as I asked, girl.'

Kensa did not move. Her right palm hovered over his leg. She longed to press it down, to make him cry out and suffer and writhe. 'I was a child,' she said. In her other hand was the hagstone, clutched tight enough to click her knuckles in their sockets.

'You will do as I command—'

Kensa raised her voice. 'Do you *know* who I am?!'

'Yes.'

Sir George raised his head an inch from his pillow, then brought it down again, sighing loudly. 'Alexander Rowe,' he said. 'I know you're his.' His voice was a grumble. Kensa could hear the exhaustion in it, as well as discomfort. 'I need to piss,' he said, lifting his arm to her, as though she would take it, as though she would help him.

'Why did you do it?' Kensa's gaze was hard. Her body smouldering, her skin blazing.

'Where is Mrs Howard?' Sir George went to rise and faltered. 'You will go and fetch her.'

Again, Kensa did not move. He would not look at her. There was a sound from behind her and she had no doubt it came from the curate. His snores had ceased. If she was overheard, she did not care. She wanted her answers and would force them out, if needs must. Eventually, the magistrate spoke, though not with ease.

'I was younger,' said Sir George. 'I was required to prove myself and, in truth, there was ample evidence to convict Alexander Rowe.' A pained grunt split his mouth atwain. 'Once we received a convincing testimony, there was nothing else to do bar hang him: he was too dangerous and no cell could ever hold him.'

Slowly, he tried to ease his legs off the bed, the good one followed by the bad.

She did not help him. 'Testimony?'

Sir George's breathing was ragged. He braced one hand on the nightstand, while the other fumbled for the piss pot beneath his bed. When he heard Kensa's question, delayed as though he listened through water, he stilled and sat up as straight as he could manage. He looked paler for the effort.

'Has no one told you?' Oh, the pity he gave her. It stitched the question with such weight that Kensa could see its letters against the hanging curtains around the bed. 'It was a man from the Coast Guard, one Peter Skewes.'

A non-conforming syllable caught on Kensa's lips.

'You're lying,' she said, when at last she could speak, only to find him relieving himself.

Unfortunately, any response Sir George might have given her was lost – and not to his own baser needs. With no warning, he dropped the piss pot. Its fine china broke. Hot urine splattered across the floorboards and walls and Kensa's finest shoes.

She cried her outrage, a cattish yowl as she leapt back. 'If I don't get a bloody—'

Kensa's running mouth fell slack and her mind emptied.

She could not summon a single errant thought. For in the magistrate's shaking grasp, drawn from his bedside table, was a pistol.

It was aimed directly at her.

Chapter Twenty-six

There by the Grace of God

'Move!' Sir George's bellow had Kensa slip back on the puddled floor, shoulder banging against the wall. Only then did she see what he aimed at, only then did she see Isolde. Through the open window the hag came, crawling disjointedly on all fours. Her nightdress was barely there, gaping in frayed smiles and hanging in dirtied hooks about her thin limbs. She was even more decayed now. Kensa could see right into her chest, to the grey honeycomb that oozed between her ribs and the lungs which shuddered behind them. Her face was not a face as one might know it, eyes sunken pits, nose half-caved and nostrils flat.

It was her mouth Kensa hated most. It was her mouth and the sound it made.

'Eaaaaaah,' the inhale.

Open and straining, one endless note.

'Eaaaaaah,' the exhale.

As though she was forever in pain.

The hag eased inside the room, one clawed foot on the windowsill, the other on the floor. Her fingers clutched at the latticed glass and smudged her filth upon it. Slowly, her head rotated from Sir George to Kensa to the warm body closest to her: Mr Delavaud. The curate was awake, had been awake for a while, listening to matters that were not his to know. His heels scraped softly on the boards; an effort to push his weight back into his chair and create distance between himself and the hag.

As though to leave its notice. As though such a thing were possible.

The hag leapt, springing from the sill and onto the curate. At the same time, Sir George fired his pistol. The bullet missed and slammed into the wood panels beside the fireplace, creating a hole no woodworm could rival. A rank gunpowder smell flooded Kensa's senses and the shot rang in her ears in one long scream. It took the hag's attention. Her mouth halted its bite, teeth – the ones she had left – an inch from the curate's throat. She was poised over Mr Delavaud's chair, legs splayed and toes perched on his arms, pinning them, while her hands hooked his fine woollen clothing. Quick, this time, she turned her head again and it was Sir George she saw.

Kensa could do nothing. Dread kept her rooted. She forgot everything. Her bad intentions. That she had ever been brave. 'I did this,' she said softly. It was her fault. There was piss on the floor. It could well have been her own with how afraid she was. A high scream came from the door and diminished down the hallway. By the time Kensa's eyes went to its source, all she saw was a nightcap's gentle fall to the floor: Mrs Howard, a staunch denier of ghosts, who now believed in them enough to run.

'That's what I saw,' barked Sir George, fumbling in his nightstand, reloading the pistol, spilling powder, dropping his shot again and again. 'It came at me, chased me to the traps.' Metal balls rattled from his bed, hitting the floor and rolling across its uneven length.

Despite his skill as a marksman, he was not quick enough.

Isolde, in her un-death, was faster. The hag leapt, knocking back Mr Delavaud's chair, and landed on the bed's furthest end, directly on Sir George's feet. He cried out as the hag's hands pressed to his thigh, scuttling upwards. With one swipe, she knocked the pistol aside. It fell with a singular dull thud.

'Isolde,' said Kensa desperately.

There was no recognition in her milky face. How could there be? Whatever had crept into the room with them did not resemble the wise woman. This was an unnatural being and Kensa could feel a pull around it, her own will manifested – her desire not to be alone – and the Old Ways warped inwards, wrong enough to snag at her joints and hair and teeth.

A rougher pull came, this time from the curate, who dragged Kensa from the bedside.

'Stay close behind me, Miss Rowe.' Mr Delavaud fumbled in his clothing and withdrew a small wooden cross. As he thrust it forwards, he began to pray, quickly. It must have been Latin, for his words seemed stale to Kensa, a dead-language sound. He may as well have sung a sea shanty. 'Is it – is it working?'

'No,' said Kensa. 'Did you think it would?'

'Not really,' he admitted.

Sir George strained back into his pillows as the hag eased her face into his. He had one hand on her swollen neck and the other on her scalp, which peeled hair and skin fragments readily over him and did nothing to keep her at bay. He was failing. The hag was winning. No strength remained inside him and new blood spilled across the sheets, seeping from his bandaged thigh. His breathing was hard and he had grown pale again, weak again.

He could not last, not long.

A forgotten instinct recalled Kensa's bone-handled knife. As soon as she pulled it from her belt, she sensed its power: the Pact. It reached to her, its keeper. The tighter she held it, the louder it became, singing to the air around it. Even that small action, the unsheathing, was enough. As soon as the blade hit her palm, the hag sensed it, righted herself and turned to Kensa, not in a way any person might turn. Each part moved separately, foot attempting to step first, chin twisting around, shoulders clicking into place last.

'Go,' ordered Kensa. 'I shan't have another curate murdered, not so soon after the last.'

Mr Delavaud baulked. 'I beg your pardon?'

Kensa tugged forcefully at his elbow. 'Run, I can do this!'

There was no time. There never was. Mr Delavaud was thrown aside as the hag stilted from the bed. Her strength was unknowable. She hurled the curate off his feet and into the ceiling, leaving him to drop as a doll might when a child is done with play. Kensa stepped back and the fire nipped at her calves and chewed on her dress.

'I don't want to hurt you,' said Kensa.

Did she have a choice? She held the knife high.

What remained of Isolde flinched, bared her remaining teeth and seemed, at once, afraid. *Click.* From the floor came the pistol once again, this time in the curate's hands. He levelled it at the hag, whose strange keening sounds had morphed into one single word:

'Pleeeeaaaa—'

Arms open, Isolde waited – sunken eyes shuttering closed – for the shot to hit. This time, it did. Mr Delavaud fired the weapon and his aim was true. It blew a fistful of matter from the hag's chest and across the bedspread, Kensa's cheek, the walls. Bone, old blood and corrupted honey. And still, Isolde remained upright. Her bent fingers went to the new cavity and probed the hole with curiosity. If any expression could be seen on the hag's features, Kensa would have sworn it was despair. At living, at standing, at death which would not come.

'Don't let her escape!' Kensa launched herself forwards and never got there.

A hand hooked around her waist and kept her back. Mr Delavaud had a firm grip, one she failed to break. With one talon cradling her wound, the hag fled. She hobbled from the room by the open window and leapt out into the canopy, blurring through the trees the same way she had come to them.

Kensa shoved at the arm that bound her. 'We need to go after her.'

'Are you mad?'

The curate would not let Kensa go. He was firm and stronger than he seemed. It took every ounce of self-discipline, forever in short supply, not to elbow him in the stomach. Or bite him, though lately there had been more than enough wise women sinking their teeth into the men of Portscatho for her liking.

Sir George released one long sigh – as though all the air that had ever entered his body was being released in one go – and fainted. Kensa attended to him immediately, the second she was released. He would live. Exhaustion was his largest fight and though his wound had settled, the binding needed replacing.

'It will do till morning,' said Kensa.

'What in Christ's name *was* that?' Mr Delavaud panted, yet his hand was steady where it held the pistol.

'She was a friend, once,' said Kensa.

'Come again?' Although the curate was wary, the healer was warier: he was the one with the weapon. 'Who befriends creatures such as that?'

Kensa could not lie to him. What could she say that he would believe? What's more, she did not know if she could trust him – or trust that he would not hurt her. For that reason, she was as honest as she could be. She kept to the facts: her mentor was dead and her mentor was not dead, the danger was mounting and their safety was at risk should they fail to contain the hag. She did mention the Bucka in vague terms, with due respect for his faith, though he did not seem disturbed by the Father of Storms' mention. In fact, he nodded, the name seemingly familiar.

'If I had not seen it, I would not believe it,' he said.

His long fingers kept possession of the pistol and expertly fetched shot after shot from the ground. Each round sphere rattled in his palm. In their number, Kensa saw a warning. Remembered what she had said to him earlier that day. Men like him had once killed women like her. Had she told her story well enough or did he hear another within it?

'I can fix this,' said Kensa.

Mr Delavaud did not reply.

'I can do it,' said Kensa.

Mr Delavaud did not reply.

At last, she confessed, 'I may need your help.'

Mr Delavaud's eyes met hers at last. She could not read them. A ready sweat began to rise across her chest. He reached for the powder horn Sir George had left on his bed, marked with a family crest and a century's thumbprints. He had shot one wise woman tonight. Would he shoot another? Kensa shied away and towards the window. She did not know whether to leap from it or close it. In the end, she chose the latter.

'How do we kill it?'

The question flew at Kensa as though it were a hungry bird. Sharp-beaked and demanding. She knew she had to destroy Isolde and had come to that realisation when she last spoke to Jack. To hear it, though, the word – *kill* – was hard to swallow.

'If that were me, if I was no longer myself,' continued the curate, 'I would want to be blasted from here to kingdom come. So how do we kill it?'

'I don't know,' said Kensa.

Isolde had seemed to fear the bone-handled knife, though Kensa doubted she could ever get close enough to the hag to make a mark. Even if she did, could she do it? Push the blade through flesh and bone and honeycomb, and whatever else had made a home in that putrid body?

Yes, she thought, *and Jack would never forgive me.*

Because whenever he looked at her, he'd see a woman as monstrous as what she'd created. And wasn't she? Strange, to break one's own heart having never even risked it.

'When I was a child, I was told stories about the West Country and my uncle's odd relations,' said Mr Delavaud, flicking a glance to Sir George. Uncle? 'About the Cornish and their wilder strokes, about the sea with a man's face. I had assumed it a children's fable, yet now I know it to be my history.' She'd been wrong, then, about no salt in his blood. Instead, he had too much for her liking.

'There's truth enough in nursery rhymes, sir,' said Kensa warily.

There, on his oval face, a smile. He was not like any holy man she had ever met.

'You're enjoying this,' she accused.

Mr Delavaud pulled on his coat, gave one glance to the snoring magistrate, and turned on his heel. 'I thought I'd be bored when I was carted off to this dull backwater village with its fishwives and farmers,' he said brightly, 'and I am exceptionally glad to be wrong.'

Kensa was quick to follow. 'You were sent here as a punishment?'

The curate looked over his shoulder and grinned at her boyishly. Surprisingly, she found herself missing the blundering and oafish Mr Aldridge. At least he had been predictable.

*

A heavy BANG, BANG, BANG reverberated around Trewense Manor. As dark as it had been in the day, it was darker now. There was no light, only an impenetrable expanse. Fearing a hag around every corner, Kensa had run back to Sir George's room and stolen the one candle burning, its flame shielded from loss by her cupped hand. Ahead, the curate had already groped his way down the staircase and to the main hall. Under the uneasy light, the chequered floor bounced and heaved. Kensa had gone to walk past it, towards the servants' entrance, until her newfound companion corrected her. He went to stride out the way he'd come in, through the expansive front door. He paused, however, when the BANG, BANG, BANG rang anew from the other side.

'Mr Delavaud—'

'Call me Pious,' he corrected. 'I think we can lose the formalities.'

Kensa raised her eyebrows. 'Your parents called you *Pious?*'

'I am the third son,' he said, 'intended for the Church since birth and given a name to suit.'

'Kensa means "first" if that helps?'

'You know, it actually does.' The racket beyond continued, as though an unyielding force was slamming itself again and again into the wood, eager to reach inside. 'Get behind me,' he said, 'and keep the flame high.'

She did as he told her. Pious handled the pistol as an old friend, over-confident and with one ear cocked for his game bird. The curate took hold of the large key in the large lock of the large door. With his free hand, he turned it, leapt back and aimed.

Jack came spilling through the entrance, shoulder first. Kensa's body acted before her brain, as she threw the candle forwards, hurling it at Pious at the same moment in which he fired. There was a dull noise as the shot went wide, while hot wax spilled across Kensa's knuckles and the curate's skull. Both cried out as Jack barrelled straight into the other man. Their tussle was brief, though dramatic, with neither one relenting till they had their adversary by the scruff. Only then did the pair stop, staring at one another in the wild-eyed night. When one went to move, the other tightened his grip, bravado forcing neither to let go first.

Kensa was shocked to find Jack on his back, weakened as he was from Isolde's earlier attack and her own blade. He had never been known to lose a fight, rare though they were. Even he seemed surprised, jerking away from Kensa when she put a hand on his shoulder.

'Jack, it's me,' she said, prompting the curate to let go. Kensa pulled the miner up and found him solid, unmoving. 'Did he get you?' She ran her hands down his torso, searching for a shot-shaped hole and finding nothing. Only hard muscle, his ribs expanding and contracting, the rough shirt he wore and the stains it had gathered that day.

He was close and closer still, forehead briefly against her temple. 'No, I . . .' He trailed off, squeezing her hand quickly, then releasing it. With that same action, he stepped back and it could have been across the county, for the distance he gave her.

She was more glad to see him than she realised. Had they been alone, she would have told him as such. Apologised and begged forgiveness. Been humble, revealed what feelings she knew to be unspoken between them, ones neither would dare utter. But, they were not alone and Kensa could not bring her voice to line up with her heart and she wondered if ever she would.

Slowly, the men regarded one another. Neither quite turning their back, as alert as two cockerels in a fighting ring.

'We lost Isolde's tracks in the woods and heard a ruckus from the house, saw her climb out of the window,' said Jack, glancing back to where Elowen stood on the wide stone steps.

The fair-haired girl held the sole surviving chicken under one arm. 'Where is she now?'

'Gone,' said the curate unhelpfully.

In the dull light, the sisters gravitated towards one another.

'Are you all right?' Elowen held the bird tightly. Its small eyes glinted as two wet jewels. 'What happened?'

'Isolde attacked us,' a deep breath, 'and then the curate chased her off,' another inhale, 'and Sir George's alive and I think he'll be fine,' she puffed out her cheeks, 'and I saw a man's parts from the waist down,' finished Kensa, in a hurry to loosen the last confession, for it seemed important to speak it now, lest she forget.

'Oh,' said Elowen, who frowned towards Pious.

'I am not certain about them,' said Kensa, waving her hands and grazing a beak. 'It's only, it seems a little—'

'I have never been interested,' agreed Elowen.

'It's not *that*, I don't know!'

Cluck, said the chicken.

A lengthy silence found the hall, which seemed to be concentrated in Jack's corner. Pious cleared his throat loudly and each person – and chicken – tried to speak at once.

It was Kensa's voice which won out.

'I think it's time we warned the village,' she said, conceding at last, worn down to the bone and marrow and further than that. 'I cannot risk anyone else.'

A high, wailing sound cut her off: a beast in distress.

'It's found the stables,' said Pious.

He did not tarry. Neither did Jack. It took Kensa and her sister a few extra steps to catch up with the men and, when they did, the hag was already gone. In one pen was a large horse with a bloodied dent in its rear. Jack went straight for it, doing what he could to soothe it.

Behind them, marked by a warning owl's shriek, fled a shape. It burst from the treeline and ran out along the narrow path which led from Trewense Manor. Though it moved with a dog's lolloping gait, it held a woman's form. One that was on its way to Portscatho.

Chapter Twenty-seven

A Man's Work

In the stable block were three distinct scents: the comfort of fresh hay, the tang of horse manure and blood – horse blood – which seemed stronger, heavier, than a man's. Kensa could do little for the injured mare. There was no time to properly examine it and its feverish kicks would surely injure her too. From what she could tell, its wound was superficial.

'There are other serviceable horses in the stable aside from mine,' said Pious authoritatively. 'We'll ride to the village and, if we're swift, intercept that devil on the way.'

A pregnant silence followed and Kensa shared a look with her fellow Portscatho dwellers. The curate moved with such ease around the animal, checking buckles and reins and equine equipment that only he had knowledge of.

When no one else took a mount, Elowen said, 'We don't know how to ride.'

Pious laughed good naturedly, then paused, realised this was no joke and skimmed a piercing glance down his companions.

'Right, then I can take one other with me.'

Kensa knew it must be she.

The moon was in its gibbous form and offered half-light to their small party. Even in its wan glow, she was exposed. And on Jack's face was an expression she rarely encountered – quiet hostility – yet it was centred on Pious, not on her, intensifying whenever the curate addressed her or seemed overly familiar. It was strange talking to a man such as Pious, who had advantages she did not. There was lazy power in his speech, in his genteel air. It was not unlike the Bucka's and Kensa found her insides squirm at the thought, confusion butting against odd emotions she could not quite place. If he was nephew to Sir George, then weren't they related – he and the Bucka? Uncomfortable, yet determined, she slid her steps into Pious's own, halting only when Jack's hand – it would always be his, for no other had one as calloused – caught her wrist.

Kensa's skin tightened across her cheekbones.

'You're going to kill her,' said Jack, speaking on his aunt. 'Aren't you?'

'Yes.'

'Good, because I can't do it.'

'She's already gone,' said Kensa, gentle as she could.

'I know, it's only, I can't.' Jack stumbled over the vowels and consonants as hazards on a rocky path. 'I can't be the one to do it.'

This was it, Kensa thought. What Isolde had tried to teach her, without ever seeming to. To be a woman, whether wise or foolish, was to carry what others could not. Exactly as a child shucks its coat into its mother's arms on a warm day, this was her weight to hold.

'You won't have to,' promised Kensa. She interlaced her fingers with his. Breathless, suddenly, dizzy with an emotion she'd yet to place. It was a second's contact in the manor's shade, hounded and soon halted by another man's footsteps and the loud crunch of hoof-beat upon the ground.

Pious interrupted, his horse – saddled and ready – a large mass among them. The mare whinnied, impatient as its rider.

'Here,' said the curate, reaching out to take Kensa away.

The curate slotted his hands together beneath the saddle for her to step upon. Jack did not let her go, not instantly. He skimmed a thumb over her mouth and pulled back, the contact hot as kiln-set clay inside her.

'Jack?' His name was a question on her lips. Yet, still, he did not tell her what she wished to hear. Even now, he could not meet her.

'Miss Rowe,' said Pious impatiently.

She nodded, numbly, falling to where the curate stood and allowing herself to be manoeuvred onto the horse. Kensa sat enshrined in the clergyman's arms, skirts hitched and her legs over the saddle's sides. Her eyes could not leave Jack's. She wanted to tell him everything. Selfish thoughts she had entertained about him and, at the same time, she never wanted to speak them. Because what did it matter? He'd had his chance and didn't take it, didn't take her.

Pious kicked his heels into the mare's sides. It surged ahead, sending Kensa and Pious with it, onward and into the night. The healer almost slipped off, until the curate righted her, his thighs bracketing her own. Elowen's bright hair was all Kensa could see behind her as the distance grew between them. Jack had already turned away. Were this any other occasion, she would have been excited, for she had never ridden a horse before. Instead, she knew grief. At what she had lost and would lose in the hours to come.

Pious was strong, and not in the way Jack was strong. He had a wiry strength and his arms were solid as they closed around her to grip the reins. Kensa was jostled between them, newly anxious as the ground raced beneath her, faster than she had ever known it. Being on horseback was to be as fast as the tide, and she could feel its dangers here. The pair made good speed. Around them, the trees thinned the further they galloped from Trewense Manor. Her sit-bones were already bruised and her legs sore from clenching. She could have sworn she heard the curate laugh and she thought he seemed very unlike any holy man should be.

There was no sign that the hag was ahead or behind or even if she had come this way. To her left: a teal flash. It came from the hedgerows, the ones that bordered the dirt track between the farmers' fields. In the night were storm-black shapes, with large wings that blotted out the silvered clouds. At first, she thought them gulls. They were not. When they first dived at their heads, Kensa could not mistake their form.

'Cormorants,' she said, leaning into Pious's chest.

'What?' He swore, loudly, as a hard beak flew at them. Only his arm, a fleshy shield, kept her safe.

'Birds,' shouted Kensa, who knew this to be the Bucka's doing.

It was hard to discern their number. One swooped at her, though it did not catch her face. It went to snatch her belt and almost succeeded, tearing at the leather band which held the bone-handled knife. She gripped it, hard. Among their gulp was a bird whose eyes were brighter than the others, glowing a malevolent blue. Yes, she knew their hue. This was her knife. Isolde had given it to her. No beak or feather or hand, however cold and full of salt, would take it from her now.

'Miss Rowe,' said Pious, with the tone of a man forced to repeat himself. 'Hold the damned reins.' He pushed them into Kensa's hands and fumbled in his coat. His free arm came round Kensa's waist and secured her, tightly. In a steady arc, he pulled Sir George's pistol free, aimed and fired. A cry split the cormorants as one tumbled down to the road to lie there, unmoving. Its feathered form was soon swallowed by the dark. The other birds quickly dispersed and veered away, the moon chalking their wingtips as though drawn by an artist's hand. One cormorant remained, its teal eye level with Kensa's for only a moment, until it too vanished with the others. *The Bucka*. In his jewelled gaze there had been an unspoken promise.

Was he right? Were they alike? Was she as monstrous as he?

Pious snatched the reins from Kensa's grasp and spurred them faster. Beneath them, the mud track was scarcely visible and the horse slipped on occasion. There was no sign of Isolde, no ragged streak or howling scream. Dim lights began to emerge ahead as Portscatho drew nearer, slanting down the hillside and into the sea. Exhausted, the horse slowed its pace, lungs straining. Its beating heart pulsed beneath Kensa's thighs and sweat sheened its flanks, dampening her skirts.

'I will head to the church and ring the bell at St Gerrans,' said Pious, as its spire came into view. He was unsteady, they both were. 'It will be easier to protect the village if everyone is in one place.'

'Not everyone will go,' said Kensa, shrinking back slightly, Pious's breaths loud against her temple. 'There's the Methodists who'd never set foot across the threshold and those who cannot climb the hill, who are old or bed-bound or sick.'

'Then if we have to choose—'

'No.' Kensa cut off his words.

A community was not a community if it left the weakest behind. As an apprentice to the wise woman, she had learned quickly what it was to see her people and their many differences. Not that she remembered them half the time and not that it changed her behaviour much. After all, she was still stubborn and incredibly argumentative, though she argued with everyone equally.

And she had betrayed them equally, too, every single one.

'I can't do this,' said Kensa suddenly, as Pious brought their mount to a stop. He had bypassed St Gerrans and brought them to the Jennings' inn. Cheerful sounds filtered through its small, dirty windows and she could hear Old Sal's familiar rants, relaying her relation to ancient Turkish royalty which the village had heard a hundred times before.

Pious was first to swing a leg off and over, landing on the

sloping road with practised precision. Only his fast reflexes prevented Kensa's ungraceful foot from clipping his forehead. 'Are you afraid the hag will come for you? If it does, I'll be here.'

'No.'

'Then what?'

'Everything,' she said limply. 'Failing.'

Kensa was carefully eased off the horse. Her legs buckled for a moment and the curate steadied her. He was ready to take command. She wanted to let him, to have him do it and spare her own skin. Besides, he had the same function in Portscatho as she did, though his healing was spiritual, not physical.

'If you don't try, you've failed anyway,' he said reasonably.

'I'm sorry.'

Pious nodded, absently, his tall boots already at the door to The Plume. In his hand was the pistol and he seemed as attached to it as she was to the bone-handled knife. 'Apologies are for afterwards,' he said, 'and only when there's no other option.'

Kensa hung back as he entered the inn, standing in the doorway, unseen. When Pious took charge, there was an odd comfort in it. To have a man speak for her, reassure her, take responsibility. She could agree, for once, that it was nice not to argue. Was this what it was to be a wife? As tired and scared and frightened as she was, she could see the appeal at last, to be taken charge of. To hide in a man bigger than her. *Jack.* To be his, and he hers. It was weakness, a moment's weakness, tepid and selfish and tempting.

'I must be heard,' announced Pious, at a volume that disrupted even the loudest drinker.

Jeers were swallowed into pint mugs. An instant quiet fell. Unease passed over curled lips and bent necks. The inn did not get his sort often. Their customers were the low-born land-workers, seafarers and occasional soldier. Pious's slightly pompous air carded the hackles on Kensa's neck, yet not enough to take her inside with him.

This would not go well.

'I would have you cover your windows and block your doors,' came his instruction, 'for there's danger afoot.'

'Speak plainly,' said Mr Jennings, bushy brows – the only hair upon his head – lowering down to his small eyes.

'There's a wolf about Portscatho.' He did not say the village's name as the locals did, too crisp and measured on his tongue. 'What's more, it seeks to kill.' Shocked exclamations rose to meet his announcement. 'I ask the frail and infirm to barricade themselves in their homes, while the rest help me and Miss Rowe hunt this hound.'

Sir George's groundskeeper, far into his cups, stood and did so with a leaning wobble. 'He's lying, he is,' he sniffed. 'It ain't no wolf, it's a woman, stinks o' the grave. She ate my grouse and killed the magistrate.'

'He's not dead,' corrected Kensa, too late. Rumour had spread hours ago, the workers from Trewense having long since stoked the gossiping fires within the village and beyond. On went the groundskeeper, talking on tales and mentioning the apprentice.

'Kensa?' Old Sal scoffed her name and the weight of the inn's stares followed it. 'I've been around long enough to know who to blame for such foul practice,' continued the fishwife, glittering with excitement as her mouth ran on, slurring on occasion. 'This'll be your doing, will it, girl?'

'I didn't mean to,' she croaked.

'It's as I warned. See, she's exactly as her father! His badness trailed after him and now here's hers, come to bring harm. On the day she were born, I swear I saw a—'

What could Kensa's reply be that wasn't an agreement?

Old Sal was right.

It was all the confirmation the village needed, for Alexander Rowe's reputation outlived him and brought due fear. Aghast cries sang up, fingers pointed, further questions were shouted at the curate than could be answered. Young Robert, who had been unable to hobble to Bohortha for the funeral service, squeezed Kensa's shoulder as he eased past her, out the door.

'No one pays Old Sal any mind these days,' he said reassuringly, yet with disappointment beneath his kindness.

Kensa called after him. 'You'll be safe?'

'I'll stay inside and knit,' he said, with false levity, 'can't risk losing the other leg, can I?'

Rather than his usual ascent, he took a downwards path and she only hoped he went to visit his sweetheart. No sooner had he left than a firm hand closed around Kensa's arm and dragged her fully into the inn, hemmed by chipped furniture and hissed jibes. Pious had relayed what he knew and, worse, much of what Kensa had told him at Trewense Manor. The curate had no control, his protests drowned out in the general chaos and fright.

'If it's Rowe's daughter who's summoned this fiend, it's her we give to it,' said Farmer Hayle. 'Tie her to the water pump in the road, let her see her workings done to herself.'

Kensa tried to pull her arm free and failed. 'Pious?'

Nothing, only shock. That he was not listened to, that his rank held no bearing against mob rule.

'It's what was done to a witch in Llanddona when she cursed the dogs,' encouraged Old Sal. 'As soon as the last bite o' her was gone, the hounds calmed.'

Mr Jennings began to untie a rope from a beer barrel behind the bar. The healer renewed her struggle. A long debate ensued about what to do with her, while the hag paraded about the night. Kensa told them. Begged them to listen, until Pious took over. The louder the curate argued, the larger the revolt against him. Who was this caddish rakefire to tell them how to be? He was no Mr Aldridge, who always kept the wise women in check.

A rope grazed Kensa's wrist, tight and coarse, as she kicked her fury. Her fingers went to the bone-handled knife and never got there. Even if it had, what would she do with it? She could not hurt these people, they were *her* people. Next came talk on piling wood, on duckings and those past torments as had been rained upon anyone who did not fit the norm. Though it had been a long while since any such killings had been done on their land, the punishments were well remembered, spoken with gleeful tongues. Centuries could pass and a mob would always know how to kill a witch.

Pious, however, had no such qualms about raising his weapon. The gun shone in the dull, tallow light. 'I do not wish to injure, though I will if I must.'

A bottle swung and smashed over his head. Glass scuffed

Kensa's cheek. A tiny shard, a sliver of a cut. Gone was the pistol, wrested from his hand, as he crumpled. Heaving, tugging, forceful hands dragged both healer and unconscious curate onto the street.

'I swear—' began Kensa, only to find the protest shook from her throat.

She tripped, knee skimming the ground, and was hauled up again. She could not get her legs to work. Was this what her father knew as he was taken to the scaffold? One or two villagers fled, stealing to their homes with a guilty look back. In their silence, they were as culpable as those who tied Kensa's and Pious's wrists together and to the village pump, torches swinging and lips with them, until silence came. If the worst happened, Portscatho would be without a healer. Who, then, would care for them all if Kensa died?

Mr Jennings, Farmer Hayle and Old Sal were the ringleaders, who stood back from a small crowd and observed their work. The curate barely stirred, though he was slowly coming round. Kensa's teeth chattered together. It was in this awkward pause that unease fell. Kensa saw it, their ready hands now limp.

'This isn't right,' said Kensa, though her tone was firm. She refused to beg. In that way, at least, she was her father's daughter.

'Don't listen or else she'll charm your ears,' said Old Sal.

'I couldn't charm a pig to mud and you know it,' spat Kensa.

'Yet there's evil here tonight,' said Farmer Hayle. 'Who raised it if not you?'

She glowered and her tongue stilled. Behind them, outside

the inn's entrance, Pious's horse whinnied its unhappiness. The assembled villagers took this as a sign and, in clumps, drifted apart. Mr Jennings hesitated enough to place the pistol a small distance away.

'It'll give you a chance,' he said, as though she had the hands or reach to grasp it.

Kensa watched her neighbours go, pulled at the ropes which did not slacken and leaned as best she could, into the curate's side. It was a quiet night – ink-black and thinly clouded – and even the sea was still, as though to listen for a scream: for the hag and her terror. An hour must have gone by, though the creature never came. No lone shape in a tattered nightdress was seen. Had the hag travelled further? Why, she could be halfway to Truro by now and all she need do was tear a single throat.

'Mr Delavaud,' said Kensa, then, when he did not answer, 'Pious?'

A groan and the curate, on his knees, arms raised and bound, finally regained his senses enough to speak. 'Where's my pistol?'

'Here, for the good it'll do,' said Kensa.

'Can't you untie these ropes?' Pious tugged at the restraints futilely, as though she had not been attempting the same. 'If you're a witch, isn't there a spell or a familiar who could chew us free?'

'Or you could ask God for help,' she countered dully.

Pious thinned his lips. 'This is your fault.'

'You're the one who tried to lie to the villagers,' said Kensa. 'Did you think us halfwits who'd believe our betters over common sense?'

His pointed silence betrayed that he, in fact, did. Around them came hammering sounds as residents barred their doors or boarded their windows. Nothing else, no wails a hag might offer to the night. 'Any sign of it?'

'No.'

Kensa sank her head into her elbow, lest he see her cry. Was this how she would die? If so, she deserved it. She bit down on the sensitive flesh of her bicep, seeking a pinch and the clarity it brought. A short distance away was her mother's house. If she called, would Derwa hear or was she too sleepy with drink to wake?

'At least it's not the bore you feared,' remarked Kensa, thinking on the curate's earlier words.

'It appears I spoke with haste.' Pious twisted his wrists again, to no avail. 'I should think a quiet clergyman's existence would be far preferable to this.' His attention struck on her middle and stayed there.

'What're you doing?' Kensa asked, sharply, till she understood his focus. On her belt was the bone-handled knife, though she could not reach it. Perhaps he could?

'Raise your leg onto my shoulder and we'll ease your waist towards—'

'I shall do no such thing,' she baulked.

'How else can we get free? If I get to the knife, I'll cut us loose,' explained Pious, with a slow and patronising insistence.

Kensa shuffled a little closer and raised her ankle half-heartedly above his knee. 'Could you at least close your eyes?'

Pious crouched and his fine boots creaked with the strain. 'If I do that, I won't be able to see.'

'You're not going to *see* anything!'

From the high bend in the main road through Portscatho came a shout. Flat and dry-sounding. It was Mr Skewes. Kensa's bearing stiffened. An intense fury squeezed her skull until her vision went fuzzy at the edges. He wore his Coast Guard's uniform: a long navy coat with a short dagger at his side. It was not an official uniform, only a degree smarter than the usual fare worn by the villagers in Portscatho. His post was hardly an official one either. It had been given to him by the naval patrols from the Falmouth coast, who needed a man to report on the smuggling which ran along Percuil River's eastern flank. These days there was little crime to report, or it had been so since the hanging of Alexander Rowe.

At his side was Young Robert, who nodded as he limped past them, as though he had done Kensa a favour. As though he had not brought her father's killer.

'Well,' said Mr Skewes.

Only that word, unsurprised to find her tied to the water pump. Duty bid him to free her, which he did, and Pious next. Kensa wished she were a snake, secretive and vengeful, filled with venom enough to kill. To think she had lived under one roof with him, had eaten at the same table as him, had let him near Derwa. The bone-handled knife at her belt was heavy again and she thought unspeakable things, none she would ever admit to anyone. The pistol scraped the road as it was raised once again into the curate's hand.

Not far behind him were Jack and Elowen, the latter hastily – quietly – tucking the chicken through Derwa's front door as surreptitiously as possible. Good, the pair seemed whole enough and Kensa's relief was heavy in her chest. Elowen's mouth was slack with tiredness. She eyed her father, for once equally as wary as her sister. As for Jack, Kensa could not look at him long, fearing he'd see the darkest thoughts she harboured. It was enough to know he hadn't sustained any further injuries, even though his shirt was wrinkled and stained.

'I find my only daughter barely able to stand, with talk about a beast loose in the village. I should've known you'd be the cause ...' began Mr Skewes's tirade, until a strange and lumbering sight interrupted him.

A sheep, throat torn and bleeding, stumbled into the road. It sank onto its forelegs, bleated once, then died with a slump to the floor. She knew who it belonged to.

Oh, sweet one, come homeward.

Kensa flinched as though a jellyfish had run its compass down her skin. Why would Isolde come to Portscatho with its cob-walled houses and warning bells and obstacles? She seemed hungry, desperate to eat and going for livestock. Thus far, she had decimated chickens, hunted grouse and gone after horses. Wouldn't sheep be next?

'The Weaver,' said Kensa, with alarm that rose with the welts at her wrists. 'We've warned everyone else and forgotten him.'

Chapter Twenty-eight

Like Father, Like Daughter

In the years Kensa had lived with Elowen, she had never once seen her disobey her father. That was why everyone liked her, the fair-haired child who was ever so compliant. It was for the opposite reason that no one liked Kensa, because she rarely took instruction. Tonight, however, the youngest daughter would not submit.

Mr Skewes said, 'Get yourself inside with your mother.'

As if on cue, Derwa appeared in her doorframe, muzzy with sleep. 'Elowen?' Behind her, a chicken clucked.

'Here is what will happen,' said the young woman to her father, quick to understand the situation. 'You will stay here and protect the village and Ma, while we see that the Weaver is safe.'

Mr Skewes was taken aback. 'If you even think about . . . '

Their argument was a short one and it was due to Elowen's verbosity. When had she become so clever? Kensa was not clever. Her belly was a lump against her spine, as though it wished to shrink away from her intentions. She found herself speaking up, though she did not realise why until afterwards.

'We might need you,' she said to Mr Skewes, her voice entirely level. 'Come with us.'

Turning in her mind was what Sir George had told her and the threat which would be waiting, the same threat she could push onto Mr Skewes. What would he make of the hag? With the years that had passed, had he forgotten his role in killing Kensa's father? Did he think she would not discover his sins? It had been well over a decade since she had witnessed Alexander Rowe's hanging, yet the memory was louder in her mind than it had ever been. Elowen tried to meet Kensa's eye. She refused it and stared at the Coast Guard with an expression too measured ever to belong to her.

'I already said I would,' retorted Mr Skewes, nodding to himself, though he'd said no such thing. Quickly it was decided: Kensa, Elowen, Jack, Pious and Mr Skewes would go to the Weaver's farm, not a mile away.

'Please be careful,' said Derwa to her children, then to Mr Skewes, 'Keep them safe.'

To do him credit, the Coast Guard nodded, pressing a kiss to the woman's cheek. Kensa turned away from it, scowling, ushering their party onwards.

The five took a rarely used path along the coast and upwards, where the trees thickened and the soil was prone to subsidence. Mr Skewes's lantern swayed as an uneasy pendulum through the night. Due to the wind that oft whipped the coast, the only shrubs to survive here were hawthorn. No blossom remained on them now and their leaves clung to the outer edges, presented with a thousand thorns.

The first dead sheep appeared on the path. It had been pulled in two and pushed back together, poorly, with its insides arranged on its outsides. Elowen released a high sound from her throat. Kensa kept walking. She led the party onwards, unfeeling, even to the shock at catching her foot on a tree root and bumping her palms on the path.

Jack hefted her up with his good arm, silent, ears pricked for a lumbering, beastly movement. 'Kensa?' He caught her hand in his. He did not need to voice his questions, she understood them all the same.

And turned away.

The usual gloaming sounds were absent. No crickets sang in the long grass and no birds called the hour. The hill they climbed sloped to a sudden drop behind them, as though the land had forgotten its shape and faltered at the end. Ahead was another sheep and another and another, dead. When Kensa strained her eyes, further shapes appeared, and she stopped straining. These small woollen heaps led the way along the sloping meadow and to the Weaver's hut. One ewe was still alive, its breath hot and shaking as it trembled out its last moments.

'Who has a knife?' It was Jack who asked. He was unarmed, Kensa realised. She had never considered him so, for his fists seemed weapons enough. Yet with his injuries, his usual defence was next to useless. Why had she allowed him to come?

He stood no chance against the coming horrors. Even so, he would never have stayed behind.

Mr Skewes reluctantly parted with his dagger. It was a short gleaming length, never used, and handed over with utmost care. Quickly and with mercy, Jack delivered the dying sheep to whatever end waited, whether its reaper wore a man's cloak or ewe's wool – or both. With that gruesome task done, Jack returned the bloodied weapon to its owner.

Overhead, the sky was filled with a dozen cormorants. Kensa could not see their shapes with clarity, only dark obstructions which occasionally took the moon from sight. Their grumbling cries rose higher and higher.

Pious met them with his altar voice, or what Kensa thought it would sound like, calm and meditative: 'And flocks shall lie down in the midst of her, all the beasts of the nations: both the cormorant and the bittern shall lodge in the upper lintels of it; their voice shall sing in the windows; desolation shall be in the thresholds: for he shall uncover the cedar work.'

Kensa asked, 'What does that mean?'

'Nothing good,' he replied.

Another sound rose above the bird calls. Distress, an animal in pain, and then an absence where that sound should be. Even the birds stilled their cries, only for a keening wail – a man's wail – to replace them: the Weaver.

Kensa ran, surging past the green-leafed hawthorn. At the hill's midpoint, the sheep farmer stood with flaming torch in hand. Before him was the hag and, under her mangled grasp, another sheep too far gone to save now. In the light – moon, torch, lanterns – there were endless masses around the sheep farmer's hut, as though the animals had run there for safety: fallen half-clumped clouds, smeared with a wet sheen.

BANG, came the gun as Pious fired. It was not a straight shot towards the hag, this was a wild firing, thrown into the air, lest it hit the Weaver. The noise was enough to distract the hunched shape, whose gnashing teeth froze over a broken neck. In the small hours in which Kensa had been away from the hag, she looked worse. Although her frame held a human base, she moved in a frameless way.

Pious was the fastest. His long legs took him to where the Weaver stood, waving his torch in grief and despair. Elowen came second, though she struggled, Mr Skewes hard on her heels, his mouth slack with the fear it held.

'Inside,' yelled Kensa, waiting until last, bringing up the rear with Jack.

Struggling, the men pulled the Weaver, who was strong despite his age, into the small hut he called a home. His flaming torch was lost outside and tumbled downwards into the dry grass. The door to the hut, although it lacked any real lock, was closed and barred behind them. It shuddered as the hag threw herself against the wood. Over and over and over. Jack and Pious leaned against it, while Mr Skewes held his blade in one hand and his daughter in the other.

In their temporary sanctuary, the Weaver's sobs were loud enough to smother their collective breaths. His loss fed Kensa's guilt, until she could barely concentrate. She thought Jack had spoken to her, though she could not be sure. Despite his fervent tone, his brows were harshly drawn – in concern or anger, she did not know – and she was too frightened to ask. Elowen was looking at her, silent as always, her thoughts her own. Kensa wished they were hers, that she could have Elowen's clever mind. That way, she would know what to do and could think, somehow, could think through this.

'We're all going to die,' said Mr Skewes. 'Aren't we? Tell me—'

'Oh, not *all*,' said Pious. 'Logically, it's quite likely a few of us will live to see the morning.' He cleared his throat as another hard thump hit the door and sent wood splintering. 'That was meant to sound reassuring.'

A burning scent pulled the air from their lungs, as fire began to catch on the thatch above their heads, spread by the Weaver's discarded torch. Embers drifted down to rake Kensa's face, hot enough to singe her lashes.

'This is my fault,' she said, looking across the tiny room to Elowen. 'I shouldn't even be a wise woman; this wasn't meant to be me.' Again came another pounding as the door was struck. 'You found the Morgawr on the beach that morning, Elowen, it should have been you.' Kensa had never spoken this truth aloud, though it was one she entertained often. 'I took what was yours and Isolde didn't even realise.'

Quiet. How long had it been quiet? The repeated slams had ceased. For a moment, Kensa thought the creature would leave and find an easier target, until the scrabbling began. A persistent shovelling at their feet. The Weaver's hut was small and poorly constructed. As soon as the hag's hands began to scoop earth from an outside corner, the walls began to shift. Elowen shrieked as a rotting arm came through a small dent beneath the stonework. Illumination poured from the hole and from the burning roof and grass beyond, as the fire caught, as the fire spread, as the hut fell.

The whip-quick flames were too bright to look at, red and angry, while the smoke was bitter on Kensa's tongue. Stones toppled, bellied inwards. Wooden beams snapped and burning thatch rained down onto the six standing inside the hut. Jack heaved the bar from the door and pushed Elowen through first, Mr Skewes following with the Weaver, and Kensa not far behind. With an aching groan, the hut collapsed. Stonework tumbled down. Rubble caught her back and almost sent her prone. A scream – Kensa's own, she realised – for not everyone had got out.

'Jack!' She couldn't lose him. He was the only thing she had left, the one thing in her life that felt like hers. Hoarse, smoke reaching into her lungs, she called to him. 'Jack?'

Elowen tried to take her wrist. Kensa yanked it free. Her bruised hands were on the fallen masonry. She began to dig and heave stone away, muscles straining, mouth cracked and dry with dread. Her own pants deafened her. No reply met her calls. *Jack, Jack, Jack.* She could not relent, she would not stop until she knew if he was alive – or dead.

'Come on,' snapped Mr Skewes, wrenching Elowen to the shelter offered by the sheepcote. It was only the Weaver who stayed behind. None could say where the hag was. Under the debris, perhaps? With her Jack—

'Stop,' said the Weaver, and he must have called it a hundred times and Kensa not heard him. He closed his fingers over hers and paused them. 'If the remaining stone falls, it'll kill them – if they're not already ... well ...'

Kensa shook her head. Yet her actions stilled. 'Jack,' she repeated, and he answered, finally, muffled, at a bulge in the broken hut's edge.

'Kensa.' A heaving, ragged cough. 'I'm here, we're all right,' he added unconvincingly. 'It's only caved on one side and we're alive, though we're trapped and the hag's gone.'

'Is Pious—'

'He's breathing,' said Jack.

'I can get them out,' said the Weaver, pushing Kensa aside. 'I made this home and I can unmake it.'

Fire spiralled across the heaped thatch, which had fallen and folded as ungainly as an unmade bed. Charred air coiled from its growing mass and thickened, flying as cormorants across her body with the same menace as the ever-circling birds above.

Behind her, Kensa heard a cry. It came from Mr Skewes.

'Good,' she said and hated herself for it. 'Good,' again, because it was not good and she was not good and what she'd said in the hut was true. She had no right to be a wise woman. This was a role she had stolen and Portscatho – and Cornwall with it – would suffer. Yes, she was her father's daughter and, yes, she was as much a thief and a killer as he was. Now she could finally admit it.

A flame caught her dress. It dallied at the black hem and began to raise it. She did not put it out. Kensa sensed the hag's presence as she might her own pulse. She had made this creature, had she not? Poured herself – the worst parts she carried – into it. In her attempts to stave off grief, she had crafted a monster that knew her better than anyone.

Perhaps that was why it went after Mr Skewes.

At the sheepcote's entrance, the hag paused, its black and bird-like eyes meeting Kensa's, waiting, as though for instruction. *Do it*, she thought and stole the impulse back in a second, but a second was all it took. Isolde crawled inside. Kensa could not speak. Her feet were rooted to the ground, while her back was warmed by the blazing night and her own slow burning.

There was another witness to her failings. He stood behind one hawthorn bank and watched this take place. His eyes, of course, were teal. Glowing sparks rose around him, while smoke encircled his wrists and slid along his jaw. She expected him to be grinning through the ashes, yet he seemed as lost and vacant as she was. Inside the sheepcote, a man was fighting for his life and Kensa could only listen as the Bucka listened. If the Pact was to break tonight, would this be the death to do it?

She wanted to scream. Instead, it was her sister who did.

Elowen.

To think Kensa had lost her own father and here she was about to take another's.

'Not like this,' she said to herself, to the Bucka. 'Not like this.'

That low fire on her clothes dampened. Was it her own will that had done it? She did not know, for the Old Ways worked in balance and she was only unbalance now.

In the sheepcote, Elowen hid behind Mr Skewes, whose dagger was lost. Beneath their feet, straw was shaped in lumps and blotched with blood. There was a deep cut along Mr Skewes's face and chest, which bled freely. As for the hag, she was low to the ground, crouched as a dog, legs poised and bent and ready.

Kensa had no weapon to throw. And then she did, she always did. Kensa reached into her pocket for the hagstone she kept there, the one which belonged to her father. If she threw it now, she'd never find it again. There were some things worth losing. She hurled it, hitting the hag's head at the same time as it leapt forwards. The blow knocked her off course, sending her tumbling into the straw, the small holey pebble lost with her. Slowly, the hag palmed itself to standing and turned to face Kensa, who withdrew the bone-handled knife. When the hag's eyes rested upon it, there was a shiver, a trembling which gripped the creature and spread from knuckle to tailbone. Fear. Hadn't the hag done this earlier at Trewense Manor and the cottage, coiling into itself and away from the knife? Kensa considered the cormorants, who had tried to pluck this very blade from her belt when she rode with Pious.

There had to be a reason.

The hag retreated, circling Kensa and bounding out the door, into the darkness. No shot had truly harmed the ever-walking creature. Perhaps the bone-handled knife would stop it where nothing else had. Only, how could the weapon succeed in Kensa's hand when it belonged to another? This duty and this right and this role was Elowen's, and Kensa never should have taken it. If there was a time to right a wrong, to give another her destiny, it was now.

Chapter Twenty-nine

Choice

In the sheepcote, Mr Skewes bent forwards on his knees, heaving into the thick straw. He seemed thin. He seemed his age. It was hard to hate another person whose failings were worn so openly. Elowen swung her legs forwards, kicking through the dry grass, to where Kensa stood.

'I thought you wouldn't come,' she said, then wrapped her arms around her sister.

Kensa could not speak. She had thought the same and yet, here she was, holding Elowen as tightly as she could.

'I am sorry,' said Kensa.

'No, you came,' said Elowen, tearful. 'That's what matters.'

The raging heat – a burning wall inching ever closer – mixed with the night's warmth, pushed sweat down Kensa's neck and between her breasts. Her dress, the same one she had worn to the funeral, stuck to her body uncomfortably. No darning would save it, no wash either.

'I can never make amends,' said Kensa, as she pulled back. With sure movements, she grasped Elowen's hand and pushed the bone-handled knife into her sister's palm. She wanted it gone. She wanted the guilt taken from her. 'This should be yours, it should have always been yours.' Confusion marked the fairer girl's face, until Kensa continued, 'You are the wise woman here. This role should have gone to you, not to me.' And then a sob. 'I can't do this, I can't.'

Elowen did not take the knife. Instead, her fingers remained slack and Kensa could not loosen her own grasp, lest the blade fall and be lost between them.

'That's not true,' said Elowen.

'It *is* true,' urged Kensa. 'You found the Morgawr. Isolde meant to choose you, she would have done, if—'

'I don't *want* to be a wise woman.' Elowen frowned the same way their mother frowned, a thin line pleating her brows together in a pattern which would form a permanent crease with age, should they live beyond this night. 'I've never been well, I could not have coped with the responsibility. Besides, I don't – and never will – want it.'

Kensa didn't understand and told her as much.

Elowen shook her head. 'How could I heal people when I can't even heal myself?'

'You would have managed,' said Kensa.

'I didn't want to and I don't want to, that's the point. You think I want to prepare salves and pierce boils? I'd much rather *you* do those horrible things, especially after how mean you've been to me,' said Elowen drily. 'Tell me, right now, do you want to be our wise woman?'

Kensa did not give her answer right away, though it came readily to her mouth, waiting to be spoken. It was hard to want, it was hard to admit to herself that, 'Yes,' she wished this was her calling, as though confessing the truth would deprive her of it.

'Then you are, don't you see?' Elowen brushed the silly tears from Kensa's cheeks. 'There is no fate we don't choose, for the most part. I refuse to believe otherwise and I refuse to take that knife.'

'You're good at this,' said Kensa, sniffling, though she was not yet convinced.

'Besides,' said Elowen, 'you're not telling me anything Isolde didn't know.' At her sister's confusion, the younger girl continued, 'We spoke on it, on what had taken place. She never asked me to be a wise woman and I wouldn't have accepted if she had.' Elowen grinned. 'She was a clever old bag and chose you for a reason, Kensa. It's about time you chose yourself.'

'I ...' At last, the new wise woman of Portscatho closed her own hands firmly around the bone-handled knife. Not all Elowen's words had met their mark, though many had. The others would need to be thought on, turned over and polished as pebbles in her mind, if any future for thinking was possible.

'I love you,' said Kensa. 'Even when I hated you, I loved you.'

'I know that.' Elowen smiled. 'You're mine – we're each other's.'

The smoke grew stronger, stinging their eyes. A small

distance away, Mr Skewes was hurriedly scooping through the straw in an attempt to find his lost blade. Kensa's eyes hardened when she looked at him.

Fire caught the sheepcote's roof and licked at the ground beneath them. Kensa, Elowen and Mr Skewes, who had finally retrieved his Coast Guard's talisman, were pushed out into the open by the burning mass. True to his word, the Weaver had pulled stone aside and freed Jack and Pious from the collapsed hut, though the latter was unsteady on his feet and his hair darkened with blood. Kensa scanned Jack's form with a fierce intensity. His temple was scuffed with mud, the knee on his trousers ripped through and stained, yet he could walk. On the sloping meadow in which they stood, bound with speedwell and sea thrift, was a crouched shape: the hag. In its claws was an unlucky cormorant, the bird's neck broken and its body victim to the monster's appetite.

'We can shelter here,' said Jack, heaving Pious along with the Weaver's help, as their small band fled to a gap in the hawthorn.

The copse tunnelled around a path, a small channel cupped by thorns, which acted as a shield. Upon stepping inside it, Kensa could've been in the Morgawr's throat with how constricting it was. Its branches were thick with foliage and flower, their colours turned amber in the fire-lit night. No large animal could easily get through and, should the hag wish to pursue them, theirs would be the higher ground. Jack had a burning wooden beam in one hand, while the Weaver held Pious's stolen pistol. Kensa had a firm grip on her knife and Mr Skewes held aloft his own, for as much use as it was.

At first, the hag went straight for them, only to be repelled by the flaming torch. It tried again and reeled back, screamed, its remaining hair catching and burning out, too damp to set aflame. And then it vanished, scuttling away into the dark-not-dark, lit by the burning flames which had begun to creep towards their shelter.

A rustling, quiet at first, then clatteringly loud, shook the hawthorn.

'It's above us,' murmured Pious, who held one gnarled branch for support. 'It's coming.'

The Weaver's expression was a solid one. 'Let it,' he growled. 'I'll see it dead.'

Kensa surveyed the bone-handled knife. It no longer seemed an ungainly weight in her palm. Instead, it had become an extension of her. One she had finally accepted.

Jack pushed his way towards her and used his bulk to shelter her from the shaking canopy above. She wanted to kiss him. She knew she'd never get the chance. How many people would die here, tonight, if she let them? Although the Pact would break with one life, Kensa was certain the hag would take far more than that until it was finally laid to rest. In the blade's shine she saw her own tired reflection and a truth she had known for hours now. Whatever need be done, she would do alone. She would risk no one else. Of course, they – the others – would not let her. The gallant Jack, the clever curate, even the skittish Mr Skewes, and especially not the bright, beautiful Elowen, would ever see her come to harm.

At once, the hag's clawing hand slashed down to scrape Mr Skewes's eye, eliciting a scream. No sooner did the hag strike than she disappeared in a shake of hawthorn. None could see where she – it – watched and waited.

In the tumult that followed, Kensa placed herself apart, further down the spiky tunnel. With her resolution came a strange unanchored sensation. She took one, last final look at Jack – cast in golden light, standing between her and the hell she'd wrought – and called to another.

'Gerent,' she said, using a name she had once heard her mentor speak, using the name she had seen engraved on the plaque at the old manor, using a dead name which held power.

She summoned him and he was summoned.

A pale hand, cold as sea, extended from the thick hawthorn at her side. Behind it was the Bucka, who beckoned her through a parting of thorns.

'No one need pay for your folly,' he said gently. 'No one but you.'

The Father of Storms towered over her. Thin branches cast shadows against his colourless face, appearing as cracks in his visage. Her own breath flew up as vapour, despite the heat, purely from her nearness to him.

Kensa nodded, frightened, yet determined.

'If you die,' he explained, 'the others need not.'

'Are you lying to me?'

'Isolde will take no one else if she takes you, I will ensure it.'

Kensa swayed towards him, to that enigmatic figure in an eel-skin coat. A man who had plagued her dreams and glittered her nightmares. Whose legend had scared her as a child and whose presence now marked her as grown. There were shouts near by, her companions' attention elsewhere, far from her and better for it.

'You are the wise woman, are you not? Sacrifice is your nature,' said the Bucka earnestly. 'Come with me.'

It was too easy a choice.

Kensa put her hand into his and was pulled through the hawthorn, which parted for her and her alone. Branches caught on her hair and her dress and her skin, though the scratches it left were shallow, the trees reluctant to pain her when there was further pain to come. Kensa feared that should she release the Bucka's hand, she would be trapped in a thorny cell for ever, held within the trees until she became them. She heard her sister call her name, voices reaching through the clawing folds, then silence, as the branches closed behind her, as impenetrable as any barricade.

When at last the Bucka's hard grip released her, Kensa stood in a clearing. Beneath her shoes were mud and roots, curved into a gentle sloping bowl. Around her was a cage of hawthorn, too thick to allow her exit. It was akin to being trapped inside a giant bird's nest, with no exit or entrance. She did not think she was in Portscatho or its surrounds any more. This place was different. It seemed to exist and not exist, in time or outside it. And though she could not see it, the sea was *loud*. A rushing, thunderous sound, pulling on the salt in her veins and stirring her pulse to beat in her ears.

Overhead came a rattling movement as slowly, slowly, slowly the trees peeled back to create a circular gap. Through it, stars blinked softness to the sky. Until they were blotted out. A shape, a scurrying, crab-like shape which belonged to the hag.

It spidered into the clearing and, with a sound like keening, the hawthorn mended itself. Kensa was firmly trapped with the creature she had made and with the Bucka, who watched from the treeline, serene and almost disinterested, as though he had forgotten tonight's happenings would kill them both.

'Give me the blade,' said the Bucka, 'and all will be as it should.'

Kensa's palm was damp with perspiration and her knuckles stiff with the gripping of it. 'It's important, isn't it?' *Yes.* Because it was power – her power. Now that she'd accepted her role as wise woman, as the Pact's keeper, the bone-handled knife was more than a simple weapon or tool.

'I can keep the hag trapped in here and protect the village,' continued the Bucka. 'Give the blade to me, Kensa, and submit.'

It was not the first time he had spoken her name, a name meaning first, though it was the first time she heard it. 'Why not take it yourself?' No sooner did Kensa ask the question than she learned its answer. It was said in a whisper, as though the Old Ways, at last, had come to greet her. 'You can't, can you? Because now I know it's mine, it can only be given, not stolen.' And she realised, then, that the only way to kill the hag, to stop all this, was by the blade she carried. No, she would not give it to him. Because in the giving would be giving up. Accepting that she was no longer a protector, a healer, that she had failed and that every bad word ever aimed her way – from herself and others – was right.

'Kensa—'

'No,' she said. 'No,' again.

She would not bend to him.

Slowly, the hag slunk around the clearing's sides, hooking her hands and feet onto the hawthorn, head turning round as though on an axle. Next came the arching back, as it readied itself to pounce.

Kensa raised the bone-handled knife.

She was ready.

The Bucka made a chiding noise with his tongue and, whip-quick, the hag pounced. Kensa was not whip-quick, she was not even quick. In her weariness, she threw herself sideways and the hag still caught her, its broken hands latching onto her leg. She kicked out, aiming a heel squarely in the hag's head, which snapped at an odd angle. Enough to grant her freedom. Eerily, the hag took its hands to its skull and clicked it back into place. The bowled clearing shrank with each passing breath. Kensa could see no way through the hawthorn. When her shoulders hit the spiked wood, it blinked and lashed out with a sharp beak. Within the branches were hundreds upon hundreds of cormorants, their blue-green eyes regarding her with glassy indifference, their bodies dark enough to mistake for shadows. When she listened, she could hear their growling calls, as menacing as distant thunder.

Kensa tried to hack her way out. She did not want to die, she did not want to die like this. Yet her blade was for cutting flesh, not hawthorn, and her blows only chipped her latticed prison. It was one thing to agree to meet her final moments, it was another to accept it.

Kensa pleaded, 'Don't do this, Isolde; please, don't do this.'

Unalive and unending in her hunger, the hag came walking,

crawling, bellying towards her. There was nothing left of Isolde to reply.

The hag leapt again and, as before, Kensa was not fast enough. Its biting hands clawed into her hair and pulled her head back. A puckered mouth went for her throat, as though to rip it free. Kensa screamed and lashed out with the knife, almost cutting herself in the process. Her back hit the ground and the hag began to pull, wrenching her along the ground by her hair. Roots bruised her back and her scalp prickled in agony. With a twist that burned her shoulders, Kensa swung her arm up. She could not reach the hag. She could only reach herself. Kensa hacked at her own muddied tresses and sheared off a good fistful. Reddish tangles fell about her and it bought her time and mobility enough to get onto her feet. It did nothing to deter the hag, who sprang onto Kensa's chest, arms wrapping around her neck. She couldn't breathe and stumbled forwards, into the hawthorn's spikes. From the trees, the cormorants' biting beaks found them both, distracting the hag enough to loosen its grip. Kensa was free, coughing, her head pounding fit to burst.

'We can both go,' said the Bucka. He spoke from the treeline, he was the treeline, his eel-skin coat moulded into the wood, his form no form at all. 'Together we can leave this place.'

'I don't want to,' said Kensa.

'You will,' he promised.

Hawthorn shrank again around her, pushing her closer to the hag. She slashed out with the knife. It caught the hag's wrist, leaving its hand swinging like the lid to a jewellery box, revealing a wet stump.

'I changed my mind, I want to go back,' said Kensa, for even though it seemed selfish, she could not stand to be here without them, without the others, without her sister, without Jack. 'I don't want to be alone when I—'

'To be first is to be alone,' said the Bucka sadly, head bowed forwards as though in prayer. 'You realised as much on the shore when the Morgawr died.'

'No.'

She wanted to hear Elowen's call, feel Jack's pull, even Mr Skewes's scorn. Whenever she had been at a death bed, she had provided comfort and she wished it for herself now. Anything other than sacrifice, anything other than solitude.

'A guv kolon, deus tre,' she sang to herself.

Oh, sweet one, come homeward.

'KENSA,' came a distant shout, her sister's, as though she had raised it.

There were hot flashes through the hawthorn, a sign that the fire had spread, a warning that it was coming closer. Kensa was dizzy. Perspiration sheened her skin.

'Elowen, Elowen, Elowen—'

Come find me.

Again, the hawthorn began to tangle, thickening around her. The larger the fear grew in Kensa, the more knotted the trees became. She was tired and knew that Death never tires, and it reached for her now, almost welcome. The slobbering hag, briefly deterred by its injury, began its predatory approach once more.

'It will be easy, I promise,' said the Bucka, as though to persuade her and himself. 'Close your eyes and it will be over.'

Kensa's feet struggled to grip the earth, for the Bucka moved it. He used his sway over water to push the trees closer around her and even pulled on the water within Kensa's blood. An internal tug that channelled every ounce of terror he had ever summoned within her. It stirred the shame she harboured and the same ill feelings he had used to manipulate her, to persuade her to summon this hag. Kensa realised, then, that the Bucka was not all-powerful. He was using her, even now, as he had always done. Theirs was the Pact between Land and Sea. If he was the latter, she was the former. Here, with soil beneath them, he could do little unless he did it through her. Why, he had never really touched her. She had done everything. The Bucka was nothing more than a shade she lent power to.

'I am more earth than he is,' she said, to herself, to him, to the binding hedge.

And the Land – and its thorns – answered her. Gradually, the hawthorn began to recede, pulling away from her with a slow, steady progress.

'Kensa,' said the Bucka, in warning.

She put the blade to her forearm and summoned a banishment.

He came behind her now, his mass as hard as granite rock, as brutal as the cliffs which could dash a head in two. Here came the tide, here came the hag, jaw clicking open – impossibly open – and broken teeth ready to bite. The creature's weight was blindingly heavy as it leapt, feet trying to find a hold on Kensa, hand grasping at her neck where the asrai had marked her, bending down to feast.

The Bucka remained rooted, standing over her, watching

as the tearing began, a pain that Kensa heard first and felt second. Even then, adrenalin kept the worst at bay as she collapsed. Onto the Land, the Land which held her, knew her, and would not be cowed. She was the wise woman – and her wisdom was fierce.

'There you are,' shouted the Weaver, whose torch swung in a fiery arc, slamming into the hag's head, forcing the Bucka several paces away and catching Kensa's face, though freeing her nonetheless. There was more fire, too, as behind Elowen and her father and Jack and Pious, came the flames which took apart the landscape. The hillside was ablaze, the sky bleached with an eerie light as cloud and ash merged.

It was a battle and then it was not, too difficult to track and happening too fast.

Pious and Elowen raised Kensa to her feet. She found she could not speak easily. Her throat was beating agony into her blood. 'The Weaver—'

It was too late. Slurps and a lapping persistence came from the hag, who crouched over the sheep farmer. 'No!' Kensa threw herself forwards and, with her remaining strength, plunged the bone-handled knife into Isolde's back. Pushed it right through to where its bitter heart lay. And she thought on her teacher, on the lessons she had imparted, on the love she had for the older woman, on every silly joke shared, now lost for ever. This was what she had tried to escape. *Grief*. Why did it hurt this much? To lose and have to keep going. How could anyone ever bear to love with the loneliness that came after? She missed her friend. Life was harder now. Couldn't it be as it was before? Or did she finally have to grow up?

Snot and tears and blood slicked Kensa's hands.

It was enough, it was enough.

To have been wanted.

There was little resistance in Isolde's flesh, which sank away under such a blow. A gentle noise, a hum in a wounded chest, sighed from the hag. Then, it crumpled, folding down and forwards, broken face sliding into roots and earth, unmoving.

It was done, Kensa could sense it. Whatever sinister intentions had kept the hag tethered to immortality were gone. She had given the hag her rest, at last. The Weaver, too, was dying. His neck lay open and blood poured freely, pooling around his head in a red circle. Pious swore loudly, speaking words he had once thought to give Sir George hours prior. Kensa knelt beside the sheep farmer, put her hands over his wound and knew it was useless. She could not heal this. Instead, she sang and she cried and she sang and he died.

And with him went the Pact.

Chapter Thirty

The Pact

Kensa's spine collapsed from beneath her. She sprawled over the Weaver. Her chest was as malleable as an overripe apple. A burrowing sensation sent pain through her tissue and bone and sinew, as though a slim finger was pulling a pip from her core, wrenching it free with one long nail. The Pact's splintering was a physical sensation. She screamed and another cry mixed in with hers, lower, gravelled, belonging to the Bucka. Ignoring her sister's voice and the hands which reached for her, Kensa turned to him. He, too, was on his knees, breathing erratically as though he had suddenly remembered how to. Jet-black feathers, a cormorant's feathers, began to push from his skin, coating him as thickly as fish scales. Through them, Kensa could see a window to his face, the blue veins rising in his body and his eyes, those bright eyes burning wild colours.

'Yes,' was all he said and Kensa saw he was crying.

She was too, though for another reason divorced from his relief.

'Thank ...'

He trailed off, words fading to a seabird's croak as the trees around them began to part and subside. Wings pushed from his arms, half-eel, half-cormorant, and he surged up with a graceless movement. In the coming fire-glow, which took the moon from the sky, Kensa saw him fly or fall or sail or soar down the hillside.

The Pact was broken. He was dying.

'I failed,' said Kensa, slumping onto her backside, arms limp and blood-stained beside her, palms stuck with grit. 'It's done.' Far below them, the sea began to rage. No bindings held it in place and Kensa could hear its unravelling. 'Portscatho is going to be washed away.'

At last, Kensa raised her gaze to meet her sister's, whose face was pressed close to hers. 'We cannot let it,' said Elowen.

'Come on,' urged Jack, grabbing at Kensa's elbow.

It was him, only him, who reached through her guilt and brought her to her senses.

An impulse had the wise woman, if she was still that, grab the bone-handled knife from the hag's back. It seemed duller now and lighter in her hand. Only a simple tool, nothing special, its power gone.

Around them, the fire had grown to a monstrous size: a red-winged shape curving up the landscape, hot enough to hurt even at this distance. It was closing in and to stay was to die, to stay was to be burned alive. The Weaver's body was abandoned with Isolde's, as Kensa limped her way out. The sea cracked and whirled as though it were a beast bucking its bridle. Elowen's hand was tight in her father's, as Mr Skewes hopped down the low path, to where the village waited at the mercy of the waves.

It would be dawn soon and the sky was weak with it, losing colour at the horizon. Portscatho's residents were no longer in their homes. Their faces were drawn and solemn. Did they feel it too? *Yes.* The answer came to Kensa as soon as she asked it, as though given by the land itself, boundless with no Pact to hold it. Those who lived beside the sea could feel its pull, their bodies knowing no circadian rhythm, only high and low and middling tide. As she met the harbour, Kensa saw every single villager staring at the waves, which rose and rose and rose and never seemed to fall, spearing up in high foaming spikes. Kensa approached them, hearing her mother's call and trusting Mr Skewes to keep her safe.

From the bubbling sea came Merrin, her body dressed in glittering salt. 'I will eat no more bloated corpses after a ship's wrecking,' she said, her shrill voice carrying to Kensa. 'Instead, I will eat fresh and I will start with you.'

At the uncresting shoreline, the creatures who had survived in its depths – sickly, hungry, vengeful – began to emerge. Those old stories, on harpies and selkies and horse-fish, proved true. From the sea came a hundred sloping beasts, each one having been driven from the land by man. Even the kraken came, its thick tentacles rooting to the sand. Now, at last, their time to take back their home had come. Merrin led them, breaking into a sprint, which was met with a pistol shot. Pushing through the villagers came Pious, came Mr Skewes, came Branok and even Derwa, hefting whatever weapons could be found, and they were not alone. A few miners and fishermen took up arms, though the rest stayed back or fled or watched with mounting horror. And there was Jack, wielding a heavy metal hook, stealing a glance from her. In his brief nod was a promise she couldn't decipher.

The asrai's walk slowed as she neared Kensa, spiked teeth flashing. Her sinister attention spied the curate and there she found her new target. Oh, she was strong and beautiful and terrible and Kensa was tired and spent and frail. Elowen fared little better. Neither could intervene. It was the end and the two sisters waited on the sand to meet it.

Elowen closed her fingers around Kensa's. 'We can finish this,' said the younger woman resolutely. 'I knew what would happen the day we found the Morgawr on the beach, for she told me, the Morgawr told me what to do,' Elowen continued sagely. 'I stand before our wise woman and I carry the Sight of the first.' She reached out with her free hand. 'Where is the bone-handled knife, the same one as formed the Pact?'

Kensa shook her head numbly. 'What are you doing?'

'I have dreamed of this moment over and over, never knowing what it meant,' said Elowen. 'In the vision, you are a child, barely able to walk, or a young woman as you are now. Sometimes, I see you as Isolde was, old and white-haired, while I am forever unchanging, always this age, at this place.' Her fair hair was burned off at one side and her body scraped and cut. 'We will renew the Pact. You and I. Together.'

Below their feet was shingle and shell. Further along lay a cold shape covered in feathers. It was the Bucka, who had met his demise at last. Water streamed around him, washing him slowly from their gaze and into the waiting ocean.

I'd wish him back, she thought, *if only so he could see what he'd done.*

'He is gone,' said Kensa. 'He cannot be bound to the Sea again.'

'But *I* can,' said Elowen. 'I was never meant to live, not like this. I was kept alive by a wise woman's will and a cruel man's promise. It is *your* will now that shall give me new purpose.'

Kensa shook her head, horrified, while a mounting dread threatened to buckle her knees.

One large wave began to rise higher than the rest, holding its breath and waiting to crash. It was taller than several houses put together. When it came down, the whole village would be lost. Kensa could feel the Land eager to push back beneath her boots, each pebble shard and scallop fragment vibrating with the effort to do so. It had no direction, neither the sea nor the land, both ripped from their moorings.

If the sisters were successful, Elowen would become a monster, the way the Bucka had been a monster. Forever un-dying, trapped within the creeks and bays and waterways that hemmed their home.

'I can't lose you,' said Kensa.

'You won't.' Elowen's features were luminous as the sun, and, as though remembering it was due, the dawn burst from its holding. 'We can make this Pact our own.'

The last one was made in hate and fear, whereas this would

be Kensa's as much as it was Elowen's. And it would be formed in love, as the sea is loved on the first hot day in spring.

'Do it now,' said Elowen. 'Let me guide you.'

Kensa withdrew her knife.

In the sunrise, the sky had fallen to bronzed light to match the burning hills above Portscatho. The ground was loose with heat and ash, the air tasting coarse on the tongue. Around them, men heaved, their backs bent and scythes cutting through the dangers which met them from the shoreline. At times failing, at times falling, as bone and flesh met shell and pincer. Jack's shape was there, then gone, lost in the frenzy. It was the same as on harvest day, with honed metal sending whispers through golden stems, while women bundled sheaths behind them. Now, all the women held was hope and chain and anchor, any tool as could be used to defend their homes.

In Kensa's mind, she no longer stood on the sand beside her sister. Instead, she stood in wheat, holding the land's spirit, to begin the Crying of the Neck. At one blink, the sisters were in a field, at another, in the sea. Reality flexed and roiled, dancing between two points as a swallow between two stars. The ever-crying storm was raging, the sea transformed into a wicked beast, talons and claws growing in might. Within seconds it would be ready and strong enough to wash the village away: the sisters could not wait.

At the field's centre, in the last field, was Elowen. 'Will you help me?'

Kensa was at once young and old, fair and weathered. 'Won't it hurt?'

'Yes,' said Elowen, whose features were smiling though mournful.

Around them stood the villagers, on the harbour, in the fields, the two places existing as one. Kensa's brazen hair caught in the rising wind and she pushed the blade down as she had seen Isolde do once, into her own wrist and along the vein. Elowen held her arm out too, the mark repeated, blood falling down their skin to meet at their clasped hands.

It was not enough.

Old Sal had been the one to tell them both about the spirit who lay in the harvest at reaping. Kensa felt it now. A power that was maid and mother and crone combined, the sugar in the bees and their honey, the strength in the ivy and the gold in the wheat. Around them, the hooks and scythes, the creatures and bloodshed, paused to listen.

'Crying the Neck is a tradition,' said Elowen, 'the land's spirit waits in the last field for reaping and must be bundled into one fistful, a neck, to be slit.'

Slowly, she bent Kensa's fingers around the standing wheat. The bone-handled knife was heavy in Kensa's grasp.

'I can't,' Kensa said. 'I can't,' again, 'I can't.'

'What 'ave 'ee?' came the cries from the men, new tongue and old tongue singing together. 'Pandr'eus genes?'

Next the reply, sung loudly in the rising light: 'A neck, a neck, a neck!'

The sun was risen now, had always been rising, to thread the sisters' binding around them. Neither one was fully grown, their bodies teetering towards womanhood and too young for their burdens. Elowen's hair was fine and liquid.

It brushed as brine over Kensa's hands as she took her place behind her sister. It was time, and time had waited for this. For the reaping and her sister's throat, open.

Kensa's own blade pressed through fair skin and spilled a new sea around them. Saltwater ran down Elowen's front, her dress, Kensa's hand, as the Pact thickened their blood. Land and Sea came to meet them. It pushed into the cut in Kensa's arm, filling the line at Elowen's throat as blood spilled, as water spilled from her open neck. Her eyes – already blue – did not change: they'd already been so bright, uncanny in their vibrancy. Kensa should have known from the start what she would become, simply by looking into those eyes.

Elowen gave one last look to her sister and turned from the shore, a shore again, no golden wheat to ground them. She walked towards the waves, to place her heart into the ocean, where no one – be they woman or man or wiser than that – could ever find it. No sooner did the swell hit her ankles than she began to change. Elowen's hair rose around her as though she already lay underwater. Limpets crawled from the sand to merge with her body, leaving their shells to serrate her collar, her spine, her hips. And when she vanished, it was in a shimmering cloud, as only the finest salt can give.

As quickly as they had risen, the storms died, the waves receded and the wise woman, and every one after, had no sway over them.

Chapter Thirty-one

The Mother of Storms

Elowen had been gone a whole month. Since the Pact had been made and the Sea had taken her, there had been no sign of the fair-haired girl. Each day, when she was done with her duties, Kensa went to the harbour side and waited. Today, she shucked off her responsibilities, dogged by Fox – or Lowarn, as the Bucka had called her – until she reached more populated areas. With a parting nose to her calf, the vixen turned back to the undergrowth and waited for Kensa's return to the cottage. Often, she thought on Isolde. Had the crone known this would happen? Possibly, her onions were shrewd enough and now under Kensa's watch.

The morning was butter weather, with thick fog spread as fat into every earthen cradle. It would not last. Summer had arrived. Kensa walked along the curving harbour wall and sat down, the sea a gentle rhythm beneath her. The stonework was numbing to her rear and she knew she'd long for this coolness later, when the earth had soaked up the day's heat and sang it out, almost burning to the touch.

For the first time, Kensa did not sit here alone. Another came to join her, his lanky legs bending comically as he took a seat not too far from her, though not too close either.

'She was born clutching a shell,' said Mr Skewes.

He seemed set to talk on and Kensa remained silent, staring down into the mist-dipped horizon and waiting for the sun to burn it away.

'It was Old Sal who delivered her. I wouldn't have the wise woman do it, I was too scared. In her hand, in Elowen's tiny hand, was a winkle,' he continued, voice wobbling. 'I think I knew then what she'd be. Course, I was told it was nothing, only birthing matter.' Mr Skewes bobbed his head fiercely and patted a pocket sewn into his shirt, into every shirt he had ever worn, painstakingly stitched by Derwa. 'I knew what it was and it'd lead to this, as did your mother – though she'll grieve for her daughter nonetheless.'

Kensa's mouth was firm. Although it was Elowen who tied them together, their relationship had always been a fraying one and Kensa pulled on those errant threads now.

'You never told me what you did to my father,' said Kensa. 'Even though you were the one who sent him to the gallows.'

Mr Skewes's tongue poked at his teeth, his nervous habits plainly visible in the early light. 'He was a murderer and a crook and a rapist and a drunk,' said the Coast Guard. 'And the worst he did, well, I kept it from Derwa.'

Kensa's jaw clenched, though she did not speak.

'If your father had not met the rope, he would have sent others to a worse end, your mother and you included.'

'You don't know that.'

Mr Skewes released a heavy breath. 'I do not ask forgiveness,' he said. 'I loved Derwa and I wanted to protect her and … and do more than that, I'll admit. When I took the Coast Guard position, I knew the village'd turn on me, being inclined to side with the smugglers or being smugglers themselves. That were never Derwa. She always had a smile for me, talked to me when others turned their backs – and when I saw what Rowe did to her, the bruises and how he spoke to her, taking what money she had and leaving her with nought, I couldn't stand it. I never thought she'd want me, and when she did, well, I told Sir George what I knew. It was the only way I thought I could help her – and you.'

Tears fell down Kensa's cheeks, falling as clear, hot baubles onto her skirt. 'Am I like him?' With what she had done, there was much she wished she could undo.

'You're stubborn,' said Mr Skewes. 'I suppose you're brave, as he was.' He looked at her and it was not unkindly. 'No, you do not take after him. Whoever you are, Kensa, you are a woman all yourself, exactly as your sister is.'

In the cresting light, as the waves sang gold and gulls found height, a shape walked from the water. Tall, serene and glowing as the tide tops on the brightest days. Her skin was bluish, her eyes bluer still. The two figures at the harbour knew her at once – and when they smiled with joy, the sea and all her bounty smiled back.

✳

'It's a letter,' said Elowen, as a courier's heels vanished from the doorway at the cottage in Bohortha. August had brought a burning heat and, in the afternoon's height, neither sister could stir much enthusiasm. When pressed, Elowen could provide coolness with a touch, though it drained her to do it. Gone was the Sight which had ravaged her body, its task done. She had yet to master the Sea's ways and her time on shore was limited, especially in such fair weather.

Kensa sank down onto what had once been the Bucka's chair, while Elowen perched on the footstool nearest the window, summoning a cool breeze as she stroked the last surviving chicken, sitting contentedly on her lap.

With the Pact taking a new form, oddities had begun to emerge. The books on the shelves misbehaved at the slightest touch, until Kensa could not tell bad from good. What's more, the animals in the surrounding woodland had begun to grow tame and Kensa found she could keep a bloom alive for long past its flowering months.

One thing that had not altered was the relationship between Kensa and Elowen. Despite their lengthy spells of separation, the sisters still behaved like sisters.

And that was how their mother treated them. Although she had a wise woman and a sea god as her children, Derwa behaved no differently, as though this was their youthful fancy and they'd leave it behind, eventually. 'You'll grow out of it,' she'd repeat whenever the pair visited her, stroking Elowen's odd, salted hair. Kensa did not argue, understanding what her mother needed. If she thought her daughters too far beyond her reach, she would lose herself, too, and so she did not comment on Elowen's changed appearance or Kensa's growing reliance on the Old Ways. It was safer that way, to pretend.

Elowen's voice was deeper, stranger. 'No one has sent us a letter before.'

'I know,' snapped Kensa. She flipped the paper and showed it to Elowen, revealing only one name on the back which surely did not begin with an 'E'. 'You mean no one has sent me a letter before.'

Not even Mr Skewes had ever received such an item, for he was not deemed important enough for such correspondence. The paper had a strange and foreign smell to it, which did not belong in Portscatho. Its wax seal was heavy and Kensa had no desire to break it, as pretty as it was, for fear she would never hold such a thing again.

'Can I see it?'

'No,' said Kensa, hastily breaking the seal, lest her sister do it first.

Inside was a neat and sloping script, which read:

You are instructed to journey to Bodmin
where the Witch Meet will hold its Summer Hasting.
An assessment will take place to determine your suitability as wise
woman to those residing on the southern tip where the River Fal lies.

Kensa had learned of the Bodmin Witch Meet from Isolde, who herself was summoned there once yearly. Now it was Kensa's turn and she could not deny her nervousness. With the letter were clear directions across Bodmin Moor, with a crude map depicting stone boundary markers and the winding De

Lank River. The word 'assessment' grated. She thought on the events in the orchard, years ago.

'I cannot go there with you,' said Elowen, frustrated. 'I cannot leave this shore.'

'Jack will take me,' said Kensa, her cheeks warming at the thought.

It was on this subject that Elowen did not tease. Although Kensa and Jack had seen one another, the pair had never been alone. The Weaver and Isolde had needed to be buried and their funerals conducted – for a second time on the latter's part – the village cleared and the fires seen to on the hills, as well as the removal of dead sheep. There had not been the moment or the space with which to speak together. Even if it had been granted, Kensa did not know what she'd say, which was exactly the predicament she faced on the morning Jack accompanied her to Bodmin.

The pair arranged a lift on a cart heading from Tregony to Truro, though what it carried the owner would not say. He was pleased enough to have a wise woman and the mine owner's son travel with him, which did not put Jack's mind at rest. This was the furthest Kensa had ever been from home and it bit her nerves as thin as her nails, forever worried at her teeth. Naturally, Jack handled everything, even accommodation at a nearby tavern. Kensa was assigned her own room and, as a woman travelling alone with a man, she was given a few sideways glances. None, however, would argue with a man Jack's size.

That being said, Bodmin was a place where wise women gathered and, when Kensa's role became common knowledge, she woke to a trinket or two outside her door in payment for any healing which may ever need take place at the tavern. She accepted the gifts – mittens shot through with bright threads and the straightest sewing needle she had ever seen – with grace.

Their final stretch took them past standing stones carved with old symbols, which pulled on Kensa's skirts as a winding finger. She relished the breeze in the early morning, for it was unlike any she had known before: the Old Ways were present here, though their power was different. In the distance, wild ponies thundered across the moors, while large rocky tors stretched high. When they were far enough through Bodmin Moor, she and Jack parted ways with the cart and its horses, to continue on foot. Occasionally, Jack cleared his throat to speak and then remained silent, prolonging the awkwardness between them.

At last, they reached Delford Bridge, a low, flat walkway in stone, which held a centuries-old age to it. The running water of the De Lank River was beautifully clear and necessary on such a hot day, cooling against Kensa's feet and brow as she paddled. Jack too, stripped off his socks and boots, wading up to his knees in the water. Swifts dipped to find their mirror in the river's surface, seeking their breakfast, while an otter splashed idly in the reeds near by.

'I'll wait here,' said Jack, for behind them and not far off was a low stone building in a squat circle where Kensa had been told to present herself.

She was early – it was not yet midday – though she approached anyway in the hope that the sooner she arrived, the sooner she could leave.

Kensa glanced behind her, once, to see Jack shucking off his shirt at the river's edge. It seemed he meant to swim. She snapped her head forwards and did not dare look again. A different heat pierced her, as straight and fine as the sewing needle wrapped safely within her father's satchel, which she wore across her body.

The door to the small circular building was open. Granite stone had been arranged high, beneath a rush-thick roof. A stunted hawthorn tree sat by the entrance, while rowan had been affixed to the low mantel above the threshold. Kensa entered, and only upon stepping inside did she hear voices.

'That is not what I meant, Billy.'

'She should never have done it!'

'That being the case, we cannot—'

The wise women who Kensa had seen in the orchard turned to stare at her. She rocked on her heels and cleared her scarred throat, which had become quite suddenly dry. The small room was tight with burning sage, which hung in running shapes over their heads, as wild as the nearby horses.

'I'm early,' said Kensa.

'Yes,' said Eadain, mouth poised and unfeeling. She wore a long navy gown with a white leather waistcoat. 'I am the one who summoned you to our circle at Bodmin to stand trial.'

Kensa immediately stepped back. 'Trial?'

A hand shot out from the shadows at her right, where a previously unseen woman crouched, her prominent teeth and tight bodice prompting Kensa to recall her name: Honour of Newquay. Her grip wrapped itself around Kensa's forearm. Eadain walked briskly, her skirts running in a sweeping motion as she closed the door. Trapped inside, the burnt herbs stung Kensa's eyes, hardened and weary.

'I sensed the Old Ways break and reform themselves, against the solemn agreements made between the Bodmin Witches,' said Eadain. 'Tell me, Miss Rowe, was this your doing?'

'Yes.' Kensa wrenched her arm free and brushed her fingers over the bone-handled knife, a habit whenever a threat presented itself. If the coven noticed, none spoke. She had suspected she would meet their ire. Yet her nerve held out. 'It had to be done.'

Eadain never reclaimed her seat, choosing to stand over her chosen victim. 'Why?'

A wariness rose about Kensa's shoulders.

Everything she spoke next, with difficulty, tipped a scale in her favour or against it. Haltingly, the wise woman of Portscatho explained what had taken place. Perhaps she should have been less honest. Lies no longer sat well on her tongue. She wanted to voice the truth and pull it from others, which was what she did. Often, there were murmurs and gasps from those assembled, whose shadows took on strange shapes behind them, as though they held a private conversation in another place.

Eadain's eyes were piercing. She looked down her hawkish nose. 'Why should *you* be allowed to remain in service to *your* community?' When she spoke it was with emphasis on certain words, as though in that distinction was a secret test: one she wished Kensa to fail. 'Your actions put us in danger.' Eadain appeared at first impassive, though there was a certain shape to her lips, to her brows. Behind her voice were unfathomable impulses, and none of them good. 'Do you deny it?'

'No,' said Kensa, squaring her shoulders.

'No,' repeated Eadain '*no*,' emphasising it to their small gathering with shock that was not as convincing as it should have been.

One thing became clear to Kensa. This woman – this witch – was enjoying their talk and the discomfort she draped over others. Naturally, she hid it, though not well. Kensa recognised the bullish nature in herself, her desire to protect herself and protrude thorns. This, however, was different and unsettling.

'Leave her be,' said a stout individual, Hawise of the Lizard, whose bonnet was perpetually in danger of falling from her grey curls. 'I'll speak for her.'

'She's earned her right to her wisening,' said another, Uzella of Lostwithiel, who fanned herself with a lazy hand. 'It's rare one can make an error and mend it as she has done. Surely, it's better to fail and right oneself than never know either?'

'I suppose it'll be entertaining, whatever happens,' added Billy, the herbalist of Mevagissey.

Eadain expelled a derogatory hum from her throat, finely edged and, one could guess, oft used. 'Let us not forget that the sea god who guarded the waters fed by the River Fal is gone and has been replaced by a mere child.'

Kensa snorted and raised her chin. 'On land you'll be safe with such words,' she cautioned. 'Though I would not speak them in sight of the sea or that mere child will see you at the bottom of it.' Admittedly, Elowen could never harm another, yet the Bodmin Witches did not know that. 'Isolde chose me to be the wise woman of Portscatho.'

Kensa faltered. Her late mentor's old advice returned to her. Once, she had been instructed to pretend well enough, to seem capable even when she was not. This was a wise woman's role and one the others in this room performed too, seeming authoritative and in command, even when doubting. She could see it. Invisible veils pulled on, a pretence that could be peeled away if one knew what to look for.

'I chose me,' said Kensa, at last, standing a little straighter, 'I am enough.'

And when she spoke it, she found she believed it.

In fact, she need not pretend at all.

By the time Kensa returned to Jack, he wore a peculiar expression. Determined, yet vulnerable, as though he had set his mind to something – and it was not long before she realised he'd set it upon her. She grinned, a little unsure, and he returned it. Eager for a final dip prior to heading home, Kensa stripped off her shoes and hitched up her skirts.

And if she lifted the fabric higher than was deemed appropriate, Jack did not chide her.

And if Jack watched her, intently, she did not chide him either.

It was settled, approved by the Bodmin Witches Meet. At least, by the majority. There was one obstinate refusal, which was easily overridden. Kensa was and would remain the wise woman of Portscatho. However, there was one other concern that sat heavy upon her and it had nothing to do with witches.

It was summer's height and all who saw her knew it. The wind was blowing from the south, warm and hot and heavy.

A midday sun was combing heat from the earth and burning through her soles where they touched the road. By the coast it would be cooler and, in the sea, cooler still.

'You're wet,' said Kensa, as Jack waded along the shallows towards her.

He stepped closer and she meant to push him away, she truly did. Because his hair, grown out a little, was dripping onto her nose, and his skin was brackish from the river. Yet there was no one in sight and no one to sight them. Finally, the two were alone. Kensa raised her hands onto his bare shoulders and his own strayed to her hips, to where her dress bunched at the sides. Jack's warmth contrasted with the chilled water, as he stood flush against her. She watched the uncertainty play across his lips – and with a second's bravery she stole it – chased it away with her own mouth, with a kiss, which was certain enough for them both. And when his tongue met hers, she was too happy to care about her own clumsiness or inexperience. Because they were together and he tasted like all the summers she'd ever known and had yet to meet.

'Again,' said Kensa, breathlessly, and for once Jack did as she asked.

Epilogue

Mist from the hills and mist from the sea blurred the oyster boats which trailed alongside Falmouth Harbour on a cold September morning. Weighty metal dredging frames were heaved from the boats' sides and plonked into the water. At the River Fal's bed, they pulled along the mud, raising silt that ran away into the ocean. Upon their recovery, each frame was stacked high with oyster and crab and shell and cultch, the stones and grit which form an oyster's bed. That last material was thrown back to sea, to allow further oysters to grow and thrive, ready to be harvested later.

One boat, however, began to struggle.

It was a small vessel with the name *Bryluen* painted on its side. The dredging frame would not come up, at least, not without a great heaving. Straining, the two occupants – a father and son – began to lift the dredging frame together.

'It'll be caught on an anchor,' said the son to his father.

Instead, it was caught on a man.

His arm was hooked into the dredging frame and, to the son's surprise, the man was alive. With one last effort, the oyster catchers pulled him onto the boat, exchanging wary looks between them. No good came from a haul such as this. At least it did not have a fish tail or a lion's head, as had been shared in stories at their drinking hole.

The sodden man's skin was bare and shining wet, one arm marked and bruised from his rise from the seabed. He seemed shocked by them, the reddened marks, as though he had forgotten what it was to feel them. When he was finally placed on his back, he vomited water onto the boat's boards and across the oyster catchers' boots, clutching the centre thwart for support. This, too, seemed to surprise him. He moved oddly, startled by each sensation that reached his mottled fingertips.

How long had he been gone? From the weight of the silt in his mouth, he wagered a year. It had been quiet, peaceful, unending – and terrible for it. Worse, almost, than being tethered to the sea. Without its pull on his veins, he was anchorless, as though he could rise above the seafarers who stared at him, not knowing yet to be afraid.

A remembrance of a woman's voice rang in his mind – Kensa's – along with the single wish she'd made in his dying breaths, while magic had been loosed from its binding:

I'd wish him back, if only so he could see what he'd done.

And she had. And here he was. Mortal.

'Tell me your name, sailor?'

Slowly, the man who was once the Bucka lifted his eyes. Ones as blue as the sea, as blue as the sky, as blue as a cormorant's as he stretches his wings and steels himself for the hunt.

Author's Letter

The Salt Bind owes a debt to my mother. She was raised on tales about her Cornish family and it led her to scour censuses, archives and church records to find the people she – and I – came from: market gardeners, groundspeople, a maid in service to the Sprys, and the odd poacher or two. These were working people, not the rich gentry, and I was fascinated by them. I have spent many a blustery day on Cornwall's shores and sensed a connection; learning that my ancestors came from here explained a great deal. Eventually, I knew I had to write their story.

Years ago, as a journalism student at Bournemouth University, I spent numerous weeks in the local library seeking old records about smugglers along Alum Chine, as well as pre-Christian beliefs in the South West. Seeds were planted and the folklore around the Roseland Peninsula nurtured them. What began as regular holidays turned into frequent research trips, where I sat on Towan Beach or roamed the creek paths above Portscatho, writing this novel. While travelling to St Mawes on Place Ferry, a tourist warned me about the Morgawr, a sea serpent whose death begins our tale. Further insights came from the Gerrans Parish Heritage Centre, its volunteers and archivists, as well as local history groups and ecclesiastical communities. I am thankful to The National Trust who protect and nurture the coastal landscape which features in the novel: the paths Kensa walks are the ones we can traverse today.

One inspiration for Elowen came from a chronic illness, especially relevant during the recent COVID-19 pandemic. Often when we get sick, we look for answers. In reality, they can be hard to come by. In fiction, we can invent them. Although Elowen's value was occasionally overlooked by characters such as Old Sal, her strength and wisdom were paramount to the story.

The Cornish Language Programme helped with *The Salt Bind*'s translations and enabled me to access the words my own ancestors may have spoken. Naturally, any and all mistakes are mine. As for witchcraft and healing business, visits to The Boscastle Witch Museum were greatly beneficial, especially when creating Isolde's cottage in Bohortha (with particular reference to fertility charms).

Numerous writers have been captivated by the county, and their work greatly influenced me, from *Rambles Beyond Railways* by Wilkie Collins to the folktales recorded by William Bottrell. I am even named after one of Daphne du Maurier's infamous characters (as was the family dog Maxim) and her bond to the land is well established.

Admittedly, I have taken *many* liberties with the location and its history, as writers do when spinning their yarns. Although I have borrowed much from Cornwall's rugged shores through this novel's creation, it was with good intentions. *The Salt Bind* exists as a love letter to a land that is tied to my soul and whose magic runs in my veins.

Kernow Bys Vyken!

Acknowledgements

Firstly, I want to thank my parents. Mum, you took me walking. It was your escape and you gave it to me: a path to elsewhere, a wardrobe door to a different destiny. Our footsteps are in this novel. Dad, your work as a projectionist at The Astra in Laarbruch, Germany, as well as your penchant for endless episodes of *Star Trek: The Next Generation*, taught me stories could ask questions and push boundaries. Secondly, I'd like to thank my brother. Mark, you'll find pieces of us in these pages. Growing up, figuring it out, sibling things – thanks for your unwavering encouragement, for being an ear to the first stories I ever told.

Next, I want to thank my friends. Lucy Sharp, my confidante and champion, you told me, 'Just because our sort doesn't do this kind of thing, doesn't mean you can't.' I should've believed you sooner. Alyson Kissner, the first to know Kensa's story, who bolstered me through the darkest days. I am indebted to your patience, especially on the morning I burst into your room with my latest plot and promised this was surely it (and wasn't I right?). Endless love to the Spook Crew, for Anna Viaene's infamous dance moves and Jacques Tsiantar's innumerable pasta dishes. Alycia Pirmohamed, a guardian who offered me a shield when I needed it.

I have been blessed with a community who have supported me and cheered me on, with immense love to Valentina Aparicio, Wanda Cassidy, Elly Grayson and Agata Świętek. Also, cheers to Trang Thanh Tran for their early advice when I was querying this novel. You are all beloved to me. For the late nights, the film clubs, the books we promised to read and discuss and then abandoned for wine and gossip – a coven all our own.

Endless gratitude to the Bridge Awards, who named me their Emerging Writer in 2020. The Weaver's introductory chapter in the sheepcote hasn't changed much since I wrote it at Moniack Mhor (room six) during a residency made possible through the award's generous gift. I've met numerous writers at that centre who've helped me develop my craft and confidence: thanks to early feedback from Daniel Shand, Rob Magnuson Smith and Andrew Miller.

To the Melbourne Literature Festival and my hosts, Emerging Writers' Festival, your funding also powered this work; I am endlessly grateful to you faraway friends. Next, All Stories, whose founder, Catherine Coe, had a vision to help different books into the world, including mine. Tilda Johnson's solid advice through this mentorship scheme was instrumental to the manuscript's development. And to the Creative Scotland team I owe a debt; being awarded the Individual Open Fund altered the trajectory of my life and enabled me to complete this work.

The Salt Bind owes so much to my agent Alex Cochran. He saw to the novel's heart and strengthened it – his guidance has been invaluable. Further gratitude to the C&W team. Thanks, also, to my editor – the talented Christina Demosthenous – and the whole crew at Dialogue. There was no other group of Renegade(s) I would have entrusted Kensa's story to.

Lastly, I want to thank the storytellers – past and present – who enriched my world by sharing theirs. And to you, the reader, I am grateful you picked up this tale, which pays homage to wind-swept friendships, to old knowledge, to life and the living of it.

Bringing a book from manuscript to what you are reading is a team effort.

Renegade Books would like to thank everyone who helped to publish *The Salt Bind* in the UK.

Editorial
Christina Demosthenous
Eleanor Gaffney

Contracts
Stephanie Evans
Sasha Duszynska Lewis
Isabel Camara

Sales
Megan Schaffer
Kyla Dean
Dominic Smith
Sinead White
Georgina Cutler-Ross
Kerri Hood
Jess Harvey
Natasha Weninger-Kong

Design
Ella Garrett
Sara Mahon
Sasha Egonu

Production
Narges Nojoumi
Kelly Llewellyn

Operations
Jairiza Rivera

Finance
Chris Vale
Jonathan Gant

Audio
Rabeeah Moeen

Copy-Editor
Alison Tulett

Proofreader
Karyn Burnham